PENGUIN BOOKS

BEAUTIFUL REDEMPTION

'*Beautiful Creatures* is gorgeously crafted, atmospheric and original. I devoured it' – Melissa Marr, *New York Times* bestselling author of *Wicked Lovely*

'A lush Southern gothic whose memorable, eccentric characters draw you into their captivating world' – Holly Black, *New York Times* bestselling author of The Spiderwick Chronicles

'A hauntingly delicious dark fantasy, a cast of fascinating characters, a rich Gothic setting – this debut novel is one to watch' – Cassandra Clare, *New York Times* bestselling author of The Mortal Instruments series

D0415826

BEAUTIFUL REDEMPTION

BY

KAMI GARCIA &
MARGARET STOHL

PENGUIN BOOKS

Published by the Penguin Group
Penguin Books Ltd, 80 Strand, London WC2R ORL, England
Penguin Group (USA) Inc., 375 Hudson Street, New York, New York 10014, USA
Penguin Group (Canada), 90 Eglinton Avenue East, Suite 700, Toronto, Ontario, Canada M4P 2Y3
(a division of Pearson Penguin Canada Inc.)
Penguin Ireland, 25 St Stephen's Green, Dublin 2, Ireland (a division of Penguin Books Ltd)
Penguin Group (Australia), 707 Collins Street, Melbourne, Victoria 3008, Australia
(a division of Pearson Australia Group Pty Ltd)
Penguin Books India Pvt Ltd, 11 Community Centre, Panchsheel Park, New Delhi – 110 017, India
Penguin Group (NZ), 67 Apollo Drive, Rosedale, Auckland 0632, New Zealand
(a division of Pearson New Zealand Ltd)
Penguin Books (South Africa) (Pty) Ltd, Block D, Rosebank Office Park, 181 Jan Smuts Avenue,
Parktown North, Gauteng 2193, South Africa

Penguin Books Ltd, Registered Offices: 80 Strand, London WC2R ORL, England

penguin.com

First published in the USA by Little, Brown and Company 2012
Published in Great Britain in Razorbill, an imprint of Penguin Books Ltd, 2012
Reprinted by Penguin Books 2013

008

Text copyright © Kami Garcia, LLC, and Margaret Stohl, Inc., 2012
Cover copyright © Hachette Book Group, Inc., 2012
Cover design by David Caplan
Cover image copyright © Michael Trevillion/Trevillion Images
All rights reserved

The moral right of the authors has been asserted

Set in 10.5/15.5pt Sabon
Printed in Great Britain by Clays Ltd, St Ives plc

British Library Cataloguing in Publication Data
A CIP catalogue record for this book is available from the British Library

ISBN: 978-0-141-33527-8

www.greenpenguin.co.uk

MIX
Paper from
responsible sources
FSC® C018179
FSC
www.fsc.org

Penguin Books is committed to a sustainable
future for our business, our readers and our planet.
This book is made from Forest Stewardship
Council™ certified paper.

ALWAYS LEARNING   **PEARSON**

For our fathers,
Robert Marin and Burton Stohl,
who taught us to believe
we could do anything,
and
our husbands,
Alex Garcia and Lewis Peterson,
who made us do the one thing
we never thought we could.

Death is the beginning of Immortality.

— MAXIMILIEN ROBESPIERRE

Beginning Again

Other people had flying dreams. I had falling nightmares. I couldn't talk about it, but I couldn't stop thinking about it either.

About him.

Ethan falling.

Ethan's shoe dropping to the ground, seconds before.

It must have come off when he fell.

I wondered if he knew.

If he'd known.

I saw that muddy black sneaker dropping from the top of the water tower every time I closed my eyes. Sometimes I hoped it was a dream. I hoped I'd wake up, and he'd be waiting out in the driveway, in front of Ravenwood, to take me to school.

Wake up, sleepyhead. I'm almost there. That's what he would've Kelted.

I'd hear Link's bad music coming through the open window, before I even saw Ethan behind the wheel.

That's how I imagined it.

I'd had nightmares about him a thousand times before. Before I knew him, or at least knew he was going to be Ethan. But this wasn't like anything I'd ever seen in any nightmare.

It shouldn't have happened. It wasn't how his life was supposed to be. And it couldn't be how my life was supposed to be.

That muddy black sneaker wasn't supposed to drop.

Life without Ethan was something worse than a nightmare.

It was real.

So real that I refused to believe it.

⁓ૐ

February 2nd
Nightmares end.
That's how you know they're nightmares. This—
Ethan— everything—it isn't ending, has no sign
of ending.
I felt—I feel—like I'm stuck.

2

Like it's my life that shattered when he—when
everything else ended.
It broke into a thousand tiny pieces.
When he hit the ground.

I couldn't stand to look at my journal anymore. I couldn't write poetry; it hurt to even read it.

It was all too true.

The most important person in my life died jumping off the Summerville water tower. I knew why he did it. Knowing why didn't make me feel any better.

Knowing he did it for me only made me feel worse.

Sometimes I didn't think the world was worth it.

Saving.

Sometimes I didn't think I was worth it either.

Ethan thought he was doing the right thing. He knew it was crazy. And he didn't want to go, but he had to anyway.

Ethan was like that.

Even if he was dead.

He saved the world, but he shattered mine.

What now?

BOOK ONE

Ethan

⊰ CHAPTER 1 ⊱

Home

A blur of blue sky over my head.

Cloudless.

Perfect.

Just like the sky in real life, only a little more blue and a little less sun in my eyes.

I guess the sky in real life isn't actually perfect. Maybe that's what makes it so perfect.

Made it.

I squeezed my eyes shut again.

I was stalling.

I wasn't sure I was ready to see whatever was out there to

see. Of course the sky looked better—Heaven being what it was and all.

Not to assume that's where I was. I'd been a decent guy, as far as I could tell. But I had seen enough to know that everything I thought about everything had pretty much been wrong so far.

I had an open mind, at least by Gatlin's standards. I mean, I'd heard all the theories. I had sat through more than my share of Sunday school classes. And after my mom's accident, Marian told me about a Buddhism class she took at Duke taught by a guy named Buddha Bob, who said paradise was a teardrop inside a teardrop inside a teardrop, or something like that. The year before that, my mom tried to get me to read Dante's *Inferno*, which Link told me was about an office building that caught fire, but actually turned out to be about a guy's voyage into the nine circles of Hell. I only remember the part my mom told me about monsters or devils trapped in a pit of ice. I think it was the ninth circle of Hell, but there were so many circles down there that after a while they all sort of ran together.

After what I'd learned about underworlds and otherworlds and sideways worlds, and whatever else came in the whole triple-layer cake of universes that was the Caster world, that first glimpse of blue sky was fine by me. I was relieved to see there was something that looked like a cheesy Hallmark card waiting for me. I wasn't expecting pearly gates or naked cherub babies. But the blue sky, that was a nice touch.

8

I opened my eyes again. Still blue.

Carolina blue.

A fat bee buzzed over my head, climbing high into the sky—until he banged into it, just as he had a thousand times before.

Because it wasn't the sky.

It was the ceiling.

And this wasn't Heaven.

I was lying in my old mahogany bed in my even older bedroom at Wate's Landing.

I was home.

Which was impossible.

I blinked.

Still home.

Had it been a dream? I desperately hoped so. Maybe it was, just like it had been every single morning for the first six months after my mom died.

Please let it have been a dream.

I reached down and searched the dust under my bed frame. I felt the familiar pile of books and pulled one out.

The Odyssey. One of my favorite graphic novels, though I was pretty sure Mad Comix had taken a few liberties with the version Homer wrote.

I hesitated, then pulled out another. *On the Road.* The first sight of the Kerouac was undeniable proof, and I rolled to one side until I could see the pale square on my wall where, until a few days ago—was that all it had been?—the tattered map had hung, with the green marker lines circling all the places from my favorite books I wanted to visit.

It was my room, all right.

The old clock on the table next to my bed didn't seem to be working anymore, but everything else looked about the same. It must be a warm day, for January. The light that came flooding in from the window was almost unnatural—sort of like I was in one of Link's bad storyboards for a Holy Rollers music video. But aside from the movie lighting, my room was exactly the way I'd left it. Just like the books under my bed, the shoe boxes holding my whole life story were still there lining my walls. Everything that was supposed to be there was there, at least as far as I was concerned.

Except Lena.

L? You there?

I couldn't feel her. I couldn't feel anything.

I looked at my hands. They seemed all right. No bruises. I looked at my plain white T-shirt. No blood.

No holes in my jeans or my body.

I went to my bathroom and looked at myself in the mirror above my sink. There I was. Same old Ethan Wate.

I was still staring at my reflection when I heard a sound from downstairs.

"Amma?"

My heart felt like it was pounding, which was pretty funny, since when I woke up, I wasn't even sure it was beating. Either way, I could hear the familiar sounds of my house, coming

10

from down in the kitchen. Floorboards creaked as someone moved back and forth in front of the cupboards and the burners and the old kitchen table. Same old footsteps, going about the same old business as usual in the morning.

If it was morning.

The smell of our old frying pan on the burner came wafting up from downstairs.

"Amma? That's not bacon, is it?"

The voice was clear and calm. "Sweetheart, I think you know what I'm cooking. There's only one thing I know how to cook. If you can call it that."

That voice.

It was so familiar.

"Ethan? How much longer are you going to make me wait to give you a hug? Been down here a long time, darling."

I couldn't understand the words. I couldn't hear anything except the voice. I'd heard it before, not that long ago, but never like this. As loud and clear and full of life as if she was downstairs.

Which she was.

The words were like music. They chased all the misery and confusion away.

"Mom? Mom!"

I raced down the stairs, three at a time, before she could answer.

❧ CHAPTER 2 ❧

Fried Green Tomatoes

There she was, standing in the kitchen in her bare feet, her hair the same as I remembered—half up, half down. A crisp white button-down shirt—what my dad used to call her "uniform"—was still covered with paint or ink from her last project. Her jeans were rolled at her ankles like always, whether or not it was in style. My mom never cared about stuff like that. She was holding our old, black iron frying pan filled with green tomatoes in one hand and a book in the other. She had probably been cooking while she read, without looking up. Humming some part of a song she didn't even realize she was humming and probably couldn't hear.

That was my mom. She seemed exactly the same.

Maybe I was the only one who had changed.

I took a step closer, and she turned toward me, dropping the book. "There you are, my sweet boy."

I felt my heart turning inside out. Nobody else called me that; they wouldn't want to and I wouldn't let them. Just my mom. Then her arms caught me, and the world folded around us as I buried my face in her hug. I breathed in the warm smell and the warm feeling and the warm everything that was my mom to me.

"Mom. You're back."

"One of us is." She sighed.

That's when it hit me. She was standing in my kitchen, and I was standing in my kitchen, which meant one of two things: Either she had come back to life, or . . .

I hadn't.

Her eyes filled with something—tears, love, sympathy— and before I knew it, her arms were around me again.

My mom always understood everything.

"I know, sweet boy. I know."

My face found its old hiding place in the crook of her shoulder.

She kissed the top of my head. "What happened to you? It wasn't supposed to be like this." She pulled back so she could see me. "None of it was supposed to end this way."

"I know."

"Then again, it's not like there's a right way to end a person's life, is there?" She pinched my chin, smiling down into my eyes.

13

I had memorized it. The smile, her face. Everything. It was all I had left during the time she was gone.

I'd always known she was alive somewhere, in some way. She had saved Macon and sent me the songs that shepherded me through every strange chapter of my life with the Casters. She'd been there the whole time, just like she had when she was alive.

It was only one moment, but I wanted to keep it that way as long as I could.

I don't know how we got to the kitchen table. I don't remember anything except the solid warmth of her arms. But there I sat, in my regular chair, as if the past few years had never even happened. There were books everywhere—and from the looks of it, my mom was partway through most of them, as usual. A sock, probably fresh from the laundry, was stuck in *The Divine Comedy*. A napkin poked halfway out of *The Iliad*, and on top of that a fork marked her place in a volume of Greek mythology. The kitchen table was full of her beloved books, one pile of paperbacks higher than the next. I felt like I was back in the library with Marian.

The tomatoes sizzled in the pan, and I breathed in the scent of my mother—yellowing paper and burnt oil, new tomatoes and old cardboard, all laced through with cayenne pepper.

No wonder libraries made me so hungry.

My mom slid a blue and white china platter onto the table between us. Dragonware. I smiled because it had been her favorite. She dropped hot tomatoes onto a paper towel, sprinkling pepper across the plate.

"There you go. Dig in."

I tucked my fork into the nearest slice. "You know, I haven't eaten one of these since you—since the accident." The tomato was so hot it burned my tongue. I looked at my mom. "Are we—is this—?"

She returned the look blankly.

I tried again. "You know. Heaven?"

She laughed, pouring sweet tea into two tall glasses—tea being the only other thing my mom knew how to make. "No, not Heaven, EW. Not exactly."

I must have looked worried, like I thought we had somehow ended up in the other place. But that couldn't be right either, because—as cheesy as it sounded—being with my mom again was Heaven, whether or not the universe thought of it that way. Then again, the universe and I hadn't agreed on much lately.

My mom pressed her hand against my cheek and smiled as she shook her head. "No, this isn't any kind of final resting place, if that's what you mean."

"Then why are we here?"

"I'm not sure. You don't get a user's manual when you check in." She took my hand. "I always knew I was here because of you—some unfinished business, something I needed to teach you or tell you or show you. That's why I sent you the songs."

15

"The Shadowing Songs."

"Exactly. You kept me plenty busy. And now that you're here, I feel like we were never apart." Her face clouded over. "I always hoped I would get to see you again. But I hoped I would be waiting a lot longer. I'm so sorry. I know it must be terrible for you right now, leaving Amma and your father. And Lena."

I nodded. "It sucks."

"I know. I felt the same way," she said.

"About Macon?" The words came tumbling out of my mouth before I could stop them.

Her cheeks went red. "I guess I deserved that. But not everything that happens in a mother's life is something she needs to discuss with her seventeen-year-old son."

"Sorry."

She squeezed my hand. "You were the person I didn't want to leave, most of all. And you were the person I worried about leaving, most of all. You and your father.

"Your father, thankfully, is in the exceptional care of the Ravenwoods. Lena and Macon have him under some powerful Casts, and Amma's spinning stories of her own. Mitchell has no idea what's happened to you."

"Really?"

She nodded. "Amma tells him you're in Savannah with your aunt, and he believes it." Her smile wavered, and she looked past me into the shadows. I knew she must be worried about my dad, despite whatever Casts he was under. My sudden departure from Gatlin was probably hurting her as much as it was me—standing by and watching it all happen, without being able to do anything about it.

"But it's not a long-term solution, Ethan. Right now everyone is just doing the best that they can. That's usually how it is."

"I remember." I'd been through it once before.

We both knew when.

She didn't say anything after that, just picked up a fork of her own. We ate together in silence for the rest of the afternoon, or for a moment. I couldn't tell which was which anymore, and I wasn't sure it mattered.

We sat out on the back porch picking shiny-wet cherries out of the colander and watching the stars come out. The sky had faded to a darkish blue, and the stars appeared in crazy bright clusters. I saw stars from the Caster sky and the Mortal sky. The split moon hung between the North Star and the Southern Star. I didn't know how it was possible to see two skies at once, two sets of constellations, but it was. I could see everything now, like I was two different people at the same time. Finally, an end to the whole Fractured Soul thing. I guess one of the perks of dying was having both halves of my soul back together.

Yeah, right.

Everything had come together now that it was over, or

maybe because it was over. I guess life was like that sometimes. It all looked so simple, so easy from here. So unbelievably bright.

Why was this the only solution? Why did it have to end like this?

I leaned my head against my mom's shoulder. "Mom?"

"Sweetheart."

"I need to talk to Lena." There it was. I'd finally said it. The one thing that had kept me from being able to exhale all day. The thing that had made me feel like I couldn't sit down, like I couldn't stay. Like I had to get up and go somewhere, even if I had nowhere to go.

As Amma used to say, the good thing about the truth is it's true, and there's no arguing with the truth. You may not like it, but that doesn't make it any less true. That's all I had to hold on to right about now.

"You can't talk to her." My mom frowned. "At least, it's not easy."

"I need to tell her I'm okay. I know her. She's waiting for a sign from me. Just like I was waiting for a sign from you."

"There's no Carlton Eaton to run your letter over to her, Ethan. You can't send a letter from this world, and you can't get to hers. And even if you could, you wouldn't be able to write one. You don't know how many times I wished it was possible."

There had to be a way. "I know. If it was, I would've heard from you more."

18

She looked up toward the stars. Her eyes shone with reflected light as she spoke. "Every day, my sweet boy. Every single day."

"But you found a way to talk to me. You used the books in the study, and the songs. And I saw you that night I was at the cemetery. And in my room, remember?"

"The songs were the Greats' idea. I suppose because I had been singing to you since you were a baby. But everyone's different. I don't think you can send anything like a Shadowing Song to Lena."

"Even if I knew how to write one." My songwriting skills made Link look like one of the Beatles.

"It wasn't easy for me, and I'd been kicking around here a whole lot longer than you have. And I had help from Amma, Twyla, and Arelia." She squinted up at the twin skies. "You have to remember, Amma and the Greats have powers that I know nothing about."

"But you were a Keeper." There had to be things she knew that they didn't.

"Exactly. I was a Keeper. I did what the Far Keep asked me to do, and I didn't do what the Far Keep didn't want me to do. You don't mess with them, and you don't mess with their record of things."

"*The Caster Chronicles*?"

She picked a cherry from the bowl, examining it for spots. She took so long to answer, I was starting to think she hadn't heard me. "What do you know about *The Caster Chronicles*?"

"Before Aunt Marian's trial, the Council of the Far Keep came to the library, and they brought the book with them."

She put the old metal colander down on the step beneath us. "Forget about *The Caster Chronicles*. All of that doesn't matter anymore."

"Why not?"

"I'm serious, Ethan. We're not out of danger, you and I."

"Danger? What are you talking about? We're already—you know."

She shook her head. "We're only partway home. We've got to find out what's keeping us here, and move on."

"What if I don't want to move on?" I wasn't ready to give up. Not as long as Lena was waiting for me.

Once again, she didn't answer for a long time. When she did, my mom sounded about as dark as I'd ever heard her. "I don't think you have a choice."

"You did," I said.

"It wasn't a choice. You needed me. That's why I'm here— for you. But even I can't change what happened."

"Yeah? You could try." I found myself crushing a cherry in my hand. The juice ran red between my fingers.

"There's nothing to try, Ethan. It's over. It's too late." She barely whispered, but it felt like she was shouting.

Anger welled up inside me. I hurled a cherry across the yard, then another, then the whole bowlful. "Well, Lena and Amma and Dad need me, and I'm not just going to give up. I feel like I shouldn't be here—like this is all a huge mistake." I

20

looked at the empty bowl in my hands. "And it's not cherry season. It's winter." I looked up at her, my eyes blurring with tears, though all I could feel was anger. "It's supposed to be winter."

My mom put her hand on mine. "Ethan."

I pulled away. "Don't try to make me feel better. I missed you, Mom. I did. More than anything. But as happy as I am to see you, I want to wake up and have this not be happening. I understand why I had to do it. I get it. Fine. But I don't want to be stuck here forever."

"What did you think was going to happen?"

"I don't know. Not this." Was that the truth? Had I really thought I could get out of sacrificing my own good for the good of the world? Did I think the One-Who-Is-Two thing was a joke?

I guess it was easier to play the hero. But now that it was real—now that I had to own up to an eternity of what and who I'd lost—suddenly it didn't seem so easy.

My mom's eyes welled up, worse than mine. "I'm so sorry, EW. If there was a way I could change things, I would." She sounded as miserable as I felt.

"What if there is?"

"I can't change everything." My mom looked down at her bare feet on the step below her. "I can't change anything."

"I'm not ready for some stupid cloud, and I don't want to get my wings when some stupid bell rings." I threw the metal bowl. It went clattering down the stairs, rolling across the back lawn. "I want to be with Lena and I want to live and I want to go to the Cineplex and eat popcorn until I'm sick and drive too fast and get a ticket and be so in love with my girl-friend that I make a total fool out of myself every day for the rest of my life."

"I know."

"I don't think you do," I said, louder than I'd intended. "You had a life. You fell in love—twice. And you had a fam-ily. I'm seventeen. This can't be the end for me. I can't wake up tomorrow and know that I'm never going to see Lena again."

My mother sighed, sliding her arm around me and pulling me close.

I said it again because I didn't know what else to say. "I can't."

She rubbed my head like I was a sad, scared little kid. "Of course you can see her. That's the easy part. I can't guarantee you can talk to her, and she won't be able to see you, but you can see her."

I looked at her, stunned. "What are you talking about?"

"You exist. We exist here. Lena and Link and your father and Amma, they exist in Gatlin. It's not that one plane of existence is more or less real. They're just different planes. You're here and Lena's there. In her world, you'll never be fully present. Not like you were. And in our world, she'll never be like us. But that doesn't mean you won't be able to see her."

"How?" At that moment, it was the only thing I wanted to know.

"It's simple. Just go."

"What do you mean, go?" She was making it sound easy, but I had a feeling there was more to it.

"You imagine where you want to go, and then you just go."

It didn't seem possible, even though I knew my mom would never lie to me. "So if I just wish myself to Ravenwood, I'll be there?"

"Well, not from our back porch. You have to leave Wate's Landing before you can go anywhere. I think our homes have the Otherworld equivalent of a Binding on them. When you're at home, you're here with me and nowhere else."

A shiver went down my spine as she said the words. "The Otherworld? Is that where we are? What it's called?"

She nodded, wiping her cherry-stained hand on her jeans.

I knew I wasn't anywhere I'd been before. I knew it wasn't Gatlin, and I knew it wasn't Heaven. Still, something about the word seemed farther away than anything I'd ever known. Farther even than death. Even though I could smell the dusty concrete of our back patio and the fresh cut grass stretching beyond it. I could feel the mosquitoes biting and the wind moving and the splinters of the old wooden steps at my back. All it felt like was loneliness. It was just us now. My mom, and me, and my backyard full of cherries. Some part of me had been waiting for this ever since her accident, and another part of me knew, maybe for the first time, it would never be enough.

"Mom?"

"Yes, sweet boy?"

"Do you think Lena still loves me, back in the Mortal realm?"

She smiled and tousled my hair. "What kind of silly question is that?"

I shrugged.

"Let me ask you this. Did you love me when I was gone?"

I didn't respond. I didn't have to.

"I don't know about you, EW, but I knew the answer to that question every day we were apart. Even when I didn't know anything else about where I was or what I was supposed to be doing. You were my Wayward, even then. Everything always brought me back to you. Everything." She smoothed my hair out of my face. "You think Lena's any different?"

She was right.

It was a stupid question.

So I smiled and took her hand and followed her inside. I had things to figure out and places to go—that much I knew. But some things I didn't have to figure out. Some things hadn't changed, and some things never would.

Except me. I had changed, and I would give anything to change back.

CHAPTER 3

This Side or the Next

Go on, Ethan. See for yourself."

I didn't look back at my mom when I reached for the doorknob.

Even though she was telling me to go, I was still uneasy. I didn't know what to expect. I could see the painted wood of the door, and I could feel the smooth iron of the handle, but I had no way of knowing if Cotton Bend was on the other side.

Lena. Think about Lena. About home. This is the only way.

Still.

This wasn't Gatlin anymore. Who knew what was behind that door? It could be anything.

I stared down at the knob, remembering what the Caster Tunnels had taught me about doors and Doorwells.

And portals.

And seams.

This door might look normal enough—any Doorwell looked pretty much like the next—but that didn't mean it was. Like the *Temporis Porta*. You never knew where you were going to end up. I'd learned that the hard way.

Quit stalling, Wate.

Get on with it.

What are you, chicken? What do you have to lose now?

I closed my eyes and turned the knob. When I opened them, I wasn't staring at my street—not even close.

I found myself on my front porch in the middle of His Garden of Perpetual Peace, Gatlin's cemetery. Right in the middle of my mother's plot.

The cultivated lawns stretched out in front of me, but instead of headstones and mausoleums decorated with plastic cherubs and fawns, the graveyard was full of houses. I realized I was looking at the homes of the people buried in the cemetery, if that's even where I was. Old Agnes Pritchard's Victorian was planted right where her plot should have been, with the same yellow shutters and crooked rosebushes that hung over the walkway. Her house wasn't on Cotton Bend, but her little rectangle of grass in Perpetual Peace was directly across from my mom's plot—the spot where Wate's Landing was sitting now.

26

Agnes' house looked almost exactly as it had in Gatlin, except her red front door was gone. In its place was her weathered cement headstone.

AGNES WILSON PRITCHARD
BELOVED WIFE, MOTHER & GRANDMOTHER
MAY SHE SLEEP WITH THE ANGELS

The words were still etched into the stone, which fit perfectly into the painted white doorframe. It was the same at every house as far as I could see—from Darla Eaton's restored Federal to the peeling paint of Clayton Weatherton's place. All the doors were missing, replaced by the gravestones of the dearly departed.

I turned around slowly, hoping to see my own white door with the haint blue trim. But instead I was staring at my mother's headstone.

LILA EVERS WATE
BELOVED WIFE AND MOTHER
SCIENTIAE CUSTOS

Above her name, I saw the Celtic symbol of Awen—three lines converging like rays of light—carved into the stone. Aside from being large enough to fill the doorway, the headstone was the same. Every nicked edge, every faded crack. I ran my hand over the face of it, feeling the letters beneath my fingers.

My mom's headstone.

Because she was dead. I was dead. And I was pretty sure I had just stepped out of her grave.

That's when I started to lose it. I mean, can you blame a guy? The situation was a little overwhelming. There's not much you can do to prepare for something like that.

I pushed on the gravestone, pounding on it as hard as I could until I felt the stone give way, and I stepped back inside my house—slamming the door behind me.

I stood against the door, breathing in as much air as I could. My front hall looked exactly the same as it had a moment ago.

My mom looked up at me from the front stairs. She had just opened *The Divine Comedy*; I could tell by the way she was still holding her sock bookmark in one hand. It was almost like she was waiting for me.

"Ethan? Changed your mind?"

"Mom. It's a graveyard. Out there."

"It is."

"And we're—" The opposite of alive. It was just starting to sink in.

"We are." She smiled at me because there wasn't really anything else she could say. "You stand there as long as you need to." She looked back down at her book and flipped a page. "Dante agrees. Take your time. It is only"—she flipped a page—" '*la notte che le cose ci nasconde.*' "

"What?"

" 'The night that hides things from us.' "

I stared at her as she continued to read. Then, seeing as there weren't that many options, I pulled the door open and stepped out.

It took me a while to take it all in, the way it takes your eyes a while to adjust to sunlight. As it turns out, the Otherworld was just that—an "other world"—a Gatlin right in the middle of the cemetery, where the dead folks in town were having their own version of All Souls Day. Except it seemed like this one lasted a lot longer than a day.

I stepped off my porch and onto the grass just to be sure it was really there. Amma's rosebushes were planted where they had always been, but they were blooming again, safe from the record-breaking heat that had killed them when it hit town. I wondered if they were blooming in the real Gatlin, too.

I hoped so.

If the Lilum kept her promise, they were. I believed she did. The Lilum wasn't Light or Dark, right or wrong. She was truth and balance in their purest forms. I didn't think she was capable of lying, or she would've sugarcoated the truth for me a little. Sometimes I wished she would have.

I found myself wandering across the freshly trimmed lawns, weaving between the familiar houses scattered throughout the cemetery like a tornado had lifted them right out of Gatlin and dropped them here. And not just houses—there were people here, too.

I tried heading toward Main Street, instinctively looking for Route 9. I guess I wanted to hike to the crossroads, where I could take a left up the road to Ravenwood. But the Otherworld didn't work that way, and every time I reached the end of the rows of graveyard plots, I found myself back where I started. The graveyard just kept going in circles. I couldn't get out.

That's when I realized I needed to stop thinking in terms of streets and start thinking in terms of graves and plots and crypts.

If I was going to find my way back to Gatlin, I wasn't going to walk there. Not on any kind of Route 9. That was pretty clear.

What had my mom said? *You imagine where you want to go, and then you just go.* Was that really all that was standing between Lena and me? My imagination?

I closed my eyes.

L—

"Whatcha doin' there, boy?" Miss Winifred looked up from sweeping her porch a few houses away. She was in the pink-flowered housecoat she wore most days back when she was alive. When *we* were alive.

I stared. "Nothing. Ma'am."

Her headstone was behind her, a magnolia tree etched above her name and underneath the word *Sacred*. There were a lot of those around here, magnolias. I guess the magnolia carvings were the red doors of the Otherworld. You were nobody without one.

Miss Winifred noticed me staring and stopped sweeping for a second. She sniffed. "Well, get on with it, then."

"Yes, ma'am." I could feel my face turning red. I knew I wouldn't be able to imagine myself anywhere else with those sharp old eyes on me.

Turns out, even in the streets of the Otherworld, Gatlin was no place for the imagination.

"And stay off my lawn, Ethan. You'll trample my begonias," she added. That was all. As if I had wandered onto her property back home.

"Yes, ma'am."

Miss Winifred nodded and went back to sweeping her porch like it was just another sunny day on Old Oak Road, where her house was sitting right now back in town.

But I couldn't let Miss Winifred stop me.

I tried the old concrete bench at the end of our row of plots. I tried the shadowy place behind the hedges along the edge of Perpetual Peace. I even tried sitting with my back up against the railing of our own plot for a while.

I was no closer to imagining my way to Gatlin than I was to imagining myself back into the grave.

Every time I closed my eyes, I got this spirit-killing, bone-crushing fear that I was dead in the ground. That I was gone and that I would never be anywhere again, except at the bottom of a water tower.

31

Not back home.

Not with Lena.

Finally, I gave up. There had to be another way.

If I wanted to get back to Gatlin, there was someone who just might know how.

Someone who made it her business to know everything about everyone and, for about the last hundred years, always had.

I knew where I needed to go.

I followed the path down to the oldest section of the graveyard. Some part of me was afraid I was going to see the blackened edges where the fire had burned through the roof and Aunt Prue's bedroom. But I didn't need to worry. When I saw it, the house was exactly the way it looked when I was a kid. The porch swing was rattling and swaying gently in the breeze, a glass of lemonade sitting on the table beside it. Just how I remembered it.

The door was carved out of good Southern blue granite; Amma had spent hours choosing it herself. "A woman as right as your aunt deserves the right marker," Amma had said. "And anyhow, if she isn't happy, I'll never hear the end a it." Both were probably true. At the top of the gravestone, a delicate angel with outstretched hands was holding a compass. I was willing to bet there wasn't another angel in all of Perpetual Peace, or maybe any cemetery in the South, that was holding a compass. Carved angels in the Gatlin graveyard held on to every kind of flower, and some even held on to the gravestones like they were life vests. None held a compass—never a compass. But for a woman who had spent her life secretly mapping the Caster Tunnels, it was right.

Under the angel was an inscription:

PRUDENCE JANE STATHAM
THE BELLE OF THE BALL

Aunt Prue had picked out the inscription herself. Her note said she wanted another "e" on *Ball*—making it *Balle*, which wasn't even a word. According to Aunt Prue, it sounded more French that way. But my dad made the point that Aunt Prue, being a patriot, shouldn't have minded having her last words written out in plain old Southern American English. I wasn't so sure, but I also wasn't about to enter into that particular conversation. It was just one part of the extensive instructions she'd left for her own funeral, along with a guest list that required a bouncer at the church.

Still, it made me smile just looking at it.

Before I even had the chance to knock, I heard the sound of dogs yipping, and the heavy front door swung open. Aunt Prue was standing in the doorway, her hair still in pink plastic curlers, one hand on her hip. There were three Yorkshire terriers weaving around her legs—the first three Harlon Jameses.

"Well, it's 'bout time." Aunt Prue grabbed me by the ear

33

quicker than I had ever seen her move when she was alive, and yanked me into the house. "You were always stubborn, Ethan. But what you did this time ain't right. I don't know what in the Good Lord's Myst'ry got inta you, but I've got a mind ta send you out front ta get me a switch." It was a charming custom from Aunt Prue's day, to let a kid pick the switch you planned to whip them with. But I knew as well as Aunt Prue did that she would never hit me. If she was going to, she would have already done it years ago.

She was still twisting my ear, and I had to bend down because she was only half my height. The whole posse of Harlon Jameses were still yipping, trailing after us as she dragged me toward the kitchen. "I didn't have a choice, Aunt Prue. Everyone I loved was going to die."

"You don't have ta tell me. I watched the whole thing, and I was wearin' my good spectacles!" She sniffed. "And ta think, folks used ta say I was the mell-o-dramatic one!"

I tried not to laugh. "You need your glasses here?"

"Just used ta them, I guess. Feel nekkid without 'em now. Hadn't figured on that." She stopped walking and pointed a bony finger at me. "Don't you try changin' the subject. This time you've made a bigger mess than a blind housepainter."

"Prudence Jane, why don't you stop hollerin' at that boy?" An old man's voice called from the other room. "What's done is done."

Aunt Prue pulled me back into the hall, without loosening

34

her grip on my ear. "Don't you tell me what ta do, Harlon Turner!"

"Turner? Wasn't that—" As she yanked me into the living room, I found myself face to face with not one but all five of Aunt Prue's husbands.

Sure enough, the three younger ones—most likely her first three husbands—were eating corn nuts and playing cards, the sleeves of their white button-down shirts rolled up to the elbows. The fourth one was sitting on the couch reading the newspaper. He looked up and acknowledged me with a nod, shoving the little white bowl toward me. "Car nut?"

I shook my head.

I actually remembered Aunt Prue's fifth husband, Harlon— the one Aunt Prue had named all her dogs after. When I was a kid, he used to carry around sour lemon hard candy in his pocket, and he'd sneak me a couple during church. I ate them, too, lint and all. There was no telling what you'd eat in church, bored out of your skull. Link once drank a whole mini-bottle of Binaca breath spray during a talk on the atonement. Then he spent the whole afternoon and part of the evening atoning for that, too.

Harlon looked exactly the way I remembered. He threw his hands up, a sure sign of surrender. "Prudence, you're near 'bout the most ornery woman I've ever met in my en-tire life!"

It was true, and we all knew it. The other four husbands looked up, a mixture of sympathy and amusement on their faces.

Aunt Prue let go of my ear and turned to face her latest late husband. "Well, I don't recollect askin' you ta marry me, Harlon James Turner. So I reckon that makes you the most foolish man I've ever met in *my* en-tire life!" The ears of the three tiny dogs perked up at the sound of their name.

The man reading the paper stood up and patted poor old Harlon on the shoulder. "I think you ought ta let our little firecracker have some time ta herself." He dropped his voice. "Or you may end up passin' on a second time."

Aunt Prue seemed satisfied and marched back to the kitchen with the three Harlon Jameses and me following dutifully. When we reached the kitchen, she pointed to a chair at the table and busied herself pouring two tall glasses of sweet tea. "If I had known I'd have ta live with the five a those men, I'd have thought twice 'bout gettin' married at all."

And here they were. I wondered why—until I figured out it was better not to. Whatever unfinished business she had with her five husbands and about as many dogs, I sure didn't want to know.

"Drink up, son," Harlon said.

I glanced at the tea, which looked pretty appealing even though I wasn't the least bit thirsty. It was one thing when my mom was cutting me up a fried tomato. I hadn't thought twice about eating anything she handed me. Now that I had passed through the graveyard to visit my dead aunt, it occurred to me that I didn't know the rules, or anything about the way things worked over here—wherever *here* was. Aunt Prue noticed me staring at the glass. "You can drink it, not that you need ta. But it's different on the other side."

"How?" I had so many questions that I didn't know where to start.

"Can't eat or drink over there, back in the Mortal realm, but you can move things. Just yesterday, I hid Grace's dentures. Dropped 'em right down in the Postum jar." It was just like Aunt Prue to find a way to drive her sisters crazy from the grave.

"Wait—you were over there? In Gatlin?" If she could go see the Sisters, then I could get back to Lena. Couldn't I?

"Did I say that?" I knew she'd have the answer. I also knew she wouldn't tell me a thing if she didn't want me to know.

"Yeah, actually. You did."

Tell me how I can find my way back to Lena.

"Well now, just for the teeniest minute. Nothin' ta get all hopped up 'bout. Then I skee-daddled back ta the Garden here, lickety-split."

"Aunt Prue, come on." But she shook her head, and I gave up. My aunt was every bit as stubborn in this life as she'd been in the last. I tried a new subject. "The Garden? Are we really in His Garden of Perpetual Peace?"

"Darn tootin'. Every time they bury someone, a new house shows up on the block." Aunt Prue sniffed again. "Can't do a thing ta stop 'em from comin' either, even if they ain't your kind a folks."

I thought about the headstones instead of doors, all the

cemetery plot houses. I'd always thought the layout of His Garden of Perpetual Peace was kind of like our town, what with the good plots all lined up one way and the questionable graves pushed out near the edges. Turns out the Otherworld wasn't any different.

"Then why don't I have one, Aunt Prue? A house, I mean."

"Young 'uns don't get houses a their own unless their parents outlive 'em. And after seein' that room a yours, I don't see as how you could keep a whole house clean anyway." I couldn't really argue with her on that.

"Is that why I don't have a gravestone?"

Aunt Prue looked away. There was something she didn't want to tell me. "Maybe you should ask your mamma 'bout that."

"I'm asking you."

She sighed heavily. "You aren't buried at Perpetual Peace, Ethan Wate."

"What?" Maybe it was too soon. I didn't even know how much time had passed since that night on the water tower. "I guess they haven't buried me yet."

Aunt Prue was wringing her hands, which was only making me more nervous.

"Aunt Prue?"

She took a sip of her sweet tea, stalling. At least it gave her hands something to do. "Amma isn't takin' your leavin' well, and Lena's no better. Don't think I don't keep an eye on them two. Didn't I give Lena my good old rose necklace, so I can get a feel for her every now and again?"

The image of Lena sobbing, of Amma screaming my name right before I jumped, flashed through my mind. My chest tightened.

Aunt Prue kept on talking. "None a this was supposed ta happen. Amma knows it, and she and Lena and Macon are havin' a heap a trouble with your passin'."

My passing. The words sounded strange to me.

A horrible thought surfaced in my mind. "Wait. Are you saying they didn't bury me?"

Aunt Prue put her hand to her heart. "Of course they buried you! They did it straightaway. They just didn't bury you in the Gatlin cemetery." She sighed, shaking her head. "Didn't even have a proper memorial, I'm 'fraid. No ushers, no sermons. No Psalms or Lamentations."

"No Lamentations? You sure know how to hurt a guy, Aunt Prue." I was kidding, but she only nodded, grim as the grave.

"No program. No funeral potatoes. Nothin' so much as a supermarket biscuit. Not even a book a remembrances. Might as well a stuck you in one a them shoe boxes in your bedroom."

"Then, where did they bury me?" I was starting to get a bad feeling.

"Over at Greenbrier, by the old Duchannes graves. Stuck you in the mud like a possum-bitten house cat."

"Why?" I looked at her, but Aunt Prue glanced away. She was definitely hiding something. "Aunt Prue, answer me. Why did they bury me at Greenbrier?"

She looked right at me, crossing her arms over her chest defiantly. "Now, don't get yerself all bowed up. It was jus' the tiniest excuse for a service. Nothin' ta write home 'bout." She sniffed. "On account a none a the folks in town knowin' you passed."

"What are you talking about?" There was nothing folks in Gatlin came out for like a funeral.

"Amma told everyone there was an E-mergency with your aunt in Savannah, and you went on down there to help her."

"The whole town? They're pretending I'm still alive?" It was one thing for Amma to try to convince my grieving dad I was still around. For her to try to convince the whole town was more than crazy, even for Amma. "What about my dad? Won't he figure out something's going on, when I never come home? He can't think I'm down in Savannah forever."

Aunt Prue stood up and walked over to the counter, where a Whitman's Sampler was already opened. She turned the lid over, inspecting the diagram that listed the type of chocolate nestled in each brown wrapper. Finally, she chose one and took a bite.

I looked at her. "Cherry Cordial?"

She shook her head, showing me. "Messenger Boy." The rectangular chocolate boy was missing his head now. "I'll never know why folks waste their money on fancy candy. If you ask me, these are the best durned chocolates on this side or the other."

"Yes, ma'am."

Sugared up on drugstore candy, she laid the truth on me. "The Casters put a Charm on your daddy. He doesn't know you're a bit dead either. Every time it looks like he might be sniffin' 'round ta the truth, the Casters double up that Charm till he doesn't know up from down. It ain't natural, if ya ask me, but not much 'round Gatlin is. Whole place's gone downright cattywampus." She held out the half-eaten box of candy. "Now have yourself somethin' sweet. Chocolate makes everything better. Molasses Chew?"

I was buried at Greenbrier so Lena and Amma and my friends could keep it a secret from everyone, including my father—who was under the influence of a Cast so powerful that he didn't know his own son was gone, just like my mom said.

There wasn't enough chocolate in the world to make this better.

⊰ CHAPTER 4 ⊱

Catfish Crossin'

Getting Aunt Prue to say the one thing you wanted her to say, right when you wanted her to say it, was like thinking you could ask the sun to shine. At some point, and probably sooner than later, you had to admit you were at her mercy. I had to, anyway.

Because I was.

I couldn't stomach one more waxy chocolate, washed down with one more glass of sweet tea, while one more little dog stared at me, to get at the one thing I needed to know. All I could do was start begging.

"I have to go to Ravenwood, Aunt Prue. You have to help me. I have to see Lena."

My aunt sniffed and tossed the box of chocolates back down on the counter. "Oh, I see, now I *have ta have ta have ta*? Someone died and made you the Gen'ral? Next you'll be thinkin' you need a statue and a green all your own." She sniffed again.

"Aunt Prue—" I gave up. "I'm sorry."

"I reckon you are."

"I just need to know how to get to Ravenwood." I knew I sounded desperate, but it didn't matter, because I was. I hadn't been able to walk there or imagine myself there. There had to be another way.

"You know you get more bees with honey, sugar. Crossin' over from one side ta the next hasn't done much ta improve your manners, Ethan Wate. Bossin' an old woman like that."

I was losing patience with my aunt. "I said I'm sorry. I'm kind of new at this, remember? Can you please help me? Do you know anything about how to get from here to Ravenwood?"

"Do you know I'm bone tired a this conversation?"

"Aunt Prue!"

She clamped her teeth shut and stuck out her chin, the way Harlon James did when he got a lock on a bone.

"There has to be a way I can see her. My mom came to visit me twice. Once in a fire Amma and Twyla made in a graveyard, and once in my own room."

"Pretty powerful stuff, crossin' like that. Then again, your mamma's always been stronger than most folks. Why don'tcha ask her?" She looked irritated.

43

"Crossing?"

"Crossin' over. Not for the faint a heart. For most a us, you just can't get there from here."

"What's that supposed to mean?"

"It means you can't make preserves till you learn how ta boil water, Ethan Wate. Gotta put in the time. Get used ta the water 'fore you jump in." Not that Aunt Prue could ever bottle anything that wouldn't burn a hole in your bread, according to Amma.

I crossed my arms, annoyed. "Why would I jump into boiling water?"

She glared at me, fanning herself with a folded piece of paper the way she had on the thousand Sundays when I drove her to church.

The rocker stopped. Bad sign.

"I mean, *ma'am*." I held my breath until the rocker started to squeak again. This time I lowered my voice. "If you know something, please help me. You said you went to see Aunt Grace and Aunt Mercy. And I know I saw you when I was at your funeral."

Aunt Prue twisted her mouth like her dentures were hurting. Or like she was trying to keep her thoughts to herself. "You had your whole mess a split-up souls back then. You could see all sorts a things a Mortal ain't supposed ta see. I ain't seen Twyla since that day either, and she's the one who crossed me over in the first place."

"I can't figure this out on my own."

" 'Course you can. You can't just show up 'round here and 'spect ta do whatcha like, easy as bad pie in a box. That's all part a crossin'. It's like fishin'. Why would I just hand you the catfish when I should be teachin' you how ta fish?"

I put my head in my hands. At that particular moment, I would have been plenty fine with bad pie in a box. "And where can a guy learn to catch a catfish around here?"

There was no answer.

I looked up to see Aunt Prue dozing in her rocking chair, the folded paper she'd been fanning herself with resting in her lap. There was no waking Aunt Prue from one of her naps. Not before, and probably not now.

I sighed, gently taking the makeshift fan out of her hand. It unfolded partway, revealing the edge of a drawing. It looked like one of her maps, only half-drawn, more of a doodle than anything else. Aunt Prue couldn't sit still long without starting to sketch out her whereabouts, even in the Otherworld.

Then I realized it wasn't a map of His Garden of Perpetual Peace—or if it was, the graveyard world was bigger than I thought.

This wasn't just any map.

It was a map of the *Lunae Libri*.

"How can there be a *Lunae Libri* in the Otherworld? It's not a grave, right? Nobody died there?"

My mom didn't look up from her copy of Dante. She hadn't looked up when I swung open the front door either. She couldn't hear a word anyone said when she was lost in those pages. Reading was her own version of Traveling.

I stuck my hand between her face and the yellowed pages, wiggling my fingers. "Mom."

"What?" My mom looked as startled as a person could look when you hadn't actually snuck up on them.

"Let me save you some time. I saw the movie. The office building catches fire." I closed the book and held out Aunt Prue's folded paper. My mom took it, smoothing it out in her hands.

"I knew Dante was ahead of his time." She smiled, turning over the paper.

"Why was Aunt Prue drawing this?" I asked, but she didn't answer. She just kept staring at the paper.

"If you're going to start asking yourself why your aunt does anything, you'll be busy for the rest of eternity."

"Why did she need a map?" I asked.

"What your aunt needs is to find someone else to talk to besides you."

That was all she said. Then she gave up, standing and slipping her arm around my shoulders. "Come on. I'll show you."

I followed my mom right down the street that wasn't a street, until we came to a plot that wasn't just a plot, and a familiar grave that wasn't even a grave. I stopped walking as soon as I saw where we were.

My mom laid her hand on Macon's gravestone, a wistful smile creeping across her face. She pushed on the stone, and it swung open. Ravenwood's front hall stood there, ghostly and deserted, as if nothing had changed except that Lena's family had gone to Barbados or something.

"So?" I couldn't bring myself to step inside. What use was Ravenwood without Lena or her family? It almost made me feel worse to be here in her home and still so far away.

My mom sighed. "So. You're the one who wanted to go to the *Lunae Libri.*"

"You mean the secret stairway into the Tunnels? Will it lead into the *Lunae Libri*?"

"Well, I don't mean the Gatlin County Library." My mom smiled.

I pushed past her into the hallway and took off running. By the time she caught up to me, I had made it all the way to Macon's old room. I flipped up the carpet and yanked open the trapdoor.

There they were.

The invisible stairs leading down into the Caster darkness.

And beyond, the Caster Library.

⊰ CHAPTER 5 ⊱

Another Lunae Libri

Darkness, it turns out, is about as dark as usual no matter what world you're in. The invisible steps beneath the trapdoor—the same ones I'd stumbled and climbed and half-fallen my way down so many times before—were every bit as invisible as they'd ever been.

And the *Lunae Libri*?

Nothing had changed about the moss-covered, rocky passageways that led us there. The long rows of ancient books, scrolls, and parchments were hauntingly familiar. Torches still threw unsteady flickering shadows across the stacks.

The Caster Library looked the same as always, even though now I was far, far away from every living Caster.

Especially the one I loved most.

I grabbed a torch from the wall, waving it in front of me. "It's all so real."

My mom nodded. "It's exactly as I remember it." She touched my shoulder. "A good memory. I loved this place."

"Me too." This was the only place that had offered me any hope when Lena and I faced the hopeless situation of her Sixteenth Moon. I looked back at my mom, half-hidden in the shadows.

"You never told me, Mom. I didn't know anything about you being a Keeper. I didn't know anything about this whole side of your life."

"I know. And I'm so sorry. But you're here now, and I can show you everything." She took my hand. "Finally."

We made our way into the darkness of the stacks, with only the torch between us. "Now, I'm no reference librarian, but I know my way around these stacks. On to the scrolls." She looked at me sideways. "I hope you never touched any of these. Not without gloves."

"Yeah. I got that down, the first time I burned all my skin off." I grinned. It was strange to be here with my mom, but now that I was, I could tell the *Lunae Libri* had been every bit hers, as much as it was Marian's.

She grinned back. "I guess that's not a problem anymore."

I shrugged. "Guess not."

She pointed to the nearest shelf, her eyes bright. It was good to see my mom back in her natural habitat.

She reached for a scroll. "C, as in *crossing*."

After what seemed like hours, we had made zero headway.

I groaned. "Can't you just tell me how to do this? Why do I have to look it up for myself?" We were surrounded by piles of scrolls, stacked all around us on the stone table at the very center of the *Lunae Libri*.

Even my mom seemed frustrated. "I already told you. I just imagine where I want to go, and I'm there. If that doesn't work for you, then I don't know how to help you. Your soul isn't the same as mine, especially not since it was fractured. You need help, and that's what books are for."

"I'm pretty sure this isn't what books are for—visitations from the dead." I glared at her. "At least, that's not what Mrs. English would say."

"You never know. Books are around for lots of reasons. As is Mrs. English." She yanked another stack of scrolls into her lap. "Here. What about this one?" She pulled open a dusty scroll, smoothing it with her hands. "It's not a Cast. It's more like a meditation. To help your mind focus, as if you were a monk."

"I'm not a monk. And I'm not any good at meditating."

"Clearly. But it wouldn't hurt you to try. Come on, focus. Listen."

She leaned over the parchment scroll, reading aloud. I read along over her shoulder.

> "In death, lie.
> In living, cry.
> Carry me home
> to remember
> to be remembered."

The words hovered in the air, like a strange silvery bubble. I reached out to touch them, but they faded out of sight as quickly as they had appeared.

I looked at my mom. "Did you see that?"

My mom nodded. "Casts are different in this world."

"Why isn't it working?"

"Try it in the original Latin. Here. Read it for yourself." She held the paper closer to the torch, and I leaned toward the light.

My voice shook as I said the words.

> *"Mortuus, iace.*
> *Vivus, fle.*
> *Ducite me domum*
> *ut meminissem*
> *ut in memoria tenear."*

I closed my eyes, but all I could think about was how far I was from Lena. How her curling black hair twisted in the

Caster breeze. How the green and the gold flecks lit her eyes, as bright and dark as she was.

How I'd probably never see her again.

"Oh, come on, EW."

I opened my eyes. "It's no use."

"Concentrate."

"I'm concentrating."

"You're not," she said. "Don't think about where you are now. Don't think about what you've lost—not the water tower or anything that came after it. Keep your head in the game."

"I am."

"No, you're not."

"How do you know?"

"Because if you were, you wouldn't be standing here. You would be halfway home, with one foot back in Gatlin."

Would I? It was hard to imagine.

"Close your eyes."

I closed them obediently.

"Repeat what I say," she whispered.

In the silence, I heard her words inside my mind, like she was speaking aloud to me.

We were Kelting, my mother and I. In death, from the grave, in a faraway world. It seemed familiar between us, something from long ago, something we had lost.

Carry me home.

Carry me home, I said.

Ducite me domum.

Ducite me domum, I said.

To *remember*.

Ut meminissem, I said.

And be *remembered*.

Ut in memoria tenear, I said.

You remember, my son.

I remember, I said.

You will remember.

I will always remember, I said.

I am the one, I said.

You will—

I will—

Remember…

⊰ CHAPTER 6 ⊱

Silver Button

I opened my eyes.

I was standing in the front hallway of Lena's house. It worked. I had crossed. I was back in Gatlin, in the world of the living. I was overwhelmed with relief; it was still here.

Gatlin remained. Which meant Lena remained. Which meant everything I'd lost—everything I'd done—hadn't been for nothing.

I leaned against the wall behind me. The room stopped spinning, and I lifted my head and looked around at the old plaster walls.

The familiar flying staircase. The shining lacquered floors.

Ravenwood.

The real Ravenwood. Mortal, solid, and heavy beneath my feet. I was back.

Lena.

I closed my eyes and fought away the prickling tears.

I'm here, L. I did it.

I don't know how long I stood frozen in place, waiting for a response, like I thought she was going to come running around the corner and into my arms.

She didn't.

She didn't even feel me Kelting.

I drew in a deep breath. The enormity of it all was still hitting me.

Ravenwood looked different than the last time I was here. It wasn't really a surprise—Ravenwood was always changing—but even so, I could tell from the black sheets hanging over all the mirrors and windows that this time things had changed for the worse.

It wasn't just the sheets. It was the way the snow fell from the ceiling, even though I was inside. The cold white drifts piled in the doorways and filled the fireplace, swirling into the air like ash. I looked up to see the ceiling crowded with storm clouds that wound all the way up the stairwell to the second floor. It was pretty cold even for a ghost, and I couldn't stop shivering.

Ravenwood always had a story, and that story was Lena's. She controlled the way the house looked with her every mood. And if Ravenwood looked like this...

Come on, L. Where are you?

I couldn't help but listen for her to answer, even though all I heard was silence.

I made my way through the slick ice of the front hall until I reached the familiar sweep of the grand front stairwell. Then I climbed the white steps, one at a time, all the way to the top.

When I turned to look down, there were no footprints at all.

"L? You in there?"

Come on. I know you can feel me here.

But she didn't say anything, and as I slipped through the cracked doorway into her bedroom, it was almost a relief to see she wasn't inside. I even checked the ceiling, where I had once found her lying along the plaster.

Lena's bedroom had changed again, like it always did. This time the viola wasn't playing by itself, and there wasn't writing everywhere, and the walls weren't glass. It didn't look like a prison, the plaster wasn't cracked, and the bed wasn't broken.

Everything was gone. Her bags were packed and neatly stacked in the center of the room. The walls and the ceiling were completely plain, like an ordinary room.

It looked like Lena was leaving.

I got out of there before I could think what that would mean for me. Before I tried to figure out how I would visit her in Barbados, or wherever she was going.

It was almost as hard to think about as leaving her the first time around.

I found my way out through the massive dining room where I had sat on so many other strange days and nights. A thick layer of frost covered the table, leaving a dark, wet rectangle on the carpet immediately below. I slipped through an open door and escaped out to the back veranda, the one that faced the sloping green hill leading to the river—where it wasn't snowing at all, just overcast and gloomy. It was a relief to be back outside, and I followed the path behind the house until I came to the lemon trees and the crumbling stone wall that told me I was at Greenbrier.

I knew what I was looking for the second I saw it.

My grave.

There it was, among the bare branches of the lemon trees, a mound of fresh soil lined with stones and covered with a sprinkling of snow.

It didn't have a headstone, only a plain old cross made of wood. The new dirt hill looked like something less than a final resting place, which actually made me feel better, rather than worse, about the whole thing.

The clouds overhead shifted, and a glimmer from the grave caught my eye. Someone had left a charm from Lena's necklace on the top of the wooden cross. The sight of it made my stomach flip over.

It was the silver button that had fallen off her sweater the night we first met in the rain on Route 9. It had gotten caught in the cracked vinyl of the Beater's front seat. In a way, it felt like we had come full circle now, from the first time I saw her to the last, at least in this world.

Full circle. The beginning and the end. Maybe I really had picked a hole in the sky and unraveled the universe. Maybe there was no kind of slipknot or half hitch or taut-line that could ever keep it all from coming undone. Something connected my first glimpse of the button to this one, even though it was just the same old button. Some small bit of universe had stretched from Lena to me to Macon to Amma to my dad and my mom—and even Marian and my Aunt Prue—back to me again. I guess Liv and John Breed were in there somewhere, and maybe Link and Ridley. Maybe all of Gatlin was.

Did it matter?

When I saw Lena for the very first time at school, how could I possibly have known where this was all headed? And if I had, would I have changed a single thing? I doubted it.

I picked up the silver button carefully. The second my fingers touched it they moved more slowly, as if I had plunged my hand to the bottom of the lake. I felt the weight of the worthless tin like it was a pile of bricks.

I put it back on the cross, but it rolled off the edge, falling onto the mounded dirt of the grave. I was too tired to try to move it again. If someone else was here, would they have seen the button move? Or did it only seem like that to me? Either way, that button was hard to look at. I hadn't thought about what it would feel like to visit my own grave. And I wasn't ready to rest, in peace or not.

I wasn't ready for any of this.

I'd never really thought past the whole dying-for-the-sake-of-the-world part of things. When you're alive, you don't dwell on how you're going to spend your time once you're dead. You just figure you're gone, and the rest will pretty much take care of itself.

Or you think you're not really going to die. You're going to be the first person in the history of the world who doesn't have to. Maybe that's some kind of lie our brains tell us to keep us from going crazy while we're alive.

But nothing's that simple.

Not when you were standing where I was.

And nobody's any different from anyone else, not when you come right down to it.

These are the kinds of things a guy thinks about when he visits his own grave.

I sat down next to my headstone and flopped back on the hard soil and grass. I plucked a single blade poking through the scattering of snow. At least it was coming in green. No dead, brown grass and lubbers now.

Thank the Sweet Redeemer, as Amma liked to say.

You're welcome. That's what I'd like to say.

I looked at the grave next to me and touched the fresh, cold soil with my hand, letting it fall through my fingers. Not a bit dry either. Things really had changed around Gatlin.

I was brought up a good Southern boy, and I knew better than to disturb or disrespect any grave in town. I had walked circles around graveyards, trailing my mom carefully to avoid accidentally putting a stray foot on someone's sacred plot.

It was Link who didn't know better than to lie on top of the graves and pretend to sleep where the dead were resting. He wanted to practice—that's what he said. A dry run. "I want to see what the view is like from down there. You wouldn't want a guy to head out for the rest a his life without knowin' where it was all takin' him in the end, would you?"

But when it came to graves, it was a different thing to worry about disrespecting your own.

That's when a familiar voice caught in the wind, surprising me with how close it was. "You get used to it, you know."

I followed the voice a few graves over, and there she was, red hair blowing wild. Genevieve Duchannes. Lena's ancestor, the first Caster who had used *The Book of Moons* to try to bring back someone she loved—the original Ethan Wate. He was my great-great-great-great-uncle, and it hadn't worked out any better for him than it had for me. Genevieve failed, and Lena's family was cursed.

The last time I saw Genevieve, I was digging up her grave with Lena, looking for *The Book of Moons*.

"Is that—Genevieve? Ma'am?" I sat up.

She nodded, curling and uncurling a loose strand of hair with her hand. "I thought you might be coming around. I wasn't sure when. There's been a lot of talk." She smiled.

"Though your kind tends to stay in Perpetual Peace. Casters, we go where we like. Most of us stay in the Tunnels. I feel better here."

Talk? I bet there was, though it was hard to imagine a town full of ghostly Sheers doing the talking. More like my Aunt Prue, probably.

Her smile faded. "But you're just a boy. It's worse, isn't it? That you're so young."

I nodded in Genevieve's direction. "Yes, ma'am."

"Well, you're here now, and that's what matters. I suppose I owe you, Ethan Lawson Wate."

"You don't owe me anything, ma'am."

"I hope to repay the debt one day. Returning my locket meant the world to me, but I don't think you'll see much gratitude from Ethan Carter Wate, wherever he may be. He always was a bit stubborn that way."

"What happened to him? If you don't mind my asking, ma'am." I'd always wondered about Ethan Carter Wate— after he came back to life for only a second. I mean, he was the beginning of all of this, everything that had happened to Lena and me. The other end of the thread we pulled, the one that had unraveled the entire universe.

Didn't I have a right to know how his story ended? It couldn't have been much worse than mine, could it?

"I don't really know. They took him away to the Far Keep. We couldn't be together, but I'm sure you know that. I learned it myself, the hard way," she said, her voice sad and far away.

Her words caught in my mind, snagging on others I'd tried to push off until now. The Far Keep. The Keepers of *The Caster Chronicles*—the same ones my mom refused to talk about. Genevieve didn't look like she wanted to elaborate either.

Why didn't anyone want to talk about the Far Keep? What were *The Caster Chronicles* really about?

I looked from Genevieve to the lemon trees. Here we were, at the site of the first big fire. It was the place where her family's land had burned, and where Lena tried to face off against Sarafine for the first time.

Funny how history repeated itself around here.

Funnier still how I was about the last person in Gatlin to figure that out.

But I had learned a few things the hard way myself. "It wasn't your fault. *The Book of Moons* sort of plays tricks on people. I don't think it was ever meant for Light Casters. I think it wanted to turn you—" She shot me a look, and I stopped talking. "Sorry, ma'am."

She shrugged. "I don't know. For the first hundred years or so, I felt that way. Like that book had stolen something from me. Like I'd been duped..." Her voice trailed off.

She was right. She had gotten the short stick.

"But good or bad, I made my own choices. They're all I have now. It's my cross to bear, and I'll be the one to bear it."

"But you did it out of love." So did Lena and Amma.

"I know. That's what helps me bear it. I just wish my Ethan

didn't have to bear it, too. The Far Keep is a cruel place." She looked down at her grave. "What's done is done. There's no cheating death any more than you can cheat *The Book of Moons*. Someone always has to pay the price." She smiled sadly. "I guess you know that, or you wouldn't be here."

"I guess I do."

I knew it better than anyone.

A twig snapped. Then a voice called out, even louder.

"Stop following me, Link."

Genevieve Duchannes disappeared at the sound of the words. I didn't know how she did it, but I was so startled that I felt myself start slipping away, too.

I clung to the voice—because it was familiar, and I would've recognized it anywhere. And because it sounded like home, chaos and all.

It was the voice that anchored me in the Mortal realm now, the same way it had kept my heart bound to Gatlin when I had been alive.

L.

I froze. I couldn't move, even though she couldn't see me.

"You tryin' to give me the slip?" Link was stomping around behind Lena, trying to catch up with her as she made her way through the lemon trees. Lena shook her head like she was trying to shake Link.

Lena.

She pushed through the brush, and I caught a glimpse of gold and green eyes. That was it; I couldn't help myself.

63

"Lena!" I shouted as loud as I could, my voice ringing across the white sky.

I took off running across the stubbly frozen ground, through the weeds and all the way down the rocky path. I flung myself into her arms…and went flying to the ground behind her.

"I'm not just trying. I'm *giving* you the slip." Lena's voice floated over me.

I had almost forgotten. I wasn't really here, not in a way she could feel. I lay back on the ground, trying to catch my breath. Then I propped myself up on my elbows, because Lena was really there, and I didn't want to miss a second of it.

The way she moved, the tilt of her head, and the soft lilt of her voice—she was perfect, full of life and beauty and everything I couldn't have anymore.

Everything that didn't belong to me.

I'm here. Right here. Can you feel me, L?

"I wanted to check on him. I haven't been out here all day. I don't want him to be lonely, or bored, or mad. Whatever he's feeling." Lena knelt next to my grave, next to me, grabbing at handfuls of cold grass.

I'm not lonely. But I miss you.

Link rubbed his hand through his hair. "You just went to check on his house. Then you checked on the water tower and your bedroom, and now you're checkin' on his grave. Maybe you should find somethin' to do other than checkin' on Ethan."

"Maybe you should find something to do other than bothering me, Link."

"I promised Ethan I'd look after you."

"You don't understand," she said.

Link looked as annoyed as Lena seemed frustrated. "What are you talkin' about? You think I don't understand? He was my *best friend* since kindergarten."

"Don't say it like that. He's still your best friend."

"Lena." Link wasn't getting anywhere.

"Don't Lena me. Out of everyone, I thought you would understand how things work around here." Her face was pale, and her mouth looked funny, like she was about to smile or cry, only she couldn't decide which.

Lena, it'll be okay. I'm right here.

But even as I thought about it, I knew nobody could fix this. The truth was, the moment I stepped off that water tower everything changed, and nothing was going to change back.

Not anytime soon.

I never knew how bad it would feel from this side. At least for me. Because I could see it all, but I couldn't do a thing to change it.

I reached for her hand, sliding my fingers around hers. My hands slipped right through, but if I really concentrated, I could still feel them, heavy and solid.

For the very first time, nothing shocked me. No burning. It wasn't like sticking my fingers in an electrical outlet.

I guess being dead will do that for you.

"Lena, help me out here. I don't speak chick—you know that—and Rid isn't here to translate."

"*Chick*?" Lena shot him a withering look.

"Aw, come on. I barely speak English, unless we're talkin' about the Lowcountry kind."

"I thought you went looking for Ridley," Lena said.

"I did, all through the Tunnels. Everywhere Macon sent me and a few places he'd never let me go. Holy hell—I haven't found anyone who's seen her."

Lena sat down and straightened the line of rocks around my grave. "I need her to come back. Ridley knows how it all works. She'll help me figure out what to do."

"What are you talkin' about?" Link sat down next to her, and next to me.

Just like old times, when the three of us would sit together on the bleachers at Jackson High. They just didn't know it.

"He's not dead. Just like Uncle Macon wasn't dead. Ethan will come back—you'll see. He's probably trying to find me right now."

I squeezed her hand. She was right about that, at least.

"Don't you think you'd be able to tell, if he was?" Link sounded a little doubtful. "If he was here, don't you think he'd give us a shout-out or somethin' like that?"

I tried her hand again, but it was no use.

Will you two pay attention?

Lena shook her head, oblivious. "It's not like that. I'm not saying he's sitting here next to us or something."

But I was. Sitting next to them or something.

Guys? I'm right here?

Even though I was Kelting, I felt like I was shouting.

"Yeah? How do you know where he is or isn't? If you're so sure and all?" Link's Sunday school background wasn't helping him out here. He was probably busy imagining houses made of clouds, and cherubs with wings.

"Uncle Macon said that new spirits don't know where they are or what they're doing. They barely know how they died or what happened to them in real life. It's upsetting, suddenly finding yourself in the Otherworld. Ethan might not even know who he is yet, or who I am."

I knew who she was. How could I forget something like that?

"Yeah? Well, say you're right. If that's the case, you have nothin' to worry about. Liv told me that she'd find him. She has that watch a hers all tweaked up, like some kind a Ethan Wate–ometer."

Lena sighed. "I wish it was that simple." She reached for the wooden cross. "This thing's crooked again."

Link looked frustrated. "Yeah? Well, there's no merit badge for grave diggin'. Not in Gatlin's pack meetin's."

"I'm talking about the cross, not the grave."

"You're the one who wouldn't let us get a stone," Link said.

"He doesn't need a gravestone when he's not—"

Then her hand froze, because she noticed. The silver button wasn't where she'd left it.

Of course it wasn't. It was where I dropped it.

"Link, look!"

"It's a cross. Or two sticks, dependin' on how you look at it." Link squinted. He was starting to tune out; I could tell by the glazed look in his eyes, the one I'd seen on every school day.

"Not that." Lena pointed. "The button."

"Yep. It's a button, all right. Any way you slice it." Link was staring at Lena like she was suddenly the dense one. It was probably a terrifying thought.

"It's my button. And that's not where I put it."

Link shrugged. "So?"

"Don't you get it?" Lena sounded hopeful.

"Not usually."

"Ethan's been here. He moved it."

Hallelujah, L. It's about time. We were making some progress here.

I held my arms out to her, and she threw her arms around Link and hugged him tight. Figures.

She pulled back from Link, excited.

"Hey now." Link looked embarrassed. "It could have been the wind. It could have been—I don't know—wildlife or somethin'."

"It wasn't." I knew the mood she was in. There was nothing anyone could say to change her mind, no matter how irrational it seemed.

"Seem pretty sure a that."

"I am." Lena's cheeks were pink, and her eyes were bright. She opened her notebook, unclipping the Sharpie from her charm necklace with one hand. I smiled to myself, because I'd given her that Sharpie at the top of the Summerville water tower, not so long ago.

I winced at the thought now.

Lena scribbled something and ripped out the page of her notebook. She used a rock to hold the note on top of the cross.

The paper fluttered in the cool breeze but remained where she'd left it.

She wiped a stray tear and smiled.

The paper had only one word on it, but we both knew what it meant. It was a reference to one of the first conversations we'd ever had, when she told me what it said on the poet Bukowski's grave. Only two words: *Don't try.*

But the torn piece of paper on my grave was christened with only one word, in all caps. Still damp and still smelling like Sharpie.

Sharpie and lemons and rosemary.

All the things that were Lena.

TRY.

I will, L.
I promise.

Crosswords

As I watched Link and Lena disappear toward Ravenwood, I knew there was one more place I needed to go, one person I had to see before I went back. She owned Wate's Landing more than any Wate ever would. She haunted that place even in full flesh and blood.

Part of me was dreading it, imagining how torn up she must be. But I needed to see her, all the same.

Bad things had happened.

I couldn't change that, no matter how much I wanted to.

Everything felt wrong, and even seeing Lena didn't make it feel right.

As Aunt Prue would say, things had gone cattywampus.

Whether in this realm or any other, Amma was always the one person who could set me straight.

I sat on the curb across the street, waiting for the sun to go down. I couldn't get myself to move. I didn't want to. I wanted to watch the sun dip behind the house, behind the clotheslines and the old trees and the hedge. I wanted to watch the sunlight fade and the lights in the house go on. I watched for the familiar glow in my dad's study, but it was still dark. He must be teaching at the university, as if nothing had happened. That was probably good, better even. I wondered if he was still working on his book about the Eighteenth Moon, unless restoring the Order had brought an end to that, too.

There was a light in the kitchen bay window, though.

Amma.

A second light flickered through the small square window next to it. The Sisters were watching one of their shows.

Then, in the dwindling light, I noticed something strange. There were no bottles on our old crepe myrtle. The one where Amma hung empty, cracked glass bottles to trap any evil spirits that happened to float our way and to keep them from getting in our house.

Where could the bottles have gone? Why wouldn't she need them now?

I stood up and walked a little closer. I could see through

71

the kitchen window to where Amma sat at our old wooden table, probably doing a crossword. I could imagine the #2 pencils scratching, could almost hear them.

I crossed the lawn and stood in the driveway, just outside the window. For once I figured it was a good thing no one could see me, because peeping in windows at night in Gatlin is what made even decent folks want to get out their shotguns. Then again, there were lots of things that made folks around here want to get out their shotguns.

Amma looked up and out into the darkness, like a deer in the headlights. I could have sworn she saw me. Then real headlights flashed behind me, and I realized it wasn't me Amma was looking at.

It was my dad, driving my mom's old Volvo. Pulling right through me and into the driveway. As if I wasn't there.

Which, in a whole lot of ways, I wasn't.

I stood in front of the house that I had spent so many summers repainting, and reached out to touch the brushstrokes next to the door. My hand slipped partway through the wall.

It disappeared inside, kind of like when I shoved it through the Charmed door of the *Lunae Libri*, the one that only looked like a regular old grating.

I pulled my hand out and stared at it.

Looked fine to me.

I stepped closer, into the side wall of the house, and found myself trapped. It kind of burned, like walking into a lit fireplace. I guess slipping my hand through was one thing, but getting my body into the house was another.

I went around to the front door. Nothing. I couldn't even kick a foot partway through. I tried the window above the kitchen table, and the one over the sink. I tried the back windows and the side windows and even the cat door that Amma had installed for Lucille.

No luck.

Then I figured out what was going on, because I went back to the kitchen window and saw what Amma was doing. It wasn't the *New York Times* crossword puzzle, or even *The Stars and Stripes* one. She had a needle, not a pencil, in one hand, and a square of cloth instead of paper in the other. She was doing something I'd seen her do a thousand times, and it wasn't going to improve anyone's vocabulary or keep anyone's mind New York City sharp.

It had to do with keeping people's souls safe—Gatlin County safe.

Because Amma was sewing a little bundle of ingredients into one of her infamous charm bags, the kind I had found in my drawers and beneath my mattress and sometimes even in my own pockets. Considering that I couldn't step foot in the house, she must have been sewing them nonstop since I jumped off the water tower.

As usual, she was using her charms to protect Wate's Landing, and there was no getting past any one of them. The salt snaking its way across the windowsill was even thicker than usual. For the first time, there was no doubt that her crazy protections kept our house haint-free. For the first time, I noticed the strange glow of the salt, as if whatever powered it leaked into the air around the windowsills.

Great.

I was rattling the screen out back, when I caught a glimpse of the stairwell leading down to Amma's canning pantry. I thought about the secret door at the back of that little room of storage shelves, the one that had probably been used for the Underground Railroad. I tried to remember where the tunnel came out—the one where we'd found the *Temporis Porta*, the magical door that opened into the Far Keep. Then I remembered the tunnel's trapdoor opening to the field across Route 9. It had gotten me out of the house before; maybe it could get me in this time.

I closed my eyes and thought about that spot, as hard as I could. It didn't work before, when I'd tried to imagine myself somewhere. But that didn't mean I couldn't try again. My mom said that's how it worked for her. Maybe all I had to do was picture myself somewhere hard enough, and I'd find my way there. Kind of like the ruby slippers in *The Wizard of Oz*—only without the actual slippers.

I thought about the fairgrounds.

I thought about the cigarette butts and the old weeds and the hard dirt with the imprints of long-gone carnival booths and trailer hitches.

Nothing happened.

I tried again. Still nothing.

I wasn't sure how your average Sheer did it. Which left me ten kinds of stuck. I almost gave up and walked, figuring if I could make it out to Route 9, I could hitch a ride on the back of an unsuspecting pickup truck.

Just when it seemed impossible, I thought about Amma. I thought about wanting to get inside my house so badly I could taste it, like a whole plate of Amma's pot roast. I thought about how much I missed her, how I wanted to hug her, take a good scolding, and untie her apron strings, like I had my entire life.

The minute those thoughts formed clearly in my mind, my feet started to buzz. I looked down, but I couldn't see them. I felt like a seltzer tablet someone had dropped into a glass of water, like everything around me was starting to bubble and fizz.

Then I was gone.

I found myself standing in the tunnel, right across from the *Temporis Porta*. The ancient door looked as forbidding to me in death as it had in life, and I was happy to leave it behind as I made my way through the tunnel and toward Wate's Landing. I knew where I was going, even in the dark.

I ran the whole way home.

I kept running until I shoved my way through the pantry door, up the stairs, and into the kitchen. Once I got past the problem of the salt and the charms, the walls didn't seem like a big deal—or feel like much of one either.

It was like walking in front of one of the Sisters' endless slide shows, where you step in front of the projector during the hundredth photo of the cruise ship, and suddenly you look down and the ship is cruising right over you. That's what a wall felt like. Just a projection, as unreal as a photograph from someone else's trip to the Bahamas.

Amma didn't look up as I approached. The floorboards didn't squeak for the first time ever, and I thought about all the times I would've appreciated that—when I was trying to sneak out of that kitchen or my house, out from beneath Amma's watchful eye. It required a miracle, and even then it usually didn't work.

I could have used a few Sheer skills back when I was alive. Now I would give anything for someone to know I was actually here. Funny how things work out like that. Like they say, I guess you really do have to be careful what you wish for.

Then I stopped in my tracks. Actually, the smells coming from the oven stopped me.

Because the kitchen smelled like Heaven, or the way Heaven should smell—since I was thinking about it a lot more these days. The two greatest smells on earth. Pulled pork with Carolina Gold, that was one of them. I'd know Amma's famous golden mustard barbeque sauce anywhere, not to mention the slow-cooked pork that gave up and fell to pieces at the first touch of a fork.

76

The other smell was chocolate. Not just chocolate, but the densest, darkest chocolate around, which meant the inside of Amma's Tunnel of Fudge cake, my favorite of all her desserts. The one she never made for any contest or fair or family in need—just for me, on my birthday or when I got a good report card or had a rotten day.

It was my cake, like lemon meringue was Uncle Abner's pie.

I sank into the nearest chair at the kitchen table, my head in my hands. The cake wasn't for me to eat. It was for her to give, an offering. Something to take out to Greenbrier and leave on my grave.

The thought of that Tunnel of Fudge cake laid out on the fresh dirt by the little wooden cross made me want to throw up.

I was worse than dead.

I was one of the Greats, but a whole lot less great.

The egg timer went off, and Amma pushed back her chair, spearing the charm bag with her needle one last time and letting it drop to the table.

"Don't want your cake to dry out now, do we, Ethan Wate?" Amma yanked open the oven door, and a blast of heat and chocolate shot out. She stuck her quilted mitts in so far I worried she was going to catch fire herself. Then she yanked out the cake with a sigh, almost hurling it onto the burner.

"Best let it cool a bit. Don't want my boy burnin' his mouth."

Lucille smelled the food and came wandering into the kitchen. She leaped onto the table, just like always, getting the best vantage point possible.

When she saw me sitting there, she let out a horrible howl. Her eyes caught me in a fixed glare, as if I'd done something deeply and personally offensive.

Come on, Lucille. You and me, we go way back.

Amma looked at Lucille. "What's that, old girl? You got somethin' to say?"

Lucille yowled again. She was ratting me out to Amma. At first I thought she was just trying to be difficult. Then I realized she was doing me a favor.

Amma was listening. More than listening—she was scowling and looking around the room. "Who's there?"

I looked back at Lucille and smiled, reaching out to scratch her on the top of her head. She twitched beneath my hand.

Amma swept the kitchen with her eagle eye. "Don't you be comin' in my house. Don't need you spirits comin' around. There's nothin' here left to take. Just a lot a broken-down old ladies and broken hearts." She reached slowly toward the jar sitting on the counter and took hold of the One-Eyed Menace.

There it was. Her death-defying, all-powerful wooden spoon of justice. The hole in the middle looked even more like an all-seeing eye tonight. And I had no doubt it could see, maybe as well as Amma. In this state—wherever I was—I could see plain as day that the thing was strangely powerful. Like the salt, it practically glowed, leaving a trail of light where she waved it in the air. I guess things of power came in all shapes and sizes. And when it came to the One-Eyed Menace, I'd be the last one to doubt anything it could do.

I shifted uncomfortably in my chair. Lucille shot me another look, hissing. Now she was getting bratty. I wanted to hiss right back at her.

Stupid cat. This is still my house, Lucille Ball.

Amma looked my way, as if she was seeing straight into my eyes. It was eerie, how close she came to knowing right where I was. She raised the spoon high above the both of us.

"Now you listen. I don't take kindly to you stickin' your nose inta my kitchen, uninvited. You either get outta my house, or you make yourself known, you hear? I won't have you intrudin' on this family. Been through nearabout enough already."

I didn't have much time. The smell from Amma's charm bag was making me kind of sick, to tell the truth, and I didn't have a whole lot of experience at haunting—if this even qualified. I was completely out of my league.

I stared at the Tunnel of Fudge cake. I didn't want to eat it, but I knew I had to do something with it. Something to make Amma understand—just like Lena and the silver button.

The more I thought about that cake, the more I knew what I had to do.

I took a step toward Amma and her cake, ducking around the defensive spoon—and stuck my hand into the fudge, as far as I could. It wasn't easy—it felt like I was trying to grab a handful of cement minutes before it hardened into actual pavement.

But I did it anyway.

I scooped out a big piece of chocolate cake, letting it topple off the side and slide onto the burner. I might as well have taken a bite out of it—that's pretty much what the gaping hole in the side of the cake looked like.

One giant ghostly bite.

"No." Amma stared, wide-eyed, holding the spoon in one hand and her apron in the other. "Ethan Wate, is that you?"

I nodded, even though she couldn't see me. She must have felt something, though, because she lowered the spoon and dropped into the chair across from me, letting the tears flow like a baby in the cry room at church.

Between the tears I heard it.

Just a whisper, but I heard it as clearly as if she had shouted my name.

"My boy."

Her hands were shaking as she held on to the edge of the old table. Amma might be one of the greatest Seers in the Lowcountry, but she was still a Mortal.

I had become something else.

I moved my hand over hers, and I could have sworn she slipped her fingers between mine. She rocked in her chair a little, the way she did when she was singing a hymn she loved or was just about to finish a particularly hard crossword.

"I miss you, Ethan Wate. More than you know. Can't bear to do my puzzles. Can't recall how to cook a roast." She wiped her hand across her eyes, leaving it on her forehead like she had a headache.

I miss you, too, Amma.

"Don't go too far from home, not just yet. You hear me? I've a few things to tell you, one a these days."

I won't.

Lucille licked her paw and rolled it over her ears. She hopped down from the table and howled one last time. She started to walk out of the kitchen, stopping only to look back at me. I could hear what she was saying, as clearly as if she was speaking to me.

Well? Come on, already. You're wasting my time, boy.

I turned and gave Amma a hug, reaching my long arms all the way around her tiny frame, as I had so many times before.

Lucille stopped and cocked her head, waiting. So I did what I'd always done when it came to that cat. I got up from the table and followed.

⇥ CHAPTER 8 ⇤

Broken Bottles

Lucille scratched at the door to Amma's room, and it slid open. I slipped through the crack in the door right after the cat.

Amma's room looked better and worse than it did the last time I saw it, the night I jumped off the water tower. That night, the jars of salt, river stones, and graveyard dirt—the ingredients in so many of Amma's charms—were missing from their places on the shelves, along with at least two dozen other bottles. Her "recipe" books had been scattered across the floor, without so much as a single charm or doll in sight.

The room had been a reflection of Amma's state of mind— lost and desperate, in a way that hurt to remember.

Today it looked completely different, but as far as I could

tell, the room was still full of what she was feeling on the inside, the things she didn't want anyone to see. The doors and windows were laden with charms, but if Amma's old charms were as good as they come, these were even better—stones intricately arranged around the bed, bundles of hawthorn tied around the windows, strands of beads decorated with tiny silver saints and symbols looped around the bedposts.

She was working hard to keep something out.

The jars were still crowded together the way I remembered them, but the shelves weren't bare anymore. They were lined with cracked brown, green, and blue glass bottles. I recognized them immediately.

They were from the bottle tree in our front yard.

Amma must have taken them down. Maybe she wasn't afraid of evil spirits anymore. Or maybe she just didn't want to catch the wrong one.

The bottles were empty, but each one was stopped up with a cork. I touched a small bluish-green one with a long crack down one side. Slowly, and with about as much ease as if I was pushing the Beater all the way up the hill to Ravenwood on a summer day, I edged the cork out from the rim of the bottle, and the room began to fade....

The sun was hot, swamp mist rising like ghosts over the water. But the little girl with the neat braids knew better. Ghosts were made of more than steam and mist. They were as real as she was, waiting for her ancient grandmamma or her aunties to call them up. And they were just like the living.

Some were friendly, like the girls who played hopscotch and cat's cradle with her. And others were nasty, like the old man who paced around the graveyard in Wader's Creek whenever there was thunder. Either way, the spirits could be helpful or ornery, depending on their mood and what you had to offer. It was always a good idea to bring a gift. Her great-great-great-grandmamma had taught her that.

The house was just up the hill from the creek, like a weatherworn blue lighthouse, leading both the dead and the living back home. There was always a candle in the window after dark, wind chimes above the door, and a pecan pie on the rocker in case someone came calling. And someone always came calling.

Folks came from miles and miles to see Sulla the Prophet. That's what they called her great-great-great-grandmamma, on account of how many of her readings came to pass. Sometimes they even slept on the little patch of grass in front of the house, waiting for the chance to see her.

But to the girl, Sulla was just the woman who told her stories and taught her to tat lace and make a butter piecrust. The woman with a sparrow that would fly in the window and sit right on her shoulder, like it was a branch on an old oak.

When she reached the front door, the girl stopped and smoothed her dress before she went in.

"Grandmamma?"

"I'm in here, Amarie." Her voice was smooth and thick—"Heaven and honey," the men in town called it.

The house was only two rooms and a small cooking space. The main room was where Sulla worked, reading tarot cards and tea leaves, making charms and roots for healing. There were glass canning jars all over, full of everything from witch hazel and chamomile to crows' feathers and graveyard dirt. On the bottom shelf was one jar Amarie was allowed to open. It was full of buttery caramels, wrapped in thick wax-coated paper. The doctor who lived in Moncks Corner brought them whenever he came by for ointments and a reading.

"Amarie, you come on over here now." Sulla was fanning a deck of cards out on the table. They weren't the tarot cards the ladies from Gatlin and Summerville liked her to read. These were the cards Grandmamma saved for special readings. "You know what these are?"

Amarie nodded. "Cards a Providence."

"That's right." Sulla smiled, her thin braids falling over her shoulder. Each one was tied with a colored string—a wish someone who visited her was hoping would come true. "Do you know why they're different from tarot cards?"

Amarie shook her head. She knew the pictures were different—the knife stained with blood. The twin figures facing each other with palms touching.

"Cards a Providence tell the truth—the future even I don't want to see some days. Dependin' on whose future I'm readin'."

The little girl was confused. Didn't tarot cards show a true future if a powerful reader was interpreting the spread? "I thought all cards show the truth if you know how to make sense a them."

The sparrow flew in from the open window and perched on the old woman's shoulder. "There's the truth you can face and the truth you can't. You come over here and sit down, and I'll show you what I mean." Sulla shuffled the cards, the Angry Queen disappearing into the deck behind the Black Crow.

Amarie walked around to the other side of the table and sat down on the crooked stool where so many folks waited to see their fate.

Sulla flicked her wrist, fanning the cards out in one swift motion. Her necklaces tangled together at her throat—silver charms etched with images Amarie didn't recognize, hand-painted wooden beads strung between bits of rock, colored crystals that caught the light when Sulla moved. And Amarie's favorite—a smooth black stone threaded through a piece of cord that rested on the hollow of Sulla's neck.

Grandmamma Sulla called it "the eye."

"Now pay attention, Little One," Sulla instructed.
"One day you'll be doin' this on your own, and I'll be
whisperin' to you from the wind."

Amarie liked the sound of that.

She smiled and pulled the first card.

The edges of the vision blurred, and the row of colored bottles came back into view. I was still touching the cracked bluish-green one and the cork that had unleashed the memory—one of Amma's, trapped like a dangerous secret she didn't want to escape into the world. But it wasn't dangerous at all, except maybe to her.

I could still see Sulla showing her the Cards of Providence, the cards that would one day form the spread that showed her my death.

I pictured the faces of the cards, especially the twins, face to face. The Fractured Soul. My card.

I thought about Sulla's smile and how small she looked compared to the giant she seemed to be as a spirit. But she wore the same intricate braids and heavy strands of beads snaking around her neck in both life and death. Except the cord with the black stone—I didn't remember that one.

I looked down at the empty bottle, pushing back the cork and leaving it on the shelf with the others. Did all these bottles hold Amma's memories? The ghosts that were haunting her in ways the spirits never would?

I wondered if the night of my death was in one of those bottles, shoved down deep where it couldn't escape.

I hoped so, for Amma's sake.

Then I heard the stairs creak.

"Amma, you in the kitchen?" It was my dad.

"I'm in here, Mitchell. Right where I always am before supper," Amma answered. She didn't sound normal, but I didn't know if my dad could tell.

I followed the sound of their voices back through the hall. Lucille was sitting at the other end waiting for me, her head tilted to the side. She sat straight like that until I was inches away from her, and then she stood up and sauntered off.

Thanks, Lucille.

She'd done her job, and she was through with me. Probably had a saucer of cream and a fluffy pillow waiting for her in front of the television.

I guessed I wasn't going to be able to spook her again.

As I rounded the corner, my dad was pouring himself a glass of sweet tea. "Did Ethan call?"

Amma stiffened, her cleaver poised over an onion, but my dad didn't seem to notice. She started chopping. "Caroline has him busy waitin' on her. You know how she is, classy and sassy, just like her mamma was."

My dad laughed, his eyes crinkling in the corners. "That's true, and she's a terrible patient. She must be driving Ethan crazy."

My mom and Aunt Prue weren't kidding. My dad was under the influence of a serious Cast. He had no idea what had happened. I wondered how many of Lena's family members it took to pull this off.

Amma reached for a carrot, lopping the end off before she even got it on the cutting board. "A broken hip's a lot worse than the flu, Mitchell."

"I know—"

"What's all that racket?" Aunt Mercy called from the living room. "We're tryin' ta watch *Jeopardy!*"

"Mitchell, get on in here. Mercy's no good at the music questions." It was Aunt Grace.

"You're the one who thinks Elvis Presley is still alive," Aunt Mercy shot back.

"I most certainly do. He can dance himself a mean jive," Aunt Grace shouted, catching every third word at best. "Mitchell, hurry on up. I need a witness. And bring some cake with you."

My dad reached for the Tunnel of Fudge cake on the counter, still warm from the oven. When he disappeared down the hall, Amma stopped chopping and rubbed the worn gold charm of her necklace. She looked sad and broken, cracked like the bottles lined up on the shelves in her bedroom.

"Be sure and let me know if Ethan calls tomorrow," my dad shouted from the living room.

Amma stared out the window for a long time before she spoke, barely loud enough for me to hear. "He won't."

89

⊰ CHAPTER 9 ⊱

The Stars and Stripes

Leaving Amma behind was like stepping away from a fire on the coldest night of winter. She felt like home, safe and familiar. Like every scolding and every supper I'd ever had, everything that had been me. The closer I was to her, the warmer I felt—but in the end, it made the cold feel that much colder when I walked away.

Was it worth it? Feeling better for a minute or two, knowing that the cold would still be out there waiting?

I wasn't sure, but for me it wasn't a choice. I couldn't stay away from Amma or Lena—and deep down, I didn't think either one of them wanted me to.

Still, there was a silver lining, even if it was a little

tarnished. If Lucille could see me, that was something. I guess it was true what people said about cats seeing spirits. I just never figured I would be the one to prove it.

And then there was Amma. She hadn't exactly seen me, but she'd known I was there. It wasn't much, but it was something. I had been able to show her, just like I'd been able to show Lena I was at my grave.

It was exhausting, taking a chunk out of a cake or moving a button a few inches. But it had gotten the message across.

In a way, I was still here in Gatlin, where I belonged. Everything had changed, and I didn't have the answers for how to fix that. But I hadn't gone anywhere, not really.

I was here.

I existed.

If only I could find a way to say what I really wanted to say. There was just so much I could do with a Tunnel of Fudge cake and an old cat and a random charm on Lena's necklace.

To tell you the truth, I was feeling downright woebegone. As in, stuck in the doldrums without a map, Ethan Wate.

W. O. E. B. E. G. O. N. E.

Nine across.

That's when it came to me. Not so much an idea as a memory—of Amma sitting at our kitchen table, all hunched over her crossword puzzles with a bowl of Red Hots and a pile of extra-sharp #2 pencils. Those puzzles were how she kept things right, figured things out.

In that moment it all came together. The way I saw an

opening on the basketball court or figured out the plot at the beginning of a movie.

I knew what I had to do, and I knew where I had to go. It was going to require a little more than scooping out a cake or pushing around a button, but not much more.

More like a few strokes of a pencil.

It was time I paid a visit to the office of *The Stars and Stripes*, the best and only newspaper in Gatlin County.

I had a crossword puzzle to write.

There wasn't a single grain of salt lining any window at *The Stars and Stripes* office, any more than there was a single grain of truth in the paper itself. There were, however, swamp coolers in every window. More swamp coolers than I had ever seen in one building. They were all that remained of a summer so hot that the whole town had almost dried up and blown away, like dead leaves on a magnolia tree.

Still, no charms, no salt, no Bindings or Casts or even a cat. I slipped in as easy as the heat had. A guy could get used to this kind of access.

Inside the office, there wasn't much more than a few plastic plants, a reenactment calendar that hung crookedly on the wall, and a high linoleum counter. That's where you stood with your ten dollars when you wanted to put an ad in the paper to hawk your piano lessons or new puppies or the old plaid couch that had been sitting in your basement since 1972.

That was about it until you got behind the counter, where three little desks stood in a row. They were covered with papers—exactly the papers I was looking for. This was what *The Stars and Stripes* looked like before it became an actual newspaper—when it was still something closer to the town gossip.

"What are you doing in here, Ethan?"

I turned around, startled, my hands up at my sides as if I'd just been busted for breaking and entering—which, in a way, I had.

"Mom?"

She was standing behind me in the empty office, on the other side of the counter.

"Nothing." It was all I could say. I shouldn't have been surprised. She knew how to cross. After all, she was the one who'd helped me find my way back to the Mortal realm.

Still, I hadn't expected to find her here.

"You're not doing 'nothing,' unless you've decided to become a journalist and report on life from the Great Beyond. Which, considering how many times I tried to get you to join the staff of *The Jackson Stonewaller*, doesn't seem likely."

Yeah, okay. I had never wanted to eat my lunch in there with the school newspaper staff. Not when I could be in the lunchroom with Link and the guys from the basketball team.

The things I thought were important back then seemed so stupid now.

"No, ma'am."

"Ethan, please. Why are you here?"

"I guess I could ask you the same question." My mom shot me a look. "I'm not looking for a job at the paper. I just want to help out on one little section."

"That's not a good idea." She spread her hands on the counter in front of me.

"Why not? You were the one sending me all those Shadowing Songs. It's practically the same thing. This is just a little more—direct."

"What are you planning to do? Write Lena a want ad and publish it in the paper? 'Wanted, one Caster girlfriend. Preferably named Lena Duchannes'?"

I shrugged. "That wasn't exactly what I had in mind, but it could work."

"You can't. You can barely pick up a pencil in this realm. You don't have physics working on your behalf as a Sheer. Around here, picking up a feather is harder than dragging a two-by-four down the street with your pinkie."

"Can *you* do it?"

She shrugged. "Maybe."

I looked at her meaningfully. "Mom, I want her to know I'm all right. I want her to know I'm here—like you wanted to let me know when you left the code in the books in the study. Now I have to find a way to tell her."

My mom walked around the counter slowly, without saying a word for a long minute. She watched as I moved across the room toward the piles of newsprint.

"Are you sure about this?" She sounded hesitant.

"Are you going to help me or not?"

She came and stood next to me, which was her way of answering. We began to read the next issue of *The Stars and Stripes*, laid out all over every surface. I leaned over the papers on the nearest desk. "Apparently, the Ladies Auxiliary of Gatlin County is starting a book club called the Read & Giggle."

"Your Aunt Marian is going to be thrilled to hear that; the last time she tried to start a book club, nobody could agree on a book, and they had to disband after the first meeting." My mom had a wicked glint in her eye. "But not until they voted to spike the lemonade with a big box of wine. Just about everyone agreed on that."

I kept going. "Well, I hope the Read & Giggle doesn't end up the same way, but if it does, don't worry. They're also starting a table tennis club called the Hit & Giggle."

"And look at that." She pointed over my arm. "Their supper club is called the Dine & Giggle."

I stifled a laugh, pointing. "You missed the best one. They're renaming the Gatlin Cotillion to—wait for it—the Wiggle & Giggle."

We went through the rest of the paper, having about as good a time as two Sheers stuck in a small-town newspaper office could ask for. It was like a scrapbook of our life together, all glued onto a whole bunch of newsprint. The Kiwanis Club was getting ready for its annual pancake breakfast, where the pancakes were raw and liquid in the middle, the way my dad liked them best. Gardens of Eden had won Main Street Window of the Month, which it did pretty much every month, since there weren't all that many windows on Main anymore.

It only got better as we read on. A wild hen was roosting in the Santa's sled that Mr. Asher had put up as part of his light-up lawn display, which was awesome, because the Ashers' holiday displays were infamous. One year Mrs. Asher even put lipstick on Emily's Baby Cuddles Jesus because she didn't think his mouth showed up well enough in the dark. When my mom tried to ask her about it with a straight face, Mrs. Asher said, "You can't just expect to shout hosannas and have everyone get the message, Lila. Lord have mercy, half the folks around here don't even know what hosanna means." When my mom pressed her further, it was obvious Mrs. Asher didn't either. After that, she never invited us to her house again.

The rest of it was the news you'd expect around here, the kind that never changed even when it always changed. Animal Control had picked up a lost cat; Bud Clayton had won the Carolina Duck-Calling Contest. The Summerville Pawnshop was running a special, Big B's Vinyl Siding and Windows was shutting down, and the *Quik-Chik* Leadership Scholarship competition was heating up.

Life goes on, I guess.

Then I saw the page for the crossword puzzle and slid it toward me as quickly as I could. "There."

"You want to do the crossword puzzle?"

"I don't want to do it. I want to write one for Amma. If she saw it, she'd tell Lena."

My mom shook her head. "Even if you could manage to get the letters the way you want them on the page, Amma won't see it. She doesn't take the paper anymore. Not since you—left. She hasn't touched one of her puzzles in months."

I winced. How could I have forgotten? Amma had said it herself while I was standing in the kitchen at Wate's Landing.

"What about a letter, then?"

"I've tried it a hundred times, but it's nearly impossible. You can only use what's already on the page." She studied the paper in front of us. "Actually, it might work because you can drag the letters around on the draft. See, how they're laying it out on the table?"

She was right. The way the puzzle worked, the letters were cut into a thousand tiles, like a Scrabble board. All I had to do was move the paper around.

If I was even strong enough to do that.

I looked at my mom, more determined than ever. "Then we'll use the crossword, and I'll make Lena see it."

Moving the letters into place was like digging up a rock from the Sisters' garden, but my mom helped me. She shook her head as we stared at the page. "A crossword puzzle. I don't know why I didn't think of that."

I shrugged. "I'm just not very good at writing songs."

In its current state, the crossword was barely half-finished, but the staff around here probably wouldn't mind too much if I helped them along. After all, it looked like the Sunday edition, the biggest day for *The Stars and Stripes*—at least for the crossword. Between the three of them, they'd probably be relieved that someone else had taken it on this week. I was surprised they didn't have Amma in here writing the puzzles for them already.

The only hard part would be getting Lena to take an interest in this puzzle at all.

Eleven across.

P. O. L. T. E. R. G. E. I. S. T.

As in, apparition or phantasm. A spectral being. A spirit from another world. A ghost. The vaguest shadow of a person, the thing that comes to you in the night when you think no one is looking.

In other words, the thing you are, Ethan Wate.

Six down.

G. A. T. L. I. N.

As in, parochial. Local. Insular. The place we're stuck, whether in the Otherworld or the Mortal one.

E. T. E. R. N. A. L.

As in, endless, without stopping, forever. The way you feel about a certain girl, whether you're dead or alive.

L. O. V. E.

As in, how I feel about you, Lena Duchannes.

T. R. Y.

As in, as hard as I can, every minute of every day.

As in, I got your message, L.

Then I felt overwhelmed by the thought of how much I'd lost, of everything that stupid fall off the water tower had cost me, and I lost control and loosened my grip on Gatlin. First my eyes filled, and then the letters blurred away, drifting into nothing as the world vanished beneath my feet and I was gone.

I was crossing back. I tried to remember the words from the scroll—the ones that had brought me here—but my mind couldn't focus on anything at all.

It was too late.

Darkness surrounded me, and I felt something like wind whipping across my face, howling in my ears. Then I heard my mother's voice—steady as the grip of her cool hand on mine.

"Ethan, hold on. I've got you."

CHAPTER 10

Snake Eyes

I felt my feet touch something solid, like I had just stepped off a train and onto the platform at the station. I saw the floorboards of our front porch, then my Chucks standing on them. We'd crossed back, leaving the living world behind us. We were back where we belonged, with the dead.

I didn't want to think about it like that.

"Well, it's 'bout time, seein' as I finished watchin' all your mamma's paint dry more than an hour ago."

Aunt Prue was waiting for us in the Otherworld, on the front porch of Wate's Landing—the one in the middle of the cemetery.

I still wasn't used to the sight of my house here instead of the mausoleums and weeping angel statues that dominated

Perpetual Peace. But standing by the railing, with all three Harlon Jameses sitting at attention around her feet, Aunt Prue looked pretty dominant, too.

More like mad as a hornet.

"Ma'am," I said, scratching my neck uncomfortably.

"Ethan Wate, I've been waitin' on you. Thought you'd only be gone a minute." The three dogs looked just as irritated. Aunt Prue nodded at my mother. "Lila."

"Aunt Prudence." They regarded each other warily, which seemed strange to me. They had always gotten along when I was growing up.

I smiled at my aunt, changing the subject. "I did it, Aunt Prue. I crossed. I was . . . you know, on the other side."

"You might a let a person know, so they didn't wait on your porch for the best part a the day." My aunt waved her handkerchief in my general direction.

"I went to Ravenwood and Greenbrier and Wate's Landing and *The Stars and Stripes*." Aunt Prue raised an eyebrow at me, as if she didn't believe it.

"Really?"

"Well, not by myself. I mean, with my mom. She might have helped some. Ma'am."

My mom looked amused. Aunt Prue did not.

"Well, if you want a preacher's chance in Heaven ta get yourself back there, we need ta talk."

"Prudence," my mom said in a strange tone. It sounded like a warning.

I didn't know what to say, so I just kept talking. "You mean about crossing? Because I think I'm starting to get the hang—"

"Stop yappin' and start listenin', Ethan Wate. I'm not talkin' 'bout practicin' any crossin'. I'm talkin' 'bout crossin' back. For good, ta the old world."

For a second, I thought she was teasing me. But her expression didn't change. She was serious—at least as serious as my crazy great-aunt ever was. "What are you talking about, Aunt Prue?"

"Prudence." My mom said it again. "Don't do this."

Don't do what? Give me a chance to get back there?

Aunt Prue glared at my mother, easing herself down the stairs one orthopedic shoe at a time. I reached out to help her, but she waved me off, stubborn as ever. When she finally made it to the carpet of grass at the base of the stairs, Aunt Prue stepped in front of me. "There's been a mistake, Ethan. A mighty big one. This wasn't supposed ta happen."

A tremor of hope washed over me. "What?"

The color drained out of my mom's face. "Stop." I thought she was going to pass out. I could barely breathe.

"I won't," said Aunt Prue, narrowing her eyes behind her spectacles.

"I thought we decided not to tell him, Prudence."

"You decided, Lila Jane. I'm too old not ta do as I please."

"I'm his mother." My mom wasn't giving up.

"What's going on?" I tried to wedge myself between them, but neither one of them would look my way.

Aunt Prue raised her chin. "The boy's old enough ta decide somethin' that big on his own, don'tcha think?"

"It's not safe." My mom folded her arms. "I don't mean to be firm with you, but I'm going to have to ask you to go."

I'd never heard my mother talk to any of the Sisters like that. She might as well have declared World War III for the Wate family. It didn't seem to stop Aunt Prue, though.

She just laughed. "Can't put the molasses back in the jar, Lila Jane. You know it's the truth, and you know you got no right keepin' it from your boy." Aunt Prue looked me right in the eye. "I need you ta come on with me. There's someone you need ta meet."

My mom just looked at her. "Prudence..."

Aunt Prue gave her the kind of look that could wilt and wither a whole flower bed. "Don't you *Prudence* me. You can't stop this thing. And where we're goin' you can't come, Lila Jane. You know well as I do that we both got nothin' but the boy's best interest at heart."

It was a classic Sisters' face-off, the kind where before you blinked, you were already past the point where nobody came out ahead.

A second later, my mom backed off. I would never know what happened in that silent exchange between them, and it was probably better that way.

"I'll wait for you here, Ethan." My mom looked at me. "But you be careful."

Aunt Prue smiled, victorious.

103

One of the Harlon Jameses began to growl. Then we took off down the sidewalk so fast I could barely keep up.

I followed Aunt Prue and the yipping dogs to the outer limits of Perpetual Peace—past the Snows' perfectly restored Federal-style manor house, which was situated in exactly the same spot their massive mausoleum occupied in the cemetery of the living.

"Who died?" I asked, looking at my aunt. Seeing as there wasn't anything on earth powerful enough to take down Savannah Snow.

"Great-great-grandpappy Snow, 'fore you were even half-way inta diapers. Been here a long time now. Oldest plot in the row." She picked her way down the stone path that led around back, and I followed.

We headed toward an old shed behind the house, the rotted planks barely holding up the crooked roof. I could see tiny flecks of faded paint clinging to the wood where someone had scraped it clean. There was no amount of scraping that could disguise the shade that trimmed my own house in Gatlin—haint blue. The one shade of blue meant to keep the spirits away.

I guess Amma was right about the haints not caring much for the color. As I looked around, I could already see the difference. There wasn't a graveyard neighbor in sight.

"Aunt Prue, where are we going? I've had enough of the Snows to last more than one lifetime."

She glowered at me. "I told you. We're goin' ta call on someone who knows more than me 'bout this mess." She reached for the splintered handle of the shed. "You just be thankful I'm a Statham, and Stathams get on with all kinds a folks, or we wouldn't have a soul ta help us sort things out." I couldn't look at my aunt. I was too scared I would start laughing, considering she got along with just about no kinds of folks, at least not in the Gatlin I was from.

"Yes, ma'am."

She stepped inside the shed, which didn't look like anything more than an ordinary shed. But if I'd learned anything from Lena and my experiences in her world, it was that things aren't always what they seem.

I followed Aunt Prue—and the Harlon Jameses—inside and closed the door behind us. The cracks in the wood let in just enough light for me to see her turn around in the shed. She reached for something in the dim light, and I realized it was another handle.

A hidden Doorwell, like the ones in the Caster Tunnels.

"Where are we going?"

Aunt Prue paused, her hand still resting on the iron pull. "Not all folks are lucky enough ta be buried in His Garden of Perpetual Peace, Ethan Wate. The Casters, I reckon they got as much right ta the Otherworld as we do, don'tcha think?"

Aunt Prue pushed the door open easily, and we stepped out onto a rocky coastline.

There was a house balancing dangerously on the edge of a cliff. The weathered wood was the same sad shade of gray as the rocks, as if it had been painstakingly carved from them. It was small and simple and hidden in plain sight, like so many things in the world I'd left behind.

I watched as the waves crashed against the face of the cliff, reaching toward the house but ultimately failing. This place had stood the test of time, defying nature in a way that seemed impossible.

"Whose house is that?" I offered Aunt Prue my arm, helping her navigate the uneven ground.

"You know what they say about curiosity and cats. May not kill ya, but it'll get ya inta a heap a trouble around here, too. Though trouble seems ta find you even when you ain't lookin' for it." She gathered her long flowered skirt in her other hand. "You'll see soon enough."

She wouldn't say another word after that.

We climbed a treacherous stairway carved into the side of the cliff. Where the rock wasn't reinforced with splintering boards, it crumbled away under my feet, and I almost lost my footing. I tried to remind myself that I wasn't about to go plummeting to my death, seeing as I was already dead. Still, it didn't help as much as you'd think it would. That was another thing I'd learned from the Caster world: There always seemed to be something worse around the next corner. There was always something to be afraid of, even if you hadn't figured out exactly what it was yet.

When we reached the house, all I could think was how much it reminded me of Ravenwood Manor, though the two buildings didn't resemble each other in any way. Ravenwood was a Greek Revival–style mansion, and this was a single-story clapboard. But the house seemed aware of us as we approached, alive with power and magic, like Ravenwood. It was surrounded by crooked trees with slanted branches that had been beaten into submission by the wind. It looked like the kind of twisted drawing you'd find in a book meant to terrify children into having nightmares. The kind of book where kids were trapped by more than just witches and devoured by more than wolves.

I was thinking it was a good thing I no longer needed to sleep, when my aunt marched up the walk. Aunt Prue didn't hesitate. She walked right up to the door and pounded the oxidized brass ring three times. There was writing carved around the doorframe. It was Niadic, the ancient language of Casters.

I backed up, letting all the Harlon Jameses go in front of me. They growled their tiny dog growls at the door. Before I had a chance to examine the writing more closely, the door creaked open.

An old man stood in front of us. I assumed he was a Sheer, but that wasn't a distinction worth making here—we were all spirits of one kind or another. His head was shaved and scarred, faint lines overlapping in a vicious pattern. His white

107

beard was cut short, his eyes covered by dark wraparound glasses.

A black sweater hung from his skinny frame, which was partially hidden behind the door. There was something frail and worn out about him, like he had escaped from a work camp, or worse.

"Prudence." He nodded. "Is this the boy?"

"'Course it is." Aunt Prue shoved me forward. "Ethan, this here is Obidias Trueblood. Go on in."

I extended my hand. "It's nice to meet you, sir."

Obidias held up his right hand, which had been hidden behind the door. "I'm sure you'll understand if we don't shake." His hand was severed at the wrist, a black line marking the place where it had been cut. Above the mark, his wrist was severely scarred, as if it had been punctured over and over again.

Which it had.

Five writhing black snakes extended from his wrist to the point where his fingers would normally have reached. They were hissing and striking at the air, curling around one another.

"Don't worry," Obidias said. "They won't hurt you. It's me they enjoy tormenting."

I couldn't think of anything to say. I wanted to run.

The Harlon Jameses growled even more loudly, and the snakes hissed back. Aunt Prue scowled at all of them. "Puh-lease. Not you, too."

I stared at the snake hand. Something about it was familiar.

How many guys with snakes for fingers could there be? Why did I feel like I knew him?

It hit me, and I realized who Obidias was—the guy Macon had sent Link to see in the Tunnels. Last summer, right after the Seventeenth Moon. The guy who'd died right in front of Link after Hunting bit him, in his house, this house—at least the Otherworld version of it. Back then I thought Link was exaggerating, but he wasn't.

Not even Link could have made this up.

The snake that replaced Obidias' thumb wrapped itself around his wrist, stretching its head toward me. Its tongue flicked in and out, the little fork flying.

Aunt Prue pushed me across the threshold, and I went stumbling, only inches from the snakes. "Go on in. You aren't afraid of a few itty-bitty little garden snakes, are you?"

Was she kidding? They looked like pit vipers.

I turned awkwardly toward Obidias. "I'm sorry, sir. It—they just caught me off guard."

"Don't give it another thought." He waved off the apology with a twist of the wrist on his good hand. "It's not something you see every day."

Aunt Prue sniffed. "I've seen a stranger thing or two." I stared at my aunt, who looked as smug as if she shook a new snake hand every day of her life.

Obidias closed the door behind us, but not before checking the horizon in every direction. "You came alone? You weren't followed?"

Aunt Prue shook her head. "Me? Nobody can follow me." She wasn't kidding.

I looked back to Obidias. "Can I ask you something, sir?" I had to know for sure if he'd met Link, if he was the same guy.

"Of course."

I cleared my throat. "I think you met a friend of mine. When you were alive, I mean. He told me about someone who looked like you."

Obidias held out his hand. "You mean a man with five snakes for a hand? There probably aren't many of us."

I wasn't sure how to say the next part. "If it was my friend, he was there when you—you know. Died. I'm not sure it matters, but if it does, I'd like to know."

Aunt Prue looked at me, confused. She didn't know any of this. Link had never told anyone but me, as far as I knew.

Obidias was watching me, too. "Did this friend of yours happen to know Macon Ravenwood?"

I nodded. "He did, sir."

"Then I remember him well." He smiled. "I saw him deliver my message to Macon after I passed. You can see a great deal from this side."

"I guess so." He was right. Because we were dead, we could see everything. And because we were dead, it didn't matter what we could see. So the whole seeing-things-from-the-grave concept? Majorly overrated. All you ended up seeing was more than you wanted to in the first place.

I'm pretty sure I wasn't the first guy who would've traded

seeing a little less for living a little more. I didn't say that to Edward Snakehands, though. I didn't want to think about how much I had in common with a guy whose fingers had fangs.

"Why don't we make ourselves more comfortable? We have a lot to talk about." Obidias ushered us further into the living room—really the only room I could see, except for a small kitchen and a lone door at the end of the hall, which must have led to the bedroom.

It was basically one gigantic library. Shelves extended from the floor to the ceiling, a battered brass library ladder attached to the highest shelf. A polished wooden stand held a huge leather volume, like the dictionary we had in the Gatlin County Library. Marian would've loved this place.

There was nothing else in the room aside from four thread-bare armchairs. Obidias waited for Aunt Prue and me to sit down before he chose a chair opposite ours. He removed the dark glasses he was wearing, and his eyes locked on mine.

I should have known.

Yellow eyes.

He was a Dark Caster. Of course.

That made sense, if he really was the guy from Link's story. But still, now that I thought about it, what was Aunt Prue doing, taking me to see a Dark Caster?

Obidias must have realized what I was thinking. "You didn't think there were Dark Casters here, did you?"

I shook my head. "No, sir. I guess I didn't."

"Surprise." Obidias smiled grimly.

Aunt Prue swooped in to save me. "The Otherworld's a place for unfinished business. For folks like me and you and Obidias here, who aren't ready ta move on just yet."

"And my mom?"

She nodded. "Lila Jane more than anyone. She's been kickin' around here longer than the whole lot a us."

"Some can cross freely between this world and others," Obidias explained. "We all eventually get to our destination. But those of us whose lives were cut short before we could right the wrongs haunting us, we remain here until we find that moment of peace."

He didn't have to tell me. I already knew it for myself—crossing was complicated business. And I hadn't felt anything remotely peaceful. Not yet.

I turned to Aunt Prue. "So you're stuck here, too? I mean, when you aren't crossing back to visit the Sisters? Because of me?"

"I can leave if I set my mind ta it." She patted my hand, as if to remind me I was silly to think there was ever anyone or anything that could keep my aunt from a place she wanted to go. "But I'm not goin' anywhere till you're back home, where you belong. You're a part a my unfinished business now, Ethan, and I 'cept that. I mean ta make things right." She patted my cheek. "Besides, what else am I gonna do? I got myself Mercy and Grace ta wait for, don't I?"

"Back home? You mean to Gatlin?"

"Ta Miss Amma, and Lena, and all our kin," she answered.

"Aunt Prue, I could barely cross to visit Gatlin, and even then nobody could see me."

"That's where you're wrong, boy." Obidias spoke up, and one of his angry-looking snakes sank its fangs into his wrist. He winced, pulling a piece of black material shaped like a mitten out of his pocket. He dropped the hood over the hissing snakes, using two pieces of cord at the bottom to tighten it. The snakes shifted and thrashed beneath the fabric. "Now, where was I?"

"Are you okay?" I was a little distracted. It's not every day that a guy, or even a Sheer, gets bitten by his own hand. At least I hoped it wasn't.

But Obidias didn't want to talk about himself. "When I heard about the circumstances that brought you to this side of the veil, I sent word to your aunt immediately. Your aunt and your mother."

My Aunt Prue clicked her tongue impatiently.

That explained my aunt wanting to bring me here—and my mother not wanting her to. Just because you told any two people in my family the same piece of news, that didn't mean they'd agree about what they'd heard. My mom used to say the people in the Evers family were about the most hog-minded, mule-stuck bloodline you could find—and the Wates were worse. A pack of wasps fighting over the nest—that's what my dad called the Wate family reunions.

"How did you hear about what happened?" I tried not to stare at the snakes twisting beneath the black hood.

"News travels fast in the Otherworld," he said, hesitating. "More importantly, I knew it was a mistake."

"I told you, Ethan Wate." Aunt Prue looked mighty satisfied.

If it was a mistake—if I wasn't supposed to be here—maybe there was a way to fix it. Maybe I really could go home.

I wanted so badly for it to be true, the same way I had wanted this to be a dream I could wake up from. But I knew better.

Nothing was ever how you wanted it to be. Not anymore. Not for me.

They just didn't understand.

"It wasn't a mistake. I chose to come, Mr. Trueblood. I worked it out with the Lilum. If I didn't, the people I loved, and lots of others, were going to die."

Obidias nodded. "I know all of that, Ethan. Just like I know about the Lilum and the Order of Things. I'm not questioning what you did. What I'm saying is that you never should've had to make that choice. It wasn't in the *Chronicles*."

"*The Caster Chronicles*?" I had only seen the book once, in the archive when the Council of the Far Keep came to question Marian, yet it was the second time I'd heard the subject come up since I got here. How did Obidias know about it? And whatever any of it meant, my mom hadn't exactly wanted to elaborate.

"Yes." Obidias nodded.

"I don't understand what that has to do with me."

He was silent for a moment.

"Go on, tell him." Aunt Prue was giving Obidias True-blood the same forceful look she always gave me right before she made me do something crazy, like bury acorns in her yard for baby squirrels. "He deserves ta know. Set it right."

Obidias nodded at Aunt Prue and looked back at me with those golden-yellow eyes that made my skin crawl almost as much as his snake hand did. "As you know, *The Caster Chronicles* is a record of everything that has happened in the world. But it is also a record of what might be—possible futures that have not come to pass."

"The past, the present, and the future. I remember." The three weird-looking Keepers I saw in the library and during Marian's trial. How could I forget?

"Yes. In the Far Keep, those futures can be altered, trans-forming them from *possible* futures to *actual* ones."

"Are you saying the book can change the future?" I was stunned. Marian had never mentioned any of this.

"It can," Obidias answered. "If a page is altered, or one is added. A page that was never intended to be there."

A shiver moved up my back. "What are you saying, Mr. Trueblood?"

"The page that tells the story of your death was never part of the original *Chronicles*. It was added." He looked up at me, haunted.

"Why would someone do that?"

"There are more reasons for people's actions than the num-ber of actions that are actually set in motion." His voice was distant, full of regret and sorrow I would never have expected from a Dark Caster. "The important thing is that your fate—this fate—can be changed."

Changed? Could you save a life once it was over?

I was terrified to ask the next question, to believe there was a way I could get back to everything I lost. To Gatlin. To Amma.

Lena.

All I wanted was to feel her in my arms and hear her voice in my head. I wanted to find a way back to the Caster girl I loved more than anything in this world, or any world.

"How?" The answer didn't actually matter. I would do whatever I had to, and Obidias Trueblood knew it.

"It's dangerous." Obidias' expression was a warning. "More dangerous than anything in the Mortal world."

I heard the words, but I couldn't believe them. There was nothing more terrifying than staying here. "What do I have to do?"

"You'll have to destroy your own page in *The Caster Chronicles*. The one that describes your death."

I had a thousand questions, but only one mattered. "What if you're wrong, and my page was there all along?"

Obidias stared down at what was left of his hand, the snakes rearing and striking even under the cloth. A shadow passed across his face.

He raised his eyes to meet mine.

"I know it wasn't there, Ethan. Because I'm the one who wrote it."

⊰ CHAPTER 11 ⊱

Darker Things

The room went quiet, so quiet you could hear the house creak as the wind pushed against it. So quiet you could hear the snakes hiss almost as loudly as Aunt Prue's asthma and my pounding heart. Even the Harlon Jameses slunk away, whimpering behind a chair.

For a second, I couldn't think. My mind was completely blank.

There was no way to process this—to understand why a man I had never met would change the course of my life, so irreparably and violently.

What the hell did I do to this guy?

I finally found the words, at least some of them. There were others I couldn't say in front of Aunt Prue, or she'd wash my mouth out with more than soap and probably make me suck down a bottle of Tabasco, too. "Why? You don't even know me."

"It's complicated—"

"Complicated?" My voice started rising, and I pulled myself up out of my chair. "You ruined my life. You forced me to choose between saving the people I loved and sacrificing myself. I hurt everyone I care about. They had to put a Cast on my own father to keep him from going crazy!"

"I'm sorry, Ethan. I wouldn't have wished this on my worst enemy."

"No. You just wished it on some seventeen-year-old kid you'd never met." This guy wasn't going to help me. He was the reason I was stuck in this nightmare in the first place.

Aunt Prue reached out and took my hand. "I know you're angry, and you've got more right than anyone ta be. But Obidias can help us get you back home. So you need ta sit down here and listen ta what he's got ta say."

"How do you know we can trust him, Aunt Prue? Every word that comes out of his mouth is probably a lie." I pulled my hand away.

"You listen here, and you listen good." She yanked on my arm harder than I would've expected, and I sank back down into the chair next to her. She wanted me to look her in the eye. "I've known Obidias Trueblood since before he was Light or Dark, before he'd done wrong or right. Spent the better part a my days walkin' the Caster Tunnels with the Truebloods and my daddy." Aunt Prue paused and glanced at Obidias. "And he saved me a time or two down there. Even if he wasn't smart enough ta save himself."

I didn't know what to think. Maybe my aunt had charted the Tunnels with Obidias. Maybe she could trust him.

But that didn't mean I could.

Obidias seemed to know what I was thinking. "Ethan, you may find this hard to believe, but I know what it's like to feel helpless—to be at the mercy of decisions that you didn't make."

"You have no idea how I feel." I heard the anger in my voice, but I didn't try to hide it. I wanted Obidias Trueblood to know I hated him for what he'd done to me and the people I loved.

I thought about Lena leaving the button on my grave. He didn't know what that felt like—for me or Lena.

"Ethan, I know you don't trust him, and I don't blame you." Aunt Prue was playing hardball now. This meant something to her. "But I'm askin' you ta trust me and hear him out."

I locked eyes with Obidias. "Start talking. How do I get back?"

Obidias took a long breath. "As I said, the only way to get your life back is to erase your death."

"So if I destroy the page, I go home—right?" I wanted to be sure there were no loopholes.

No calling a moon out of time, no splitting the moon in half. No curses that kept me from leaving, once the page was gone.

He nodded. "Yes. But first you have to get to the book."

"You mean from the Far Keep? The Keepers had it with them when they came for my Aunt Marian."

"That's right." He looked at me, startled. I guess he hadn't expected me to know anything about *The Caster Chronicles*.

"So what are we doing sitting around here talking? Let's get on with it." I was halfway out of my chair before I realized Obidias wasn't moving.

"And you think you'll just walk in there and take the page?" he asked. "It's not that easy."

"Who's going to stop me? A bunch of Keepers? What do I have to lose?" I tried not to think about how terrifying they had seemed when they came for Marian.

Obidias pulled the hood off his hand, and the snakes hissed and struck one another. "Do you know who did this to me? A 'bunch of Keepers' who caught me trying to steal my page from the *Chronicles*."

"Lord have mercy," Aunt Prue said, fanning herself with her handkerchief.

For a second, I didn't know if I believed him. But I recognized the emotion playing out on his face, because I was feeling it myself.

Fear.

"Keepers did that to you?"

He nodded. "Angelus and Adriel. On one of their more generous days." I wondered if Adriel was the big one who had shown up in the archive with Angelus and the albino woman. They were the three strangest-looking people I'd seen in the Caster world. At least until today.

I looked at Obidias and his snakes.

"Like I said, what can they do to me now? I'm already dead." I tried to smile, even though it wasn't funny. It was the opposite of funny.

Obidias held out his hand, the snakes jerking and stretching as they tried to reach me. "There are things worse than death, Ethan. Things that are darker than the Dark Casters. I should know. If you are caught, the Keepers will never let you leave the library at the Far Keep. You will be their scribe and their slave, forced to rewrite the futures of innocent Casters… and Mortal Waywards who are Bound to them."

"Waywards are supposed to be pretty rare. How many can there be to write about?" I had never met another one, and I'd met Vexes and Incubuses and more kinds of Casters than I ever wanted to.

Obidias leaned forward in his chair, cloaking his cruelly deformed hand once again. "Perhaps they aren't as rare as you think. Maybe they just don't live long enough for the Casters to find them."

There was an undeniable truth in his words that I couldn't explain. I guess there was some part of me that knew a lie would have sounded different. Another part knew I'd always been in danger, one way or another—with or without Lena.

Whether I was meant to jump off a water tower or not.

Either way, the fear in his voice should've been proof enough.

"Okay. So I won't get caught."

Aunt Prue's face was filled with concern. "Maybe this isn't the best idea. We should go on back ta my house and think

121

on it. Talk ta your mamma about it. She's waitin' on us, I reckon."

I squeezed her hand. "Don't worry, Aunt Prue. I know a way in. There's a *Temporis Porta* in an old tunnel beneath Wate's Landing. I can get in and out before the Keepers ever realize I was there."

If I could walk through walls in the Mortal realm, I was pretty sure I could step through the *Temporis Porta*, too.

Obidias broke the end off a thick cigar. His hand was shaking as he lit the match and held it up. He took a few puffs, until it glowed a steady orange. "You can't enter the library at the Far Keep through the Mortal realm. You have to enter through the seam." He delivered the news as calmly as if he was giving me directions to the local Stop & Steal, to pick up some milk.

"You mean the Great Barrier?" It seemed like a strange place for a door to the Far Keep's inner sanctum. "I can handle it. I did it once, and I can do it again."

"What you've done is nothing compared to what you're about to do. The Great Barrier is just one place you can get to from the seam," Obidias explained. "You can cross into other worlds from there that will make the Barrier feel like home."

"Just tell me how to get there." We were wasting time, and every second we sat around talking was another second away from Lena.

"You have to cross the Great River. It runs through the Great Barrier, all the way to the seam. It forms the border between the realms."

"Like the River Styx?"

He ignored me. "And you can't cross unless you have the river eyes—two smooth black stones."

"Are you kidding?"

He shook his head. "Not at all. They're very rare and hard to come by."

"River eyes. Got it. I can find a couple rocks."

"*If* you get across the river, and that's a big if, you'll still have to make it past the Gatekeeper before you can get into the library."

"How do I do that?"

Obidias took a puff from the cigar. "You have to offer him something he can't refuse."

"What exactly would that be?" Aunt Prue asked, as though she might have whatever it was tucked in her pocketbook. Like the Gatekeeper would be interested in three linty breath mints, some nondairy creamer, and a wad of folded-up Kleenex.

"It's always different. You'll have to figure it out when you get there," Obidias said. "He has…eclectic taste." He didn't say any more on the subject.

An offering. Eclectic taste. Whatever the hell that meant.

"Okay. So I have to find the black stones and get across the Great River," I said. "Figure out what the Gatekeeper guy wants and give it to him to get inside the library. Then find *The Caster Chronicles* and destroy my page." I paused, because the question I was about to ask was the most important detail, and I wanted to get it straight. "If I do all that and don't get caught, I'll get back home—my real home? How do I do that? What happens after I destroy the page?"

Obidias looked at Aunt Prue and back to me. "I'm not sure. It's never happened, as far as I know." He shook his head. "It's a chance, nothing more. And not even a good one…"

"Nothin's certain, Ethan Wate, 'cept for that you had a shot at a life a your own, and the Keepers stole it from you."

I stood up before they could finish talking.

Lena was waiting, in my room or hers, by the crooked cross stuck in the grass at my gravesite or somewhere else. But she was waiting—that's what mattered.

If I had a chance in hell to get back home, I'd take it.

I'm trying, L. Don't give up on me.

"I need to get going, Mr. Trueblood. I have a river to cross."

Aunt Prue opened her pocketbook and pulled out a faded map, covered with shapes that didn't represent any continent, country, or state I'd ever seen. This was more than a doodle on the back of an old church program. I knew what Aunt Prue's maps were like, and I knew how important they had been to me before—the last time I found my way to the seam, for Lena's Seventeenth Moon.

"I've been workin' on it since I got here, jus' a little bit here and there. Obidias told me you'd be needin' it." She shrugged. "Reckoned it was the least I could do."

I leaned down and hugged her. "Thanks, Aunt Prue. And don't be worried."

"I'm not," she lied. But she didn't need to be.

I was worried enough for both of us.

⊰ CHAPTER 12 ⊱

Still Here

After we got back to our side of the Otherworld—Harlon Jameses and all—I didn't go home. I left Aunt Prue at her house and walked the streets—more like the rows—of His Garden of Perpetual Peace.

Peace wasn't exactly what I was feeling.

I stopped in front of Wate's Landing. It looked every bit the same as when I left, and I knew my mom was inside. I wanted to talk to her. But there were other things I had to do first.

I sat down on the front steps, closing my eyes.

"Carry me home."

What was it?

To remember. And be remembered.

Ducite me domum.

Ut meminissem.

Ut in memoria tenear.

I remember Lena.

Not the water tower.

What came before.

I remember Ravenwood.

Let Ravenwood remember me.

Let Ravenwood—

Carry me—

I was lying in the dirt in front of Ravenwood, half-stuck beneath a rosebush and an overgrown camellia hedge. I had crossed again—and this time, all on my own.

"I'll be damned." I laughed, relieved. I was getting pretty good at this whole being-dead thing.

Then I practically ran up the old veranda steps. I had to see if Lena had gotten the message—my message. My only problem was that no one bothered to do the crossword in *The Stars and Stripes*, not even Amma. I had to find a way to get them to look at that paper, if they hadn't already.

Lena wasn't in her room, and she wasn't at my grave either. She wasn't in any of the usual places we used to go.

Not in the lemon grove or the crypt, where I'd died the first time.

I even looked in Ridley's old room, where Liv was asleep in Ridley's creaking four-poster bed. I was hoping she'd be able to sense that I was there with her Ethan Wate—ometer. No such luck. That's when I realized it was nighttime in Gatlin, the real Gatlin, and there was absolutely no correlation between time that passed in the Otherworld and Mortal time. I felt like I'd only been gone a few hours—and here it was, the middle of the night.

I didn't even know what day it was, come to think of it.

Worse yet, when I leaned over Liv's face in the moonlight, it looked like she had been crying. I felt guilty, since there was a strong possibility I was the reason for the tears, unless she and John had had a fight.

But that was unlikely, because when I looked down, I was standing right in the middle of John Breed's chest. He was curled up next to the bed, on the worn pink shag carpeting.

Poor guy. As many times as he had screwed up in the past, he was good to Liv, and for a while he believed he was the One Who Is Two. It's hard to hold a grudge against a guy who tried to give his life to save the world. If anyone understood that, it was me.

It wasn't his fault the world wouldn't have him.

So I stepped off his chest as quickly as I could, and vowed to be a little more careful where I put my feet in the future. Not that he'd ever know.

As I moved through the rest of the house it seemed completely vacant. Then I heard the crackling of a fireplace and followed the sound. At the bottom of the stairs, straight off the front hall, I found Macon sitting in his cracked leather chair by the fire. True to form, where there was Macon, there was also Lena. She was sitting at his feet, leaning against the ottoman. I could smell the Sharpie she was writing with. Her notebook lay open on her lap, but she was barely looking at it. Drawing circles over and over, until the page looked like it was ripping apart.

She wasn't crying—far from it.

She was plotting.

"It was Ethan. It had to be. I could feel him there with us, like he was standing right next to his grave."

Had she seen the crossword? Maybe that was why she was so fired up. I looked around the study, but if she'd read the paper, there was no sign of it. A stack of old newspapers filled a brass bin next to the fireplace; Macon used them for kindling. I tried to lift a single page of newsprint, and I could barely make a corner flutter.

I wondered if I would've been able to figure out the crossword without a more experienced Sheer like my mom helping me.

Amma didn't need to worry so much about the haint blue and the salt and the charms. This whole haunting thing wasn't as easy as it was cracked up to be.

Then I noticed how sad Macon looked, studying Lena's face. I gave up on the newspaper and focused harder on their conversation.

"You may have felt the essence of him, Lena. A burial site is a powerful place, no doubt."

"I don't mean I felt something, Uncle Macon. I felt him. Ethan, the Sheer. I'm sure of it."

The smoke from the fire curled out from the grating. Boo lay with his head in Lena's lap, the flames reflecting in his dark eyes.

"Because a button fell onto his grave?" Macon's voice didn't change, but he sounded tired. I wondered how many of these conversations he'd endured since I died.

"No. Because he moved it." Lena didn't give up.

"What about the wind? What about someone else? Wesley could have bumped it off, considering he is not the most graceful of creatures."

"It was only a week ago. I remember it perfectly. I know it happened." She was even more stubborn than he was.

A week ago?

Had that much time passed in Gatlin?

Lena hadn't seen the paper. She couldn't prove I was still here, not to herself or my family or even my best friend. There was no way to explain about Obidias Trueblood and all the complications in my life, not while she didn't even know I was in the room with her.

"What about since then?" Macon asked.

She looked troubled. "Maybe he's gone. Maybe he's up to something. I don't know how it works in the Otherworld." Lena stared into the fire as if she was looking for something. "It's not just me. I went to see Amma. She said she felt him in the house."

"Amma's feelings are not to be trusted when it comes to Ethan."

"What's that supposed to mean? Of course Amma can be trusted. She's the most trustworthy person I know." Lena looked furious, and I wondered how much she actually knew about that night at the water tower.

He didn't say a word.

"Isn't she?"

Macon closed his book. "I can't see the future. I'm not a Seer. All I know is Ethan did what needed to be done. The whole realm—Dark and Light—will always be grateful to him."

Lena stood up, ripping the ink-stained page from her notebook. "Well, I'm not. I understand he was very brave and noble and whatever, but he left me here, and I'm not sure it was worth it. I don't care about the universe and the realm and saving the world, not anymore. Not without Ethan."

She tossed the ripped page into the fire. The orange flames leaped up around it.

Uncle Macon spoke as he watched the fire. "I understand."

"Really?" Lena didn't seem to believe him.

"There was a time when I put my heart above all else."

"And what happened?"

"I don't know. I got older, I suppose. And I learned that things often are more complicated than we think."

Leaning against the mantel, Lena stared into the fire.

"Maybe you just forgot what it feels like."

"Perhaps."

"I won't." She looked at her uncle. "I won't ever forget."

She twisted her hand, and the smoke rose up until it curled around her and took shape. It was a face. It was my face.

"Lena."

My face disappeared at the sound of Macon's voice, fading away into streaks of gray cloud.

"Leave me alone. Let me have what little I can, what I have left of him." She sounded fierce, and I loved her for it.

"Those are only memories." There was sadness in Macon's voice. "You have to move on. Trust me."

"Why? You never did."

He smiled sadly, staring past her into the fire. "That's how I know."

I followed Lena up the stairs. Though the ice and snow had melted away since my last visit to Ravenwood, a thick gray fog hung throughout the house, and the air was colder.

Lena didn't seem to notice or care what was going on around her, even though her breath was curling up toward her face in a quiet white cloud. I noticed the dark rings under her eyes, the way she looked as thin and as frail as she had when Macon died. She wasn't the same person she had been then, though—she was someone much stronger.

She had believed Macon was gone forever, and we found a way to bring him back. I knew deep down she couldn't hold out for any less of a fate for me.

Maybe Lena didn't know I was here, but she knew I wasn't gone. She wasn't giving up on me yet. She couldn't.

I knew, because if I was the one left behind, I couldn't have either.

Lena slipped into her room, past the pile of suitcases, and crawled into bed without even taking off her clothes. She waved her fingers, and her door slammed shut. I lay down next to her, my face on the edge of her pillow. We were only inches apart.

The tears began to roll down her face, and I thought my heart would break, just watching her.

I love you, L. I always will.

I closed my eyes and reached for her. I wished, desperately, that there was something I could do. There had to be some way I could let her know I was still here.

I love you, Ethan. I won't forget you. I'll never forget you, and I'll never stop loving you.

I heard her voice uncurl inside my head. When I opened my eyes, she was staring right through me.

"Never," she whispered.

"Never," I said.

I wrapped my fingers in the curls of black hair and waited until she fell asleep. I could feel her nestled up next to me.

I had to make sure she found that newspaper.

As I followed Lena down the stairs the next morning, I was starting to feel a) like some kind of stalker and b) like I was losing my mind. Kitchen sent out as big a breakfast as ever—but thankfully, now that the Order wasn't broken and the world wasn't about to end, the food wasn't so raw that the sight of it made you want to throw up.

Macon was waiting for Lena at the table, and he was already digging in. I still wasn't used to the sight of him eating. There were biscuits this morning, baked with so much butter it came bubbling up through cracks in the dough. Thick slices of bacon crowded against an Amma-sized mountain of scrambled eggs. Berries piled inside a big piece of pastry crust that Link, before his Linkubus days, would have swallowed whole in one bite.

Then I saw it. *The Stars and Stripes* was folded at the bottom of a whole stack of newspapers—from about as many countries as I could name.

I reached for the paper just as Macon reached for the coffeepot, shoving his hand right through my chest. It felt cold and strange, like I'd swallowed a piece of ice. Maybe like brain freeze from an ICEE, only in my heart rather than in my head.

I grabbed the paper with both hands and pulled on it as hard as I could. One edge slowly peeked out from beneath the pile.

Not good enough.

I looked up at Macon and Lena. Macon had his head buried

in a newspaper called *L'Express*, which looked like it was written in French. Lena had her eyes glued to her plate, like the eggs were going to reveal an important truth.

Come on, L. It's right here. I'm right here.

I yanked the paper harder, and it slid all the way out from the pile and fluttered onto the floor.

Neither one of them looked up.

Lena stirred milk into her tea. I reached for her hand with mine, squeezing it until she dropped the spoon, splashing tea onto the tablecloth.

Lena stared at her teacup, flexing her fingers. She leaned down to blot the tablecloth with her napkin. Then she noticed the paper on the floor, where it had landed next to her foot.

"What's this?" She picked up *The Stars and Stripes*. "I didn't know you subscribed to this paper, Uncle M."

"I do. I find it's helpful to know what's going on in town. You wouldn't want to miss, I don't know, the latest diabolical plan of Mrs. Lincoln and the Ladies Auxiliary." He smiled. "Where would the fun be in that?"

I held my breath.

She tossed it over, facedown on the table.

The crossword was on the back. The Sunday edition, just like I'd planned it back in the office of *The Stars and Stripes*.

She smiled to herself. "Amma would do this crossword in about five minutes."

Macon looked up. "Less than that, I'm sure. I believe I could do it in three."

"Really?"

"Try me."

"Eleven across," she said. "Apparition or phantasm. A spectral being. A spirit from another world. A ghost."

Macon looked at her, his eyes narrowing.

Lena leaned over the paper, holding her tea. I watched as she began to read.

Figure it out, L. Please.

It was only when the teacup began to shake and fell to the carpet that I knew she'd gotten it—not the crossword but the message behind it.

"Ethan?" She looked up. I leaned closer, holding my cheek against hers. I knew she couldn't feel it; I wasn't back with her, not yet. But I knew she believed I was there, and for now that's all that mattered.

Macon stared at her, surprised.

The chandelier above the table began to sway. The room brightened until it was blindingly white. The enormous dining room windows began to crack into hundreds of glass spiderwebs. Heavy drapes flew against the walls like feathers in the wind.

"Darling," Macon began.

Lena's hair curled in every direction. I closed my eyes as window after window began to shatter like fireworks.

Ethan?

I'm here.

Above everything, that was all I needed her to know.

Finally.

135

⊰ CHAPTER 13 ⊱

Where the Crow Carries You

Lena knew I was there. It was hard to drag myself away, but she had figured out the truth. That was the main thing. Amma and Lena. I was two for two. It was a start.

And I was exhausted.

Now I had to find my way back to her for good. I crossed back in about ten seconds flat. If only the rest of the way was that easy.

I knew I should go home and tell my mom everything, but I also knew how worried she'd be about me going to the Far Keep. From what Genevieve and my mom and Aunt Prue and Obidias Trueblood had said, the Far Keep seemed like the last place a person would voluntarily go.

Especially a person with a mother.

I cataloged everything I needed to do, everywhere I needed to go. The river. The book. The river eyes—two smooth black stones. That's what Obidias Trueblood said I needed. My mind kept going back to it, over and over.

How many smooth black stones could there be in the world? And how was I going to know which ones happened to be the eyes of the river, whatever that even meant?

Maybe I'd find them on the way. Or maybe I'd already found them, and I didn't even know it.

A magical black rock, the eye of the river.

It sounded strangely familiar. Had I heard it before?

I thought back to Amma, to all the charms, every tiny bone, every bit of graveyard dirt and salt, every piece of string she'd given me to wear.

Then I remembered.

It wasn't one of Amma's charms. It was from the vision I saw when I opened the bottle in her room.

I had seen the stone hanging around Sulla's neck. Sulla the Prophet. In the vision Amma had called it "the eye."

The river's eye.

Which meant I knew where to find it and how to get there—as long as I could figure out how to find my way to Wader's Creek on this side.

It couldn't be avoided, intimidating as it was. It was time to pay a visit to the Greats.

I unfolded Aunt Prue's map. Now that I knew how to read the map, it wasn't that hard to see where the Doorwells were marked. I found the red X on the Doorwell that led to Obidias' place—the one at the Snow family crypt—so after that I went looking for every red mark I could find.

There were plenty of red Xs, but which of those Doorwells would take me to Wader's Creek? Their destinations weren't exactly marked like exits on the interstate—and I didn't want to stumble into any of the surprises that could be waiting for a guy behind Otherworld door number three.

Snakes for fingers might be getting off easy.

There had to be some kind of logic. I didn't know what connected the Doorwell behind the Snow family plot to the rocky path that had taken me to Obidias Trueblood, but there had to be something. Seeing as we were all related to one another around here, that something was probably blood.

What would connect one of these plots in His Garden of Perpetual Peace to the Greats? If there was a liquor store in the graveyard—or a buried coffin full of Uncle Abner's Wild Turkey, or the ruins of a haunted bakery known for lemon meringue pie—he wouldn't have been far behind me.

But Wader's Creek had its own graveyard. There wasn't a crypt or a plot for Ivy, Abner, Sulla, or Delilah in Perpetual Peace.

Then I found a red X behind what my mom had said was one of the oldest tribute markers in the graveyard, and I knew it had to be the one.

So I folded up the map and decided to check it out.

Minutes later, I found myself staring at a white marble obelisk.

Sure enough, the word SACRED was carved into the crumbling veined stone, right above a gloomy-looking skull with empty eyes that stared at you straight on. I never understood why a single creepy skull marked a handful of Gatlin's oldest graves. But we all knew about this particular tribute, even though it was tucked away on the far edge of Perpetual Peace, where the heart of the old graveyard sat, long before the new one was built up around it.

The Confederate Needle—that's what folks around Gatlin called it, not because of its pointed shape but because of the ladies who had put it there. Katherine Cooper Sewell, who founded the Gatlin chapter of the Daughters of the American Revolution—probably not long after the Revolution itself— had seen to it that the DAR raised enough money for the obelisk before she died.

She had married Samuel Sewell.

Samuel Sewell had built and run the Palmetto Brewery, the first distillery in Gatlin County. Palmetto Brewery made one thing and one thing only.

Wild Turkey.

"Pretty smart," I said, circling to the back of the obelisk, where the twisted wrought iron fencing bowed and broke into pieces. I didn't know if I would've been able to see it back home, but here in the Otherworld, the trapdoor of a Doorwell cut into the base of the rock was plain as day. The rectangular outline of the entrance snaked between rows of engraved shells and angels.

I pressed my hand against the soft stone and felt it give way beneath me, swinging from sunlight into shadow.

A dozen uneven stone steps later, I found myself on what sounded like a gravel pathway. I made my way around a turn in the passage and caught sight of light pooling in the distance. As I got closer, I smelled swamp grass and waterlogged palmettos. There was no mistaking that smell.

This was the right place.

I reached a warped wooden door, propped halfway open. Nothing could keep out the light now—or the hot, sticky air, which only got hotter and stickier as I climbed the steps on the other side of the door.

Wader's Creek was waiting for me. I couldn't see past the first fringe of tall cypress trees, but I knew it was there. If I followed the muddy path in front of me, I would find my way to Amma's home away from home.

I pushed through the palmetto branches and saw a row of tiny houses, just off the edge of the water.

The Greats. It had to be.

As I made my way down the path, I heard voices. On the nearest veranda, three women were crowded around a table with a deck of cards. They were fussing and swatting at one another the way the Sisters did when they played Scrabble.

I recognized Twyla from a distance. I suspected she was going to join the Greats when she died on the night of the Seventeenth Moon. Still, it was strange to see her here, hanging out on the porch and playing cards with them.

"Now, you can't throw that card, Twyla, and you know it. You think I can't see you cheatin'?" A woman in a colorful shawl pushed the card back toward Twyla.

"Now, Sulla. You may be a Seer, *cher*. But there's nothin' there to see," Twyla responded.

Sulla. That's who she was. Now I recognized her from the vision—Sulla the Prophet, Amma's most famous ancestor of all.

"Well, I think you're both cheatin'." The third woman tossed her cards down and adjusted her round glasses. Her shawl was bright yellow. "And I don't want ta play with either one a you." I tried not to laugh, but the scene was too familiar; I might as well be home.

"Don't you be such a sourpuss, Delilah." Sulla wagged her head.

Delilah. She was the one in the glasses.

A fourth woman was sitting in a rocking chair at the edge of the porch, with a hoop in one hand and a needle in the other. "Why don't you go on in and cut your old Aunt Ivy a slice a pie? I'm busy with my stitchin'."

Ivy. It was weird to finally see her in person after the visions.

"Pie? Ha!" An old man laughed from his rocking chair—a bottle of Wild Turkey in one hand and a pipe in the other.

Uncle Abner.

I felt like I knew the man personally, though we'd never met. After all, I'd been in the kitchen when Amma made him more than a hundred pies over the years—maybe a thousand.

The giant crow flew down and landed on Uncle Abner's shoulder. "Won't find any pie in there, Delilah. We're runnin' low."

Delilah stopped, one hand on the screen door. "Why would we be runnin' low, Abner?"

He nodded in my direction. "I'm guessin' Amarie's busy bakin' for him now." He emptied his pipe, tapping the old tobacco over the side of the porch railing.

"Who, me?" I couldn't believe Uncle Abner was actually talking to me. I took a step closer to all of them. "I mean, hello, sir."

He ignored me. "I'm guessin' I won't be seein' another lemon meringue unless it's the boy's favorite, too."

"Are you gonna stand there starin' or come on over here already?" Sulla had her back to me, but she still knew I was there.

Twyla squinted into the sunlight. "Ethan? That you, *cher*?"

I walked toward the house, as much as I felt like staying where I was. I don't know why I was so nervous. I hadn't expected the Greats to seem so regular. They could've been any group of old folks, hanging out on the porch on a sunny afternoon. Except that they were all dead.

"Yeah. I mean, yes, ma'am. It's me."

Uncle Abner stood up and walked over to the railing to get a better look. The enormous crow was still perched on his shoulder. It flapped its wings, and he didn't even flinch. "Like I said, we won't be gettin' any pie—or much else—now that the boy's up here with us."

Twyla waved me over. "Maybe he'll share a bit a his with you."

I climbed up the scuffed wooden steps, and the wind chimes tapped against one another. There wasn't so much as a breeze.

"He's a spirit, all right," Sulla said. There was a tiny brown bird hopping around the table. A sparrow.

"'Course he is." Ivy sniffed. "Wouldn't be up here otherwise."

I gave Uncle Abner and his scavenger a wide berth.

When I was close enough, Twyla jumped up and threw her arms around me. "Can't say I'm happy you're here, but I am happy to see you."

I hugged her back. "Yeah, well, I'm not all that happy to be here either."

Uncle Abner took a swig of whiskey. "Then why'd you go and jump off that fool tower?"

I didn't know what to say, but Sulla answered before I had to think of anything. "You know the answer to that, Abner, about as well as you know your own name. Now stop givin' the boy a hard time."

The crow flapped its wings again. "Somebody should," Uncle Abner said.

Sulla turned and gave Uncle Abner the look. I wondered if that was where Amma had learned it. "Unless you were strong enough to stop the Wheel a Fate yourself, you know the boy didn't have a choice."

Delilah brought a wicker chair over for me. "Now, you come on and sit down here with us."

Sulla was still flipping cards, but these were ordinary playing cards.

"Can you read those, too?" It wouldn't have surprised me.

She laughed, and the sparrow chirped. "No, we're just playin' gin." Sulla slapped down her cards. "Speakin' a that—gin."

Delilah pouted. "You always win."

"Well, I've won again," Sulla said. "So why don't you sit down here, Ethan, and tell us what brings you 'round our way."

"I'm not sure how much you know."

She lifted her eyebrows.

"Okay, so you probably already know that I went to see Obidias Trueblood, this old—"

"Mmm hmm." She nodded.

"And if he's telling the truth, there's a way I can get back home." I was stumbling over my words. "I mean, to the home where I was alive."

"Mmm hmm."

"I have to get my page from—"

"*The Caster Chronicles*," she finished for me. "I know all that. So why don't you go on and say what you need from us."

144

I was sure she knew, but she wanted me to ask anyway. It was only proper.

"I need a stone." I thought about the best way to describe it. "This will probably sound strange, but I saw you wearing it once, in kind of a dream. It's shiny and black...."

"This one?" Sulla held out her palm. There it was. The black stone I saw in my vision.

I nodded, relieved.

"Darn right you do." She pressed the rock into my hand, closing my fingers around it. It pulsed with a kind of strange warmth that seemed to come from inside.

Delilah looked at me. "You know what that is?"

I nodded. "Obidias said it's called a river's eye, and I need two of them to get across the river."

"Then I reckon you're one short," Uncle Abner said. He hadn't moved from the railing. He was busy packing his pipe with dry leaf tobacco.

"Oh, there's another one." Sulla smiled knowingly. "Don't you know?"

I shook my head.

Twyla reached over and took my hand. A smile spread across her face, her long braids slipping over her shoulder as she nodded. "*Un cadeau*. A gift. I remember when I gave it to Lena," she said in her heavy French Creole accent. "River's eye is a powerful stone. Brings luck and a safe journey." As she spoke, I saw the charm from Lena's necklace. The smooth black rock she always wore hanging from the chain.

145

Of course.

Lena had the second stone I needed.

"You know how to get to the river and get on your way?" Twyla asked, dropping my hand.

I pulled Aunt Prue's map out of my back pocket. "I have a map. My aunt gave it to me."

"Maps are good," Sulla said, looking it over. "But birds are better." She made a clicking noise with her tongue, and the sparrow fluttered onto her shoulder. "A map can lead you astray if you don't read it right. A bird always knows the way."

"I wouldn't want to take your bird." She had already given me the stone. It felt like I was taking too much. Plus, birds made me nervous. They were like old ladies but with sharper beaks.

Uncle Abner took a long puff of his pipe and walked toward us. Even though he wasn't looming over me from the sky, he was still taller than me. He had a slight limp, and I couldn't help but wonder what caused it.

He hooked his finger around one of the suspenders attached to his loose brown pants. "Then take mine."

"Excuse me, sir?"

"My bird." He cocked his shoulder, and the huge crow's feathers ruffled. "If you don't wanna take Sulla's bird—which I understand, since it's not much bigger than a field mouse—then take mine."

I was scared to stand next to that vulture-sized crow. I definitely didn't want to take it anywhere with me. But I had to be careful, because he was offering me something he valued, and I didn't want to insult him.

I *really* didn't want to insult him.

"I appreciate it, sir. But I don't want to take your bird either. It seems…" The crow squawked loudly. "Really attached to you."

The old man waved off my concern. "Nonsense. Exu is smart, named for the god of the crossroads. He watches the doors between worlds and knows the way. Don't you, boy?"

The bird sat proudly on the man's shoulder as if he knew Uncle Abner was singing his praises.

Delilah walked over and held out her arm. Exu flapped his wings once, dropping down to land on her. "The crow is also the only bird that can cross between the worlds—the veils between life and death, and places far worse. That old heap a feathers is a powerful ally, and a better teacher, Ethan."

"Are you saying he can cross over to the Mortal realm?" Was that really possible?

Uncle Abner blew the thick pipe smoke in my face as he spoke. "'Course he can. There and back, there and back again. Only place that bird can't go is underwater. And that's only 'cause I never taught him to swim."

"So he can show me the way to the river?"

"He can show you a lot more than that if you pay attention." Uncle Abner nodded at the bird, and it took off into the sky, circling above our heads. "He behaves best if you give a gift every now and again, just like the god I named him after."

147

I had no idea what kinds of gifts to offer a crow, a voodoo god, or a crow named after one. I got the feeling regular birdseed wasn't going to cut it.

But I didn't have to worry, because Uncle Abner made sure I knew. "Take some a this." He poured whiskey into a dented flask and handed me a small tin. It was the same one he had opened to fill his pipe.

"Your bird drinks whiskey and eats tobacco?"

The old man frowned. "Just be glad he doesn't like eatin' scrawny boys that don't know their way 'round the Otherworld."

"Yes, sir." I nodded.

"Now you get outta here and take my bird and that stone." Uncle Abner shooed me away. "I won't get any a Amarie's pie with you hangin' 'round here."

"Yes, sir." I put the tobacco tin and the flask in my pocket with the map. "And thank you."

I started down the stairs and stepped off the porch. I turned back to take one last look at the Greats, gathered around a card table, sewing and fussing, scowling and drinking whiskey, depending on which one of them you were talking about. I wanted to remember them this way, like regular people who were great for reasons that had nothing to do with seeing the future or scaring the hell out of Dark Casters.

They reminded me of Amma and everything I loved about her. The way she always had the answers and sent me off with something strange in my pocket. The way she scowled at me when she was worried, and reminded me of all the things I still didn't know.

Sulla stood up and leaned over the porch rail. "When you see the River Master, you be sure to say I sent ya, you hear?"

She said it like I should know what she was talking about. "River Master? Who is that, ma'am?"

"You'll know him when you see him," she said.

"Yes, ma'am." I started to turn away.

"Ethan," Uncle Abner called, "when you get home, tell Amarie I'm expectin' a lemon meringue and a basket a fried chicken. Two big, fat drumsticks.... Make that four."

I smiled. "I will."

"And don't forget to send my bird back. He gets ornery after a while."

The crow circled above me as I made my way down the stairs. I had no idea where I was going, not even with a map and a tobacco-eating bird that could cross over between worlds.

It didn't matter if I had my mom, Aunt Prue, a Dark Caster who had escaped from the very place I was trying to break into, and all the Greats, with Twyla thrown in for good measure.

I had one stone now, and the more I thought about Lena, the more I realized I'd always known where to find the other one. She never took it off her charm necklace. Maybe that's why Twyla had given it to her when she was a little girl—for some kind of protection. Or for me.

After all, Twyla was a powerful Necromancer. Maybe she'd known that I'd need it.

I'm coming, L. As soon as I can.

I knew she couldn't hear me Kelting, but I listened for her voice in the back of my mind anyway. As if the memory of it could somehow replace hearing her.

I love you.

I imagined her black hair and her green and gold eyes, her beat-up Chucks and her chipped black nail polish.

There was only one thing left to do, and it was time for me to do it.

⊰ CHAPTER 14 ⊱

Messed-Up Things

It didn't take me long to retrace my steps to the Confederate Needle, and I found my own way to *The Stars and Stripes* this time around. I was crossing like an old Sheer now. Once I got the hang of it—a certain way of letting my mind do the work for me without focusing on anything at all—it seemed as easy as walking. Easier, since I wasn't actually walking.

And once I was there, I knew what to do, and I could do it myself. In fact, I was actually looking forward to it. I'd done a little thinking ahead of time. I could see why Amma liked crossword puzzles so much. Once you got the right mind-set, they were sort of addictive.

When I found my way into the office—past Swamp Cooler

City—the mock-up of the current issue was on one of the three little desks, right where it had been last time. I fanned open the papers. This time I found the crossword puzzle without much trouble.

This puzzle was even less finished than the last one. Maybe the staff was getting lazy, now that they knew there was a chance someone else would do it for them.

Either way, Lena would be reading the crossword puzzle. I picked up the nearest letter and pushed it into place.

Four down.

O. N. Y. X.

As in, a black stone.

Nine across.

T. R. I. B. U. T. A. R. Y.

As in, a river.

Six down.

O. C. U. L. U. S.

As in, an eye.

Eight across.

C. H. A. R. I. S. M. A.

As in, charm.

M. A. T. E. R.

As in, my own. Lila Jane Evers Wate.

S. E. R. I. O. U. S.

As in, grave.

That was the message. I need the black stone—the eye of a river, and the one you wear on your charm necklace. And I need you to leave it for me at my mother's grave. I couldn't spell it out any clearer than that.

At least not in this edition of the paper.

By the time I finished, I was exhausted, as if I'd been running sprints all afternoon on the basketball court. I didn't know how much time would need to pass in the Otherworld before Lena got my message in this one. I only knew that she'd get it.

Because I was as sure of her as I was of myself.

―❧―

When I got home to the Otherworld—to my house, or my mom's grave, whatever you wanted to call it—there it was, waiting for me on the doorstep.

She must have left it on my mother's grave, like I asked.

I couldn't believe it had worked.

Lena's black-rock charm from Barbados, the one she always wore around her neck, sat in the middle of the doormat.

I had the second river stone.

A wave of relief settled over me. It lasted about five seconds, until I realized what the stone also meant.

It was time to go. Time to say good-bye.

So why couldn't I bring myself to say it?

"Ethan." I heard my mom's voice, but I didn't look up.

I was sitting on the floor of the living room, my back to the couch. I had a house and a car in my hands, stray pieces of my mom's old Christmas town. I couldn't take my eyes off the car.

"You found the lost green car. I never could."

She didn't answer. Her hair looked even messier than usual. Her face was streaked with tears.

I don't know why the town was set out on the coffee table like that, but I put down the house and moved the tiny green tin car farther along the table. Away from the toy animals, the church with the bent steeple, and the pipe-cleaner tree.

Like I said, time to go.

Part of me wanted to take off running the second I heard about what I had to do to get back to my old life. Part of me didn't care about anything but seeing Lena again.

But as I sat there, all I could think about was how much I didn't want to leave my mom. How much I'd missed her, and how quickly I had gotten used to seeing her in the house, hearing her in the next room. I didn't know if I wanted to give that up again, no matter how badly I needed to go back.

So all I could do was just sit there and look at that old car and wonder how something that had been lost for so long could be found again.

My mom took a breath, and I closed my eyes before she could say a word. It didn't stop her. "I don't think it's wise, Ethan. I don't think it's safe, and I don't think you should be going. No matter what your Aunt Prue says." Her voice wavered.

"Mom."

"You're only seventeen."

"Actually, I'm not. What I am now is nothing." I looked up at her. "And I hate to break it to you, but it's a little late for that speech. You have to admit that safety might not be my biggest concern at the moment. Now that I'm dead and everything."

"Well, if you say it like that." She sighed and sat down on the floor next to me.

"How do you want me to say it?"

"I don't know. Passed on?" She tried not to smile.

I half-smiled back. "Sorry. Passed on." She was right. Folks didn't like saying *dead*, not where we were from. It was impolite. As if saying it somehow made it true. As if words themselves were more powerful than anything that could actually happen to you.

Maybe they were.

After all, that's what I had to do now, wasn't it? Destroy the words on a page in some book in a library that had changed my Mortal destiny. Was it really so far-fetched to think that words had a way of shaping a person's whole life?

"You don't know what you're getting yourself into, sweetheart. Maybe if I had figured it out for myself, before all this, you wouldn't even be here. There wouldn't have been a car accident, and there wouldn't have been a water tower—" She stopped.

"You can't keep things from happening to me, Mom. Not even these things." I leaned my head back along the edge of the couch. "Not even messed-up things."

155

"What if I want to?"

"You can't. It's my life, or whatever this is." I turned to look at her.

She leaned her head on my shoulder, holding the side of my face close with her hand. Something she hadn't done since I was a kid. "It's your life. You're right about that. And I can't make a decision like this for you, however much I want to. Which is very, very much."

"I kind of figured that part out."

She smiled sadly. "I just got you back. I don't want to lose you again."

"I know. I don't want to leave you either."

Side by side, we stared at the Christmas town, maybe for the last time. I put the car back where it belonged.

I knew then that we would never have another Christmas together, no matter what happened. I would stay or I would go—but either way, I would move on to somewhere that wasn't here. Things couldn't be like this forever, not even in this Gatlin-that-wasn't-Gatlin. Whether or not I was able to get my life back or not.

Things changed.

Then they changed again.

Life was like that, and even death, I guess.

I couldn't be with both my mom and Lena, not in what was left of one lifetime. They would never meet, though I had already told them everything there was to tell about the other. Since I got here, my mom had me describe every charm on

Lena's necklace. Every line of every poem she'd ever written. Every story about the smallest things that had happened to us, things I didn't even know I remembered.

Still, it wasn't the same as being a family, or whatever we could have been.

Lena and my mom and me.

They would never laugh about me or keep a secret from me or even fight about me. My mom and Lena were the two most important people in my life, or afterlife, and I could never have both of them together.

That's what I was thinking when I closed my eyes. When I opened them, my mom was gone—as if she'd known I couldn't leave her. As if she'd known I wouldn't be able to walk away.

Truthfully, I didn't know if I could have done it, myself.

Now I'd never find out.

Maybe it was better that way.

⁓

I pocketed the two stones and made my way down the front steps, closing the door carefully behind me. The smell of fried tomatoes came wafting out the door as it shut.

I didn't say good-bye. I had a feeling we'd see each other again. Someday, somehow.

Aside from that, there wasn't anything I could tell my mom that she didn't already know. And no way to say it and still walk out the door.

She knew I loved her. She knew I had to go. At the end of the day, there wasn't much more to say.

I don't know if she watched me go.

I told myself she did.

I hoped she didn't.

◄ CHAPTER 15 ►

The River Master

A_s I stepped inside the Doorwell, the known world gave way to the unknown world more quickly than I expected. Even in the Otherworld, there are some places that are noticeably more other than others.

The river was one of them. This wasn't any kind of river I'd seen in the Mortal Gatlin County. Like the Great Barrier, this was a seam. Something that held worlds together without being in any one of them.

I was in totally uncharted territory.

Luckily, Uncle Abner's crow seemed to know the way. Exu flapped overhead, gliding and hanging in circles above me, sometimes landing on high branches to wait for me if I fell too far behind. He didn't seem to mind the job either; he tolerated our quest with only the occasional squawk. Maybe he enjoyed getting out for a change. He reminded me of Lucille that way, except I didn't catch her eating little mice carcasses when she was hungry.

And when I caught him looking at me, he was really looking at me. Every time I started to feel normal again, he would catch my eye and send shivers down my spine, like he was doing it on purpose. Like he knew he could.

I wondered if Exu was a real bird. I knew he could cross between worlds, but did that make him supernatural? According to Uncle Abner, it only made him a crow.

Maybe all crows were just creepy.

As I walked farther, the swamp weeds and cypress trees jutting out of the murky water led to greener grass beyond the bank, grass so tall I could barely see over it in places.

I wove through the grass, following the black bird in the sky, trying not to remember too much about where I was going or what I was leaving behind. It was hard enough not to imagine the look on my mother's face when I walked out the door.

I tried desperately not to think about her eyes, about the way they lit up when she saw me. Or her hands, the way she waved them in the air as she talked, as if she thought she could pull words out of the sky with her fingers. And her arms, wrapping around me like my own house, because she was the place where I was from.

I tried not to think about the moment the door closed. It would never open again, not for me. Not like that.

It's what I wanted. I said it to myself as I walked. It's what she wanted for me. To have a life. To live.

To leave.

Exu squawked, and I beat back the tall brush and the grass.

Leaving was harder than I ever could've imagined, and part of me still couldn't believe I had done it. But as much as I tried not to think about my mom, I tried to keep Lena's face in my mind, a constant reminder of why I was doing this—risking everything.

I wondered what she was doing right now.... Writing in her notebook? Practicing the viola? Reading her battered copy of *To Kill a Mockingbird*?

I was still thinking about it when I heard music in the distance. It sounded like...the Rolling Stones?

Part of me expected to push through the grass and see Link standing there. But as I edged closer to the chorus of "You Can't Always Get What You Want," I realized it was the Stones, but it definitely wasn't Link.

The voice wasn't bad enough, and too many of the notes were right.

It was a big guy, wearing a faded bandanna tied around his head, and a Harley-Davidson T-shirt with scaly wings across the back. He was sitting at a plastic folding table like the ones the bridge club used back in Gatlin. With his black shades and long beard, he looked like he should be riding an old chopper instead of sitting next to a riverbank.

Except for his lunch. He was spooning something out of a plastic Tupperware container. From where I was, it looked like intestines or human remains. Or...

The biker belched. "Best chili-ghetti this side a the Mississippi." He shook his head.

Exu cawed and landed on the edge of the folding table. An enormous black dog lying on the ground next to it barked but didn't bother to get up.

"What're you doing around here, bird? Unless you're looking to make a deal, there's nothing for you here. An' don't even think I'm letting you get into my whiskey this time." The biker shooed Exu off the table. "Go on. Shoo. You tell Abner I'm ready to deal when he's ready to play."

As he waved the crow off the table, and Exu disappeared into the blue sky, the biker noticed me standing at the edge of the grass. "You out sightseeing, or are you looking for something?" He tossed the remains of his lunch into a small white Styrofoam cooler and picked up a deck of playing cards.

He nodded my way, shuffling the cards from hand to hand.

I swallowed hard and stepped closer as "Hand of Fate" started playing on the old transistor radio sitting in the dust. I wondered if he listened to anything besides the Rolling Stones, but I wasn't about to ask. "I'm looking for the River Master."

The biker laughed, dealing a hand as if someone was sitting on the other side of the table. "River Master. I haven't heard that one in a while. River Master, Ferryman, Water Runner—I go by a lot of names, kid. But you can call me Charlie. It's the one I answer to *when* I feel like answering."

I couldn't imagine anyone getting this guy to do anything he didn't feel like doing. If we were in the Mortal realm, he would probably be a bouncer at a biker bar or a pool hall where people were dragged out for breaking bottles over one another's heads.

"Nice to meet you...Charlie," I choked. "I'm Ethan."

He waved me over. "So what can I do for you, Ethan?"

I walked over to the table, careful to give the giant creature on the ground a wide berth. It looked like a mastiff, with its square face and wrinkled skin. Its tail was bandaged with white gauze.

"Don't mind old Drag," he said. "He won't get up unless you're carrying some raw meat." Charlie grinned. "Or unless you *are* raw meat. Dead meat like you, kid—you're off the hook."

Why didn't that surprise me?

"Drag? What kind of name is that?" I reached out toward the dog.

"Dragon. The kind that breathes fire and chews your hand off if you try to pet him."

Drag looked at me, growling. I moved my hand back to my pocket.

"I need to cross the river. I brought you these." I laid the river eyes on the padded card table. It really did look like the ones at the bridge club.

Charlie glanced at the stones, unimpressed. "Good for you. One for the way there, one for the way back. That's like showin' a bus driver your bus ticket. Still don't make me want to get on no bus."

"It doesn't?" I swallowed. So much for my plans. Somehow I had thought this was all working out too easily.

Charlie looked me over. "You play blackjack, Ethan? You know, twenty-one?"

I knew what he meant. "Um, not really." Which wasn't entirely true. I used to play with Thelma, until she started cheating as badly as the Sisters did at Rummikub.

He pushed my cards toward me, flipping a nine of diamonds on top of the first one. My hand. "You're a smart boy—I bet you can figure it out."

I checked my card, a seven. "Hit me." That's what Thelma would have said.

Charlie seemed like a risk-taker. If I was right, he probably respected other people who did the same. And what did I have to lose?

He nodded approvingly, flipping a king. "Sorry, kid, that's twenty-six. You're over. But I would've taken the hit, too."

Charlie shuffled the deck and dealt us each another hand.

This time I had a four and an eight. "Hit me."

He flipped a seven. I had nineteen, which was hard to beat. Charlie had a king and a five sitting in front of him. He had to take a hit, or I would win for sure. He pulled a card from the top of the deck. A six of hearts.

"Twenty-one. That's blackjack," he said, shuffling again.

I wasn't sure if this was some kind of test or if he was just bored out here, but he didn't seem anxious to get rid of me anytime soon. "I really need to get across the river, si—" I stopped myself before I called him "sir." He lifted an eyebrow. "I mean, Charlie. See, there's a girl—"

Charlie nodded, interrupting. "There's always a girl." The Rolling Stones started crooning "2,000 Light Years from Home." Funny.

"I need to get back to her—"

"I had a girl once. Penelope was her name. Penny." He leaned back in his chair, smoothing his scraggly beard. "Eventually she got tired of hanging around here, so she took off."

"Why didn't you go with her?" The second I asked the question, I realized it was probably too personal. But he answered anyway.

"I can't leave." He said it matter-of-factly, flipping cards for both of us. "I'm the River Master. It's part of the gig. Can't run out on the house."

"You could quit."

"This isn't a job, kid. It's a sentence." He laughed, but there was a bitterness that made me feel sorry for him. That and the folding card table and the lazy dog with the messed-up tail.

Then "2,000 Light Years from Home" faded out, replaced by "Plundered My Soul."

I didn't want to know who was powerful enough to sentence him to sit by what, for the most part, looked like a pretty unimpressive river. It was slow and calm. If he wasn't hanging out here, I probably could've swum across.

"I'm sorry." What else could I say?

"It's okay. I made my peace with it a long time ago." He tapped on my cards. An ace and a seven. "You want a hit?"

Eighteen again.

Charlie had an ace, too.

"Hit me." I watched as he turned the card between his fingers.

A three of spades.

He took off his shades, ice blue staring back at me. His pupils were so light, they were barely visible. "You gonna call it?"

"Blackjack."

Charlie pushed back his chair and nodded toward the riverbank. There was a poor man's ferry waiting, a crude raft made of logs that were bound together with thick rope. It was just like the ones that lined the swamp in Wader's Creek. Dragon stretched and ambled after him. "Let's go before I change my mind."

I followed him to the rickety platform and stepped onto the rotting logs.

Charlie held out his hand. "Time to pay the Ferryman." He pointed toward the brown water. "Come on. Hit me."

I tossed the stone and it hit, without so much as a splash.

The moment he lowered the long pole to push against the river bottom, the water changed. A putrid odor rose from the surface—swamp rot, spoiled meat—and something else.

I looked down into the shadowy depths beneath me. The water was clear enough to see all the way to the bottom now, except I couldn't, because there were bodies everywhere I looked, only inches below the surface. And these weren't the writhing forms from myths and movies. They were corpses, bloated and waterlogged, still as death. Some faceup, some facedown—but what faces I could see had the same blue lips and terrifyingly white skin. Their hair fanned out around them in the water as they floated and bumped against one another.

"Everyone pays the Ferryman sooner or later." Charlie shrugged. "Can't change that."

The taste of bile rose in my throat, and it took every ounce of energy I had to keep from throwing up. The revulsion must have registered on my face, because Charlie's tone was sympathetic. "I know, kid. The smell's hard to take. Why do you think I don't make many trips across?"

"Why did it change? The river." I couldn't drag my eyes away from the waterlogged bodies. "I mean, it wasn't like this before."

"That's where you're wrong. You just couldn't see it. There are lots of things we choose not to see. Doesn't mean they aren't there, even if we wish they weren't."

"I'm tired of seeing everything. It was easier back when I didn't know anything. I barely even knew I was alive."

Charlie nodded. "Yeah. So I hear."

The wooden platform smacked against the opposite bank. "Thanks, Charlie."

He leaned on the pole, his unnaturally blue, pupil-less eyes staring right through me. "Don't mention it, kid. I hope you find that girl."

I reached my hand out cautiously and scratched Dragon behind the ears. I was happy to see my hand didn't burn off.

The huge dog barked at me.

"Maybe Penny will come back," I said. "You never know."

"The odds are against it."

I stepped onto the bank. "Yeah, well. If you're going to look at it that way, I guess you could say they're against me, too."

"You may be right. If you're headed where I think."

Did he know? Maybe this side of the river only led to one place, though I doubted it. The more I learned about the world I thought I knew and all the ones I didn't, the more everything threaded together, leading everywhere and nowhere at the same time.

"I'm going to the Far Keep." I didn't think he'd get the chance to tell any of the Keepers, since he couldn't leave this spot. Besides, there was something about Charlie I liked. And saying the words only made me feel more like they were true.

"Straight ahead. You can't miss it." He pointed into the distance. "But you have to get past the Gatekeeper."

"I heard." I had been thinking about it since my visit to Obidias' house with Aunt Prue.

"Well, you tell him he owes me money," Charlie said. "I won't wait around forever." I looked at him, and he sighed. "Well, say it anyway."

"You know him?"

He nodded. "We go way back. There's no telling how long it's been, but I'd guess a lifetime or two."

"What's he like?" Maybe if I knew more about this guy, I would have a better chance of convincing him to let me into the Far Keep.

Charlie smiled, pushing off with the pole and sending the poor man's ferry floating back into the sea of corpses.

"Not like me."

◄ CHAPTER 16 ►

A Rock and a Crow

O nce I left the river behind, I realized the road to the Gates of the Far Keep wasn't a road at all. It was more of a crude, winding path, hidden within the walls of two towering black mountains that stood side by side, creating a natural gate more ominous than anything that could've been made by Mortals— or Keepers. The mountains were slick, with razor-sharp corners that reflected the sun, as if they were made of obsidian. They looked like they were cutting black slits into the sky.

Great.

The idea of navigating a path through those jagged knife-blade cliffs was a little more than intimidating. Whatever the Keepers were up to, they definitely didn't want anyone to know about it.

Big surprise there.

Exu circled overhead now, as if he knew exactly where he was going. I picked up my pace to follow his shadow on the trail in front of me, feeling grateful for the creepy bird that was even bigger than Harlon James. I wondered what Lucille would think about him. Funny how a supernatural crow borrowed from the Greats could seem like the one familiar thing in the landscape.

Even with the help of Uncle Abner's crow, I kept stopping to consult Aunt Prue's map. Exu definitely knew the general direction of the Far Keep, but he disappeared from view every mile or so. The cliffs were high, the trail was twisted, and Exu didn't have to worry about navigating those mountains.

Lucky bird.

On the map, my path was outlined in Aunt Prue's shaky hand. Every time I tried to trace where it would lead, the path disappeared a few miles ahead. I was starting to worry that her hand had shaken a little too far in the wrong direction. Because the directions on the map didn't have me going over the mountains or between them—I was supposed to go *through* one of them.

"That can't be right."

I stared from the paper up to the sky. Exu glided from tree to tree in front of me, though now that we were closer to the mountains, the trees were that much farther apart. "Sure. Go ahead. Rub it in. Some of us have to walk, you know."

He squawked again. I waved the whiskey flask over my head. "Just don't forget who has your dinner, eh?"

He dove at me, and I laughed, sliding the flask back into my pocket.

It didn't seem so funny after the first few miles.

When I reached the sheer cliff face, I double-checked the map. There it was. A circle drawn in the hillside—marking some sort of cave entrance or a tunnel. It was easy enough to find on the map. But when I lowered the paper and tried to find the cave, there was nothing.

Just a rocky cliff face, so steep it rose into a straight vertical, cutting the trail off right in front of me. It pushed up into the clouds so high that it looked like it never ended.

Something had to be wrong.

There had to be an entrance to the tunnel somewhere around here. I felt along the cliff, stumbling over broken pieces of the shiny black rock.

Nothing.

It wasn't until I stepped back from the cliff and noticed a patch of dead brush growing along the stones that I put it together.

The brush grew in what was vaguely the shape of a circle.

I grabbed the dead overgrowth with both hands, yanking as hard as I could—and there it was. Sort of. Nothing could've prepared me for the reality of what that circle drawn on the mountain actually represented.

A small, dark hole—and by *small*, I mean *tiny*—barely big enough for a man. Barely big enough for Boo Radley. Maybe Lucille, but even that would have been cutting it tight. And it was pitch-dark inside. Of course it was.

"Aw, come on!"

According to the map, the tunnel was the only way to the Far Keep, and to Lena. If I wanted to get home, I was going to have to crawl through it. I felt sick just thinking about it.

Maybe I could go around. How long would it take to reach the other side of the mountain? Too long, that was for sure. Who was I kidding?

I tried not to think about what it would feel like to have a whole mountain fall on you while you were crawling through the middle of it. If you were already dead, could you be crushed to death? Would it hurt? Was there anything left to hurt?

The more I told myself not to think about it, the more I thought about it, and soon I was almost ready to turn back.

But then I imagined the alternative—being trapped here in the Otherworld without Lena for "infinity times infinity," as Link would say. Nothing was worth that risk. I took a deep breath, wedged my way inside, and started to crawl.

The tunnel was smaller and darker than I ever could've imagined. Once I squeezed inside, I had only a few inches of free space above me and on either side. This was worse than the time Link and I got locked in the trunk of Emory's dad's car.

I had never been scared of small spaces, but it was impossible not to feel claustrophobic in here. And it was dark—worse than dark. The only light came from cracks in the rock, which were few and far between.

Most of the time, I was crawling in complete darkness, only the sound of my breathing echoing off the walls. Invisible dirt filled my mouth, stung my eyes. I kept thinking that I was going to hit a wall—that the tunnel would just stop and I'd have to backtrack to get out. Or that I wouldn't be able to.

The ground beneath me was made of the same sharp black stone as the mountain itself, and I had to move slowly to avoid bearing down on the exposed edges of razored rubble. My hands felt like I'd shredded them to pieces; my knees, like two sacks of shattered glass. I wondered if dead people could bleed to death. With my luck, I would be the first guy to find out.

I tried to distract myself—counting to a hundred, humming the off-key tunes of some of the Holy Rollers' songs, pretending I was Kelting with Lena.

Nothing helped. I knew I was alone.

It only strengthened my resolve not to stay that way.

It's not much farther, L. I'm going to make it and find the Gates. We'll be back together soon, and then I'll tell you about how much this really *sucked.*

I fell silent after that.

It was too hard to pretend to Kelt.

My movements slowed, and my mind slowed with them, until my arms and legs moved in some kind of stiff syncopation, like the driving beat to one of Link's old songs.

Back and forth. Back and forth.

Lena. Lena. Lena.

I was still Kelting her name when I saw the light at the end of the tunnel—not a metaphoric light but a real one.

I heard Exu cawing in the distance. I felt the beginnings of a breeze, the stir of air in my face. The cold dampness of the tunnel began to give way to the warm light of the outside world.

I was almost there.

I squinted when the sunlight hit the mouth of the hole. I hadn't hauled my body out yet. But the tunnel was so dark that my eyes were having a hard time adjusting to even the smallest amount of light.

When I was only halfway out, I dropped onto my stomach with my eyes still closed, the black dirt pressing against my cheek. Exu was calling loudly, probably angry that I was taking a break. At least that's what I thought.

I opened my eyes to see the sun glinting off a pair of black-laced boots. Then the bottom of a matching wool robe came into focus.

Great.

I raised my head slowly, prepared to see a Keeper towering over me. My heart began to pound.

It looked like a man—in a way. If you ignored the fact that he was completely bald, with impossibly smooth grayish-black skin and enormous eyes. The black robe was tied at the waist with a long cord, and he—if you could call it a he—looked like some kind of miserable alien monk.

"Did you lose something?" he asked. The voice sounded so much like a man's. Like an old man, sort of sad or maybe kind. It was hard to reconcile the human features and voice with the rest of what I was staring at.

I pulled against the rock opening, yanking my legs out from the tunnel, trying to avoid bumping into whatever he was. "I—I'm trying to find the way to the Far Keep," I stammered. I tried to remember what Obidias had said. What was I looking for? Doors? Gates? That was it. "I mean, the Gates of the Far Keep." I got to my feet and tried to step back, but there was nowhere to go.

"Really?" He looked interested. Or maybe sick. Honestly, I wasn't sure it was really even a face I was looking at, so it was hard to tell what the expression meant.

"That's right." I tried to sound confident. When I stood tall, I was almost his height, which was reassuring.

"Are the Keepers expecting you?" His strange, dull eyes slitted.

"Yes," I lied.

He turned abruptly on his heel to go, his robe swinging after him.

Wrong answer.

"No," I called out. "And they'll torture me if they find me. At least that's what everyone seems to think. But there's this girl—it was all a mistake—I'm not supposed to be here—and then the lubbers came, and the Order broke, and I had to jump." My words died out, once I realized how crazy I sounded. There was no point trying to explain. It barely made sense even to me.

The creature stopped, tilting his head to the side, as if he was considering my words. Me. "Well, you've found them."

"What?"

"The Gates of the Far Keep."

I looked past him. There was nothing around but shiny black rock and clear blue sky. Maybe he was crazy. "Um, I don't see anything but mountains."

He turned and pointed. "There."

The sleeve of his robe slid down, and I caught a glimpse of an extra fold of skin flapping away from his body and disappearing under the robe.

It looked like the wing of a giant bat.

I remembered the crazy story Link told me over the summer. Macon had sent him into the Caster Tunnels to deliver a message to Obidias Trueblood. That much I'd already put together. But there was another part, about how Link was attacked by some kind of creature he ended up stabbing with his garden shears—it was grayish black and bald, with the features of a man, and deformed black bands of skin that Link was convinced were wings. "Seriously," I remembered him saying. "You don't want to face that thing in an alley at night."

I knew it couldn't be the same creature, because Link said the monster he saw had yellow eyes. And the one standing here was staring back at me with green eyes—almost Caster green. Then there was the other thing. The whole gardening-shears-to-the-chest thing.

This couldn't be him.

Green eyes. Not gold. I didn't need to be afraid, right? He couldn't be Dark, could he?

Still, it wasn't anything I'd ever seen before—and I had seen more than my share.

The creature turned around, lowering his arm that wasn't an arm. "Do you see them?"

"What?" The wings? I was still trying to figure out what he was—or wasn't.

"The Gates." He seemed disappointed by my stupidity. I guess I'd be disappointed, too, if I were him. I was feeling pretty stupid myself.

I searched in the direction he had pointed a moment ago. There was nothing there. "I don't see anything."

A satisfied smile spread across his face, as if he had a secret. "Of course you don't. Only the Gatekeeper can see them."

"Where's the—" I stopped, realizing I didn't need to ask the question. I already knew the answer. "You're the Gatekeeper." There was a River Master and a Gatekeeper. Of course there was. There was also a snake man, a whiskey-drinking crow that could fly from the land of the living to the land of the dead, a river full of bodies, and a dragon dog. It was like waking up in the middle of a game of *Dungeons & Dragons*.

"The Gatekeeper." The creature nodded, obviously pleased with himself. "I am that, among other things."

I tried not to fixate on the word *thing*. But as I looked at his charcoal-colored skin and thought about those awful wings, I couldn't stop imagining him as some terrifying cross between a person and a bat.

A real-life Batman, sort of.

Only not the kind who saves anyone. Maybe the reverse.

What if this thing doesn't want to let me in?

I took a deep breath. "Look, I know it's crazy. I left crazy behind about a year ago. But there's something I need in there. And if I don't get it, I won't be able to go home. Is there any way you can show me where the Gates are?"

"Of course."

I heard the words before I saw his face. And I smiled, until I realized I was the only one smiling.

The creature frowned, his huge eyes narrowing. He put his hands together in front of his chest, tapping his crooked fingertips. "But why would I do that?"

Exu shrieked in the distance.

I looked up to see the massive black shape circling above our heads, as if he was prepared to swoop down and attack.

179

Wordlessly, without looking up, the creature held up his hand.

Exu descended and landed on the Gatekeeper's fist, nuzzling his arm as if reunited with an old friend.

Maybe not.

The Gatekeeper looked even more frightening with Exu at his side. It was time to face facts. The creature was right. He had no reason to help me.

Then the bird squawked, almost sympathetically. The creature made a low, throaty sound—almost a chuckle—and raised a hand to smooth the bird's feathers. "You are lucky. The bird is a good judge of character."

"Yeah? What does the bird say about me?"

"He says—slow on the switchbacks, cheap with the whiskey, but a good heart. For a dead man."

I grinned. Maybe that old crow wasn't so bad.

Exu squawked again.

"I can show you the Gates, boy."

"Ethan."

"Ethan." He hesitated, repeating my name slowly. "But you have to give me something in return."

I was almost afraid to ask. "What do you want?" Obidias had mentioned that the Gatekeeper would expect some kind of gift, but I hadn't really put much thought into it.

He looked at me thoughtfully, considering the question. "Trade is a serious matter. Balance is a key principle within the Order of Things."

"The Order of Things? I thought we didn't have to worry about that anymore."

"There is always Order. Now more than ever, the New Order must be carefully maintained."

I didn't understand the details, but I understood the importance. Wasn't that how I got into this mess in the first place?

He kept talking. "You say you need something to take you home? The thing you desire most? I say, what brought you here? That is what I desire most."

"Great." It sounded simple, but he might as well have been speaking in riddles or randomly written Mad Libs.

"What do you have?" His eyes glinted greedily.

I stuffed my hands in my pockets and pulled out the one remaining river stone and Aunt Prue's map. The whiskey and the tobacco—Exu's stash—were long gone.

The Gatekeeper lifted his hairless brows. "A rock and an old map? Is that all?"

"That's what brought me here." I pointed at Exu, still perched on his shoulder. "And a bird."

"A rock *and* a crow. That is difficult to pass up. But I already have both of those things in my collection."

Exu pushed off from his shoulder and flew back up into the sky, like he was offended. Within seconds the crow disappeared.

"And now you have no bird," the Gatekeeper said matter-of-factly.

"I don't understand. Is there something specific you want?" I tried to hide the frustration in my voice.

The Gatekeeper seemed delighted by the question. "Specific, yes. Specifically, a fair trade is what I prefer."

"Could you be a *little* more specific than that?"

He tilted his head. "I don't always know what will interest me until I see it. The things that are the most valuable are often the ones you don't even know exist."

That was helpful.

"How am I supposed to know what you have already?"

His eyes lit up. "I can show you my collection if you would like to see it. There isn't another one like it anywhere in the Otherworld."

What could I say? "Yeah. That would be great."

As I followed him along the sharp black stones, I could hear Link's voice in my head. "Bad move, man. He's gonna kill you, stuff you, and add you to his collection of idiots who followed him back to his creepy cave."

This was one time I was probably safer dead than alive.

How fair and balanced was that?

The Gatekeeper slid through a narrow crack in the wall of slick black stone. It was bigger than the hole, but not by much. I moved along sideways because there wasn't enough room to turn around.

I knew this could be some kind of trap. Link had described the creature he encountered as an animal—dangerous and crazed. What if the Gatekeeper was no different, just better at hiding it? Where was that stupid crow when I needed him?

"We're almost there," he called back to me.

I could see a faint light ahead, flickering in the distance.

His shadow passed in front of it, momentarily darkening the passage as the narrow space opened into a cavernous room. Wax dripped from an iron chandelier bolted directly into the glossy stone ceiling. The walls sparkled in the candlelight.

If I hadn't just crawled through a whole mountain of the stuff, I might have been more impressed. As it was, the closeness of the cavern walls just made my skin crawl.

But when I glanced around, I realized this place was more like a museum—with an even crazier collection than what you'd find if you dug up the Sisters' whole backyard. Glass cases and shelves lined the walls, filled with hundreds of objects. It was the randomness of the collection that intrigued me, like a child had done not only the collecting but the cataloging. Intricately carved silver and gold jewelry boxes sat next to a collection of cheap children's music boxes. Shiny black vinyl records were piled in towering stacks next to one of those old-fashioned record players with a funnel speaker, like the one the Sisters used to have. A Raggedy Ann doll curled in a rocking chair, a huge green jewel the size of an apple resting in her lap. And on a center shelf, I saw an opalescent sphere similar to the one I had carried in my hand the past summer.

It couldn't be…an Arclight.

But it was. Exactly like the one Macon had given my mom, except milky white instead of midnight black.

"Where did you get that?" I walked toward the shelf.

He darted in front of me, snatching the sphere. "I told you. I'm a collector. You could say a historian. You mustn't touch anything in here. The treasures in this room cannot be replaced. I've spent a thousand lifetimes collecting them. They are all equally valuable," he breathed.

"Yeah?" I looked at a Snoopy lunch box full of pearls.

He nodded. "Priceless."

He replaced the Arclight. "All sorts of things have been offered to me at the Gates," he added. "*Most* people, and non-people, know it is only polite to bring me a gift when they come knocking." He stole a look at me. "No offense."

"Yeah, sorry. I mean, I wish I had something to give you—"

He lifted a hairless eyebrow. "Besides a rock and a crow?"

"Yeah." I scanned the rows of leather books lined up neatly on the shelves, the spines inscribed with symbols and languages I didn't recognize. The spine of a black leather book caught my eye. It looked like it said… "*The Book of Stars?*"

The Gatekeeper looked pleased and rushed to pull it down from the shelf. "This is one of the rarest books of its kind." Niadic, the Caster language I had come to recognize, looped around the edges of the cover. A cluster of stars was embossed in the center. "There is only one other like it—"

"*The Book of Moons,*" I finished for him. "I know."

His eyes widened, and he clutched *The Book of Stars* to his chest. "You know about the Dark half? No one in our world has seen it for hundreds of years."

"That's because it isn't in your world." I looked at him for a long moment before correcting myself. "Our world."

He shook his head in disbelief. "How could you possibly know that?"

"Because I was the one who found it."

For a moment, he didn't say a word. I could tell he was trying to decide if I was lying or crazy. There was nothing in his expression that made it seem like he actually believed me, but like I said, there wasn't really too much to go on—his face not really being a face and all.

"Is this a trick?" His dull green eyes narrowed. "It wouldn't serve you well to play games with me if you ever expect to find the Gates of the Far Keep."

"I didn't even know *The Book of Moons* had another half, or whatever you said. So how would I know to lie about it?"

It was true. I had never heard anyone mention it—not Macon or Marian or Sarafine or Abraham.

Is it possible they didn't know?

"As I said, balance. Light and Dark are both part of the invisible scale that is always tipping as we hang on to the edges." He ran his crooked fingers over the cover of the book. "You can't have one without the other. Sad as that might be."

After everything I had learned about *The Book of Moons*, I couldn't imagine what was within the covers of its counterpart.

Did *The Book of Stars* yield the same kind of devastating consequences?

I was almost afraid to ask. "Is there a price for using that one, too?"

The Gatekeeper walked to the far end of the room and sat down in an intricately carved chair that looked like a throne from an old castle. He lifted a Mickey Mouse Thermos, pouring a stream of amber liquid into the plastic cup, and drank half of it. There was a weariness in his movements, and I wondered how long it had taken him to amass the collection of intangibly valuable and valueless items within these walls.

When he finally spoke, he sounded like he'd aged a hundred years.

"I have never used the book myself. My debts are too steep to risk owing anything more. Though there is not much left for them to take, is there?" He threw back the rest of his drink and slammed the plastic cup on the table. Within seconds, he was pacing again, nervous and agitated.

I followed him to the other side of the room.

"Who do you owe?"

He stopped walking, pulling his robe tighter, as if he was protecting himself from an unseen enemy. "The Far Keep, of course." There was a mix of bitterness and defeat in his voice. "And they always collect their debts."

⊰ CHAPTER 17 ⊱

The Book of Stars

The Gatekeeper turned his back to me, moving instead to a glass case behind him. He examined a collection of charms—amulets hanging from long leather cords, crystals and exotic rocks that reminded me of the river stones, runes with markings I didn't recognize. He opened the cabinet and took out one of the amulets, rubbing the silver disk between his fingers. It reminded me of the way Amma touched the gold charm she wore around her neck, whenever she got nervous.

"Why don't you just leave?" I asked. "Take all this stuff and disappear?" I knew the answer even as I asked the question.

Nobody would stay here unless they had to.

He spun a large enamel globe on a tall stand next to the

cabinet. I watched as it turned, strange shapes spinning past me. They weren't the continents I was used to seeing in history class.

"I can't leave. I'm Bound to the Gates. If I venture too far from them, I'll continue to change."

He stared down at his bent, gnarled fingers. A chill rushed up my back.

"What do you mean?"

The Gatekeeper turned his hands over slowly, as if he had never seen them before. "There was a time when I looked like you, dead man. A time when I was a man."

The words were swimming around in my head, but I couldn't find a way to make them true. Whatever the Gatekeeper was—however reminiscent his features were of a man's—it wasn't possible.

Was it?

"I—I don't understand. How—?" There was no way to say what I was thinking without being cruel. And if he was a man somewhere inside there, he had suffered more than enough cruelty already.

"How did I become this?" The Gatekeeper fingered a large crystal hanging from a golden chain. He picked up a second necklace, made of rings of sugar candy, the kind you could buy at the Stop & Steal, smoothing it back down inside its velvet-lined case. "The Council of the Far Keep is very powerful. They have powerful magic at their disposal, stronger than anything I witnessed as a Keeper."

"You were a Keeper?" This thing used to be like my mom and Liv and Marian?

His dull green eyes stared back at me. "You might want to take a seat...." He paused. "I don't think you told me your name."

"Ethan." I'd told him twice now.

"It's nice to meet you, Ethan. My name is—was—Xavier. No one calls me that anymore, but you can if it makes things easier."

I knew what he was trying to say—if it made it easier to imagine him as a man instead of a monster.

"Okay. Thanks, Xavier." It sounded funny, even coming from me.

He tapped the case with his fingers, some kind of nervous habit. "And to answer your question, yes. I was a Keeper. One who made the mistake of questioning Angelus, the head—"

"I know who he is." I remembered the one named Angelus, the Keeper with the bald head. I also remembered the ruthless expression on his face when he had come after Marian.

"Then you know he's dangerous. And corrupt." Xavier watched me carefully.

I nodded. "He tried to hurt a friend of mine—two, actually. He brought one of them to the Far Keep to stand trial."

"Trial." He laughed, only there was nothing like a smile on his nothing like a face.

"It wasn't funny."

"Of course not. Angelus must have been making an example

189

of your friend," Xavier said. "I was never given a trial. He finds them dull compared to the punishment."

"What did you do?" I was afraid to ask, but I felt like I had to.

Xavier sighed. "I questioned the authority of the Council, the decisions they were making. I never should have done it," he said quietly. "But they were breaking our vows, the laws we swore to abide by. Taking things that were not theirs to Keep."

I tried to imagine Xavier in a Caster library somewhere like Marian, stacking books and recording the details of the Caster world. He had created his own version of a Caster library here, a place filled with magical objects—and a few unmagical ones.

"What kind of things, Xavier?"

He glanced around the cavernous room, panicked. "I don't think we should be talking about this. What if the Council finds out?"

"How would they?"

"They will. They always do. I don't know what more they could do to me, but they would think of something."

"We're in the center of a mountain." My second one today. "It's not like they can hear you."

He pulled the collar of the heavy wool robe away from his neck. "You would be surprised at what they can find out. Let me show you."

I wasn't sure what he meant as he moved past a heap of

broken bicycles to another glass cabinet. He opened the doors and took out a cobalt-blue sphere the size of a baseball.

"What is that thing?"

"A Third Eye." He held it in his palm carefully. "It allows you to see the past, a specific memory in time."

The color began to swirl inside the ball, churning like storm clouds. Until it cleared, and a picture came into view...

A young man was sitting behind a heavy wooden desk in a dimly lit study. His long robe appeared to be too big for him, much like the ornately carved chair he was sitting in. His hands were clasped together as he leaned heavily on his elbows. "What is it now, Xavier?" he asked impatiently.

Xavier ran his hands through his dark hair and over his face, his green eyes darting around the room. It was obvious that he was dreading the conversation. He twisted the cord of his own robe in his lap. "I'm sorry to bother you, sir. But certain events have come to my attention—atrocities that violate our vows and threaten the mission of the Keepers."

Angelus looked bored. "What atrocities are you referring to, Xavier? Has someone failed to file a report? Lost a crescent key to one of the Caster libraries?"

Xavier straightened. "We're not talking about lost keys, Angelus. Something is going on in the dungeons

191

below the Keep. At night I hear the screams, blood-curdling screams you can't—"

Angelus waved off the comment. "People have nightmares. We can't all sleep as blissfully as you. Some of us run the Council."

Xavier pushed back from his chair and stood. "I've been down there, Angelus. I know what they are hiding. The question is, do you?"

Angelus whipped around, his eyes narrowing. "What is it you think you've seen?"

The rage in Xavier's eyes was impossible to ignore. "Keepers using Dark power—Casting—as if they are Dark Casters. Conducting experiments on the living. I've seen enough to know that you must take action."

Angelus turned his back on Xavier, facing the window that overlooked the vast mountains surrounding the Far Keep. "Those experiments, as you call them, are for their protection. There is a war, Xavier. Between Light and Dark Casters, and the Mortals are caught in the middle." He turned. "Do you want to watch them die? Are you prepared to take responsibility for that atrocity? Your acts have already cost you enough, wouldn't you agree?"

"For your protection," Xavier corrected. "That is what you meant, isn't it, Angelus? Mortals are caught in the middle of the war. Or have you become something beyond Mortal?"

Angelus shook his head. "It's clear we aren't going to agree on this matter." He started to speak the words of a Cast in low tones.

"What are you doing?" Xavier pointed at Angelus. "Casting? This is not right. We are the balance—we observe and Keep the records. Keepers do not cross the line into the world of magic and monsters!"

Angelus closed his eyes and continued the incantation.

Xavier's skin seared and blackened, as if it was burnt.

"What are you doing?" he cried.

The charcoal color spread like a rash, the skin tightening as it turned impossibly smooth. Xavier screamed, clawing at his own skin.

Angelus spoke the final word of the Cast and opened his eyes in time to watch Xavier's hair fall out in tufts.

He smiled at the sight of the man he was destroying. "It seems to me that you are crossing a line right now."

Xavier's limbs started to lengthen unnaturally, bones cracking and breaking. Angelus listened. "You should consider having a bit more sympathy for monsters."

Xavier dropped to his knees. "Please. Have mercy...."

Angelus stood over the Keeper, who was almost unrecognizable. "This is the Far Keep. Removed from the Mortal and Caster worlds. The vows are the words I speak, and the laws the ones I choose." He pushed Xavier's devastated body over with his boot.

"There is no mercy here."

The images faded, replaced by the swirling blue haze. For a second, I didn't move. I felt like I had just witnessed a man's execution—and he was standing right next to me. What was left of him.

Xavier looked like a monster, but he was a good guy, trying to do the right thing. I shuddered, thinking about what could have happened to Marian if Macon and John hadn't gotten there in time.

If I hadn't made a deal with the Lilum.

At least I knew enough not to regret what I did. As bad as things were, they could have been worse. I knew that now.

"I'm sorry, Xavier." I didn't know what else to say.

He put the Third Eye back on the shelf. "That was a long time ago. But I thought you should know what they are capable of, since you are so anxious to get inside. If I were you, I would run the other way."

I leaned against the cold wall of the cavern. "I wish I could."

"Why do you want so badly to get in there?"

I was sure he couldn't think of one good reason. For me, one reason was all I needed.

"Someone added a page in *The Caster Chronicles*, and I ended up dead. If I can destroy it—"

Xavier reached his hands toward me as if he was going to grab me by the shoulders and shake some sense into me. But he drew them back before he touched me. "Do you have any idea what they'll do to you if you're caught? Look at me, Ethan. I'm one of the lucky ones."

"Lucky? You?" I shut my mouth before I accidentally made it worse. Was he nuts?

"They've done this to others, Mortals and Casters alike. It's Dark power." His hands were shaking. "Most of them have gone mad, left to wander the Tunnels or the Otherworld like animals."

It was exactly the way Link had described the creature that attacked him the night Obidias Trueblood died. But what Link had encountered wasn't an animal. It was a man, or something that had been a man once—driven crazy as his body was mutated and tortured.

I felt sick.

The walls of the Far Keep were hiding more than *The Caster Chronicles*.

"I don't have a choice. If I don't destroy the page, I can't get back home." I could almost see his mind spinning. "There has to be a Cast—something in *The Book of Stars* or one of your books that could help me."

Xavier whipped around, pointing a broken finger inches from my face. "I would never let *anyone* touch one of my books or use them to Cast! Have you learned nothing here?"

I backed up. "I'm sorry. I shouldn't have said that. I'll find another way, but I still have to get inside."

Everything about his demeanor had changed when I suggested using a Cast. "You still have nothing to offer. I can't show you the Gates unless you give me something in return."

"Are you serious?" But I could tell from his expression that he was. "What the hell do you want?"

"*The Book of Moons*," he said without hesitation. "You know where it is. That's my price."

"It's in the Mortal realm. And if you haven't noticed, I'm dead. And by the way, Abraham Ravenwood has it. He's not what you'd call a nice guy." I was beginning to think that getting past the Gates was going to be the hardest part of finding my way home, if it was even possible.

Xavier started moving toward the slit in the rock that led back to the outside. "I think we both know there are ways around that. If you want to get through the Gates, bring me *The Book of Moons*."

"Even if I could get it, why would I give you the most powerful book in the Caster world?" I practically shouted. "How do I know you won't use it to do something terrible?"

His unnaturally large eyes widened. "What could be more terrible than how I am standing before you now? Is there something worse than watching your body betray you? Feeling your bones break as you move? Do you think I can risk the trade the Book might choose to make?"

He was right. You couldn't get something from *The Book of Moons* without giving something in return. We'd all learned that, the hard way. The other Ethan Wate. Genevieve. Macon and Amma and Lena and me. The Book made the choice.

"You could change your mind. People get desperate." I couldn't believe I was lecturing a desperate man about desperation.

Xavier turned to face me, his body already partially hidden in shadow. "Because I know what it is capable of—what it could do in the hands of men like Angelus—I would never speak a word from that book. And I would be sure it never left this room, so no one else could either."

He was telling the truth.

Xavier was terrified of magic, Light or Dark.

It had destroyed him in the worst possible way. He didn't want to Cast or wield supernatural power. If anything, he wanted to protect himself and others from that kind of power. If there was anywhere *The Book of Moons* would be safe, it was here—safer than in the *Lunae Libri* or some other far-away Caster library. Safer than hidden in the depths of Ravenwood or buried in Genevieve's grave. No one would ever find it here.

That was when I decided I was going to give it to him.

There was only one problem.

I had to figure out how to get it away from Abraham Ravenwood first.

I looked at Xavier.

"How many powerful objects would you say you've got in this room, Xavier?"

"It doesn't matter. I told you—they're not to be used."

I smiled. "What if I were to tell you I could get you *The Book of Moons*, but I'd need your help? Your help, and the help of a few of your treasures?"

He made a strange expression, twisting his uneven mouth from one side to the other. I really, really hoped it was a smile.

⇥ CHAPTER 18 ⇤

Shadows

How I get there isn't as important as getting there." I said it for the fifth time.

"To this Land of the Stars and Stripes?" he asked.

"Yeah. Well, kinda. The office anyway. On Main."

He nodded. "Ah, the Mainlands. Is that past the Swamp of the Coolers?"

"The swamp coolers? Yeah. More or less." I sighed.

I tried to explain my plan to Xavier. I wasn't sure when he had been in the Mortal world last, but whenever it was, it was way before swamp coolers and newspapers. Which was kind of funny, given how much he liked lunch boxes, vinyl records, and sweets.

I picked up another ancient book, opening it to a cloud of dust and possibility—and uncertainty. I was frustrated, and sitting on the floor surrounded by Caster Scrolls in the middle of this strange creature's cave made me feel as if I was back working in the Gatlin County Library on the first day of my summer break.

I tried to think. There had to be something we could do. "What about Traveling? Can Waywards use Casts that pertain to an Incubus?"

Xavier shook his head. "I don't think so."

I leaned back against a stack of books. I was close to giving up. Once again, if Link was here, he'd lecture me about being the Aquaman of the Caster world.

"A dead Aquaman," I said to myself.

"Excuse me?"

"Nothing," I muttered.

"A dead man?" he asked.

"You don't have to rub it in."

"No, that's it. You don't need Casts that work for a Mortal. You're not a Mortal anymore. You need Casts that work for a Sheer." He flipped page after page. "An *Umbra* Cast. Sending a shadow from one world to the next. That's you, the shadow. It should work."

I thought about it. Could it be that simple?

I stared at my hand, at the flesh and bones of it.

It only looks like flesh and bones. You're not really here, not like that. You don't have a body.

What was the big difference between a Sheer and a shadow?

"I need to be able to touch something, though. It won't work unless I can get the message to Lena, and I'll need to be able to move some papers around."

He cocked his head, twisting his face into a grimace. I hoped it was his thinking face.

"Do you need to touch something?"

"That's what I just said."

He shook his head. "No, it's not. You said you need to move something. That's different."

"Does it matter?"

"Entirely." He flipped a few more pages. "A *Veritas* Cast should allow the truth to appear. As long as you're looking for the truth."

"That'll work?"

I hoped he was right.

Minutes later, any doubts I had about Xavier were gone.

I was here. I hadn't flown across the Great River, or the Great Barrier, or any other supernatural seam. I hadn't turned on the crow-vision. I was here, on Main, staring into the office of *The Stars and Stripes*.

At least, my shadow was.

I felt like Peter Pan in reverse. Like Wendy had unstitched my shadow from me instead of sewing it back to my feet.

I moved through the wall and into the darkness of the

room, only I was even darker. I had no body, but it didn't matter. I lifted my hand—the shadow of my hand—and thought the words Xavier had taught me.

I watched as the words on the page rearranged themselves. I had no time for riddles. No time for games, hidden messages.

My words were simple.

Five across.

Read, in Spanish.

L. I. B. R. O.

Two down.

Belonging to.

O. F.

Five across.

Lunae.

M. O. O. N. S.

I lowered my hand and disappeared.

My last message, all I had left to say. Lena had figured out how to send me the river rock charm, and she would know how to send the Book to me. I hoped. If not, maybe Macon would.

If Abraham still had it, and Lena could get it away from him.

There were only about a thousand other ifs in between. I tried not to think about them, and all the people they involved. Or the danger that always surrounded *The Book of Moons*.

I couldn't afford to think like that. I'd come this far, right?

She would find it, and I would find her.

It was the only Order of Things I cared about now.

BOOK TWO

Lena

⊰ CHAPTER 19 ⊱

Mortal Problems

Sometimes Link could be a real idiot.

"*Libro* what? *Book of Moons*? What does that mean?" Link looked from me to *The Stars and Stripes*, scratching his head. You would have thought I was bringing up the subject for the first time.

"Three words. It's a book, Link. I'm sure you've heard of it." It was only the book that had destroyed our lives, and the lives of all the Casters in my family before me on our sixteenth birthdays.

"That's not what I meant." He looked hurt.

I knew what Link meant.

But I didn't know why Ethan was asking for *The Book of*

Moons any more than Link did. So I just kept staring at the newspaper in the middle of the kitchen.

Amma was behind me, and she didn't say a word. She'd been that way for a while now—since Ethan. The silence was as wrong as everything else. It was strange to not hear her banging around in her kitchen. Even stranger that we were sitting around Ethan's kitchen table trying to figure out the message he'd left in today's crossword puzzle. I wondered if he could see us or knew we were here.

> *surrounded by strangers who love me*
> *(un)strangers made strange*
> *by pain*

I felt my fingers twitch, looking for the pen that wasn't there. I fought the poetry off. It was a new habit. It hurt too much to write now. Three days after Ethan left, the word NO appeared, inked in black Sharpie on my left hand. WORDS appeared on my right.

I hadn't written a word since, not on paper. Not in my notebook. Not even on my walls. It seemed like forever since I had.

How long had Ethan been gone? Weeks? Months? It was all one long blur, as if time had stopped when he left.

Everything had stopped.

Link stared up at me from where he was sitting on the kitchen floor. When he unfolded his new quarter-Incubus

206

body like that, he took up most of the kitchen. There were arms and legs everywhere, like a praying mantis, only with muscles.

Liv studied her own copy of the puzzle from the table—clipped and taped into her trusty red notebook, covered in her neatly penciled analysis—while John leaned over her shoulder. The way they moved together, you would think it hurt them *not* to touch.

Unlike Casters and Mortals.

A human and a hybrid Incubus. They don't know how good they have it. Nothing catches fire when they kiss.

I sighed, resisting the urge to Cast a *Discordia* on them. We were all here. You would have thought nothing had changed. Only one person was missing.

Which made everything different.

I folded up the morning paper, sinking into the chair next to Liv. "*Book of Moons*. That's all it says. I don't know why I keep reading it. If I read this thing any more times, I'm going to burn a hole in it with my eyes."

"You can do that?" Link looked interested.

I wriggled my fingers in front of him. "Maybe I can burn more than just paper. So don't tempt me."

Liv smiled at me sympathetically. As if the situation called for anything like a smile. "Well then, I suppose we have to think. Those are three rather specific words. So it seems the messages are changing." She sounded precise and logical, like a British version of Marian, as she always did.

207

"And?" Link sounded irritated, like he always did lately.

"So what's going on...over there?" *Where Ethan is.* Liv didn't say it. Nobody wanted to. Liv pulled the three crossword puzzles out of her notebook. "At first, it seems like he just wants you to know he is..."

"Alive? Hate to break it to you—" Link said, but John kicked him under the table. Amma dropped a pan behind me, sending it clattering toward where Link sat on the floor. "Oww. You know what I meant."

"Around," John corrected him, looking from Amma to me. I nodded, feeling Amma's hands slip down to rest on my shoulders.

I touched her hand with mine; her fingers curled tightly around it. Neither one of us wanted to let go. Especially now that it was possible Ethan wasn't gone forever. It had been weeks since Ethan had started sending me messages through *The Stars and Stripes.* It didn't matter what they said. They all said the same thing to me.

I'm here.

I'm still here.

You're not alone.

I wished there was a way I could say it to him.

I squeezed Amma's fingers harder. I tried to talk to her about it right after I found the first message, but she just muttered something about a fair trade and how it was her mess to sort out. How it was what she aimed to do, sooner or later.

But she didn't doubt me. Neither did my uncle, not any-

208

more. In fact, Uncle Macon and Amma were the only ones who really believed me. They understood what I was going through, because they had gone through it themselves. I didn't know if Uncle Macon would ever get over losing Lila. And Amma seemed to be having as hard a time without Ethan as I was. They had seen the proof, too. Uncle Macon was there when I saw Ethan's crossword for the first time. And Amma had all but seen Ethan standing in the kitchen of Wate's Landing.

I said it out loud again to everyone, for the tenth time. "Of course he's around. I told you, he's going somewhere. He's got some kind of plan. He's not just sitting there, waiting in a grave full of dirt. He's trying to get back to us. I'm sure of it."

"How sure?" Link asked. "You're not sure, Lena. Nothin's sure, except death an' taxes. And when they said it, I think they were talkin' more about stayin' dead, not comin' back again."

I didn't know why Link was having so much trouble believing that Ethan was still there, that he could come home again. Wasn't Link the one who was part Incubus? He knew as well as anyone that strange things happened around here all the time. Why was it so hard for him to believe that this particular strange thing could be happening?

Maybe losing Ethan was harder on Link than it was for the rest of them. Maybe he couldn't let himself risk losing his best friend all over again, even if it was only the idea of him. No one knew what Link was going through.

Except me.

While Link and Liv returned to arguing about whether or not Ethan was actually gone, I felt myself slipping into the fog of nagging doubts that I worked so hard to push out of my mind.

They just kept coming.

What if this whole thing really was my imagination, like Reece and Gramma kept saying? What if they were right, and it was just too hard for me to accept my life without him? And it wasn't just them—Uncle Macon wouldn't try anything to bring him back either.

And if it was real—if Ethan could hear me—what would I say?

Come home.

I'm waiting.

I love you.

Nothing he didn't already know.

Why bother?

I refused to write, but the words were hard to even think now.

words same as always
same as nothing
when nothing is the same

There was no point in saying it to myself.

John kicked Link again, and I tried to focus on the present. The kitchen and the conversation. All the things I could do for Ethan, rather than all the things I felt about him.

"Let's say, for the sake of argument, that Ethan is—around." Liv looked at Link, who kept quiet this time. "Like I said, it seemed he spent all his energy trying to convince us of that a few weeks ago."

"Right around the time you measured the energy spiking at Ravenwood," John reminded her. Liv nodded, flipping pages in her notebook.

"Or maybe Reece was just usin' the microwave," Link muttered.

"Which was the same time Ethan moved the button at his grave," I said obstinately.

"Or maybe it was just windy." Link sighed.

"Something was definitely going on." John moved his foot closer to Link, the threat of another good kick shutting Link up for a while. I thought about slapping a *Silentium* Cast on him, but it didn't seem right. Plus, knowing Link, it would take more than magic to shut him up.

Liv went back to examining the papers in front of her. "But then, quite soon, his messages began to change. It's like he figured something out. What he needed to do."

"To come home," I said.

"Lena, I know you want to think that's what's happenin'." Amma's voice was bleak. "And I felt my boy here, same as you. But we don't know which end is up. There are no easy answers, not when it comes to gettin' someone in or outta the Otherworld. Believe me, if there was an easy way, I would've already done it."

She sounded so haggard and tired. I knew she had been working on getting Ethan home as hard as I had. And I'd tried everything at first—everything and everyone. The problem was trying to get Light Casters to talk about raising the dead. And I didn't have quite the access to the Dark Casters that I used to. Uncle Macon had come for me the moment I'd set foot in Exile. I suspected he made some kind of deal with the bartender, a shifty-looking Blood Incubus who looked like he'd do anything if he was thirsty enough.

"But we don't know that's not it," I said, looking at Liv.

"True. The logical assumption would be that wherever Ethan was, he would be trying to get back." Liv carefully erased a small mark in the margin. "To where you are." She didn't look at me, but I knew what she meant. Liv and Ethan had a history of their own, and even though Liv had found something better for her with John, she was always very careful of how she spoke about Ethan, especially to me.

She tapped the pencil. "First the river rock. Now *The Book of Moons*. He must need them for something."

John pulled the last puzzle toward him. "If he needs *The Book of Moons*, it's a good sign. It has to be."

"A mighty powerful book, on this side or the other. A book like that would be worth bargaining for." Amma rubbed my shoulders as she spoke, and I felt a shiver go down my spine.

John looked at both of us. "Bargaining for what? Why?"

Amma said nothing. I suspected she knew more than she

was saying, which was usually the case. Plus, she hadn't even mentioned the Greats in weeks, which was unlike her. Especially now that Ethan was in their care, technically speaking. But I had no idea what Amma was up to any more than I knew what Ethan was planning.

I finally answered for both of us, because there was only one possible answer. "I don't know. It's not like I can ask him."

"Why not? Can't you Cast something?" John looked frustrated.

"It doesn't work like that." I wished it did.

"Some kind of Reveal Cast?"

"There's nothing to Cast it on."

"His grave?" John looked at Liv, but she shook her head. No one had an answer, because none of us had ever even contemplated anything like this before. A Cast on someone who wasn't even on this plane of existence? Short of raising the dead—which Genevieve had done to start this whole mess in the first place, and I had done again, more than a hundred years later—what could anyone do?

I shook my head. "What does it matter? Ethan wants it, and we have to get it to him. That's the important thing."

Amma chimed in. "Besides, only one kind a bargain my boy would be makin' over there. Only one thing he wants bad enough. And that would be to get himself back home again, sure as the sunrise."

"Amma's right." I looked at them. "We have to get him the Book."

Link sat up. "Are you sure, Lena? Are you absolutely death-and-taxes sure it's Ethan who's even sendin' us these messages? What if it's Sarafine? Or even Colonel Sanders?" He shuddered.

I knew who Link meant. Abraham, in his rumpled white suit and his string tie. Satan himself, at least as far as Gatlin County was concerned.

That really would be the worst-case scenario.

"It's not Sarafine. I'd know."

"Would you really know if it was her?" Link rubbed his hair, which was sticking out in a thousand different directions. "How?"

Through the window, I watched as Mr. Wate's Volvo pulled into the driveway. I knew the conversation was over, even before I felt Amma's hands stiffen on my shoulders. "I just would."

Wouldn't I?

I stared at the stupid crossword puzzle as if it could give me some kind of answer, when all it could tell me was that I knew nothing at all.

The front door opened as the back door banged shut. John and Liv must have disappeared out the back. I braced for the inevitable.

"Afternoon, kids. You waitin' for Ethan to get home?" Mr. Wate looked at Amma hopefully. Link scrambled to his feet, but I looked away. I couldn't bear to answer.

More than anything. More than you know.

"Yes, sir. Waitin's hardly the word. Bored outta my thick skull without Ethan around." Link tried to smile, but even he looked like he was about to cry.

"Cheer up, Wesley. I miss him as much as you do." Mr. Wate reached for Link's spiked hair, rubbing it with one hand. Then he opened the pantry and looked inside. "You hear anything from our boy today, Amma?"

"Afraid not, Mitchell."

Mr. Wate stopped short, frozen in place with a box of cereal in his hand. "I've half a mind to drive down to Savannah myself. It makes no sense, keeping a boy out of school this long. Something's not right." His face clouded over.

I focused my eyes on the tall, gaunt figure of Mitchell Wate, just as I had so often since Ethan died. Once he was fixed in my sight, I slowly began reciting the words of the *Oblivio* Cast that Gramma had taught me to repeat every time I saw Ethan's dad.

He stared at me, curious. My eyes didn't even flicker. Only my lips began to move, and I whispered the words as they formed in my mind.

"*Oblivio, Oblivio, Non Abest.*
Oblivion, Oblivion, He Is Not Gone."

A bubble expanded inside my chest the moment I formed the Cast, pushing past me toward Ethan's father, reaching right across the room and wrapping itself around him. The room seemed to stretch and contract, and I thought for a moment the bubble was about to pop.

Then I felt the air snap around us, and suddenly it was over, and the air was just air, and everything seemed normal again.

As normal as things could be.

Mr. Wate's eyes brightened and glazed over. He shrugged, smiling at me, sticking one hand back inside the cereal box. "Ah well, what are you going to do? He's a good kid. But if Ethan doesn't get his tail home from Caroline's soon, he's going to be mighty behind when he gets back. At this rate, he'll be doing homework all the way through spring break. You tell him that for me, will you?"

"Yes, sir. I'll tell him." I smiled, wiping at my eye before anything like a tear could fall. "I'll tell him the next time I talk to him."

That's when Amma almost threw the pan of pork chops down on the burner. Link shook his head.

I turned and fled. I tried not to think, but the words followed me, like a curse, like a hex.

oblivion eyes on a cereal box,
the warm blinds of a father
lost and last to know
lost and last to love
last boy lost

you can't see
even a bubble
once it's
popped

I fought off the words.
But you couldn't unpop a bubble.
Even I knew that.

CHAPTER 20

A Deal with the Devil

This is freakin' nuts. We don't even have the stupid *Book a Moons*. You sure *The Stars and Sucks* didn't say anythin' else?"

Link was sitting on the floor again, with only his feet sticking out from under the table—this time the one in Macon's study. We'd made no progress, but here we were again. New table. Same people. Same problems.

Only the presence of my Uncle Macon, half-hidden in the flickering shadows of the fireplace, changed the conversation. That, and the fact that we'd left Amma back at Wate's Landing to keep an eye on Ethan's father.

"I can't believe I'm actually saying this, but maybe Link's right. Even if we all agreed—even if we knew we had no choice but to get Ethan *The Book of Moons*—it still wouldn't matter. We don't know where it is, and we don't know how to get it to him." Liv said what we all were thinking.

I said nothing, twisting my charm necklace between my fingers.

It was Macon who finally answered. "Yes. Well. These things are difficulties, not impossibilities."

Link sat up. "The whole death thing, yeah, I'd say that's pretty difficult, sir. I mean, no offense, Mr. Ravenwood."

"Finding *The Book of Moons* is not out of the question, Mr. Lincoln. I'm sure I don't need to remind you where we last saw it and who last had it."

"Abraham." We all knew who he was talking about, but it was Liv who said it. "He had it with him at the Seventeenth Moon, in the cave. And he used it to bring up the Vexes, right before—"

"The Eighteenth Moon," John said quietly. None of us ever wanted to talk about the night at the water tower.

All of which just set Link off more. "Oh well. That's easy. Find the Book. How about we just find our way over to whatever backwoods swamp hole Colonel Sanders has been livin' in for the last two hundred years, and ask him real nice if he wouldn't mind handin' over his creepy book? So our dead friend can use it for who knows what, over in who knows where."

I flicked my wrist at Link, annoyed. A spark flew from the fire grating, singeing his leg.

219

He jerked away. "Cut it out!"

"Uncle Macon's right. It's not impossible," I said.

Liv played with the rubber band holding her red notebook closed—an anxious habit that meant she was thinking. "And this time Sarafine's dead. He won't have her backing him up."

Uncle Macon shook his head. "He never needed her, I'm afraid. Not really. You can't rely on him being any weaker now than he ever was. Don't underestimate Abraham."

Liv looked somber. "What about Hunting and his pack?"

Macon stared into the fire. I watched the flames grow taller, deepening into purple and red and orange. I couldn't tell if my uncle really believed me or not. I didn't know if he thought for a minute there was a way to bring Ethan back.

I didn't care what he thought, as long as he was willing to help me.

He looked at me as if he knew what I was thinking. "Hunting, though stupid, is a powerful Incubus. But Abraham alone is a formidable threat. If fear is going to stop us, we should concede failure right now."

Link huffed from the floor behind him.

Macon looked at him over his shoulder. "That is, if you're frightened."

"Who said anything about that?" Link was indignant. "I just like a better set a odds when I throw myself into a snake pit."

"It's me." John sat up and announced it, as if he'd just figured out the answer to all our problems.

"What?" Liv pulled away from him.

"I'm the one thing Abraham wants. And the only thing he can't have."

"Don't be stupid." Link groaned. "You sound like his girlfriend."

"I'm not stupid. I'm right. I thought I was the One Who Is Two, and I thought it was up to me to do...what Ethan did. But that wasn't about me. This is."

"Shut up," Link snapped.

Macon's face twisted into a frown, his green eyes darkening. I knew that expression too well.

Liv nodded. "I agree. Do as your brilliant Incubus brother says. Shut up."

John put his arm gently around her, as if he was speaking only to Liv. But I was hanging on his every word, because everything he was saying was starting to make sense. "I can't. Not this time. I'm not going to sit around and let Ethan take all the punches. For once, I'm going to get what's coming to me. Or *who*."

"And that is?" Liv wouldn't look at him.

"Abraham. If you tell him you'll make a trade, he'll come for me. He'll swap me for *The Book of Moons*." John looked at Macon, who nodded.

Link looked skeptical. "How do you know?"

John smiled weakly. "He'll come. Trust me."

Macon sighed, finally turning from the fireplace toward us. "John, I appreciate your honor and your courage. You're a fine young man, even if you have your own demons. We all do. But you should take some time to make certain this is a trade you're willing to make. It's a last course of action, nothing more."

"I'm willing." John stood up, like he was ready to enlist now.

"John!" Liv was furious.

Macon waved him into his seat. "Think it over. If Abraham does take you, it's not likely we will be able to bring you home, not anytime soon. And as much as I want to bring Ethan back—" Uncle Macon glanced over at me before continuing. "I'm not certain trading one life for another is worth the risk Abraham poses, for any of us."

Liv stepped in front of John, as if she wanted to protect him from everyone else in the room and everything else in the world. "He doesn't need time to think about it. It's a terrible plan. Absolutely horrid. The worst plan we've ever come up with. The worst plan in the history of plans." Liv was pale and shaking, but when she saw me watching her, she stopped talking.

She knew what I was thinking.

It didn't involve John jumping off the Summerville water tower. It wasn't the worst plan. I closed my eyes.

falling not flying
one lost muddy shoe
like the lost worlds
between me and you

"I'll do it," John said. "I don't like it any more than the rest of you, but this is the way it has to be."

It all sounded too familiar. I opened my eyes to see Liv, stricken. As the tears began to run down Liv's face, I felt like I was going to throw up.

"No." I heard myself say the word before I realized I was saying it. "My uncle's right. I'm not putting you through that, John. Any of you." I saw the color seep into Liv's cheeks, and she sank into the chair next to him. "It's a last-ditch effort. A last chance."

"Unless you've got another one, Lena, I think the land of last chances is right about where we are." John looked serious. He had made up his mind, and I loved him for it.

But I shook my head. "I do. What about Link's idea?"

"Link's—what?" Liv looked confused.

"My what?" Link scratched his head.

"We find our way to whatever backwoods swamp hole Abraham has been living in for the last two hundred years."

"And we ask him real nice to give us the Book?" Link looked hopeful. John looked like he thought I was having a stroke.

"No. We steal it, real nice."

Macon looked interested. "That presumes we can even find my grandfather's home. The nasty brand of Dark power he wields demands a lifestyle of secrecy, I'm afraid. Tracking Abraham down won't be easy. He keeps to the Underground."

I looked steadily back at him. "Well, as the smartest

person I know once said, these things are difficulties, not impossibilities."

My uncle smiled at me. John shook his head. "Don't look at me. I don't know where the guy lives; I was just a kid. I remember rooms without windows."

"Perfect," Link snapped. "There can't be many of those around."

Liv dropped her hand onto John's shoulder.

John shrugged. "Sorry. My childhood is one big dark cloud. I've done my best to block the whole thing out."

My uncle nodded, rising to his feet. "Very well. Then I suggest you start not with the smartest people but perhaps the oldest people. They might have a clue or two as to where you can find Abraham Ravenwood."

"The oldest people? You mean the Sisters? Do you think they remember Abraham?" My stomach tensed. It wasn't exactly scary, but it was hard to understand half the things they said—when they weren't talking crazy.

"If they can't, they're likely to invent something equally plausible. They are the closest thing my exponentially-great-grandfather has to contemporaries. Even if they're hardly what one would call contemporary."

Liv nodded. "It's worth a try."

I stood up.

"Just a conversation, Lena," Uncle Macon cautioned. "Don't get any ideas. You're not to set out on any kind of reconnaissance mission of your own. Am I perfectly clear?"

"Crystal," I said, because there was no talking to him about anything that seemed dangerous. He'd been like this since Ethan—

Since Ethan.

"I'll go with you for backup," Link said, pulling himself up from the floor of the study. Link, who couldn't add two-digit numbers, always sensed when my uncle and I were about to start fighting.

He grinned. "I can translate."

By now, I felt like I knew the Sisters as well as my own family. Though they were eccentric, to put it mildly, they were also the finest example of living history Gatlin had to offer.

That's what the people around here called it.

When Link and I walked up the steps of Wate's Landing, you could hear Gatlin's living history fighting with each other all the way through the screen door, true to form.

"You don't throw away perfectly good cut-ler-ee. That's a cryin' shame."

"Mercy Lynne. They're plastic spoons. Means you're supposed ta throw 'em away." Thelma was consoling her, patient as always. She should be sainted. Amma was the first one to say it every time Thelma broke up one of the Sisters' arguments.

"Just because *some people* think they're the queen a England doesn't give 'em a crown," Aunt Mercy responded.

Link stood next to me on the porch and tried not to laugh. I knocked on the door, but nobody seemed to notice.

"Now, what on earth is that supposed ta mean?" Aunt Grace interrupted. "Who's *some people*? Angelina Witherspoon an' all them partly nekkid stars—"

"Grace Ann! You don't speak like that, not in this house."

It didn't even slow Aunt Grace down. "—from those smutty magazines you're always askin' Thelma ta get from the market?"

"Now, girls…" Thelma started.

I knocked again, more loudly this time, but it was impossible to hear over the chaos.

Aunt Mercy was shouting. "It *means* you wash the good spoons same as you wash the bad spoons. Then you put 'em all back in the spoon drawer. Everyone knows that. Even the queen a England."

"Don't listen ta her, Thelma. She washes the garbage when you and Amma aren't lookin'."

Aunt Mercy sniffed. "What if I do? You don't want the neighbors talkin'. We're respectable, churchgoin' people. We don't smell like sinners, and there's no reason for the cans out front ta smell any different."

"Exceptin' they're full a garbage." Aunt Grace snorted.

I knocked on the screen door one more time. Link took over, banging once—and the door practically gave out, one hinge swinging down toward the porch.

"Whoops. Sorry about that." He shrugged awkwardly.

Amma appeared at the door, looking grateful for the distraction. "You ladies have some visitors." She pushed the screen open wide. The Sisters glanced up from their respective afghans, looking friendly and polite, like they hadn't been screaming bloody murder a second earlier.

I sat on the edge of a hard wooden chair, not making myself too comfortable. Link stood even less comfortably next to me.

"I reckon we do. Afternoon, Wesley. And who's there with y'all?" Aunt Mercy squinted, and Aunt Grace elbowed her.

"It's that girlfriend a Ethan's. That pretty Ravenwood gal. The one who always has her nose in a book, like Lila Jane."

"That's right. You know me, Aunt Mercy. I'm Ethan's girlfriend, ma'am." It was the same thing I said every time I came over.

Aunt Mercy harrumphed. "Well, what if it is? What're ya doin' around here now that Ethan's gone and passed on ta one world or another?"

Amma froze in the kitchen doorway. "Come again?"

Thelma didn't look up from her needlepoint.

"You heard me, Miss Amma," Aunt Mercy said.

"Wh-what?" I stammered.

"What are you talking about?" Link could barely speak.

"You know about Ethan? How?" I leaned forward in my chair.

"You think we don't catch a thing or two 'bout what's goin' on around here? Wasn't born yesterday, and we're smarter than y'all think. We know plenty 'bout the Casters, same as we do weather patterns and dress patterns and traffic patterns...." Aunt Grace wadded up her handkerchief, her voice trailing off.

"And the peach stand seasons." Aunt Mercy looked proud.

"A storm cloud's a storm cloud. This one's been workin' its way through the sky for a long time now. Near 'bout all our lives." Aunt Grace nodded at her sister.

"Seems to me any right-minded person would try to keep outta a storm like that," Amma bristled, tucking the edge of the blanket around Aunt Grace's legs.

"We didn't know you knew," I said.

"Lord have mercy, you're as bad as Prudence Jane. She thought we didn't have a clue between us 'bout her traipsin' all over underneath the County and back. Like we didn't know our daddy picked her ta keep the map. Like we didn't tell him ourselves ta pick Prudence Jane. Always thought she was the one with the steadiest hand outta all three a us." Aunt Mercy laughed.

"Sweet Redeemer, Mercy Lynne, you know our daddy woulda picked me 'fore he picked you. I only told him ta ask you on account a I didn't like my hair all curled up, the way it got in the Underground. Looked like a porkypine with a bad permanent, I swear." Aunt Grace shook her head.

Mercy sniffed. "You do swear, Grace Ann, and I'm the only one who knows it."

"You take that back." Aunt Grace pointed a bony finger at her sister.

"I will not."

"Please, ma'am. Ma'ams." What was the plural of *ma'am*? "We need your help. We're looking for Abraham Ravenwood. He has something of ours, something important." I looked from one Sister to the other.

"We need it ta—" Link corrected himself. "To bring Ethan home, lickety-split." If you hung around the Sisters long enough, you started talking like them.

I rolled my eyes.

"What're you fussin' 'bout?" Aunt Grace waved her handkerchief.

Aunt Mercy sniffed again. "Sounds like more Caster nonsense ta me."

Amma raised an eyebrow. "Why don't you catch us all up? Seein' as how we all love nonsense the way we do."

Link and I looked at each other. It was going to be a long night.

Caster nonsense or not, once Amma dragged out the Sisters' scrapbooks, wheels began turning and mouths started moving. At first Amma couldn't bear to hear the mention of Abraham Ravenwood's name, but Link kept talking.

And talking, and talking.

Still, Amma didn't stop him, which seemed like half a victory. Though talking to the Sisters themselves didn't seem anything like the other half of one.

Within the hour, Abraham Ravenwood was denounced as

the Devil, a cheat, a scoundrel, a no-goodnik, and a thief. He'd kept their daddy's daddy's daddy from the southeast corner of his old apple orchard, which was rightfully his, and his daddy's daddy from a seat on the county board, which also was rightfully his.

And on top of all that, they were more than certain that he danced with the Devil up at Ravenwood Plantation on more than one occasion, before it burned during the Civil War.

When I attempted to clarify, they didn't want to get more specific than that.

"That's what I said. He up and danced with the Devil. He made a deal. Don't like talkin' 'bout or thinkin' 'bout him neither." Aunt Mercy shook her head so violently, I thought her dentures were going to come unglued.

"Let's say you did think about him, though. Where would you picture him?" Link tried again, just as we had all night.

Finally, it was Aunt Grace who found the missing piece to the scrambled crossword puzzle the Sisters considered conversation.

"Why, at his place, a course. Anybody with a lick a sense knows that."

"Where's his place, Aunt Grace? Ma'am?" I put my hand on Link's arm, hopeful. It was the first clear sentence we'd gotten out of her in what felt like hours.

"The dark side a the moon, I reckon. Where all the Devils and Demons live when they're not burnin' down below."

My heart sank. I was never going to get anywhere with these two.

"Great. The dark side a the moon. So Abraham Ravenwood is alive and well in a Pink Floyd album." Link was getting as crabby as I was.

"That's what Grace Ann said. The dark side a the moon." Aunt Mercy looked annoyed. "Don't know why you two act like that's such a conundy-rum."

"Where, exactly, is the dark side of the moon, Aunt Mercy?" Amma sat down next to Ethan's great-aunt, taking the old woman's hands in her lap. "You know. Come on now."

Aunt Mercy smiled at Amma. "'Course I do." She glared at Aunt Grace. "'Cause Daddy picked me 'fore Grace. I know all sorts a things."

"Then, where is it?" Amma asked.

Grace snorted, pulling the photo album off the coffee table in front of them. "Young people. Actin' like they know everythin'. Actin' like we're one step from the home just 'cause we got a year or two on you." She leafed through the pages madly, as if she was looking for one thing in particular—

Which, apparently, she was.

Because there, on the last page, under a faded pressed camellia and a stretch of pale pink ribbon, was the ripped-off top of a book of matches. It was from some kind of bar or club.

"I'll be danged," Link marveled, earning himself a swat on the head from Aunt Mercy.

There it was, marked with a silvery moon.

The Dark Side o' the Moon was a place.

A place where I might be able to find Abraham Ravenwood and, I hoped, *The Book of Moons*. If the Sisters were not completely out of their minds, which was a possibility that could never be discounted.

Amma took one look at the matches and left the room. I remembered the story of Amma's visit to the bokor and knew better than to press her further.

Instead, I looked at Aunt Grace. "Do you mind?"

Aunt Grace nodded, and I pulled the antique shred of matchbook from the album page. Most of the paint was scratched off the embossed moon, but you could still see the writing. We were going to New Orleans.

—⁂—

You would have thought Link had solved the Rubik's Cube. The moment we got into the Beater, he started blasting some song from Pink Floyd's *Dark Side of the Moon* and shouting excitedly over the music.

When we slowed at the corner, I turned down the volume and cut him off. "Drop me off at Ravenwood, will you? I need to get something before I leave for New Orleans."

"Hold on. I'm comin' with you. I promised Ethan I'd keep my eye on you, and I keep my promises."

"I'm not taking you. I'm taking John."

"John? That's the somethin' you're gettin' from home?" His eyes narrowed. "No way."

"I wasn't asking your permission. Just so you know."

"Why? What's he got that I haven't?"

"Experience. He knows about Abraham, and he's the strongest hybrid Incubus in Gatlin County, as far as we know."

"We're the same, Lena." Link's feathers were getting ruffled.

"You're more Mortal than John is. That's what I like about you, Link. But it also makes you weaker."

"Who are you callin' weak?" Link flexed his muscles. To be fair, he did nearly split his T-shirt in half. He was like the Incredible Hulk of Stonewall Jackson High.

"I'm sorry. You're not weak. You're just three-quarters human. And that's a little too human for this trip."

"Whatever. Suit yourself. See if you even get ten feet through the Tunnels without me. You'll be back here, beggin' for my help, before I can say..." His face went blank. A classic Link moment. Sometimes the words just seemed to float away from him before they could make it all the way from his brain to his mouth. He finally gave up with a shrug. "Somethin'. Somethin' real dangerous."

I patted his shoulder. "Bye, Link."

Link frowned, hitting the gas pedal, and we ripped down

the street. Not the usual kind of rip for an Incubus, but then again, he was three-quarters rocker. Just the way I liked him—my favorite Linkubus.

I didn't say that, but I'm pretty sure he knew.

I changed every light green for him, all the way down Route 9. The Beater never had it so good.

⊰ CHAPTER 21 ⊱

Dark Side of the Moon

Saying we were going to New Orleans to find an old bar—
and an even older Incubus—was one thing. Actually finding
him was something different. What stood between those two
things was talking my Uncle Macon into letting me go.

I tried my uncle at the dinner table, well after Kitchen had
served up his favorite dinner, before the plates had disappeared from the endlessly long table.

Kitchen, who was never as accommodating as you'd think
a Caster kitchen might be, seemed to know it was important
and did everything I asked and more. When I walked downstairs, I found flickering candelabras and the scent of jasmine
in the air. With a flutter of my fingers, orchids and tiger lilies

bloomed across the length of the table. I fluttered them again, and my viola appeared in the corner of the room.

I stared at it, and it began to play Paganini. A favorite of my uncle's.

Perfect.

I looked down at my grubby jeans and Ethan's faded sweatshirt. I closed my eyes as my hair began to weave itself into a thick French braid. When I opened them again, I was dressed for dinner.

A simple black cocktail dress, the one Uncle Macon bought me last summer in Rome. I touched my neck, and the silver crescent moon necklace he gave me for the winter formal appeared at the base of my throat.

Ready.

"Uncle M? Dinnertime—" I called out into the hall, but he was already there next to me, appearing as swiftly as if he was still an Incubus and could rip through space and time whenever he wanted. Old habits died hard.

"Beautiful, Lena. I find the shoes an especially nice touch." I looked down and noticed my raggedy black Converse still on my feet. So much for dressing for dinner.

I shrugged and followed him to the table.

Fillet of sea bass with baby fennel. Warm lobster tail. Scallops carpaccio. Grilled peaches soaked in port. I had no appetite, especially not for food you could only find at a five-star restaurant on the Champs-Élysées in Paris—where Uncle

Macon took me at every opportunity—but he ate happily for the better part of an hour.

One thing about former Incubuses: They really appreciate Mortal food.

"What is it?" my uncle finally said, over a forkful of lobster.

"What's what?" I put down my fork.

"This." He gestured at the spread of silver platters between us, pulling the shiny dome off one overflowing with steaming, spicy oysters. "And this." He looked pointedly at my viola, still playing softly. "Paganini, of course. Am I really that predictable?"

I avoided his eyes. "It's called dinner. You eat it. Which you seem to have no problem doing, by the way." I grabbed a ridiculous flagon of ice water—where Kitchen found some of our tableware, I'd never know—before he could say anything else.

"This is not dinner. This is, as Mark Antony would say, a tantalizing table of treason. Or perhaps treachery." He swallowed another bite of lobster. "Or perhaps both, if Mark Antony were a fan of alliteration."

"No treason." I smiled. He smiled back, waiting. My uncle was many things—a snob, for one—but he wasn't a fool. "Just a simple request."

He set down his wineglass, heavy on the linen tablecloth. I waved a finger, and the glass filled itself.

Insurance, I thought.

"Absolutely not," said Uncle Macon.

"I haven't asked you anything."

"Whatever it is, no. The wine proves it. The last straw. The final pheasant feather on the proverbial fluffy feather bed."

"So you're saying Mark Antony isn't the only fan of alliteration?" I asked.

"Out with it. Now."

I pulled the matchbook cover out of my pocket and pushed it across the table so he could see it.

"Abraham?"

I nodded.

"And this is in New Orleans?"

I nodded again. He handed me back the matchbook, dabbing at his mouth with his linen napkin. "No." He returned to the wine.

"No? You were the one who agreed with me. You were the one who said we could find him ourselves."

"I did. And I will find him while you remain locked safely in your room, like the nice little girl you should be. You're not going to New Orleans alone."

"*New Orleans* is the problem?" I was stunned. "Not your ancient-but-deadly Incubus ancestor who tried to kill us on more than one occasion?"

"That and New Orleans. Your grandmother wouldn't hear of it, even if I said yes."

"She wouldn't hear of it? Or she *shouldn't* hear of it?"

He lifted an eyebrow. "I beg your pardon?"

"What about if she just doesn't hear of it? That way it's not an issue." I put my arms around my uncle. As angry as he made me, and as annoying as it was to have him pay off the Underground bartenders and ground me from various dangerous pursuits, I loved him, and I loved that he loved me as much as he did.

"How about no?"

"How about she'll be with Aunt Del and everyone in Barbados until next week, so why is this even a problem?"

"How about still no?"

At that point, I gave up. It was hard to stay angry at Uncle Macon. Impossible, even. Knowing how I felt about him was the only way I understood how hard it was for Ethan to live apart from his own mother.

Lila Evers Wate. How many times had her path crossed mine?

> we love what we love and who
> we love who we love and why
> we love why we love and find
> a falling shoelace knotted and strung
> between the fingers of strangers

I didn't want to think about it, but I hoped it was true. I hoped wherever Ethan was, he was with her now.

At least give him that.

John and I left first thing in the morning. We needed to leave early, since we were taking the long way—the Tunnels, rather than Traveling, though if I'd let him, John could have easily gotten us there in the blink of an eye.

I didn't care. I wouldn't let him. I didn't want to be reminded of the other times I'd let John carry me—all the way to Sarafine.

So we did it my way. I Cast a *Resonantia* on my viola and set it to practice in the corner while I was gone. It would wear off eventually, but it might give me enough time.

I didn't tell my uncle I was going. I just went. Uncle Macon still slept most of the day, old habits being what they were. I figured I had at least six good hours before he noticed my absence. By which I mean, before he flipped out and came after me.

One thing I'd realized in the last year was that there were some things no one could give you permission to do. All the same, it didn't mean you couldn't or shouldn't do them—particularly when it came to the big things, like saving the world, or journeying to a supernatural seam between realities, or bringing your boyfriend back from the dead.

Sometimes you had to take matters into your own hands. Parents—or uncles who are the closest thing you have to them—aren't equipped to deal with that. Because no self-respecting parent in this world or any other is going to step aside and say, "Sure, risk your life. The world is at stake here."

How would they possibly say it?

Be back by dinner. Hope you don't die.

They couldn't do it. You couldn't blame them. But it didn't mean that you shouldn't go.

I had to go, no matter what Uncle Macon said. That's what I told myself, anyway, as John and I headed into the Tunnels far beneath Ravenwood. Where, in the darkness, it could have been any time of day or year—any century, anywhere in the world.

The Tunnels weren't the scary part.

Even spending time alone with John—something I hadn't done since he'd tricked me and dragged me into going to the Great Barrier for my Seventeenth Moon—wasn't the problem.

The truth was, Uncle Macon was right.

I was more afraid of the Doorwell that stood before me and of what I would find on the other side. The ancient Doorwell that brought light flooding down onto the stone steps of the Caster Tunnel where I waited now. The one marked NEW ORLEANS. The place where Amma had basically made a pact with the Darkest magic in the universe.

I shivered.

John looked at me, his head tilted. "Why are you stopping here?"

"No reason."

"You scared, Lena?"

"No. Why would I be scared? It's just a city." I tried to put all thoughts of black magic bokors and voodoo out of my mind. Just because Ethan had followed Amma into bad times there didn't mean I was going to encounter the same Darkness. At least not the same bokor.

Did it?

"If you think New Orleans is just a city, then you've got another thing coming." John's voice was low, and I could barely see his face in the darkness of the Tunnels. He sounded as spooked as I felt.

"What are you talking about?"

"The most powerful Caster city in the country—the greatest convergence of Dark and Light power in modern times. A place where anything can happen, at any hour of the day."

"At a hundred-year-old bar for two-hundred-year-old Supernaturals?" How frightening could it be? At least that's what I tried to tell myself.

He shrugged. "Might as well start there. Knowing Abraham, it won't be as easy to find him as we think."

We started up the stairs and into the bright sunlight that would take us to the Dark Side o' the Moon.

The street—a row of shabby bars, sandwiched between more shabby bars—was deserted, which made sense, considering it was still so early in the day. It looked like all the other streets we'd seen since the Doorwell brought us up into the infamous French Quarter of New Orleans. The ornately wrought iron railings swept across every balcony and along every building, even curving around the street corners. In the stark morning light, the faded colors of the painted plaster were sun-bleached and peeling. The road was lined with trash, trash piled upon more trash—the only remaining evidence of the night before.

"I'd hate to see how it looks around here the morning after Mardi Gras," I said, looking for a way to pick through the mountain of garbage standing between me and the sidewalk. "Remind me never to go to a bar."

"I don't know. We had some good times back at Exile. You and me and Rid, causing trouble on the dance floor." John smiled and I blushed, remembering.

arms around me
dancing, hurried
Ethan's face
pale and worried

I shook my head, letting the words fall away. "An underground hole for derelict Supernaturals isn't what I was talking about."

"Ah, come on. We weren't exactly derelicts. Well, you weren't. Rid and me, we probably qualified." He pushed me toward the doorway playfully.

I shoved him back, a little less playfully. "Stop it. That was

243

a million years ago. Maybe two million. I don't want to think about it."

"Come on, Lena. I'm happy. You're—"

I shot him a look, and he cut himself off. "You will be happy again, I promise. That's why we're here, isn't it?"

I looked at him, standing there next to me in the middle of a run-down side street in the French Quarter far too early in the morning, helping me look for the not-quite-a-man John hated more than anyone in the universe. He had more of a reason to hate Abraham Ravenwood than I did. And he wasn't saying a word about what I was making him do.

Who would've thought John would end up being one of the best guys I'd ever met? And who would've thought John would end up volunteering to risk his life to bring back the love of mine?

I smiled at him, though I felt like crying. "John?"

"Yeah?" He wasn't paying attention. He was looking up at the bar signs, probably wondering how he was going to get up the nerve to go inside any of them. They all looked like serial killer hangouts.

"I'm sorry."

"Huh?" Now he was listening. Confused, but listening.

"About this. That it has to involve you. And if you don't want it to—I mean, if we don't find the Book—"

"We'll find it."

"I'm just saying, I won't blame you if you don't want to go through with it. Abraham and everything." I couldn't bear to do it to him. Not him and not Liv—no matter how much had

244

gone down between us. No matter how much she had believed she loved Ethan.

Before.

"We'll find the Book. Come on. Quit talking crazy." John kicked a clearing in the trash heap, and we made our way past the empty beer bottles, past the soggy napkins, and up to the sidewalk.

By the time we made it halfway down the block, we were looking through the open doorways to see if anyone was inside. To my surprise, there were people hiding in the woodwork—literally. Slumping inside the darkened doorways. Sweeping the trash from deserted, shadowy alleys. Even silhouetted on a few of the empty balconies.

The French Quarter wasn't that different from the Caster world, I realized. Or from Gatlin County. There was a world within a world, all hidden in plain sight.

You just had to know where to look.

"There." I pointed.

THE DARK SIDE O' THE MOON

A carved wooden sign bearing the words swung back and forth, dangling by two ancient chains. It squeaked as it moved in the wind.

Even though there was no wind.

I squinted in the bright morning light, trying to see into the shadows of the open doorway.

This Dark Side was no different from the other nearly deserted bars in the neighborhood. Even from the street, I could hear voices echoing through the heavy door.

"People are in there this early?" John made a face.

"Maybe it's not early. Maybe it's late if you're them." I locked eyes with a scowling man who was leaning against the doorframe and trying to light a cigarette. He muttered to himself and looked away.

"Yeah. Way too late."

John shook his head. "You sure this is the right place?"

For the fifth time, I handed him the book of matches. He held up the cover, comparing it to the logo on the sign. They were identical. Even the crescent moon carved into the wooden sign was an exact duplicate of the one printed on the matchbook in John's hand.

"And I was so hoping the answer would be no." He handed the matchbook back to me.

"You wish," I said, kicking a stray piece of wet napkin off my black Chucks.

He winked at me. "Ladies first."

CHAPTER 22

Bird in a Gilded Cage

It took a while for my eyes to adjust to the dim light, and even longer for the rest of me to adjust to the stench. It smelled like must and rust and old beer—old everything. Through the shadows, I could see rows of small round tables and a high brass bar, almost as tall as I was. Bottles were stacked on shelves all the way to a high ceiling—so high the long brass chandeliers seemed to dangle down from nowhere.

Dust covered every surface and every bottle. It even swirled in the air, in the few places where beams of light poked through shuttered windows.

John elbowed me. "Isn't there some kind of Cast that can keep our noses from working? Like a *Stinkus Lessus* Cast?"

"No, but I can think of a few *Shutus Upus* Casts that might be applicable right about now."

"Temper, Caster Girl. You're supposed to be Light. You know, one of the good guys."

"I broke the mold, remember? On my Seventeenth Moon, when I was Claimed Light and Dark?" I shot him a serious look. "Don't forget. I've got my Dark side."

"I'm scared." He grinned.

"You should be. Very."

I pointed to a mirrored sign on the paneling, right behind him. A silhouette of a woman was painted next to a row of words. " 'Lips that touch liquor shall not touch ours.' " I shook my head. "Clearly not the slogan of the Jackson cheer squad."

"What?" John looked up.

"I bet this place used to be a speakeasy. A hidden bar during Prohibition. New Orleans was probably full of them." I looked around the room. "That means there has to be another room, right? A room behind this room."

John nodded. "Of course. Abraham would never hang out where anyone could walk into his hideout, no matter where it is. It was one thing all our homes had in common." He looked around. "But I don't remember a place like this."

"Maybe it was before your time, and he came back here because it was somewhere no one currently alive could find him."

"Maybe. Still, something feels off about this place."

Then I heard a familiar voice.

No. A familiar laugh, sweet and sinister. There was nothing else like it in the world.

Ridley? Is that you?

I Kelted, but she didn't answer. Maybe she didn't hear, or it had been too long since we had connected in any kind of meaningful way. I didn't know, but I had to try.

I ran up the wooden staircase at the back of the bar. John was just steps behind me. As soon as I got to the room at the top, I started banging on the wall where I thought her voice had come from, high above stacks of crates and cases of bottles. The storage-room wall was hollow, and there was clearly something behind it.

Ridley!

I needed a better look. I pushed a tall stack of crates out of the way. I closed my eyes and let myself rise high into the air, until I floated parallel with the window. I opened my eyes, hovering for a second. What I saw was so surprising it knocked me right to the floor.

I could have sworn I saw my cousin, and a whole lot of makeup, and what looked like a flash of gold. Rid wasn't in danger. She was probably lying around in there, painting her nails. Sucking on a lollipop, having the time of her life.

Either that, or I was hallucinating.

I'm going to kill her.

"I swear, Rid. If you're really this crazy, if you've really gone this Dark, I'm going to jam those lollipops of yours down your throat, one ball of sugar at a time."

"What?"

I felt John's arms behind me, pulling me back to the floor.

I pointed to the wall. "It's my cousin. She's on the other side of this wall." I knocked on the wall above the nearest row of crates.

"No. No, no, no—" He started backing away, like even the mention of my cousin had him wanting to make a break for it.

I felt myself turning red. She was my cousin, and I wanted to kill her. Still, she was *my* cousin, and *I* was the one who wanted to kill her. It was a family matter. Not something John needed to worry about. "Look, John, I have to get her."

"Have you lost your mind?"

"Probably."

"If she's hanging with Abraham, she's not going anywhere. And we don't want him to find us until we figure out how to get the Book."

"I don't think he's there," I said.

"You don't *think*, or you don't *know*?"

"If he was there, wouldn't you sense something? I thought you two were connected somehow. Wasn't that how he brainwashed you or whatever?"

John looked nervous, and I felt guilty for saying it. "I don't know. It's possible." He stared up at the high window. "Okay. You get in there and see what Ridley's problem is. I'll keep an eye out for Abraham outside and make sure he doesn't come back while you're inside."

"Thanks, John."

"But don't be an idiot. If she's gone too Dark, she's too Dark. You can't change Ridley. That's one thing we've all learned the hard way."

"I know." I probably knew it better than anyone, except maybe Link. But deep down, I also knew better than anyone how much my cousin was like everyone else. How badly she wanted to fit in and be loved and have friends and be happy—just like the rest of us.

How Dark can a person like that really be?

Hadn't the New Order shown us that the price had been paid—Ethan made sure he paid it—and that things weren't as simple as we all thought they were?

Didn't I Claim myself for Dark and Light?

"You're sure you'll be all right in there?"

Is it really any different for anyone else? Even Ridley? Especially Ridley?

John poked me in the side. "Earth to Lena. Just make some kind of noise so I know you heard me, before I throw you to that lion in there."

I tried to focus. "Go. I'm fine."

"Five minutes. That's all you have," he said.

"Got it. I'll only need four."

He disappeared, and I was alone to deal with my cousin. Dark or Light. Good or evil. Or maybe just somewhere in between.

I needed a better look. I grabbed a cask of wine, pulling it over to the space beneath the window that was cut into the

251

wall. I climbed up and the cask wobbled, threatening to topple, but I managed to balance myself.

I still couldn't see.

Oh, come on.

I closed my eyes and twisted my hands into the air next to me, pushing myself up toward the ceiling. The light in the room began to flicker.

That's it.

I wasn't much for flying, but this was more like levitating. I rose, wobbling, until my Chucks were hovering a few inches above the cask.

Just a little farther. I needed one good look to let me know if my cousin was forever lost, if she had joined the Darkest Incubus alive and would never come home to me again.

One last look.

I pulled myself up, barely level with the small window.

That's when I saw the bars swerving down from the ceiling, all the way around Ridley in every direction. It was some kind of gold prison. A literal gilded cage.

I couldn't believe it. Ridley wasn't lounging on a chaise in the lap of luxury in Abraham's place. She was trapped.

She turned, and our eyes locked. Rid leaped to her feet, rattling the bars in front of her. For a second, she looked kind of like a damaged Tinkerbell, with a lot of black mascara running down her face, and even more smeared red lipstick.

She'd been crying, or worse. Her arms looked bruised,

especially around the wrists. They were marked by some kind of ropes or chains. Shackles, maybe.

The room around her clearly belonged to Abraham—at least that's what I thought, considering it looked like a mad scientist's dorm room, with a lone bed next to a crammed bookshelf. A tall wooden table was covered with technical equipment. The place could have belonged to a chemist. Even stranger, the two sides of the window didn't seem to correlate exactly, in terms of physical space. Looking through the speakeasy window was like looking through a dirty telescope, and I couldn't tell exactly where the other end lay. It could have been anywhere in the Mortal universe, knowing Abraham.

But that didn't matter. It was Ridley. It was a terrible thing to see anyone like that, but for my careless, carefree cousin, it seemed especially cruel.

I felt my hair begin to twist in the familiar Caster breeze.

> "*Aurae Aspirent*
> *Ubi tueor, ibi adeo.*
> Let the wind blow
> Where I see I go."

I began to twist into nothingness. I felt the world give way beneath me, and when I tried to reach my feet out to touch solid ground, I realized I was now standing next to Ridley.

On the outside of the golden cage.

"Cuz! What are you doing here?" she called out to me, reaching her long pink fingernails through a space in the bars.

"I guess I could say the same to you, Rid. Are you okay?" I approached the bars carefully. I loved my cousin, but I couldn't forget everything that had happened. She chose Dark and left us—Link, me, all of us. It was impossible to know whose side she was on.

Ever.

"Think it's a little obvious, don't you?" she snapped. "I've been better." She rattled the bars. "Much."

Ridley sat back down on her heels and began to cry, like we were both little kids again and someone had hurt her feelings on the playground. Which didn't happen often, and if it did, it was usually me doing the crying.

Rid was always the strong one.

Maybe that's why her tears got to me now.

I slid down to the floor across from her, taking her hand through the cage bars. "I'm sorry, Rid. I was so angry with you for not coming back when Ethan—now that Ethan—"

She didn't look at me. "I know. I heard. I feel terrible. That's when everything happened. Abraham was furious, and I only made things worse when I made the mistake of trying to leave. I just wanted to go home. But he was so angry that he threw me in here." She shook her head as if she wanted to shake off the memory.

"I mean it, Rid. I should have known that you would've come unless something stopped you."

"Whatever. More water under another watery bridge." She wiped her eyes, smearing her mascara even more. "Let's blow this place before Abraham comes back, or you'll be stuck in here with me for the next two hundred years."

"Where did he go?"

"I don't know. Usually he spends all day in his creepy lab of creatures. But there's no way to know how long he'll be gone."

"Then we'd better get on with it." I looked around the room. "Rid, have you seen Abraham with *The Book of Moons*? Is it here?"

She shook her head. "Are you kidding? I wouldn't come within ten miles of that thing, not after the way it royally screws anyone who touches it."

"But have you seen it?"

"No way. Not here. If Abraham still has it, he's not dumb enough to keep it on him. He's evil, but he's not stupid."

My heart sank.

Ridley rattled the bars again. "Hurry up! I'm really stuck. Protection Casts, from what I can tell. I'm going crazy in here...."

Then I heard a terrible crash, and a pile of equipment crates next to me toppled to the ground. Broken glass and broken wood flew everywhere—like I had upset Abraham's project for the science fair. Some sort of glowing green goop was splattered in my hair.

Whoops.

Uncle Macon was trying to untangle himself from John Breed, who had one foot caught in the remnants of a wooden crate.

"Where are we?" Uncle M stared at the cage in disbelief. "What kind of twisted place is this?"

"Uncle M?" Ridley looked as relieved as she was confused. "Were you Traveling?"

"I found him out front," John said. "He wouldn't let me go. When I tried to come back, he just sort of came along for the ride." John must have seen my face, because he got defensive. "Hey, don't look at me. I wasn't exactly planning on picking up hitchhikers."

Uncle Macon glared at John, who glared right back at him.

"Lena Duchannes!" My uncle looked angrier than I'd ever seen him. Green goop was dripping from his otherwise impeccable suit. He glanced from Ridley to me, then pointed at both of us. "You two. Come out of there this instant."

I grabbed Ridley's hand and muttered the *Aurae Aspirent* while Uncle Macon tapped his foot impatiently. A second later, my cousin and I reappeared on the outside of the cage.

"Uncle Macon," I began.

He held up his gloved hand. "Don't. Not a word." His eyes flashed, and I knew better than to keep talking. "Now. Let's focus on what we came here to do, while we still have time to do it. The Book."

John had already started pulling open boxes, scanning the shelves for *The Book of Moons*. Uncle Macon and I joined him, looking until we had searched every possible hiding place. Ridley sat sullenly on a crate, not making things easier—but not making them more difficult either. Which I took as a good sign.

From what I could see, Abraham Ravenwood appeared to be the Caster answer to Dr. Frankenstein. I couldn't recognize much beyond the occasional burner or beaker, and I had taken chemistry. And at the rate John and Uncle Macon were trashing the room, it was going to look like our search was conducted by Frankenstein's monster.

"It's not here," John said, finally giving up.

"Then neither are we." Uncle Macon straightened in his overcoat. "Home, John. Now."

Traveling was one thing. The speed at which John managed to get us home—without so much as another word from Uncle Macon—was another. I found myself out of Abraham's hideaway and back in my room before Ridley could wipe off her smeared, raccoon-y mascara.

The viola was still playing Paganini's Caprice no. 24 when I got there.

⊰ CHAPTER 23 ⊱

Dar-ee Keen

The next day it was raining, and the Dar-ee Keen was leaking as if it was finally giving up. More depressing, Uncle Macon hadn't even bothered to ground me. Apparently, the situation was hopeless enough without locking me in my room. Which was pretty hopeless.

Rain fell everywhere at the Dar-ee Keen, on the inside and out. Water dripped from the square, buzzing light fixtures. It crept down the wall like a slow stain of tears beneath the crookedly mounted Employee of the Month photograph—from the look of it, a member of the Stonewall Jackson cheer squad, of course, though they all were starting to look the same.

No one worth crying over. Not anymore.

I scanned the nearly empty diner, waiting for Link to show up. Nobody was out on a day like today, not even the flies. I couldn't blame them.

"Seriously, could you cut it out? I'm sick of the rain, Lena. And I smell like a wet dog." Link appeared out of nowhere, sliding into the opposite side of the booth. He looked like a wet dog.

"That smell has nothing to do with the rain, my friend." I smiled. Unlike John, Link was apparently human enough that the natural elements still affected him. He assumed normal Link posture, leaning back in the corner of the booth and doing his best impression of someone physically capable of falling asleep.

"It's not me," I said.

"Right. Because it's been nothin' but sunshine and kitty cats out there since December."

Thunder rumbled in the sky. Link rolled his eyes.

I frowned. "I guess you must have heard. We found Abraham's place. The Book wasn't there. At least we couldn't find it."

"Figures. Now what?" He sighed.

"Plan B. We don't really have a choice."

John.

I couldn't say it. I curled my hand into a fist on the seat next to me.

Thunder rumbled again.

Was it me? I didn't know if I was doing it or if the weather outside was doing something to me. I had lost track of myself weeks ago. I stared at the rain dripping into the red plastic bucket in the center of the room.

red plastic rain
her tears stain

I tried to shake myself out of it, but I couldn't stop looking at the bucket. The water dripped down from the ceiling rhythmically. Like a heartbeat or a poem. A list of names of the dead.

First Macon.
Then Ethan.
No.
My father.
Then Macon.
My mother.
Then Ethan.
Now John.

How many people had I lost?

How many more would I lose? Would I lose John, too? Would Liv ever forgive me? Did it even matter anymore?

I watched the raindrops bead on the greasy table in front of me. Link and I sat together in silence, in front of wadded-up waxy paper, crushed ice in plastic glasses. A cold, soggy meal nobody was even thinking of eating. If he wasn't trapped at his own dinner table, Link didn't even pretend to move the food around anymore.

Link nudged me. "Hey. Come on, Lena. John knows what he's doing. He's a big boy. We're gonna get the Book and get Ethan back, no matter how crazy your plan is."

"I'm not crazy." I didn't know who I was saying it to, Link or myself.

"I didn't say you were."

"You say it every time you have the chance."

"You don't think I want him back?" Link said. "You don't think it sucks to shoot hoops without him watchin' to tell me how bad I suck or how big my head is gettin'? I drive around Gatlin in the Beater, blastin' the tunes we used to play, and there's no reason to play them anymore."

"I get that it's rough, Link. You know I get it, more than anyone."

His eyes welled up, and he dropped his head, staring down at the greasy table between us. "I don't even feel like singin'. The guys in the band, they're talkin' about breakin' up. The Holy Rollers could end up as a bowlin' team." He looked like he was going to be sick. "At this rate, I'm gonna have nowhere to go but college, or somewhere even worse."

"Link. Don't say that." It was true. If Link went to college—even Summerville Community College—it would mean the end of the world had finally arrived, no matter how many times Ethan tried to save us all.

Had tried.

"Maybe I'm just not as brave as you are, Lena."

"Sure you are. You've survived all those years in your house with your mom, haven't you?" I tried to smile, but Link was beyond cheering up.

It was like talking to myself.

"Maybe I just gotta give up when the odds are as bad as they are now."

"What are you talking about? The odds are always this bad," I said.

"I'm the guy who gets bit. I'm the guy who gets the F and then even fails summer school."

"That wasn't your fault, Link. You were helping Ethan rescue me."

"Face it. The only girl I ever loved chose Darkness over me."

"Rid loved you. You know that. And about Ridley..." I had almost forgotten why I'd brought him here. He still didn't know. "Seriously. You don't understand. Rid—"

"I don't want to talk about her. It wasn't meant to be. Nothin's ever gone my way before. I shoulda known it wouldn't work out."

Link stopped talking because the bell over the door rang in the distance, and time stopped—in a flurry of bright pink flapper feathers and purple tin beads. Not to mention eyeliner and lip liner and anything else that could possibly be lined or shined or painted any of the colors of the cosmetic rainbow.

Ridley.

I barely thought the word before I flew halfway up out of my seat and toward her for a hug.

I knew she was coming—I was the one who'd found her at Abraham's—but it was a different thing to see her making her way safe and sound through the plastic tables of the Dar-ee Keen. I almost knocked her off her three-inch platforms. Nobody walked in heels like my cousin.

Cuz.

She Kelted it as she buried her face in my shoulder, and all I could smell was hair spray and bath gel and sugar. Glitter swirled in the air around us, knocked loose from whatever sparkly goop she'd smeared all over her body.

Dark or Light, somehow it never mattered between us. Not when it really counted. We were still family, and we were together again.

It's strange to be here without Short Straw. I'm sorry, Cuz.

I know, Rid.

Here at the Dar-ee Keen, it was all hitting home, like she finally understood what happened.

What I'd lost.

"You okay, kid?" She pulled back, looking me in the eyes.

I shook my head as my eyes started to blur. "No."

"Somebody mind fillin' me in on what's goin' on here?" Link looked like he was about to pass out, or throw up, or both.

"I was trying to tell you. We found Ridley, stuck in one of Abraham's cages."

"You know it. Like a peacock, Hot Rod." She didn't look right at Link, and I wondered if it was because she didn't want to or because she didn't dare. "A really hot one."

I would never understand what went on between the two of them. I didn't think anyone could—not even them.

"Hey, Rid." Link was pale, even for a quarter Incubus. He looked like someone had just punched him in the face.

She blew him a kiss across the table. "Looking good, Hot Rod."

He was stammering. "You look…you're lookin'…I mean, you know."

"I know." Ridley winked and turned back to me. "Let's get out of here. It's been too long. I can't do this anymore."

"Do what?" Link managed not to stammer, though his face was now as red as the plastic bucket beneath the leaking ceiling.

Ridley sighed, sticking her lollipop to one side of her mouth. "Hello? I'm a Siren, Shrinky Dink. A bad girl. I need to be back among my own."

$\sim$

"Abraham, eh? That old goat?" Ridley shook her head.

I nodded. "That's the plan." For what it was worth, if it was worth anything.

The air was dark, and the ceiling lights of Exile only seemed to make it darker, instead of adding to the light. I didn't blame Ridley for wanting to bring us here. It was the first place she always wanted to go when she was Dark.

But if you weren't Dark, it wasn't the most relaxing place in the world. You spent half the night making sure not to accidentally look anyone in the eye or smile in the wrong direction.

"And you think getting Short Straw *The Book of Moons* is going to help him un-kick the can?"

Link growled from the next seat. He insisted on coming with us for safekeeping, but I could tell he hated it here even more than I did.

"Watch it, Rid. Ethan hasn't kicked the can. He's just— bent it outta shape a little."

I smiled. I guess Link could tell me Ethan was gone all he wanted, but it wasn't the same when someone else said it.

And it meant Ridley wasn't one of us anymore, at least not for Link. She really had left him, and she really was Dark.

She was an outsider.

Link seemed to sense it, too. "I need to use the bathroom." He hesitated, unwilling to leave my side. Everyone seemed to have their own brand of bodyguard at a club like Exile. My bodyguard happened to be a quarter Incubus with a heart of gold.

Ridley waited until he was out of earshot. "Your plan sucks."

"The plan doesn't suck."

"Abraham's not going to trade John Breed for *The Book of Moons*. John isn't worth anything to him now that the Order of Things has been set right. It's too late."

"You don't know that."

"You're forgetting I've spent more time than I wanted to with Abraham in the past few months. He's been keeping himself busy. He spends every day in that Frankenstein lab of his, trying to figure out what went wrong with John Breed. He's gone back to the mad science drawing board."

"That means he'll want John back, so he'll trade us the Book. Which is exactly what we want."

Ridley sighed. "Are you listening to yourself? He's not a good guy. You don't want to hand John over to him. When Abraham's not gluing wings onto bats, he's been having secret meetings with some creepy bald guy."

"Can you be more specific? That doesn't narrow it down."

Rid shrugged. "I don't know. Angel? Angelo? Something church-y like that."

I felt sick. My glass turned to ice in my hand. I could feel the frozen particles collecting at the tips of my fingers.

"Angelus?"

She popped a chip into her mouth from the black bowl on the bar. "That's it. They're teaming up for some supersecret takedown. I never heard the details. But this guy definitely hates Mortals as much as Abraham does."

What would a member of the Council of the Far Keep be doing with a Blood Incubus like Abraham Ravenwood? After what Angelus tried to do to Marian, I knew he was a monster, but I thought he was some kind of righteous lunatic. Not someone who would conspire with Abraham.

Still, it wasn't the first time Abraham and the Far Keep seemed to have their agendas aligned. Uncle Macon had brought it up before, right after Marian's trial.

I shook my head at the thought. "We have to tell Marian. After we get that book. So unless you have a better idea, we're meeting Abraham to make the trade." I drained what was left of my frozen soda water, knocking the glass back down to the bar.

It shattered in my hand.

The room quieted around me, and I could feel the eyes— nonhuman eyes, some gold and others black as the Tunnels themselves—staring back at me. I ducked my head from view.

The bartender made a face, and I glanced at the door from the corner of my eye—half-expecting to see my Uncle Macon standing there. The bartender was staring. "Those are some eyes you've got."

Rid shot me a look. "Hers? One of them didn't take," she said casually. "You know how it goes." We waited in our seats, nervous and tense. You didn't want to attract too much attention at Exile, not when you only had one gold eye to show for it.

The bartender studied me for another moment, then nodded and checked his watch. "Yeah. I know how it goes." This time he glanced at the door. He'd probably already made the call to my uncle.

That rat.

"You're going to need all the help you can get, Cuz."

"What are you saying, Rid?"

"I'm saying it looks like I'm going to have to rescue you fools again." She flicked a piece of broken glass off the counter.

"Rescue us how?"

"You leave that to me. Turns out I'm not just another pretty face. Well, I'm that, too." She smiled, but she couldn't quite pull it off. "All this *and* another pretty face."

Even her smart mouth seemed halfhearted to me now. I wondered if Ethan's disappearance was getting to her as much as the rest of us.

My instincts were still right about one thing.

Uncle Macon showed up at the door like clockwork, and I was back home in my bedroom before I could ask her.

CHAPTER 24

The Hand That Rocks the Cradle

Ridley was waiting for us behind the farthest row of crypts, which, judging by the number of abandoned beer bottles in the bushes, was also a Gatlin County hot spot.

I couldn't imagine hanging out here willingly. His Garden of Perpetual Peace still had Abraham's fingerprints all over it. Nothing seemed to have changed since he had called up the Vexes only weeks before the Eighteenth Moon. Warning signs and yellow caution tape created a labyrinth between the broken mausoleums, uprooted trees, and cracked gravestones in the new section of the cemetery. Now that the Order of Things was repaired, the grass wasn't burning up anymore, and the lubbers were gone. But the other scars were still there if you knew where to look for them.

True to Gatlin form, the worst of the damage had already been hidden under the layers of fresh dirt Ridley was standing on now. The caskets had been reburied and the tombs sealed. I wasn't surprised. It wasn't like the good citizens of Gatlin to keep the skeletons out of the closet for long.

Rid unwrapped a cherry lollipop and waved it around dramatically. "I sold it to him. Hook, line, and stinker." She smiled at Link. "That's you, Shrinky Dink."

"You know what they say. Takes one to know one," Link shot back.

"You know I smell like frosting on a cupcake. Why don't you come on over here, and I'll show you just how sweet I can be?" She wriggled her long pink nails like claws.

Link walked over to John, who was leaning against a weeping angel that was split right down the middle. "Just callin' it like I see it, Babe. And I can smell you just fine from here."

Link was throwing Ridley more than just quarter-Incubus swagger today. Now that he'd wrapped his head around the fact that she was back, it was like he lived to trade insults with her.

Ridley turned back to me, annoyed that she hadn't gotten a bigger rise out of him. "All it took was a little trip back to N'awlins, and I had Abraham eating out of my hand."

That was hard to imagine, and John definitely wasn't buying it. "You expect us to believe you Charmed Abraham with a few Ridley pops? You and what chain of candy stores?"

Ridley pouted. "Of course not. I had to sell it. So I thought, who would be stupid enough to do whatever I say and play right into my hands?" She blew Link a kiss. "Our little Dinkubus, of course."

Link's jaw tightened. "She's full of crap."

"All I had to do was tell Abraham that I used Link and his feelings for me to infiltrate your stupid little circle and figure out your even stupider little plan. Then I complained about him keeping me caged like his prize pet. Of course, I said I couldn't blame him. Who wouldn't want me around full-time?"

"Is that a question? Because I'd be happy to answer," Link snapped.

"He wasn't mad that you broke out of your fancy birdcage?" John asked.

Ridley's voice edged up a little. "Abraham knew I wouldn't stay in there if I could find a way out. I'm a Siren; it's not in my nature to be confined. I told him I used my Power of Persuasion on his pathetic Incubus errand boy and convinced him to let me out. It didn't end well. Abraham just got a bigger cage for him."

"What else did you say?" I wanted to know if there was really a chance we were getting the Book. I twisted my charm necklace around my finger, trying not to think about the memories slipping around it.

"I broke it down for him and said I'd rather bet on him than you guys." She gave Link a sweet smile. "You know how I like a winning team. Naturally, Abraham believed every word. Why wouldn't he? It's so utterly believable."

Link looked like he wanted to throw her across the graveyard.

"And Abraham will be there? Today?" John still didn't trust her.

"He'll be there. In the flesh. Of course, I'm using the term loosely." She shuddered. "Very loosely."

"He agreed to trade me for *The Book of Moons*?" John asked.

Ridley sighed, leaning against the crypt wall. "Well, technically, I believe it went something like, 'They're stupid enough to believe you'll trade John for the Book, but of course you won't.' And then there might have been some laughing. And some drunken Casting. It's all a haze."

Link folded his arms across his chest. "The thing is, Rid, how do we know you're not saying the same thing to him? You're Dark as they come. How can we know"—he stepped protectively in front of me—"whose side you're really on?"

"She's my cousin, Link." Even as I said it, I wasn't really sure of the answer. Ridley was a Dark Caster again. The last time she offered to help me, it was a trap, and she led me right to my mother and my Seventeenth Moon.

But I knew she loved me. As much as a Dark Caster could love anyone. And as much as Rid could love anyone other than herself.

Ridley leaned closer to Link. "Good question, Shrinky Dink. Too bad I have no intention of answering it."

"One of these days, I guess I'll figure out that one for myself." Link frowned, and I smiled.

"Let me give you a little clue," Rid purred. "Today's not the day."

Then in a swirl of cotton candy body glitter, the Siren he loved to hate was gone.

───── ⸹ ─────

It was just starting to get dark when we left Liv and Uncle Macon in the study, poring over every Caster book they could find about Sheers and Ravenwood history, respectively. Liv was convinced that Ethan was trying to contact us, and she was determined to find a way to communicate with him. Every time I went down there, she was taking notes or adjusting the crazy gadget she used to measure supernatural frequencies. I think she was desperate to find a solution that didn't involve trading John for *The Book of Moons*.

I didn't blame her.

Uncle Macon was, too, even if he wouldn't admit it. He was scouring every journal and scrap of paper he could find for references to other places where Abraham could have hidden the Book.

That's why I couldn't tell them what we were doing. We already knew how Liv felt about the idea of trading John for the Book. And Uncle Macon wasn't going to trust Ridley. Instead, I told them I wanted to visit Ethan's grave, and John volunteered to go with me.

Link was waiting for John and me back at the cemetery.

The sky was dark now, and I could barely make out where a crow circled high in the air above us, shrieking, as we made our way toward the oldest part of His Garden of Perpetual Peace.

I shivered. That crow had to be some sort of omen. But there was no way of knowing which kind. Either things were going to go well, and I would end the day with *The Book of Moons* and a chance at getting Ethan back, or I'd fail and lose John in the process.

John Breed wasn't the love of my life, but he was the love of someone's life. And John and I had spent more than a few dark months together, when he and Rid seemed like the only people I could talk to. But John wasn't the same guy he was back then. He had changed, and he didn't deserve to go back to a life with Abraham. I wouldn't have wished that on anyone.

What had I become?

> *bargaining with a life*
> *that isn't mine*
> *isn't a bargain*
> *misery*
> *doesn't*
> *come*
> *cheap*

John wouldn't look at me. Even Link kept his eyes fixed on the path ahead of us. I felt like they were disappointed in me for being so selfish.

I was disappointed in myself.

It is what it is, and I am what I am. I'm no better than Ridley. I only want what I want.

Either way, it didn't stop my feet from walking.

I tried not to think about it as I followed Link and John through the trees. While most of His Garden of Perpetual Peace was in the process of being restored to its pre–Vex attack state, the same wasn't true of the older part of the graveyard. I hadn't seen it since the night the earth cracked open, covering these hills with decomposing corpses and severed bones. Though the bodies were gone, the ground was still over-turned, huge sinkholes replacing the graves that had surrounded generations of Wates since before the Civil War. Even if Ethan wasn't here.

Thank God.

"This blows." Link trudged up the hill with his garden shears in hand. "But don't worry. I got your back. He's not going to take you off to creepy-old-guy-land. Not without a fight. Not with these babies."

John shoved Link to the side. "Put those things away, rookie. You won't be able to get close enough to Hunting to clip the grass around his feet. And if Abraham sees them, he'll use them to slit your throat without even touching them."

Link shoved John back, and I ducked to avoid being knocked down the hill, as collateral damage. "Yeah, well, they helped me out on the way to that guy Obidias' place when

I took out that chicken-fried bat guy. Just don't get me killed, Caster Boy."

"Hold up a second." John, now serious, stopped walking and turned to both of us. "Abraham is no joke. You have no idea what he's capable of—I'm not sure anyone does. Stay out of the way and let me handle him. You're backup, in case Hunting or your girlfriend gives us trouble."

"Rid's on our side, remember?" I reminded him.

"At least she's supposed to be. And she's not my girlfriend." Link clenched his jaw.

"In my experience, the only side Ridley's ever on is her own." John stepped over a broken statue of a praying angel, her hands cracked at the wrists. All the broken angels around here were starting to feel like a bad omen.

Link looked annoyed, but he didn't say anything. He didn't seem to like it when anyone but him criticized Ridley. I wondered if things could ever really be over between them.

He and John navigated around the broken caskets and tree limbs, reaching an enormous sinkhole just beyond the old Honeycutt crypt. I did my best to keep up, but they were Incubuses, so there was nothing I could do, short of Casting an Incubus-cloning spell.

But soon it didn't matter, because we had nowhere left to go.

Abraham was waiting for us.

Either we had walked right into his trap or he had walked right into ours. It was almost time to find out.

Abraham Ravenwood was standing on the far side of the sink-hole. Wearing a long black coat and stovepipe hat and leaning against a splintered tree, he looked bored, as if this was an annoying errand.

The Book of Moons was tucked under his arm.

I breathed a sigh of relief. "He brought it," I said quietly.

"We don't have it yet," Link said under his breath.

Wearing a black turtleneck and a leather jacket, Hunting stood behind his great-great-great-grandfather. He was blow-ing smoke rings at Ridley. She coughed, waving the smoke away from her red dress, and gave her uncle a dirty look.

There was something disturbing about seeing her dressed in red, standing a few feet away from two Blood Incubuses. I hoped John was wrong and Ridley really was on our side—for Link's sake as much as my own.

We both loved her. And you couldn't control who you loved, even if you wanted to. That had been Genevieve's problem with Ethan Carter Wate. It had been Uncle Macon's problem with Lila, Link's with Ridley. Probably even Ridley's with Link.

Love was how all these knots started to unravel in the first place.

"You brought it," I called across to Abraham.

"And you've brought him." Abraham's eyes narrowed at the sight of John. "There's my boy. I've been so worried."

John tensed. "I'm not your boy. And you've never cared about me, so you can stop pretending."

"That's not true." Abraham acted hurt. "I've put a great deal of energy into you."

"Too much, if you ask me," Hunting said.

"No one did," Abraham snapped.

Hunting clenched his jaw and flicked his cigarette into the grass. He didn't look pleased. Which meant he would probably take that anger out on someone who didn't deserve it and didn't expect it. We were all plausible candidates.

John looked disgusted. "You mean treating me like a slave and using me to do your dirty work? Thanks, but I'm not interested in the kind of energy you put into things."

Abraham stepped forward, his black string tie blowing in the breeze. "I don't care what interests you. You serve a purpose, and when you stop serving it, you won't be useful to me anymore. I think we both know how I feel about things that aren't of any use to me." He smirked. "I watched Sarafine burn to death, and the only thing that bothered me was the ash on my jacket."

He was telling the truth. I had watched my mother burn, too. Not that I thought of Sarafine that way. But hearing Abraham talk about her like that made me feel something, even if I didn't know what.

Sympathy? Compassion?

Do I feel sorry for the woman who tried to kill me? Is that possible?

John had told me that Abraham hated Casters as much as

Mortals. I hadn't believed him until that moment. Abraham Ravenwood was cold, calculating, and evil. He really was the Devil, or the closest thing I'd ever met.

I watched as John raised his head high and called to Abraham. "Just give my friends the Book, and I'll leave with you. That was the deal."

Abraham laughed, the Book still safely tucked under his arm. "The terms have changed. I think I'll keep it after all." He nodded at Link. "And your new friend."

Ridley stopped sucking on her lollipop. "You don't want him. He's worthless—trust me." She was lying.

Abraham knew it, too. A vicious smile spread across his face. "As you wish. Then we can feed him to Hunting's dogs. When we get home."

There was a time when Link would've backed up, scared out of his mind. But that was before John bit him and his life changed. Before Ethan died and everything changed.

I watched Link standing next to John now. He wasn't going anywhere, even if he was afraid. That Link was long gone.

John tried to step in front of him, but Link held out his arm. "I can defend myself."

"Don't be stupid," John snapped. "You're only a quarter Incubus. That makes you half as strong as me, without the Caster blood."

"Boys." Abraham snapped his fingers. "This is all very moving, but it's time to get going. I have things to do and people to kill."

John squared his shoulders. "I'm not going anywhere with you unless you give them the Book. I've come into contact with some powerful Casters lately. I make my own choices now."

John collected powers the way Abraham collected victims. Ridley's Power of Persuasion, even some of my abilities as a Natural. Not to mention the ones he absorbed from all the other Casters who unknowingly touched him. Abraham had to be wondering whose power John had tapped into.

Still, I started to panic. Why hadn't we taken John back down into the Tunnels to collect a few more? Who was I to think we could take on Abraham?

Hunting glanced at Abraham, and a flash of recognition passed between them—a secret they shared.

"Is that so?" Abraham dropped *The Book of Moons* at his feet. "Then why don't you come over here and take it?"

John had to know it was some kind of trick, but he started walking anyway.

I wished Liv were here to see how brave he was. Then again, I was glad she wasn't. Because I could barely stand to watch him take another step closer to the ancient Incubus, and I wasn't the girl who loved him.

Abraham held out his hand and flicked his wrist, like he was turning a doorknob.

With that one motion, everything changed. Instantly, John grabbed his head like someone had just cracked it open from the inside, and dropped to his knees.

Abraham kept his arm in front of him, closing his fist slowly, and John jerked violently, screaming in pain.

"What the hell?" Link grabbed John's arm and yanked him to his feet.

John could barely stand. He swayed, trying to regain his balance.

Hunting laughed. Ridley was still standing next to him, and I could see the lollipop shaking in her hand.

I tried to think of a Cast, anything that would stop Abraham, even for a second.

Abraham stepped closer, gathering up the bottom of his coat to keep it from dragging in the mud. "Did you think I would create something as powerful as you if I couldn't control it?"

John froze, his green eyes fearful. He squinted hard, trying to fight the pain. "What are you talking about?"

"I think we both know," Abraham said. "I made you, boy. Found the right combination—the parentage I needed—and created a new breed of Incubus."

John staggered back, stunned. "That's a lie. You found me when I was a kid."

Abraham smiled. "That depends on your interpretation of the word *found*."

"What are you saying?" John's face was ashen.

"We took you. I did engineer you, after all." Abraham dug around in his jacket pocket and removed a cigar. "Your parents had a few happy years together. It's more than most of us get."

"What happened to my parents?" John gritted his teeth. I could almost see the rage.

Abraham turned to Hunting, who lit the cigar with a silver lighter. "Answer the boy, Hunting."

Hunting flipped the top of the lighter closed. He shrugged. "It was a long time ago, kid. They were juicy. And chewy. But I can't remember the details."

John lurched forward and ripped through the darkness.

One second he was there. The next, he was gone, sliding away in a ripple of air. He reappeared just inches in front of Abraham and wrapped his hand around the old Incubus' throat. "I'm going to kill you, you sick son of a bitch."

The tendons in John's arm tightened, but his grip didn't.

The muscles in his hand were tensing, his fingers obviously trying to close, but they wouldn't. John grabbed his wrist with his other hand, trying to brace it.

Abraham laughed. "You can't hurt me. I'm the architect of the design. Think I would build a weapon like you without a kill switch?"

Ridley stepped back, watching as John's hand loosened against his will, his fingers opening as he tried to force them closed again with his other hand. It was impossible.

I couldn't bear to watch. Abraham seemed more in control of John now than he had on the night of the Seventeenth Moon. Worse, John's awareness didn't seem to change the fact that he couldn't control his body. Abraham was pulling the strings.

"You're a monster," John hissed, still holding his wrist inches from Abraham's throat.

"Flattery won't get you anywhere. You've caused me lots of problems, boy. You owe me." Abraham smiled. "And I plan to take it out of your flesh."

He twitched his hands again, and John rose off the ground further, clutching his own neck with his hands, strangling himself.

Abraham was trying to do more than make a point. "You have outlived your usefulness. All that work for nothing."

John's eyes rolled back in his head, and his body went limp.

"Don't you need him?" Ridley shouted. "You said he was the ultimate weapon."

"Unfortunately, he's *defective*," Abraham answered.

I noticed something move in my peripheral vision a moment before I heard his voice.

"One could say the same thing about you, Grandfather." Uncle Macon stepped out from behind one of the crypts, his green eyes glowing in the darkness. "Put the boy down."

Abraham laughed, though his expression was anything but amused. "Defective? That's a compliment, coming from the little Incubus who wanted to be a Caster."

Abraham's grip on John loosened just enough for John to get some air. The Blood Incubus was focusing his anger on Uncle Macon now.

"I never wanted to be a Caster, but I'm glad to accept any fate that unburdens me from the Darkness you brought upon this family." Uncle Macon pointed a hand at John, and a wave of energy flashed across the graveyard, the blast hitting John squarely.

John yanked his hands away from his neck as his body dropped to the ground.

Hunting started toward his brother, but Abraham stopped him, clapping dramatically. "Nicely done. That's quite a party trick, son. Maybe next time you can light my cigar." Abraham's features settled in his familiar sneer. "Enough games. Let's finish this."

Hunting didn't hesitate.

He ripped through the darkness as Uncle Macon focused his green eyes on the black sky. Hunting materialized in front of his brother just as the sky exploded into a blanket of pure light.

Sunlight.

Uncle Macon had done it once before, in the parking lot of Jackson High, but this time the light was even more intense—and focused. That light coming from him had been Caster green. This time it was something stronger and more natural, as if the light came from the sky itself.

Hunting's body jerked. He reached out and grabbed his brother's shirt, taking them both to the ground.

But the killing light only intensified.

Abraham's skin went pale, the color of white ash. The light

seemed to weaken him, but not nearly as quickly as it was draining Hunting.

Even as Hunting desperately tried to stay alive, Abraham only seemed interested in trying to kill us. The old Blood Incubus was too strong, and he reached out for Uncle Macon. I knew better than to underestimate him. Even wounded, he wouldn't give up until he destroyed us all.

An overwhelming sense of panic surged inside me. I concentrated every thought, every cell on Abraham. The earth around him bucked, tearing itself from the ground like a rug being pulled out from under him. Abraham staggered and then turned his attention to me.

He closed his hand around the air in front of him, and an invisible force tightened around my throat. I felt my feet rise off the ground, my Chucks kicking below me.

"Lena!" John shouted. He closed his eyes, concentrating on Abraham, but whatever he was planning, he wasn't fast enough.

I couldn't breathe.

"I don't think so." Abraham twisted his free hand, bringing John to his knees in seconds.

Link charged Abraham, but another simple flick of the Blood Incubus' wrist sent him flying. Link's back hit the jagged stone crypt with a loud crack.

I struggled to stay conscious. Hunting was below me, his hands around Uncle Macon's neck. But he didn't seem to have enough strength left to hurt his brother. The color slowly drained from Hunting's skin, turning his body hauntingly transparent.

I gasped for breath, transfixed, as Hunting's hands slid from Uncle M's neck and he started writhing in pain.

"Macon! Stop!" he pleaded.

Uncle Macon focused his energy on his brother. The light held steady as the darkness leached out of Hunting's body and into the overturned earth.

Hunting seized, and sucked in his last breath. Then his body shuddered and froze.

"I'm sorry, brother. You left me no choice." Macon stared down at what was left before Hunting's corpse disintegrated, as if he had never existed at all.

"One down," he said grimly.

Abraham shielded his eyes, trying to determine if Hunting was really gone. The color was beginning to seep out of Abraham's skin now, but it had only made it as far as his wrists. He would kill me long before the sunlight took him out. I had to do something before we all ended up dead.

I closed my eyes, trying to push past the pain. My mind was slipping into numbness.

Thunder rumbled overhead.

"A storm? Is that all you've got, my dear?" Abraham said. "Such a waste. Just like your mother."

Anger and guilt churned inside me. Sarafine was a monster, but she was a monster Abraham had helped create. Abraham had used her weaknesses to lure her into Darkness. And I had watched her die. Maybe we were both monsters.

Maybe we all are.

"I'm nothing like my mother!" Sarafine's fate was decided for her, and she wasn't strong enough to fight it. I was.

Lightning tore across the sky and struck a tree behind Abraham. Flames raced down the trunk.

Abraham took off his hat and shook it with one hand, careful to keep the hand tethered to my throat tightly clenched. "I always say it's not a party until something catches fire."

My uncle rose to his feet, his black hair messy and his green eyes glowing even brighter than before. "I would have to agree."

The light in the sky intensified, blazing like a spotlight on Abraham. As we watched, the beam exploded in a blinding flash of white—forming two horizontal beams of pure energy.

Abraham swayed, shielding his eyes. His iron grip retracted, and my body fell to the rotting soil.

Time seemed to stop.

We all stared at the white beams spreading across the sky.

Except one of us.

Link ripped before anyone else had a chance to react—dematerializing in a split second, like he was a pro. I couldn't believe it. The only times he'd ever ripped in front of me, he practically flattened me like a pancake.

Not this time.

A crack in space opened up for him, only inches in front of Abraham Ravenwood.

Link yanked the garden shears out of the waistband of his jeans, raising them above his head. He plunged them into Abraham's heart before the old Incubus even realized what had happened.

Abraham's black eyes widened and he stared at Link, struggling to stay alive as a circle of red seeped slowly out around the blades.

Link leaned in close. "All that engineerin' wasn't for nothin', Mr. Ravenwood. I'm the best a both worlds. A hybrid Incubus with his own onboard navigation."

Abraham coughed desperately, his eyes fixed on the mostly Mortal boy who had taken him down. Finally, his body slid to the ground, the stolen science lab shears protruding from his chest.

Link stood over the body of the Blood Incubus who had hunted us for so long. The one person generations of Casters hadn't been able to touch.

Link grinned at John and nodded. "Screw all that Incubus crap. That's how you do it Mortal-style."

CHAPTER 25

Death's Door

Link stood over Abraham's body, watching as it started to disintegrate into tiny particles of nothing.

Ridley stepped up beside him, looping her arm through his. "Grab the scissors, Hot Rod. They might come in handy if I need to cut myself out of a cage sometime."

Link pulled the shears from what was left of the Blood Incubus. "I would like to take this opportunity to thank the Jackson High Biology Department. Stay in school, kids." He shoved the shears back into his jeans.

John walked over and slapped Link on the shoulder. "Thanks for saving my ass. Mortal-style."

"You know it. I got some mad skills." Link grinned.

Uncle Macon brushed off his trousers. "I don't think any-one can argue with that assessment, Mr. Lincoln. Well played. Your timing was impeccable."

"How did you know we were here?" I asked. Had Amma seen something and given us away?

"Mr. Breed was kind enough to leave a note."

I turned to John, who was kicking at the dirt with his boot. "You told him what we were doing? What about our plans? What about the part where we agreed not to tell my uncle anything?"

"I didn't. The note was for Liv," he answered sheepishly. "I couldn't just disappear without saying good-bye."

Link shook his head. "Seriously, dude? Another note? Why didn't you just leave a map?"

This was the second time John's guilty conscience and one of his notes had led Liv—or, in this case, my uncle—to him.

"You should all be grateful for Mr. Breed's sentimental inclinations," Uncle M said. "Or I'm afraid this evening could have resulted in a very unfortunate outcome."

Link elbowed John. "You're still a sap."

I stopped listening.

Why couldn't Liv keep her mouth shut?

Another voice entered my mind.

I hardly think blaming Liv for your mistakes is necessary.

I was almost too stunned to speak. My uncle had never Kelted with me before. It was a power he could only have acquired after his transition into a Caster.

"How?"

"You know my abilities are constantly evolving. This one is unpredictable, I'm afraid." He shrugged innocently.

I tried not to think. It didn't seem to stop him from scolding me.

Really? You thought you could take on Abraham alone, in a graveyard?

"But how did you know where we were?" John asked. "I didn't put that in the note."

Oh my God....

"Uncle M? Can you read minds?"

"Hardly." My uncle snapped his fingers, and Boo lumbered up the hill. Knowing my uncle, it was practically a confession.

I felt my hair lift from my shoulders as a gentle wind whipped around me. I tried to calm down. "You were *spying* on me? I thought we made a deal about that."

"*That* was before you and your friends decided you were equipped to take on Abraham Ravenwood on your own." His voice rose. "Have you learned nothing?"

The Book of Moons lay in the dirt, the moon embossed on its black leather cover facing the sky.

Link bent down to pick it up.

"I wouldn't do that, Hot Rod," Ridley said. "You don't have that much Incubus in you." She picked up the Book and touched her lollipop to his lips almost like a kiss. "Wouldn't want those pretty hands to get burned."

"Thanks, Babe."

"Don't call me—"

Link grabbed the lollipop out of her hand. "Yeah, yeah. I know."

I watched the way they looked at each other. Any idiot could see they were in love, even if they were the only two idiots who couldn't.

My chest ached, and I thought about Ethan.

the missing piece
my breath
my heart
my memory
me
the other half
the missing half

Stop.

I didn't want to write poems in my mind, especially if my uncle could hear them. I needed to send a completely different kind of message. "Rid, give it to me."

She nodded and handed me *The Book of Moons*.

The Book that nearly killed Ethan and then Uncle Macon. The Book that took more than it ever gave. Part of me wanted to set it on fire and see if it would burn, though I doubted something as mundane as fire could destroy it.

It still would have been worth a try if it prevented even one person from using the Book to hurt someone else—or themselves. But Ethan needed it, and I trusted him. Whatever he was doing, I believed he wouldn't use it to hurt anyone. And I wasn't sure he could hurt himself now.

"We have to take it to Lila's grave."

Uncle Macon studied me for a long moment, an unfamiliar mixture of sadness and worry warring in his eyes. "All right."

I recognized his tone. He was indulging me.

I started walking toward Lila Wate's grave, next to the empty plot where the good folks of Gatlin believed my uncle was buried.

Ridley sighed dramatically. "Great. More time in the creepy graveyard."

Link slung his arm over her shoulders casually. "Don't worry, Babe. I'll protect you."

Ridley looked at him suspiciously. "Protect me? You do realize I'm a Dark Caster again?"

"I like to think you're kinda on the gray side. Either way, I'll give you a pass today. I did just kill the Galactus of Incubuses."

Rid flipped her blond and pink hair. "Whatever that means."

I stopped listening and wove my way through the cemetery, *The Book of Moons* pressed against my chest. I felt the heat radiating from it, as if the worn leather cover might burn me, too.

———✺———

I knelt in front of Ethan's mother's grave. This was the spot where I'd left the black stone from my necklace for him. It seemed to work then; I could only hope it would work again. *The Book of Moons* had to be a whole lot more important than a rock.

My uncle stared at the headstone, transfixed. I wondered how long he would love her. Forever, that was my best guess.

For whatever reason, this place was a doorway I couldn't find my way through. The important thing was that Ethan could open it somehow.

He had to.

I put the Book on the grave, touching it for what I hoped would be the last time.

I don't know why you need it, Ethan. But here it is. Please come home.

I waited as if it might disappear right in front of me.

Nothing happened.

"Maybe we should leave it alone," Link suggested. "Ethan probably needs privacy or somethin' to do his ghost tricks."

"He's not a ghost," I snapped.

Link held up his hands. "Sorry. His Sheer tricks."

He didn't realize that the word didn't matter. It was the image the word called up in my mind. A pale, lifeless Ethan. Dead. The way I found him the night of my Sixteenth Moon, after Sarafine stabbed him. Panic pressed against my lungs like two hands squeezing the breath out of me. I couldn't stand to think about it.

"Let's leave it and see what happens," John said.

"Absolutely not." Uncle Macon was done indulging me. "I'm sorry, Lena—"

"What if it was Lila?"

His face clouded over at the mention of her name. The question hung in the air, but we both knew the answer.

If the woman he loved needed him, he would do anything to help—from this side of the grave or any other.

I knew that, too.

He studied me for a long moment. Then he sighed, nodding. "All right. You can try. But if it doesn't work—"

"Yeah, yeah. We can't just ditch the most powerful book in the Caster and Mortal worlds on some grave and walk away." Ridley was still perched on the headstone, smacking her gum. "What if someone finds it?"

"I'm afraid Ridley's right." Uncle Macon sighed. "I'll wait here."

"I don't think it will work if you're here, sir. You're a scary kinda person, too," Link said as respectfully as possible. "Sir."

"We are not leaving *The Book of Moons* unattended, Mr. Lincoln."

An idea took hold slowly, stretching out until it was perfectly formed. "Maybe we don't need someone to stay with the Book, but *something*."

"Huh?" Link scratched his head.

I bent down. "Boo, come here, boy."

Boo Radley stood up and shook his black fur, which was as thick as a wolf's.

I dug my fingers behind his ears. "That's my good boy."

"Not a bad idea." Rid put two fingers in her mouth and whistled.

"You really think one dog can fight off the Blood Pack if they show up?" Link asked.

Uncle Macon crossed his arms. "Boo Radley is hardly a common dog."

"Even a Caster dog can use a little help," Rid said.

A branch cracked, and something leaped from the bushes.

"Holy crap!" Link yanked the garden shears out of his waistband just as Bade's paws hit the ground.

Leah Ravenwood's enormous mountain cat growled.

Uncle M smiled. "My sister's cat. An excellent idea. She does provide a certain level of intimidation that Boo lacks."

Boo barked, offended.

"Here, kitty kitty...." Ridley reached out her hand, and Bade stalked over.

Link stared at her. "You're a total psycho."

Bade growled at Link again, and Rid laughed. "You're just mad because Bade doesn't like you, Hot Stuff."

John took a step back. "Yeah, well, I'm not petting her either."

"So we leave the Book for a little while and see what happens." I hugged Boo. "You stay here." The Caster dog sat down in front of the grave like a guard dog, and Bade came over and stretched out in front of him lazily.

I stood up, but I was having trouble forcing myself to walk away.

What if something happened to it? The Book might be Ethan's only chance to get back to me. Could I risk it?

John noticed I wasn't moving, and pointed to the rise a few yards beyond the grave. "We can hang out on the other side in case they need some backup. Okay?"

Ridley hopped off the headstone, her platforms smacking against the border of the plot. In the South, that had to be the equivalent of something like seven years of bad luck. Maybe more in Gatlin.

She draped her arm over my shoulders and waved a lollipop in front of me. "Come on. I'll tell you all about my adventures in shackles."

Link jogged up next to us. "Did you say shackles? Those are like handcuffs, right?" He seemed a little too excited about hearing the details.

"Mr. Lincoln!" Uncle M looked like he wanted to strangle him.

Link stopped in his tracks. "Uh, sorry, sir. It was just a joke. You know..."

I let Ridley drag me down the other side of the hill while Link tried to talk his way out of trouble with Uncle Macon. John trudged behind us, his boots as heavy as any Mortal's footsteps.

If I closed my eyes, I could pretend they were Ethan's.

But it was getting harder and harder to pretend. I was Kelting to him before I even realized it, the same three words over and over.

Please come home.

I wondered if he could hear me. If he was already on his way.

I counted the minutes, wondering how long we should wait before checking on the Book. Even Link and Ridley's banter couldn't distract me, which was saying a lot.

"I think all this quarter-Incubus stuff is going to your head," Ridley said.

Link flexed. "Or maybe it's taking out the baddest badass around."

Ridley rolled her eyes. "Please."

"Do you two ever stop?" John asked.

They both whipped around to look at him. "Stop what?" they asked at the same time.

I was about to tell John not to bother, when I saw a streak of black in the sky.

The crow. The same one that had watched us when we went to meet Abraham. Maybe it was following us.

Maybe it knew something.

It dipped and circled the area above Ethan's grave.

"It's the crow." I took off back up the hill.

John ripped and appeared at my side. "What are you talking about?"

Link and the others caught up to us. "Where's the fire?"

I pointed at the bird. "I think that crow has been following us."

Uncle Macon studied the bird. "Interesting."

Ridley smacked her gum. "What?"

"A Seer like Amarie would tell you that many believe crows can cross between the world of the living and the world of the dead."

We made it over the rise. Bade and Boo were staring up at the sleek black bird.

"So what? Even if it could fly from world to world, you really think that little bird could carry *The Book a Moons*?" Link asked.

I didn't know. But the crow was connected to Ethan somehow. I was sure of it.

"Why is it circling like that?" John asked.

Ridley strolled up behind us. "It's probably scared of the giant cat."

For once, she might be right.

"Bade and Boo, go home," I called. The big cat's ears perked up at the sound of her name.

Boo hesitated and looked up at Uncle Macon.

He nodded to the dog. "Go on."

Boo cocked his head. Then he turned and lumbered through the tall grass. Bade yawned, baring her huge white teeth, and followed, her tail swishing like a lion's from one of the nature shows Link was always watching on the Discovery

Channel. He blamed it on his mom, but in the last couple of months, I'd noticed him watching it by himself more than a few times.

The crow circled again and swooped toward us, landing on the headstone. Its beady black eyes seemed to be staring right at me.

"How come it's checkin' you out like that?" Link asked.

I stared back at the black bird.

Please. Take the Book or make it disappear. Whatever you have to do to get it to Ethan.

Uncle Macon looked at me from the other side of the headstone.

He can't hear you, Lena. You can't Kelt with a bird, I'm afraid.

I glared at my uncle. At this point, I would try anything.

How do you know?

The crow hopped down, its talons touching the thick leather cover for a split second before it squawked and pulled its legs up again quickly.

"I think the Book burned it," John said. "Poor guy."

I knew he was right. I felt the tears welling in my eyes. If the crow couldn't touch the Book, how would we get it to Ethan? I'd left the black stone Ethan had asked for, the one from my charm necklace, right here on the grave. I didn't know what had happened to it after that.

"Maybe the bird has nothing to do with it, and he's just a messenger or something," John offered.

I sniffled, swiping at my face. "Then what's the message?"

John squeezed my shoulder. "Don't worry."

"How are we going to get the Book to Ethan? He needs it, or he can't—" I couldn't finish. I couldn't stand to even think it.

We had risked our lives to track down Abraham Ravenwood, and we had found a way to kill him—at least Link had. *The Book of Moons* was right here at my feet, and there was no way to get it to Ethan.

"We'll figure it out, Cuz." Ridley picked up the Book, the back cover dragging across the stone. "Someone must have the answer."

John smiled at me. "Someone does. Especially when it comes to that book. Come on—let's go ask her."

A flutter of hope filled my chest. "Are you thinking what I'm thinking?"

He nodded. "It is Presidents' Day, which was still a bank holiday the last time I checked."

Ridley pulled on the bottom of her miniskirt, which didn't move an inch. "Who's thinking what, and where are we going?"

I grabbed her arm, tugging her down the hill. "Your favorite place, Rid. The library."

"It's not that bad," she said, inspecting her purple nail polish. "Except for all those books."

I didn't respond.

There was only one book that mattered right now, and my whole world—and Ethan's future—depended on it.

CHAPTER 26

Quantum Physics

From just inside the hidden grating that led into the *Lunae Libri*, I could see all the way down to the bottom of the stairs. Marian sat behind the circular reception desk, exactly where I knew she would be. Liv was pacing at the far end of the room, where the stacks began.

As we came down into the *Lunae Libri*, Liv's neck snapped up. She bolted across the room the moment she saw John.

But he was faster. John ripped, materializing in Liv's path and gathering her up in his arms. My heart broke a little as I watched the relief spread across her face. I tried not to feel envious.

"You're all right!" Liv threw her arms around John's neck.

She pulled back, her expression changing. "What were you thinking? How many times are you going to sneak off to do something completely insane?" Liv turned her scowl on Link and me. "And how many times are you going to let him?"

Link raised his hands in surrender. "Hey, we weren't even there the last time."

John leaned his forehead against hers. "He's right. I'm the one you should be angry with."

A tear rolled down her cheek. "I don't know what I would have done—"

"I'm okay."

Link puffed his chest out. "Thanks to me."

"It's true," John said. "My protégée saved our asses."

Link raised an eyebrow. "That better mean somethin' good."

Uncle Macon cleared his throat and adjusted a cuff of his crisp white shirt. "It does indeed, Mr. Lincoln. It does indeed."

Arms crossed, Marian stepped out from behind the desk. "Would someone like to tell me exactly what happened tonight?" She stared at my uncle expectantly. "Liv and I have been worried sick."

He glared at me. "As you can imagine, their little show-down with my brother and Abraham did not go according to plan. And Mr. Breed almost met an untimely end."

"But Uncle M saved the day." Ridley didn't even try to hide her sarcasm. "He gave Hunting a sunburn where the sun don't shine. Now let's get on with the part where you give us a big lecture and we all get grounded."

Marian turned to my uncle. "Is she implying—?"

Uncle Macon nodded. "Hunting is no longer with us."

"Abraham's dead, too," John added.

Marian stared at Uncle Macon as if he had just parted the Red Sea. "You killed Abraham Ravenwood?"

Link cleared his throat loudly, grinning. "No, ma'am. I did."

For a moment Marian was speechless. "I think I need to sit down," she said, her knees beginning to buckle. John rushed behind the desk to get her a chair.

Marian pressed her fingers against her temples. "You're telling me that Hunting and Abraham are dead?"

"That would be correct," Uncle Macon said.

Marian shook her head. "Anything else?"

"Just this, Aunt Marian." Ethan's nickname for her just slipped out before I realized it. I dropped *The Book of Moons* on the polished wood tabletop next to her.

Liv inhaled sharply. "Oh my God."

I stared down at the worn black leather, embossed with a crescent moon, and the weight of the moment closed in on me. My hands shook, and my legs felt like they were about to give out, too.

"I can't believe it." Marian inspected the book suspiciously, as if I were returning a late library book into her system. She would never be anything less than 100 percent librarian.

"It's the real deal." Ridley leaned against one of the marble columns.

Marian stood up in front of her desk as if trying to position herself between Ridley and the most dangerous book in the Mortal and Caster worlds. "Ridley, I don't think you belong in here."

Ridley pushed her sunglasses up on her head, yellow cat eyes blinking back at Marian. "I know, I know. I'm a Dark Caster, and I don't belong in the good guys' secret clubhouse, right?" She rolled her eyes. "I am so over this."

"The *Lunae Libri* is open to all Casters, Light and Dark," Marian answered. "What I meant is that I'm not sure you belong with us."

"It's okay, Marian. Rid helped us get the Book," I explained.

Ridley blew a bubble and waited for it to pop, the sound echoing loudly off the walls. "Helped you? If by *help*, you mean set Abraham up for you so you could get *The Book of Moons* and kill him, then, yeah, I guess I helped."

Marian stared at her, speechless. Without a word, she walked over and held up a trash can in front of Ridley's mouth. "Not in my library. Spit it out now."

Ridley sighed. "You know it's not just gum, right?"

Marian didn't move.

Ridley spit.

Marian dropped the can. "What I don't understand is why you would risk your lives for that dreadful book. I appreciate the fact it is no longer in the hands of Blood Incubuses, but—"

"Ethan needs it," I blurted out. "He found a way to contact me, and he needs *The Book of Moons*. He's trying to get back here."

"Have you gotten another message?" Marian asked.

I nodded. "In the latest *Stars and Stripes*." I took a deep breath. "I need you to trust me." I looked into her eyes. "And I need your help."

Marian studied me for a long moment. I don't know what she was thinking, or debating, or even deciding. All I know is, she didn't say a word.

I don't think she could.

Then she nodded, pulling her chair a bit closer to me. "Tell me everything."

So I started talking. We took turns filling in the blanks— Link and John all but acting out our encounter with Abraham, and Rid and Uncle Macon helping me explain our plan to trade John for *The Book of Moons*. Liv looked on unhappily, as if she could hardly bear to hear it.

Marian didn't say a word until we finished, though it was easy to read her expressions, which ranged from shock and horror to sympathy and despair.

"Is that everything?" She looked at me, exhausted by our story.

"It gets worse." I looked at Ridley.

"You mean aside from the fact that Link dissected Abraham with the giant scissors?" Rid made a face.

"No, Rid. Tell her about Abraham's plans. Tell her what you heard about Angelus," I said.

Uncle Macon's head snapped up at the sound of the Keeper's name. "What is Lena talking about, Ridley?"

"Angelus and Abraham were up to something, but I don't know the details." She shrugged.

"Tell us exactly what you know."

Ridley twisted a lock of pink hair around her finger nervously. "This Angelus guy is a nutcase. He hates Mortals, and he thinks the Dark Casters and the Far Keep should be in control of the Mortal world, or something like that."

"Why?" Marian was thinking out loud. Her fists were clenched so tightly that her knuckles were white. Marian's own trouble with the Far Keep was all too fresh in her memory.

Rid shrugged. "Ah, maybe because he's *Special K-razy?*"

Marian looked over at my uncle, a silent conversation passing between them. "We can't let Angelus gain a foothold here. He's far too dangerous."

Uncle M nodded. "I agree. We need—"

I cut him off before he could finish. "All I know is first we need to get *The Book of Moons* to Ethan. There's still a chance we can get him back."

"Do you really think so?" Marian said the words quietly, almost under her breath. Though I couldn't be certain, it seemed like only I could hear them. Still, I knew Marian believed in the impossibilities of the Caster world—she'd seen them firsthand— and she loved Ethan as much as I did. He was like a son to her.

We both wanted to believe.

I nodded. "I do. I have to."

She rose from her chair and came back around the desk, poised as ever.

"Then it's settled. We'll get Ethan *The Book of Moons*, one way or another." I smiled at her, but she was already lost in thought, looking around the library as if it held the answers to all our problems.

Which, sometimes, it did.

"There has to be a way, right?" John asked. "Maybe in one of these scrolls or one of these old books—"

Ridley unscrewed the top of her nail polish bottle, wrinkling her nose. "Goody. Old books."

"Try to have a bit more respect, Ridley. A *book* is the reason the children in the Duchannes family suffered for generations." Marian was referring to our curse.

Rid crossed her arms, pouting. "Whatever."

Marian swiped the bottle out of her hand. "Another thing I don't allow in my library." It clattered to the bottom of the trash can.

Ridley glared, but she didn't say a word.

"Dr. Ashcroft, have you ever delivered a book to the Otherworld?" Liv asked.

Marian shook her head. "I can't say that I have."

"Maybe Carlton Eaton could just run it on over." Link looked hopeful. "You could wrap it up in one a those brown paper packages, like you do for my mom's books. And, you know, circulate it or somethin'."

Marian sighed. "I'm afraid not, Wesley." Even Carlton Eaton, who had his nose in every letter in town in both the Mortal and Caster worlds, couldn't make a delivery like that.

Frustrated, Liv flipped through her little red note-book. "There has to be a way. What were the odds you could get the Book from Abraham at all? And now that we have it, we're just going to give up?" She pulled the pencil from behind her ear, scribbling and mumbling to herself. "The laws of quantum physics must allow for this sort of eventuality...."

I didn't know anything about the laws of quantum physics, but I knew one thing. "The stone from my charm necklace disappeared when I left it for Ethan. Why would the Book be any different?"

I know you took it, Ethan. Why couldn't you take the Book, too?

I realized Uncle Macon could probably hear me, and I tried to stop.

It was no use. I couldn't stop Kelting any more than I could stop the words that strung themselves together, waiting for me to write them down somewhere.

laws of physics
laws of love
of time and space
and the (in)between place
(in)between you and me
and where we are
lost and looking
looking and lost

"Maybe the Book's too heavy," Link offered. "That little black rock wasn't any bigger than a quarter."

"I'm not sure that's the reason, Wesley. Though anything is possible," Marian said.

"Or impossible." Ridley pushed her sunglasses back into place and stuck out her red tongue.

"So why can't it make the jump?" John asked.

Marian glanced at Liv's notes, considering the question. "*The Book of Moons* is a powerful supernatural object. No one really understands the scope of its power. Not the Keepers or the Casters."

"And if the origin of its magic is in the Caster world, it could be deeply rooted here," Liv said. "The way a tree is rooted to a particular spot."

"Are you saying the Book doesn't want to cross over?" John asked.

Liv tucked the pencil behind her ear. "I'm saying maybe it can't."

"Or shouldn't." Uncle Macon's tone grew more serious.

Ridley slid to the floor and stretched out her long legs. "This is so messed up. I risked my life, and now we're stuck with that thing. Maybe we need to hit the Tunnels and see if any of the other bad guys know the answer. You know—Team Dark."

Liv crossed her arms over her EDISON DIDN'T INVENT THE LIGHTBULB T-shirt. "You want to take *The Book of Moons* to a Dark Caster bar?"

"You have a better idea?" Rid asked.

"I think I do." Marian slipped her red wool jacket on.

Liv scrambled after her. "Where are you going?"

"To see someone who knows a great deal about not just that book but a world that defies the physics of both the Caster and Mortal worlds. Someone who just may have the answers we need."

My uncle nodded. "An excellent idea."

There was only one person who fit that description.

Someone who loved Ethan as much as I did. Someone who would do anything for him, even rip a hole in the universe.

⊰ CHAPTER 27 ⊱

The Cracks in Everything

Now, don't you tell me you're thinkin' a settin' foot on my front walkway, you hear?" Amma refused to let Ridley anywhere near Wate's Landing. She said so in about fifteen different ways in the first conversation we unsuccessfully tried to have with her.

"Mmmm-nnnnnnn. No Dark Casters are comin' into this house while I'm here on this sweet earth. Or after I leave it. No, sir. No, ma'am. No how."

She agreed to meet us at Greenbrier instead.

Uncle Macon hung back. "It's better this way. Amarie and I haven't seen each other since the night…it happened," he explained. "I'm not sure this is the right moment."

"So what you're saying is that you're scared of her, too?" Ridley eyed him with new interest. "Imagine that."

"I'll be at Ravenwood if you need me," he said, giving Ridley a withering stare.

"Imagine that." I smiled.

The rest of us waited inside the crumbling wall of the old graveyard. I resisted the urge to wander over to Ethan's plot, though I felt the familiar pull, the longing to be with him there. I believed, with all my heart, that there was a way to get Ethan back, and I wasn't going to stop trying until I found it.

Amma was hopeful, too, but I had seen the fear and doubt in her eyes. She had already lost him twice. Every time I took her another crossword puzzle, she was desperate to get him back.

I think Amma wasn't about to let herself believe in anything she could stand to lose again.

With the Book, though, we were one step closer.

Ridley was leaning against a tree, a safe distance from the hole in the stone wall. I knew she was just as afraid of Amma as Uncle Macon was, even if she wouldn't admit it.

"Don't say anything to her when she gets here," Link warned Ridley. "You know how she gets about that book."

Ridley rolled her eyes. "I thought Abraham was a pain. Amma's even worse."

I saw a black orthopedic lace-up step through the opening.

"Worse than what?" Amma demanded. "Worse than your manners?" She looked Ridley up and down. "Or your taste in clothes?"

313

She was wearing a yellow dress, all sunlight and sweetness, which didn't match her expression. Her grayish-black hair was twisted into a neat bun, and she was carrying a patterned quilting bag. I'd been around long enough to know there weren't any quilting supplies inside.

"Or a stitch worse than the girl who gets pulled outta Hell only to walk back into the fire on her own?" Amma watched Ridley carefully.

Ridley didn't take off her sunglasses, but I could see the shame anyway. I knew her too well. There was something about Amma that made you feel completely awful if you disappointed her—even if you were a Siren with no ties to her.

"That's not what happened," Ridley said quietly.

Amma dropped her bag on the ground. "Isn't it, then? I have it on good authority that you had a chance to be on the right side a wrong for once, and you gave it up. Did I miss somethin' in the fine print?"

Ridley shifted nervously. "It's not that simple."

Amma sniffed. "You go on tellin' yourself that if it helps you sleep at night, but don't try to sell it to me, because I'm not buyin' it." Amma pointed to the lollipop in Ridley's hand. "And all that sugar will rot those teeth right outta your head, Caster or no Caster."

Link laughed nervously.

Amma focused her eagle eye on him. "What're you laughin' about, Wesley Lincoln? You're knee deep in more trouble than the day I caught you in my basement when you were nine years old."

Link's face reddened. "It sorta finds me, ma'am."

"You know you go lookin' for it, sure as the sun shines the same on the saints as it does on the sinners." She glanced at each of us. "So what is it this time? And it better not have anythin' to do with destroyin' the balance a the universe."

"All saints, ma'am. No sinners." Link backed away an inch or two, looking at me for help.

"Spit it out. I've got Aunt Mercy and Aunt Grace at the house, and I can't leave them alone with Thelma for too long, or the three a them will order everything that comes on the shoppin' channel." Amma rarely called Ethan's great-aunts "the Sisters" anymore, now that one of them was gone.

But now it was Marian who walked over and took Amma's arm reassuringly. "It's about *The Book of Moons*."

"*We have it*," I blurted out.

Liv stepped aside, revealing *The Book of Moons* lying on the ground behind her. Amma's eyes widened. "Do I wanna know how you got it?"

Link jumped in. "Nope. I mean no, ma'am, you sure don't."

"The fact remains we have it now," Marian said.

"But we can't get it to Ethan—" I heard the desperation in my voice.

Amma shook her head and approached the Book, circling it like she didn't want to get too close. "'Course you can't.

This book is too powerful for one world. If you want to send it from the world a the livin' to the world a the dead, we'll need the power a both worlds to send it."

I wasn't sure what she meant, but I only cared about one thing. "Will you help us?"

"Not my help you need. You need help on the receivin' end."

Liv inched closer to Amma. "We left the Book for Ethan, but he didn't take it."

She sniffed. "Hmm. Ethan's not strong enough to carry that kinda weight across. He probably doesn't even know how."

"But there is someone strong enough," Marian coaxed. "Perhaps more than one someone." She was talking about the Greats.

The question was, would Amma call them?

I bit my lip.

Please say yes.

"Figured if you were callin', you were lookin' to test out just how far crazy will go." Amma opened the quilting bag and took out a shot glass and a bottle of Wild Turkey. "So I came prepared." She poured a shot and pointed to me. "You're gonna have to help, though. We need the power a both worlds, don't forget."

I nodded. "I'll do whatever I need to."

Amma nodded in the direction of Ravenwood. "You can start by gatherin' up the rest a your kin. You don't have the kinda power we need on your own."

"Rid is here, and John can help, too. He's half Caster."

Amma shook her head. "If you want that book to cross, you're gonna have to go get the rest a them."

"They're in Barbados."

"Actually, they returned a few hours ago," Marian said. "Reece stopped by the library earlier tonight. She said your grandmother wasn't fond of the humidity."

I tried not to smile. What my grandmother wasn't fond of was missing all the action, and Reece wasn't much better. With every Caster power in my extended family, I was certain they knew something was going on.

"I could ask them. But they might be tired from all the travel." I was worried enough that Uncle M was going to change his mind about all this. Adding the rest of my family into the mix fell somewhere between risky and idiotic.

Amma crossed her arms, as determined as I'd ever seen her. "What I know is that this book isn't going anywhere without them."

There was no use arguing with her. I had watched Ethan try to talk her down when her mind was made up, and he rarely succeeded. And Amma loved him more than anyone in the world. I didn't stand a chance.

Ridley nodded at me. "I'll go with you for backup."

"Your mom will freak if you just show up. I'm going to have to tell her you're back. And I should probably tell them that you've—" I hesitated. It wasn't going to be easy for anyone in my family to deal with the fact that Ridley ran back to Sarafine for her Dark Caster powers. "Changed."

Link looked away.

That wasn't the worst of it. "It's going to be hard enough to explain to Gramma why I have the Book."

Rid slung her arm over my shoulder. "Don't you know that the best way to distract someone from bad news is to give them some worse news?" She smiled, leading me toward Ravenwood. "News doesn't get much worse than me."

Link shook his head. "No kidding."

Ridley spun around and pushed her sunglasses up. "Zip it, Shrinky Dink. Or I'll make you want to rip into your mother's room and tell her you're becoming a Methodist."

"Your powers don't work on me anymore, Babe."

Ridley blew him a sticky pink kiss. "Try me."

CHAPTER 28

Caster Catfight

I opened the front door, and the air inside the house seemed to move. No—it was moving. Hundreds of butterflies fluttered through the air while others rested on the delicate antique furniture Uncle Macon had spent years collecting.

Butterflies.

What was I doing to Ravenwood?

A tiny green butterfly with streaks of gold across its wings landed on the bottom of the banister.

"Macon?" Gramma's voice called from the second floor. "Is that you?"

"No, Gramma. It's me. Lena."

She swept down the stairs in a high-neck white blouse, her

hair gathered neatly in a bun and her lace-up boots peeking out from under her long skirt. Against the perfectly restored flying staircase, she looked like a Southern belle right out of an old movie.

She glanced at the butterflies flitting around the room and gave me a hug. "I'm so glad to see you're in a good mood."

Gramma knew Ravenwood's interior constantly changed to mirror my moods. To her, a room full of butterflies meant happiness. But for me, it meant something entirely different— something I had been clinging to tightly.

Hope, borne on green and gold wings. Dark and Light, like I had become the night of my Claiming.

I touched the wire Christmas tree star on my charm necklace. I had to focus. Everything had come down to this. Ethan was out there somewhere, and there was a chance we could bring him home. I just had to convince my family to lend their powers to us.

"Gramma, I need your help with something."

"Of course, sweetheart."

She wouldn't be saying that if she knew what I was about to tell her. "What if I told you I found *The Book of Moons*?"

Gramma froze. "Why would you ask me something like that, Lena? Do you know where it is?"

I nodded.

She gathered her skirt, rushing toward the stairs. "We have to tell Macon. The sooner we get that book back to the *Lunae Libri*, the better."

"We can't."

Gramma turned around slowly, her eyes looking right through me. "Start explaining, young lady. And you can start by telling me how you found *The Book of Moons*."

Ridley stepped out from behind a marble column. "I helped her."

For one long moment, I held my breath, until it became clear Ravenwood wasn't about to fall to the ground.

"How did you get in here?" Gramma's voice was as controlled as Ridley's, maybe more. She'd been around a long time, and it would take more than my Dark-again cousin to throw her.

"Lena let me in."

There was a flicker of disappointment in my grandmother's eyes. "I see you're wearing your sunglasses again."

"It was kind of a self-preservation thing." Ridley bit her lip nervously. "The world's a dangerous place."

It was something my grandmother said to us all the time when we were kids—particularly to Ridley. I remembered something else she said, something that might delay the confession of the Abraham story long enough for me to get the Book to Ethan.

"Gramma, do you remember the deal you made with Ridley the first time she went to a party?"

She looked at me blankly. "I'm not sure I do."

"You told her not to get in a car with anyone who had been drinking."

"Certainly good advice, but I'm not sure how it relates to this situation."

"You told Rid that if she called and said her ride was drinking, you would send someone to pick her up, no questions asked." I saw a hint of recognition pass across her face. "You said she wouldn't get in trouble, no matter where she was or what she did."

Ridley leaned against the column awkwardly. "Yeah. It was like a Get Out of Jail Free card. I definitely needed one of those recently."

"Is this conversation going to explain why you two are in possession of the most dangerous book in the Caster or Mortal world?" Gramma looked skeptically from my cousin to me.

"I'm calling to tell you my ride has been drinking," I blurted out.

"Pardon me?"

"I need you to trust me and do something without asking any questions. Something for Ethan."

"Lena, Ethan is—"

I held up my hand. "Don't say it. We both know people can communicate from the other side. Ethan sent me a message. And I need your help."

"She's telling the truth. At least she thinks she is, for what it's worth." Reece was standing in the darkened doorway to the dining room. I hadn't even seen her, but she had obviously seen me. It only took a Sybil one look at your face to read it, and Reece was among the best. Finally, it was working to my advantage.

"Even if you are telling the truth, you are asking for more than just a little faith. And no matter how much I love you, I can't help you use—"

"We aren't trying to use *The Book of Moons*." I wondered if she would believe me. "We're trying to send it to Ethan."

The room was silent, and I waited for her to say something. "What would lead you to believe that's possible?"

I explained the messages Ethan had been leaving in the crosswords, but I left out the part about how we actually got our hands on *The Book of Moons*, invoking the "my ride is drunk" clause. I wouldn't get away with it forever. Eventually, Gramma would insist on an explanation. But I didn't need forever—just tonight. After we sent the Book to Ethan, Gramma could interrogate me all she wanted.

Besides, Uncle M already had first dibs on the grounding.

She listened carefully, sipping from a black porcelain tea-cup that appeared in her hand, compliments of Kitchen. She didn't offer a single word, and she didn't look away from me as I spoke.

Finally, the cup found its way back into the saucer, and I knew she had made a decision. My grandmother drew a deep breath. "If Ethan needs our assistance, we have no choice but to give it to him. After what he sacrificed for us all, it's the least we can do."

"Gramma!" Reece threw up her hands. "Listen to yourself!"

"How can she, when you're yelling?" Ridley snapped.

Reece ignored her. "You're really going to send the most powerful book in the Caster universe into the Otherworld, with no way of knowing who'll be on the other end?"

Rid shrugged. "At least you won't be there."

Reece looked like she wanted to stab Ridley with garden shears of her own.

"Ethan will be there," I argued.

Gramma hesitated, a new thought shaking her resolve. "It's not as if we are shipping a package, Lena. What if the Book doesn't end up where we intend?"

Reece looked satisfied. Ridley looked like now she was the one thinking about garden shears.

"Amma's going to call the Greats."

Gramma finished her tea, and the cup vanished. "Well, if Amarie is involved, I'm sure she has a plan. I'll get my coat."

"Wait." I looked over at Reece. "We need everyone to come. Amma says we won't have enough power unless we do this together."

Reece looked at Uncle Macon, who had sidled into the room at the first sign of the Caster family fighting. "Are you going to let her do this?"

He chose his words carefully. "On the one hand, I think this is a very bad idea."

"There." Reece smiled.

"What?" Losing my uncle's support was the one thing I had been afraid of when Amma sent me for reinforcements.

"Let him finish, girls." Gramma raised her voice.

"But," Uncle M continued, "we owe Ethan a debt we will never be able to properly repay. I watched him give his life for us, and I don't take that lightly."

I exhaled. *Thank goodness.*

"Uncle Macon—" Reece started.

He silenced her with a gesture. "This isn't up for discussion. If it weren't for Ethan, you could be powerless right now—or worse. The Order was broken, and we were only beginning to see the effects. Things were headed in a very grave direction indeed. I promise you that."

"I don't know why we're still talking about it, then." Gramma gathered her skirt and ascended the stairs. "I'll get Del, Barclay, and Ryan."

Ridley swallowed hard at the sound of her mother's name. Aunt Del was always heartsick when Ridley disappeared, and she had no idea her daughter was back. Or that she had returned as a Dark Caster.

I remembered how happy Aunt Del looked when Ridley lost her powers last summer. Being a Mortal was better than being Dark, especially in this family.

Reece turned to face her sister. "You shouldn't be here. Haven't you put everyone through enough pain?"

Ridley stiffened. "I thought you deserved a little more, Sis. Wouldn't want to leave you hanging. I mean, seeing how you've always been there for me." She said it sarcastically, but I could hear the pain. Ridley only pretended she didn't have a heart.

I heard voices, and Aunt Del appeared at the top of the staircase. Uncle Barclay's arm was wrapped tightly around her. I wasn't sure if she'd overheard us or if Gramma told her about Ridley. But I could tell by the way Aunt Del was wringing her hands that she already knew the truth.

Uncle Barclay led her down the stairs, his tall frame looming over her. His salt-and-pepper hair was combed neatly, and for once he looked like he belonged in the same era as the rest of us. Ryan trailed behind them, her long blond hair swinging in a ponytail.

When Ryan and Ridley were standing in the same room, it was impossible to ignore how much they resembled each other. In the last six months, Ryan had come to look more like a teenager than a little girl, even though she was only twelve.

Aunt Del smiled at Rid weakly. "I'm glad you're all right. I was so worried."

Ridley bit her lip and teetered on her stacked heels. "I'm sorry, you know. I couldn't exactly call."

"Abraham had Rid locked up." I blurted it out before I could stop myself. Ridley was guilty of lots of things, but it was hard to watch them judge her for something that was out of her control.

Aunt Del's face crumpled—everyone's did, except for

Reece's. She positioned herself protectively between her mother and her Dark sister.

"Is that true?" Uncle Barclay sounded genuinely concerned.

Ridley twisted a pink strand between her fingers nervously. "Yeah. He was a real prince." She Kelted to me desperately. *Don't tell them, Cuz. Not now.* "I'm fine," Ridley went on, waving off her father's concern. "Let's worry about Ethan. No one wants to hear about me and the Big Bad Wolf."

Ryan stepped closer to Ridley tentatively. "I do," she said quietly.

Rid didn't respond. Instead, she held out her empty hand.

I waited for a mouse or a lollipop to appear in her palm, some cheap trick to distract her sister from what she was now. But her hand stayed empty.

Ryan smiled and reached out her own hand, closing it around Ridley's.

I heard Aunt Del's breath catch, or maybe it was mine.

"If Lena trusts you, so do I," Ryan said. She looked at Reece. "Sisters should trust each other."

Reece didn't move, but I didn't need to be a Sybil to read her face.

Tiny cracks were already forming in the tough exterior Reece worked so hard to maintain. They were hard to see, but they were there. The beginning of something—tears, forgiveness, regret—I couldn't be sure.

It reminded me of something Marian told Ethan before everything happened. It was one of her famous quotes, by a guy named Leonard Cohen: "There is a crack in everything. That's how the light gets in."

That's what I thought of when I saw Reece's face.

The light was finally getting in.

"Lena, are you all right?" Uncle Barclay glanced at the ceiling. The crystal chandelier was swinging dangerously above us.

I took a deep breath, and it stopped immediately. *Get control of yourself.*

"I'm fine," I lied.

I composed the words in my head, even if I wouldn't let my pen write them.

bent
like the branches of a tree
broken
like the pieces of my heart
cracked
like the seventeenth moon
shattered
like the glass in the window
the day we met

I closed my eyes, trying to silence the words that wouldn't stop coming.

No.

I ignored them, forcing them out of my mind. I wasn't Kelt-

328

ing them to Uncle Macon, and I wasn't writing a word until Ethan came back.

Not a single word.

"Amarie is expecting us. We should go." Uncle Macon slipped on his black cashmere coat. "She is not a woman who appreciates being kept waiting."

Boo lumbered behind him, his thick fur blending seamlessly into the darkness of the room.

Ridley opened the door, fleeing as fast as she could. She unwrapped a red lollipop before she even made it down the steps of the veranda. She hesitated for a second near the flower bed before pocketing the wrapper.

Maybe people could change—even the ones who made the wrong choices, if they tried hard enough to make them right. I wasn't sure, but I hoped so. I had made enough bad choices myself in the last year.

I walked toward the only one that had been right.

The only one that mattered.

Ethan.

I'm coming.

CHAPTER 29

The Hands of the Dead

It's about time." Her arms crossed impatiently, Amma was staring at the opening in the old stone wall when we stepped through.

Uncle Macon was right; she didn't like to be kept waiting.

Marian gently put her hand on Amma's shoulder. "I'm sure it was difficult to round everyone up."

Amma sniffed, ignoring the excuse. "There's difficult, and then there's difficult."

John and Liv were sitting on the ground next to each other, Liv's head resting casually on John's shoulder. Uncle Barclay stepped through after me and helped Aunt Del navigate the broken pieces of the wall. She blinked hard, staring at a spot not far from Genevieve's grave. She swayed, and Uncle Barclay steadied her.

The layers of time were obviously peeling themselves back, the way they did only for Aunt Del.

I wondered what she saw. So much had happened at Greenbrier. Ethan Carter Wate's death, the first time Genevieve used *The Book of Moons* to bring him back, the day Ethan and I found her locket and had the vision, and the night Aunt Del used her powers to show us those pieces of Genevieve's past in this very spot.

But everything had changed since then. The day Ethan and I were trying to figure out how to repair the Order and I accidentally burned the grass beneath us.

When I watched my mother burn to death.

Can Aunt Del see all of it? Can she see that?

An unexpected feeling of shame washed over me, and I secretly hoped she couldn't.

Amma nodded at Gramma. "Emmaline. You're lookin' well."

Gramma smiled. "As are you, Amarie."

Uncle Macon was the last one to enter the lost garden. He lingered near the wall, an uncharacteristic and almost imperceptible unease about him.

Amma locked eyes with him, as if they were having a conversation that only they could hear.

The tension was impossible to ignore. I hadn't seen them together since the night we lost Ethan. And both of them claimed everything was *fine*.

331

But now that they were standing only feet apart, it was clear nothing was fine. Actually, Amma looked like she wanted to tear my uncle's head off.

"Amarie," he said slowly, bowing his head respectfully.

"I'm surprised you showed up. Aren't you worried some a my wickedness might stain those fancy shoes a yours?" she said. "Wouldn't want that. Not when your party shoes cost such a pretty penny."

What is she talking about?

Amma was a saint—at least that's how I'd always thought of her.

Gramma and Aunt Del exchanged glances, looking equally confused. Marian turned away. She knew something, but she wasn't saying.

"Grief makes people desperate," Uncle M responded. "If anyone understands that, I do."

Amma turned her back on him, facing the whiskey and shot glass lying on the ground next to *The Book of Moons*. "I'm not sure you understand anything that doesn't suit your purpose, Melchizedek. If I didn't think we'd need your help, I would send you packin' straight back to your house."

"That's hardly fair. I was trying to protect you—" Uncle Macon stopped when he noticed we were all staring. All of us except Marian and John, who were doing everything they could not to look at Amma or my uncle. That pretty much meant looking at the mud on the ground or *The Book of Moons*, neither of which was going to make anyone any less uncomfortable.

Amma spun back around to face Uncle Macon. "Next time, try protectin' me a little less and my boy a little more. If there is a next time."

Did she blame Uncle Macon for not doing a better job of protecting Ethan when he was alive? It didn't make any sense....

"Why are you two fighting like this?" I demanded. "You're acting like Reece and Ridley."

"Hey," said Reece. Rid just shrugged.

I shot Amma and my uncle a look. "I thought we were here to help Ethan."

Amma sniffed, and my uncle looked unhappy, but neither of them said a word.

Marian finally spoke up. "I think we're all worried. It would probably be best if we put everything else aside and focused on the issue at hand. Amma, what is it you need us to do?"

Amma didn't take her eyes off my uncle. "Need the Casters to form a circle around me. Mortals can spread out between 'em. We need the power a this world to hand that evil thing off to the ones who can take it the rest a the way."

"The Greats, right?" I hoped so.

She nodded. "If they answer."

If they answered? Was there a chance they wouldn't?

Amma pointed to the ground at my feet. "Lena, I need you to bring me the Book."

I lifted the dusty leather volume and felt the power pulsing through it like a heartbeat.

"The Book's not gonna want to go," Amma explained. "It wants to stay here, where it can cause trouble. Like your cousin there." Ridley rolled her eyes, but Amma only looked at me. "I'll call the Greats, but you need to keep a hand on it till they take it."

What was it going to do? Fly away?

"Everyone else, make that circle. Hold hands nice and tight."

After Ridley and Link bickered about holding hands, and Reece refused to hold hands with Ridley or John, they finally completed the circle.

Amma glanced over at me. "The Greats haven't been exactly happy with me. They may not come. And if they do, I can't promise they'll take the Book."

I couldn't imagine the Greats being upset with Amma. They were her family, and they had come to our rescue more than once.

We just needed them to do it one more time.

"I need the Casters to concentrate everything you got inside the circle." Amma bent down and filled the shot glass with Wild Turkey. She drank the shot and then refilled it for Uncle Abner. "I don't care what happens—you send the power my way."

"What if you get hurt?" Liv asked, concerned.

Amma stared back at Liv, her expression twisted and broken. "Can't get any more hurt than I am already. You just hold on."

Uncle Macon stepped forward, dropping Aunt Del's hand. "Would it help if I assisted you?" he asked Amma.

She pointed a shaky finger at him. "You get outta my circle. You can do your part from there."

I felt a surge of heat from the Book, as if its anger flared to meet Amma's.

Uncle Macon stepped back and joined hands with everyone else. "One day you will forgive me, Amarie."

Her dark eyes narrowed to meet his green ones. "Not today."

Amma closed her eyes, and my hair began to curl involuntarily as she spoke the words only she could.

> "Blood a my blood,
> and roots a my soul,
> I'm in need a your intercession."

The wind began to whip around me within the circle, and lightning cracked overhead. I felt the heat of the Book joining with the heat of my hands, the heat I could command—to burn and destroy.

Amma didn't stop, as if she was talking to the sky.

> "I call you to carry what I cannot.
> To see what I cannot.
> To do what I cannot."

A green glow surged from Uncle Macon's hands and spread around the circle from one hand to the next. Gramma closed her eyes, as if she was trying to channel Macon's power. John noticed and closed his eyes, too, and the light intensified.

Lightning tore across the sky, but the universe didn't open up, and the Greats didn't appear.

Where are you? I pleaded silently.

Amma tried again.

"This is the crossroads I can't cross.
Only you can take this book to my boy.
Deliver it to your world from ours."

I concentrated harder, ignoring the heat of the Book in my hands. I heard a branch break, then another. I opened my eyes, and a burst of flames sprang up outside the circle. It caught like someone had lit the wick on a stick of dynamite, tearing through the grass and creating another circle outside the first.

The Wake of Fire—the uncontrollable flames that ignited sometimes against my will. The garden was burning again because of me. How many times could this earth char before the damage was irreparable?

Amma squeezed her eyes tighter. This time she spoke the words plainly. They weren't a chant but a plea. "I know you don't wanna come for me. So come for Ethan. He's waitin' on you, and you're as much his family as you are mine. Do the right thing. One last time. Uncle Abner. Aunt Delilah. Aunt Ivy. Grandmamma Sulla. Twyla. Please."

The sky opened up, and rain poured down from the heavens. But the fire still raged, and the Caster light still glowed.

I saw something small and black circling above us.

The crow.

Ethan's crow.

Amma opened her eyes and saw it, too. "That's right, Uncle Abner. Don't punish Ethan for my mistakes. I know you been lookin' after him over there, the same way you've always looked after us down here. He needs this book. Maybe you know why, even if I don't."

The crow circled closer and closer, and the faces began to appear in the dark sky, one by one—their features carving themselves out of the universe above us.

Uncle Abner appeared first, his lined face creased by time.

The crow landed on his shoulder like a tiny mouse at the feet of a giant.

Sulla the Prophet was next, regal braids cascading over her shoulder. Strands of tangled beads rested against her chest as if they weighed nothing. Or were worth the weight.

The Book of Moons bucked in my hands, as if trying to pull free. But I knew it wasn't the Greats reaching for it.

The Book was resisting.

I tightened my grip as Aunt Delilah and Aunt Ivy appeared simultaneously, holding hands and looking down like they were evaluating the scene. Our intentions or our abilities—it was impossible to know.

But they were judging us nonetheless. I could feel it, and

the Book could, too. It tried to pull free again, singeing the skin on my palms.

"Don't let go!" Amma warned.

"I won't," I called over the wind. "Aunt Twyla, where are you?"

Aunt Twyla's dark eyes appeared before her gentle face and arms laden with bracelets. Before her braided hair knotted with charms, or the rows of earrings that marched down her ears.

"Ethan needs this!" I shouted over the wind and the rain and the fire.

The Greats stared down at us, but they didn't react.

The Book of Moons did.

I felt the pulse beating within it, the power and rage spreading through my body like poison.

Don't let go.

Images flashed in front of my eyes.

Genevieve holding the Book, speaking the words that would bring Ethan Carter Wate back for a split second—and curse our family for generations.

Amma and me speaking the same words, standing over Ethan Lawson Wate—our Ethan.

His eyes opening and Uncle Macon's closing.

Abraham standing over the Book as the fire threatened Ravenwood in the distance, his brother's voice begging him to stop, right before he killed Jonah.

I could see it all.

338

All the people this book had touched and hurt.

The people I knew and the ones I didn't recognize.

I could feel it pulling away from me again, and I screamed louder this time.

Amma grabbed the Book, her hands over mine. Where parts of her skin were touching the leather, I could feel her skin burning.

Tears formed in her eyes, but she didn't let go.

"Help us," I screamed into the sky.

It wasn't the sky that answered.

Genevieve Duchannes materialized in the darkness, her hazy form close enough to touch.

Give it to me.

Amma could see her; it was obvious from her haunted expression. But I was the only one who could hear her Kelting.

Her long red hair blew in the wind, in a way that seemed both impossible and right at the same time.

I'll take it. It doesn't belong in this world. It never did.

I wanted to hand her the Book—to send it to Ethan and to stop Amma's hands from burning.

But Genevieve was a Dark Caster. I only had to look at her yellow eyes to remember.

Amma was trembling.

Genevieve reached out her hand. What if I made the wrong choice? Ethan would never get the Book, and I would never see him again....

How do I know I can trust you?

Genevieve's heartbroken eyes stared back at me.

You'll only know if you do.

The Greats looked down at us, and there was no way to know if they were going to help. Amma's Mortal hands were burning alongside my Caster ones, and *The Book of Moons* was no closer to Ethan than when it was in Abraham Ravenwood's hands, not long ago.

Sometimes there's only one choice.

Sometimes you just have to jump.

Or let go...

Take it, Genevieve.

I pulled my hands away, and Amma's moved with mine. The Book jerked free as if it sensed its only chance at escape. It lurched toward the outer circle, where John and Link were holding hands.

The glowing green light was still in place, and John concentrated his gaze on the Book. "I don't think so."

It hit the light and ricocheted back into the center of the circle and Genevieve's waiting hands. She closed her hazy palms around it, and the Book seemed to shudder.

Not this time.

I held my breath, listening to Amma cry.

Genevieve pressed the Book against her chest and dematerialized.

My heart dropped. "Amma! She took it!" I couldn't think or feel or breathe. I had made the wrong choice. I would never see Ethan again. My knees gave out, and I felt myself falling.

I heard a rip, and an arm caught me around the waist.

"Lena, look." It was Link.

I blinked back the tears and looked at him, his free hand pointing at the sky.

Genevieve was there in the darkness, her red hair trailing behind her. She held *The Book of Moons* out to Sulla, who took it from her hands.

Genevieve smiled at me.

You can trust me. I'm sorry. I'm so sorry.

She disappeared, leaving the Greats looming in the sky behind her like giants.

Amma held her burnt hands to her chest and stared up at her family from another world. The world where Ethan was trapped. Tears ran down her cheeks as the green glow died around us.

"You take that book to my boy, ya hear?"

Uncle Abner tipped his hat to her. "Be expectin' a pie now, Amma. One a those lemon meringues will do me just fine."

Amma choked back a final sob as her legs gave out from under her.

I dropped with her, breaking her fall. I watched as the rain drowned out the fire and the Greats disappeared. I had no way of knowing what was going to happen next. There was only one thing I knew for sure.

Ethan had a chance now.

The rest was up to him.

BOOK THREE

Ethan

⊰ CHAPTER 30 ⊱

Lost Time

L. *Are you there? Can you hear me? I'm waiting. I know you'll find the Book soon.*

You wouldn't believe this place. I feel like I'm living in a ten-thousand-year-old temple, or maybe a fortress. You wouldn't believe this guy either. My friend Xavier. At least I think he's my friend. He's like a ten-thousand-year-old monk. Or maybe some kind of ancient temple wombat.

Do you know what waiting feels like in a world where no time passes? Minutes feel like centuries—eternities—only worse, because you can't even tell which is which.

I find myself counting things. Compulsively. It's the only way I know how to mark the time.

Sixty-two plastic buttons. Eleven broken strands of between fourteen and thirty-six pearls each. One hundred and nine old baseball cards. Nine AA batteries. Twelve thousand seven hundred and fifty-four dollars and three cents in coins, from six countries. Or maybe just six centuries.

More or less.

I didn't know how to count the doubloons.

This morning I counted grains of rice falling through the split seam of a stuffed frog. I don't know where Xavier finds this stuff. I made it to nine hundred ninety-nine, and then I lost my place and had to start over again.

That was how I spent today.

Like I said, a person could go crazy trying to pass the time in a place with no time. When you find The Book of Moons, *L, I'll know. I'll be out of here the second I can. I keep my stuff ready to go, by the mouth of the cave. Aunt Prue's map. An empty flask of whiskey and a tobacco tin.*

Don't ask.

Can you believe, after everything, that the Book is still coming between us? I know you're going to find it. One day. You will.

And I'll be waiting.

I'm not sure if thinking about Lena makes the time pass faster or slower. But it doesn't matter. I couldn't stop thinking about her if I tried. Which I have—playing chess with these creepy figures Xavier collects. Helping him catalog everything from bottle caps and marbles to ancient Caster volumes. Today it's stones. Xavier must have hundreds of them, ranging from raw diamonds as big as strawberries to chunks of quartz and plain old rocks.

"It's important to keep careful records of everything I have." Xavier added three hunks of coal to the list.

I stared at the rocks in front of me. Gravel, Amma would say. Just the right shade of gray for Dean Wilks' driveway. I wondered what Amma was doing right now. And my mom. The two women who raised me were in two totally different worlds, and I couldn't see either of them.

I held up a handful of dusty driveway gravel. "Why do you collect these, anyway? They're just rocks."

Xavier looked shocked. "Stones have power. They absorb people's feelings and their fears. Even their memories."

I didn't need anyone else's fears. I had enough of my own.

I reached into my pocket and took out the black stone. I rubbed the smooth surface between my fingers. This one was Sulla's. It was shaped like a thick teardrop, while Lena's was rounder.

"Here." I held it out to Xavier. "You can add it to your collection."

I was pretty sure I wouldn't need it to cross the river again. I would either find my way back home or I would never leave here. Somehow I knew that, even if I didn't know anything else.

Xavier stared at the stone for a long minute. "You keep it, dead man. Those aren't—"

After that, I couldn't make out what he was saying. My vision started to blur, Xavier's leathery black skin and the stone in my palm shifting until they started to bleed together into a single dark shadow.

Sulla sat at an old wicker table, an oil lamp illuminating the small room. A spread was laid out in front of her, the Cards of Providence lined up in two neat rows, each stamped with a black sparrow in the corner—Sulla's mark. A tall man sat across from her, his smooth head gleaming in the light.

"The Bleeding Blade. Blind Man's Rage. Liar's Promise. The Stolen Heart." She frowned and shook her head. "Can tell you, none a this is good. What you're chasin', you ain't never gonna find. And it'll be worse if you do."

The man ran his huge hands over his scalp nervously. "What's that supposed to mean, Sulla? Stop talking in circles."

"It means they're never gonna give you what you want, Angelus. The Far Keep doesn't need a spread to know you've been breakin' their rules all along."

Angelus pushed away from the table violently. "I don't need them to give me what I want. I have other Keepers behind me. Keepers who want to be more than scribes. Why should we be forced to record history when we can be the ones who make it!"

"Can't change the cards—that's all I know."

Angelus stared at the beautiful woman with the golden skin and delicate braids. "Words can change things, Seer. You just have to put them in the right book."

Something caught Sulla's eye, and she was distracted for a moment. Her granddaughter crouched behind the door, listening. On any other night, Sulla wouldn't have minded. Amarie was seventeen, older than Sulla was when she learned to read cards. Sulla didn't want the girl to see this man. There was something evil inside him. She didn't need the cards to see that much.

Angelus started to stand, his huge hands clenched into fists.

Sulla tapped a card at the top of the spread, with a pair of golden gates inked across the face. "This one here's a wild card."

The man hesitated. "What does it mean?"

"Means sometimes we make our own fate. Things the cards can't see. Depends on which side a the gate you choose."

Angelus picked up the card, crumpling it in his hand. "I've stood outside the gates long enough."

The door slammed, and Amarie stepped out from her hiding place. "Who was that, Grandmamma?"

The older woman picked up the crumpled card, smoothing it with her hands. "He's a Keeper from up north. A man who wants more than any man should have."

"What does he want?"

Sulla's eyes met Amarie's, and for a second she was not sure if she would answer the girl. "To tamper with fate. Change the cards."

"But you can't change the cards."

Sulla looked away, remembering what she'd seen in the cards the day Amarie was born. "Sometimes you can. But there's always a price."

When I opened my eyes, Xavier was standing above me, his features twisted in concern. "What did you see, dead man?"

The black stone was warm in my hand. I squeezed it tighter, as if it could somehow bring me closer to Amma. To the memories locked within its shiny black surface. "How many times has Angelus changed *The Caster Chronicles*, Xavier?"

The Gatekeeper looked away, wringing his long fingers nervously.

"Xavier, answer me."

Our eyes met, and I saw the pain in his. "Too many times."

"Why is he doing it?" What did Angelus have to gain?

"Some men want to be more than Mortal. Angelus is one of those men."

"Are you saying he wanted to be a Caster?"

Xavier nodded slowly. "He wanted to change fate. To find a way to defy supernatural law and mix Mortal and Caster blood."

Genetic engineering. "So he wanted Mortals to have powers like Casters?"

Xavier ran his abnormally long hand over his bald head. "There is no reason to have power if you are left with no one to torment and control."

It didn't make sense. It was too late for Angelus. Was he, like Abraham Ravenwood, trying to create some kind of hybrid child? "Was he experimenting on children?"

Xavier turned away, and for a long moment he was silent. "He experimented on himself using Dark Casters."

A chill ran up my spine, and I couldn't swallow. I couldn't imagine what the Keeper must have done to them. I was trying to find the right words to ask, but Xavier told me before I had a chance.

"Angelus tested their blood, tissue—I don't know what else. And he injected a serum made from their blood into his own. It didn't give him the power he wanted. But he kept trying. Each injection made him paler and more desperate."

"That sounds horrible."

He turned his deformed face back toward mine. "That was not the horrible part, dead man. That would come later."

I didn't want to ask, but I couldn't stop myself. "What happened?"

"Eventually, he found a Caster whose blood gave him a mutated version of his own power. She was Light and beautiful and kind. And I..." He hesitated.

"Did you love her?"

His features looked more human than ever before. "I did. And Angelus destroyed her."

"I'm so sorry, Xavier."

He nodded. "She was a powerful Telepath before she went mad from Angelus' experiments."

A mind reader. Suddenly I understood.

"Are you saying Angelus can read minds?"

"Only Mortal ones."

Only Mortal ones. Like mine and Liv's and Marian's.

I needed to find my page in *The Caster Chronicles* and get back home.

"Don't look so sad, dead man."

I watched the hands on Xavier's clocks turn in different directions, marking the passage of time that didn't exist here. I didn't want to tell him that I wasn't sad.

I was afraid.

I kept my eyes on those clocks, but I still couldn't keep track of the time. Sometimes it got so bad that I started to forget what I was waiting for in the first place. Too much time will do that to you. Blur the edges between your memories and your imagination until everything feels like something you saw in a movie instead of your life.

I was beginning to give up on ever seeing *The Book of Moons* again. Which meant giving up on a whole lot more than some old Caster book.

It meant giving up on Gatlin, the good and the bad of it. Giving up on Amma and my dad and Aunt Marian. Link and Liv and John. Jackson High and the Dar-ee Keen and Wate's Landing and Route 9. The place where I first realized Lena was the girl from my dreams.

Giving up on the Book meant giving up on her.

I couldn't do that.

I wouldn't.

After what had to be a few days or a few weeks—it was impossible to know—Xavier realized I was losing more than time.

He was sitting on the dirt floor inside the cave, cataloging what looked like thousands of keys. "What did she look like?"

"Who?" I asked.

"The girl."

I watched him sort the keys by size, then shape. I wondered where they came from, whose doors they opened, as I searched for the right words. "She was…alive."

"Was she beautiful?"

Was she? It was getting harder to remember.

"Yeah. I think so."

Xavier stopped sorting the keys, watching me. "What did she look like, the girl?"

How could I tell him everything was swirling in my mind, blending together in a way that made it impossible to picture her clearly?

"Ethan? Did you hear me? You have to tell me. Otherwise you will forget. That's what happens if you spend too much time here. You'll lose everything that made you who you were. This place takes it from you."

I turned away before I answered. "I'm not sure. It's all a blur."

"Was her hair gold?" Xavier loved gold.

"No," I said. I was pretty sure, though I couldn't remember why. I stared at the wall in front of me, trying to picture her face. Then a single thought came to me, and I opened my eyes. "There were curls. Lots and lots of curls."

"The girl?"

"Yes." I looked at the rocky outcroppings at the top of the cave. "Lena."

"Her name is Lena?"

I nodded as tears began to stream down my face. I was so relieved I could still remember her name.

Hurry, Lena. I don't have much time left.

—⟡—

By the time I saw the crow again, I had forgotten. My memories were like dreams, except I never slept. I watched Xavier. I counted buttons and cataloged coins. I stared at the sky.

That's what I was trying to do now, but the stupid bird kept shrieking and flapping its enormous wings.

"Go away."

He shrieked even louder.

I rolled onto my side and swatted at him. That's when I saw the Book lying in the dirt in front of me.

"Xavier," I said, my voice unsteady. "Come here."

"What is it, dead man?" I heard him call from the cave.

"*The Book of Moons.*" I picked it up, and it was warm in my hands. But my hands didn't burn. I remembered thinking they should.

As I held the Book, my memories came flooding back to me. Just as this book had brought me back from the dead once before, so now was it bringing my life back to me again. I could picture every detail. The places I'd been. The things I'd done. The people I loved.

I could see Lena's delicate face. Her green and gold eyes and the crescent-shaped birthmark on her cheek. I remembered

355

lemons and rosemary and hurricane-force winds and spontaneous combustion. Everything that made Lena the girl I loved.

I was whole again.

And I knew I had to leave this place before it claimed me forever.

I picked up the Book in both hands and carried it into the cave. It was time to make a trade.

With every step, the Book was heavy in my hands. It didn't slow me down, though. Nothing could, not now.

Not until there were no more steps to take.

The Gates of the Far Keep rose before me, straight and tall. Now I understood why Xavier was so obsessed with gold. The Gates were a filthy blackish brown, but underneath I could see the gold fighting through. They rose in forbidding spires. They didn't seem to lead anywhere a person would want to go.

"They look so evil."

Xavier followed my eyes to the tips of the spires. "They are what they are. Power is neither good nor evil."

"Maybe that's true, but this place is evil."

"Ethan. You are a strong Mortal. You have more life in you than any dead man I've met." Somehow, that wasn't a comfort. "I cannot open the Gates if you do not truly wish to go." The words sounded ominous.

"I have to go. I have to get back to Lena, and Amma, and

Link. And my dad, and Marian, and Liv, and everybody." I saw their faces, every one of them. I felt surrounded by them, by their spirits, and by mine. I remembered what it was to live among them, my friends.

I remembered what it was to live.

"Lena. The girl with the golden curls?" Xavier sounded curious.

There was no point trying to explain, not to him. I just nodded—it seemed easier.

"And you love her?" He looked even more curious about that.

"Yes." There was no doubt. "I love her beyond the universe and back. I love her from this world to the next."

He blinked, expressionless. "Well. That's very serious."

I almost felt like smiling. "Yeah. I tried to tell you. It's like that."

He stared at me for a long moment, finally nodding. "All right. Follow me." Then he disappeared up the dusty pathway in front of me.

I followed him as the path twisted into an impossibly rocky staircase. We climbed until we reached a narrow cliff that dropped away into what seemed like oblivion. When I tried to look over the edge of the rock, all I could see were clouds and darkness.

In front of me were the imposing black Gates. I couldn't see anything beyond them. But I could hear terrible sounds—chains rattling, voices wailing and crying.

"It sounds like Hell."

He shook his head. "Not Hell. Only the Far Keep."

Xavier moved in front of me, blocking my path to the Gates. "Are you sure you want to do this, dead man?"

I nodded, keeping my eyes on his disfigured face.

"Human boy. The one called Ethan. My friend." His eyes went pale and glassy, as if he was going into some kind of trance.

"What is it, Xavier?" I was impatient, but more than that I was terrified. And the longer we stood outside listening to the terrible sounds of whatever was going on inside, the worse it seemed to get. I was afraid of losing my nerve—of giving up and turning back—of wasting everything Lena had gone through to get *The Book of Moons* to me.

He ignored me. "You propose a trade, dead man? What do you offer me if I open the Gates? How do you propose to pay your way for entrance into the Far Keep?"

I just stood there.

He opened one eye, hissing at me. "The Book. Give me the Book."

I gave it to him, but I couldn't move my hands away. It was like the Book and I were one thing, yet somehow connected to Xavier as well.

"What the—"

"I accept this offering, and in return I open the Gates of the Far Keep." Xavier's body went limp, and he collapsed in a heap around the Book.

"Are you okay, Xavier?"

"Shh." The sound coming from the heap of robes was the only thing that told me he was still alive.

I heard another sound, like rocks falling or cars crashing, but really it was just the enormous Gates opening. It seemed like they hadn't been opened in a thousand years. I watched the black walls give way to the world inside.

As a rush of relief and exhaustion and adrenaline made my heart race, one thought kept running through my mind.

It has to be over soon.

This had to be the hardest part. I paid the Ferryman. I crossed the river. I got the Book. I made the trade.

I made it to the Far Keep. I'm almost home. I'm coming, L.

I could picture her face. Imagined seeing her and holding her in my arms again.

It wouldn't be long.

At least that's what I thought as I walked through the Gates.

⊰ CHAPTER 31 ⊱

Keepers of Secrets

I don't remember what I saw when I walked into the Far Keep. What I remember are the feelings. The pure terror. The way my eyes couldn't find anything—not one familiar thing—to rest on. Nothing they could understand. I was prepared in no way, by any world I'd ever encountered, for the one I was encountering now.

This place was cold and evil, like Sauron's tower in *The Lord of the Rings*. I had that same feeling of being watched, the feeling that some sort of universal eye could see what I was seeing, could sense the innermost terrors of my heart and exploit them.

As I stepped away from the Gates, tall walls loomed on

360

either side of me. They extended toward an overlook, where I could see the greater part of a city. It was as if I was looking into a valley from a high mountaintop. Beneath me, the city extended toward the horizon in a great recess of structures. As I looked more closely, I realized it didn't resemble a regular city.

It was a labyrinth, a massive, interlocking puzzle of paths carved from cut hedges. It threaded through the whole of the city between me and the golden building that rose steeply toward the horizon ahead.

The building I needed to reach.

"Have you come here to face the labyrinth? Are you here for the games?" I heard a voice behind me, and I turned to see an unnaturally pale man, like the Keepers who had appeared in the Gatlin Library before Marian's trial. He had the opaque eyes and prismatic glasses I had come to associate with the Far Keep.

Over his thin frame hung a black robe like the ones the Council members had worn when they sentenced Marian—or whatever they had planned to do, before Macon, John, and Liv stopped them.

Those were the bravest people I knew. I couldn't let them down now.

Not Lena. Not any of them.

"I'm here for the library," I answered. "Can you show me the way?"

"That's what I said. The games?" He pointed to a braid of

gold rope around his shoulder. "I'm an officer. I'm here to make sure all who enter the Keep find their way."

"Huh?"

"You want to gain entrance to the Great Keep. Is that your desire?"

"That's right."

"Then you're here for the games." The pale man pointed at the overgrown green maze below us. "If you survive the labyrinth, you'll end up there." He moved his finger until he was pointing at the gold towers. "The Great Keep."

I didn't want to find my way through a labyrinth. Everything about the Otherworld felt like one gigantic maze, and all I wanted to do was find my way out.

"I don't think you understand. Isn't there some kind of door? A place where I can walk inside without having to play any games?" I didn't have time for this. I needed to find *The Caster Chronicles* and get out. Get home.

Come on.

He slapped his hand against my arm, and I struggled to stay standing. The man was incredibly strong—Link and John strong. "It would be too easy if you could walk into the Great Keep. What would be the point of that?"

I tried to hide my frustration. "I don't know? How about to get inside?"

He frowned. "Where have you come from?"

"The Otherworld."

"Dead man, listen well. The Great Keep is not like the

Otherworld. The Great Keep has many names. To the Norse it is Valhalla, Hall of the Lords. To the Greeks it is Olympus. There are as many names as there are men who would speak them."

"Okay. I'm down with all that. I just want to find my way inside this one library. If I could just find someone to talk to—"

"There is but one way into the Great Keep," he said. "The Warrior's Way."

I sighed. "So there's no other way? Like, a doorway? Maybe even a Warrior's Doorway?"

He shook his head. "There are no doors to the Great Keep."

Of course there weren't.

"Yeah? What about a stairway?" I asked. The pale man shook his head again. "Or maybe an alley?"

He was finished with this conversation. "There is only one way in, an honorable death. And there is only one way out."

"You mean I can be more dead than this?"

He smiled politely.

I tried again. "What's that, exactly? An honorable death?"

"You face the labyrinth. It does what it will with you. You accept your fate."

"And? What's the one way out?"

He shrugged. "No one leaves unless we choose to let them leave."

Great.

"Thanks, I guess." What else was there to say?

363

"Good luck, dead man. May you fight in peace."

I nodded. "Yeah, sure. I hope so."

The strange Keeper, if that's what he was, went back to guarding his post.

I stared down at the massive labyrinth, wondering once again what I'd gotten myself into and how I could possibly get myself out.

They shouldn't call death passing on. They should call it leveling up.

Because the game only got harder once I lost. And I was more than a little worried it had only just begun.

⁂

I couldn't put it off any longer. The only way to get through this whole labyrinth thing, like most other crappy things, was to just get through it.

I would have to find a path the hard way.

The Warrior's Way, or whatever.

And fight in peace? What was that about?

My guard was up as I stumbled my way down a staircase cut out of rock. I moved deeper into the valley below, and the stairs widened into layers of steep cliffs, where green moss grew between the rocks, and ivy clung to the walls. When I reached the base of the walled stairwell, I found myself in an immense garden.

Not just a garden like the ones folks in Gatlin grew their

tomatoes in, out behind their swamp coolers. A garden in the sense of the Garden of Eden—and not Gardens of Eden, the florist over on Main Street.

It looked like a dream. Because the colors were all wrong— they were too bright, and there were too many of them. As I moved closer, I realized where I was.

The labyrinth.

Rows of hedges tangled with so many flowering bushes that they made the gardens of Ravenwood look small and shabby in comparison.

The farther I walked, the less it seemed like walking and the more it felt like bushwhacking. I pulled branches out of my face and kicked my way through the waist-high brambles and brush. Root hog or die. That's what Amma would have said. Keep trying.

It reminded me of the time I tried to walk home from Wader's Creek when I was nine. I had been poking around in Amma's craft room, which wasn't a craft room at all. It was the room where she stored the supplies for her charms. She gave me a piece and a half of her mind, and I told her I was walking home. "I can find my own way"—that's what I told her. But I didn't find my way, or any way. Instead, I wandered deeper and deeper into the swamplands, spooked by the sound of gators' tails thrashing in the water.

I didn't know Amma was following me, until I dropped to my knees and started to cry. She stepped out into the moonlight, hands on her hips. "Guess you shoulda dropped some bread crumbs if you were plannin' to run off." She didn't say anything else, just held out her hand.

"I would've found my way back," I'd said.

She nodded. "I don't doubt it for a minute, Ethan Wate."

But now, yanking dirt and thorns out of my face, I didn't have Amma to come find me. This was something I had to do on my own.

Like plowing the Lilum's field and bringing the water back to Gatlin.

Or taking a dive off the Summerville water tower.

It didn't take long for me to figure out that I was pretty much in the same boat I'd been in that day in the swamp when I was nine. I was walking down the same pathways over and over, unless some other guy was wearing the same size Converse as me. I might as well be lost on the way home from Wader's Creek.

I tried to think.

A maze is just a big puzzle.

I was going about this wrong. I needed to mark the pathways I had already taken. I needed some of Amma's bread crumbs.

I stripped the nearest bush of its leaves, stuffing them in my pockets. I reached out my right hand until it touched the wall of bushes, and I started walking. I kept my right hand on the wall of the maze and used my left to drop the waxy leaves every few feet.

It was like a giant corn maze. Keep the same hand on the

366

stalks until you dead-end. Then switch hands and go the other way. Anyone who's ever been stuck in a corn maze can tell you that.

I followed the path to the right until it dead-ended. Then I switched hands and bread crumbs. This time I reached out with my left hand, and I used stones instead of leaves.

After what felt like hours of winding my way through this particular puzzle, hitting one dead end after another and stepping over the same rocks and leaves I had used to mark my tracks, I finally reached the very center of the maze, the place where all pathways came to an end. Only the center wasn't an exit. It was a pit, with what looked like enormous mud walls. As thick rolls of white fog spread toward me, I was forced to confront the truth.

The labyrinth wasn't a labyrinth at all.

It was a dead end.

Beyond the fog and dirt, there was nothing but the impenetrable brush.

Keep moving. Keep your bearings.

I walked forward, kicking waves in the dense mist that clung to the ground around me. Just as I made some progress, my foot hit something long and hard. Maybe a stick or a pipe.

I tried to navigate more carefully, but the fog made it hard to see. It was like looking through glasses smeared with Vaseline.

As I moved closer to the center, the white mist began to clear, and I tripped again.

This time I could see what was in the way.

It wasn't a pipe or a stick.

It was a human bone.

Long and thin, it must have been a leg bone, or maybe an arm.

"Holy crap." I yanked on it, and it pulled free, sending a human skull rolling toward my feet. The dirt around me was piled high with bones, as long and bare as the one I was holding in my hand.

I let the bone drop and backed away, stumbling over what I thought was a rock. But it was another skull. The faster I ran, the more I tripped, twisting my ankle in the loops of an old hip bone, catching my Chucks on a piece of spine.

Am I dreaming?

On top of that, I had an overpowering sense of déjà vu. The feeling that I was running toward a place I'd been before. Which didn't make sense, because I had no experience with pits or bones or wandering around being dead, until now.

Still.

It felt like I'd been here, like I'd always been here, and I couldn't get far enough away. Like every path I'd ever taken was here in this maze.

No way out but through it.

I had to keep moving. I had to face this place, this pit full of bones. Wherever it was leading me. Or to who.

Then a dark shadow emerged, and I knew I wasn't alone.

Across the clearing, there was a person sitting on what looked like a box, perched on a gruesome hill of human remains. No—it was a chair. I could see the back rising higher than the rest, the arms jutting wider.

It was a throne.

The figure laughed with impossible confidence as the fog parted to reveal the corpse-ridden waste of the uneven battleground. It didn't matter to the person on the throne.

To her.

Because as the fog rolled back to reveal the center of the pit, I knew immediately who was sitting tall on a hideous throne of bones. Back made of broken backs. Arms made of broken arms. Feet made of broken feet.

The Queen of the Dead and the Damned.

Laughing so hard her black curls slithered through the air, like the snakes on Obidias' hand. My worst nightmare.

Sarafine Duchannes.

CHAPTER 32

Throne of Bones

Her dark cloak flapped in the wind like a shadow. The mist swirled around her black-buckled boots, disappearing into the darkness, as if she could draw it to her. Maybe she could. After all, she was a Cataclyst—the most powerful Caster in two universes.

Or the second most powerful.

Sarafine pushed back her cloak, letting it fall off her shoulders, around her long black curls. My skin went cold.

"Karma's a bitch, wouldn't you say, Mortal Boy?" she called across the pit, her voice confident and strong. Full of energy and evil.

She stretched luxuriously, clasping the arms of the chair in her own bony claws.

"I wouldn't say anything, Sarafine. Not to you." I tried to keep my voice even. I hadn't wanted to see her in one lifetime, let alone two.

Sarafine beckoned with one curving finger. "Is that why you're hiding? Or are you still afraid of me?"

I took a step closer. "I'm not afraid of you."

She cocked her head. "I don't know that I blame you. After all, I did kill you. A knife to the chest, in warm Mortal blood."

"Hard to remember back that far. I guess you weren't that memorable." I folded my arms stubbornly. Trying to hold my ground.

It was no use.

She rolled a ball of mist toward me, and it wrapped around me, closing the gap between us. I felt myself moving forward, powerless, as if she was dragging me by a leash.

So she still had her powers even here.

Good to know.

I stumbled over the ridge of an inhuman skeleton, something twice as big as me, with twice as many arms and legs. I swallowed. More powerful creatures than a guy from Gatlin County had met their fates here. I hoped she wasn't the reason why.

"What are you doing here, Sarafine?" I tried not to sound as intimidated as I was. I dug my feet into the dirt.

Sarafine leaned back in her throne of bones, examining the nails on one of her claws. "Me? Lately I've spent most of my time being dead, like you. Oh, wait—you were there. You watched when my daughter let me burn to death. A real charmer, that one. Teenagers. What are you going to do?"

Sarafine had no right to mention Lena. She'd surrendered that right when she walked away from a burning house with her baby daughter inside. When she tried to kill Lena like she'd killed Lena's father. And me.

I wanted to throw myself at her, but every instinct I had left told me to stay back. "You're nothing, Sarafine. You're a ghost."

She smiled when I said the word "ghost," biting the tip of one of her long black nails. "Something we have in common now."

"We don't have anything in common." I could feel my hands clenching into fists. "You make me sick. Why don't you get out of my sight?"

I didn't know what I was saying. I wasn't in any position to be ordering her around. I didn't have a weapon. No possible means of attack. No way past her.

My mind raced, but I couldn't find an advantage—and you couldn't let Sarafine get the upper hand.

Kill or be killed, that was her style. Even when it seemed like we should have moved past something as Mortal as death.

Her mouth curled into a snarl. *"Your sight?"*

She laughed, a cold sound that rippled down my spine. "Maybe your girlfriend should have thought about that before she killed me. She's the reason I'm here. If it weren't for that ungrateful little witch, I would still be in the Mortal world. Instead of stuck in the dark, battling the ghosts of lost and pathetic Mortal boys."

She was close enough now that I could see her face. She didn't look too good, even for Sarafine. Her dress was ragged and black, the bodice charred into tattered pieces. Her face was smudged with soot, and her hair smelled like smoke.

Sarafine turned toward me, her eyes glowing and white—milky with an opaque light I had never seen before.

"Sarafine?"

I took a step back—just as she struck me with a bolt of electricity, the smell of burnt flesh traveling faster than her body possibly could.

I heard a psychotic scream. Saw her face, contorted into an inhuman death mask. Sharp teeth seemed to match the dagger she held in her hand—only inches from my throat.

I winced, pulling back from the blade, but I knew it was too late. I wasn't going to make it.

Lena!

Sarafine stopped short, as if smashed backward by an invisible current. Her arms stretched toward me, her blade shaking with anger.

Something was wrong with her.

I heard the sound of chains as she fell, stumbling back toward her throne. She dropped the blade, and her long skirt kicked open, and I saw the manacles around her ankles. The chains holding her to the ground and pinning her to the throne.

She wasn't the Queen of the Underworld. She was an angry dog trapped in a kennel. Sarafine screamed, beating her fists against the bones. I moved to the side, but she didn't even look at me.

Now I understood.

I picked up a bone and tossed it at her. She didn't react until it hit the throne, falling harmlessly into the pile of debris at her feet.

She spit at me, shaking with rage. "Fool!"

But I knew the truth.

Her white eyes saw nothing.

Her pupils were fixed.

She was blind.

Maybe it was from the fire that had killed her in the Mortal world. It all came flooding back to me—the terrible end of her terrible life. She was as damaged here as she was when she burned to death. But that wasn't all. Something else had happened. Even the fire couldn't explain the chains.

"What happened to your eyes?" I watched her recoil when I said it. Sarafine wasn't one to show weakness. She was better at finding and exploiting it.

"My new look. Old blind woman, like the Fates or the Furies. What do you think?" Her lips curved over her teeth, into a growl.

It was impossible to feel sorry for Sarafine, so I didn't. Still, she seemed bitter and broken.

"The leash is a nice touch," I said.

She laughed, but it was more like the hiss of an animal. She had become something that didn't resemble a Dark Caster, not anymore. She was a creature, maybe even more of one than Xavier or the River Master. She was losing it—whatever part of our world she'd known.

I tried again. "What happened to your sight? Was it the fire?"

Her white eyes burned as she answered. "The Far Keep wanted to have their fun with me. Angelus is a sadistic pig. He thought they would even the odds by forcing me to battle without being able to see my opponents. He wanted me to know how it would feel to be powerless." She sighed, picking at a bone. "Not that it's slowed me down yet."

I didn't think it had.

I looked at the circus of bones surrounding her, the bloodstains in the dirt at her feet. "Who cares? Why fight? You're dead. I'm dead. What do we even have left to fight about? Tell this Angelus guy to go jump off a—"

"Water tower?" She laughed.

But I had a point, if you thought about it. It was starting to feel like those old *Terminator* movies between us. If I killed her now, I could imagine her skeleton dragging itself across this pit with glowing red eyes until it could kill me a thousand more times.

She stopped laughing. "Why are you here? Think about it, Ethan." She lifted her hand, and I felt my throat beginning to close. I gasped for air.

I tried to back away, but it was pointless. Even with her dog chain, she still had enough power to make my not-quite-a-life miserable.

"I'm trying to get into the Great Keep." I choked. I tried to inhale, but I couldn't get a real breath.

Am I even breathing, or am I only imagining it?

Like she said herself, she'd already killed me once. What was left?

"I just want to take my page. You think I want to be stuck here forever, wandering through a maze of bones?"

"You'll never get past Angelus. He'd die before he'd let you near *The Caster Chronicles*." She smiled, twisting her fingers, and I gasped again. Now it felt like she had a hand around my lungs.

"Then I'll kill him." I grabbed at my neck with both hands. My face felt like it was on fire.

"The Keepers already know you're here. They sent an officer to lead you into the labyrinth. They didn't want to miss out on the fun." Sarafine twisted around at the mention of the Keepers, as if she was looking over her shoulder, which we both knew she wasn't. An old habit, I guess.

"I still have to try. It's the only way I can get home."

"To my daughter?" Sarafine rattled her chains, looking disgusted. "You never give up, do you?"

"No."

"It's like a sickness." She rose from her throne, crouching on her heels like an evil, overgrown little girl, dropping the hand that was choking me. I collapsed onto a heap of bones. "You really think you can hurt Angelus?"

"I can do anything if it will get me back to Lena." I looked

376

straight into her sightless eyes. "Like I said, I'll kill him. At least part of him is Mortal. I can do it."

I don't know why I said it that way. I guess I wanted her to know, in case there was any small part of her that still cared about Lena. Any part of her that needed to hear I really would do anything under the sun to find a way back to her daughter.

Which I would.

For a second, Sarafine didn't move. "You actually believe that, don't you? It's charming, really. Shame you have to die again, Mortal Boy. You certainly amuse me."

Light flooded into the pit, as if we really were two gladiators competing for our lives.

"I don't want to fight. Not with you, Sarafine."

She smiled darkly. "You really don't know how this works, do you? The loser faces Eternal Darkness. It's simple enough." She sounded almost bored.

"There's something Darker than this?"

"Much."

"Please. I just need to get back to Lena. Your daughter. I want to make her happy. I know that doesn't mean anything to you, and I know you've never wanted to make anyone happy but yourself, but it's the only thing I want."

"I want something, too." She twisted the fog around her in her hands until it wasn't fog at all but something glowing and alive—a ball of fire. She stared right at me, even though I knew she couldn't see. "Kill Angelus."

Sarafine started to Cast, but I couldn't hear what she was saying. Fire shot from the base of her throne, spreading in all directions. It moved closer and closer, turning from orange to blue and purple flames as it ignited bone after bone.

I backed away from her.

Something was wrong. The fire was growing, spreading faster than I could run. She wasn't trying to stop the flames.

She was the one making them grow.

"What are you doing?" I shouted. "Are you crazy?"

She was in the very center of the flames. "It's a battle to the death. Absolute destruction. Only one of us can survive. And as much as I hate you, I hate Angelus more." Sarafine raised her arms over her head, and the fire grew, as if she was pulling the flames up with her.

"Make him pay."

Her cloak caught fire, and her hair started burning.

"You can't just give up!" I shouted, but I didn't know if she could hear me. I couldn't see her anymore.

I hurled myself into the fire without thinking, falling toward her through the flames. I wasn't sure I could stop, even if I wanted to. But I didn't want to.

It was Sarafine or me.

Lena or Eternal Darkness.

It didn't matter. I wasn't going to sit there and watch anyone die chained like a dog. Not even Sarafine.

It wasn't about her. It was about me.

I reached for the manacles around her ankles, beating on

the iron with a bone at the base of her throne. "We have to get out of here."

The fire had completely surrounded me, when I heard the screaming. The sound tore across the barren dirt, rising into the air over the pit. It sounded like a wild animal dying. For a second, I thought I saw the distant golden spires of the Great Keep flicker at the sound of her voice through the flames.

Sarafine's burning body arched back, writhing in pain, and started to crumble into tiny pieces of burnt skin and bone. There was nothing I could do as the flames consumed her. I wanted to close my eyes or turn away. But it seemed like someone should bear witness to her last moments. Maybe I just didn't want her to die alone.

After a few minutes that felt more like hours, I watched as the last bits of the Darkest Caster in two worlds blew into cold white ash.

It was too late to get out.

I felt the fire crawl up my arms.

I was next.

I tried to picture Lena one last time, but I couldn't even think. The pain was unbearable. I knew I was going to pass out. This was it.

I closed my eyes....

When I opened them again, the pit was gone, and I was standing in front of a quiet doorway in a still hallway, in a building that looked like a castle.

There was no pain.

No Sarafine.

No fire.

Exhausted, I wiped the ash out of my eyes and sank into a ball at the foot of the wooden doors. It was over. There were no bones beneath my feet, only marble tiles.

I tried to focus on the doors. They were so familiar.

I'd seen all of this before. It was even more familiar than the feeling I had when I saw Sarafine coming toward me.

Sarafine.

Where is she now? Where is her soul?

I didn't want to think about it, and I closed my eyes and let the tears fall. Crying for her felt impossible. She was an evil monster. No one ever felt sorry for her.

So that couldn't be it.

At least that's what I told myself, until I stopped shaking and stood up again.

The pathways of my life had doubled back on me, as if the universe was forcing me to choose them all over again. I was standing in front of the unmistakable doorway to all other doorways, to all other places and times.

I didn't know if I had the strength to go any farther, and I knew I didn't have the courage to give up. I reached out and touched the carved wood of the ancient Caster doorway.

The *Temporis Porta*.

CHAPTER 33

The Wayward's Way

I took a deep breath and tried to let the power of the *Temporis Porta* flow into me. I needed to feel something other than shock. But they felt like two regular wooden doors, even if they were about a thousand years old and framed with Niadic script, an even older lost language.

I pressed my fingers against the wood. It felt like Sarafine's blood was on my hands in this world, as my blood had been on hers in the last. It didn't matter if I had tried to stop her.

She had sacrificed herself so I would have a chance to make it to the Great Keep, even if hate was her only motivation. Sarafine had still given me a shot at getting back home to the people I loved.

I had to keep going. Like the officer at the Gates said, there was only one way into the one place I needed to go—the Way of the Warrior. Maybe this was how it felt.

Awful.

I tried not to think about the other thing. The fact that Sarafine's soul was trapped in Eternal Darkness. It was hard to imagine.

I took a step back from the broad wooden doors of the *Temporis Porta*. It was identical to the doorway I found in the Caster Tunnels beneath Gatlin. The one that took me to the Far Keep for the first time. Rowan wood, carved into Caster circles.

I placed my palms against the rough exterior of the paneling.

Just like always, they gave way beneath me. I was the Wayward, and they were the Way. These doors would open for me in this world as they had in the other. They would show their pathway to me.

I pushed harder.

The doors swung open, and I stepped inside.

There were so many things I didn't realize when I was alive. So many things I took for granted. My life didn't seem precious when I had one.

But here, I'd fought through a mountain of bones, crossed a river, tunneled through a mountain, begged and bargained and bartered from one world to another, to get myself this close to these doors and this room.

Now I just had to find the library.

One page in one book.

One page in The Caster Chronicles, *and I can go home.*

The nearness of it swirled in the air around me. I had experienced this feeling only once before, at the Great Barrier—another seam between worlds. Then, just like now, I had felt the power crackling in the air, too, the magic. I was in a place where great things could happen and did happen.

There were some rooms that could change the world.

Worlds.

This was one of them, with its heavy drapes and dusty portraits and dark wood and rowan doors. A place where all things were judged and punished.

Sarafine had promised that Angelus would come for me—that he had practically led me here himself. There was no use trying to hide. He was probably the reason I was sentenced to die in the first place.

If there was a way around him, a way to get to the library and *The Caster Chronicles*, I hadn't figured it out yet. I just hoped it would come to me, the way so many ideas had in the past when my future was at stake.

The only question was, would he come first?

I decided to take my chances and try to find the library before Angelus found me. It would have been a good plan if it had actually worked out. I had barely crossed the room when I saw them.

The Council Keepers—the man with the hourglass, the albino woman, and Angelus—appeared in front of me.

Their robes fell around them, pooling at their feet, and they barely moved. I couldn't even tell if they were breathing.

"Puer Mortalis. Is qui, unus, duplex est. Is qui mundo, qui fuit, finem attulit." When one spoke, all their mouths moved like they were the same person, or at least governed by the same brain. I had almost forgotten.

I didn't say anything, and I didn't move.

They looked at one another and spoke again. "Mortal Boy. The One Who Is Two. He Who Endeth the World That Was."

"When you say it that way, it sounds kind of creepy." It wasn't Latin, but it was the best I could come up with. They didn't respond.

I heard the murmuring of foreign voices around me and turned to see the room suddenly crowded with unfamiliar people. I looked for the telltale tattoos and gold eyes of the Dark Casters, but I was too disoriented to register anything beyond the three robed figures who stood in front of me.

"Child of Lila Evers Wate, deceased Keeper of Gatlin." The choral voices filled the great hall like some kind of trumpet. It reminded me of Beginning Band with Miss Spider back at Jackson High, only less off-key.

"In the flesh." I shrugged. "Or not."

"You have taken the labyrinth and defeated the Cataclyst. Many have tried. Only you have been—" There was a hitch, a pause, like the Keepers didn't know what to say. I took a

384

breath, half expecting them to say something like *extermi-nated*. "Victorious."

It was almost like they couldn't bring themselves to say the word.

"Not really. She kind of defeated herself." I scowled at Angelus, who was standing in the center. I wanted him to look at me. I wanted him to know that I knew what he'd done to Sarafine. How he'd chained the Caster, like a dog, to a throne of bones. What kind of sick game was that?

But Angelus didn't flinch.

I took a step closer. "Or I guess you defeated her, Angelus. At least, that's what Sarafine said. That you enjoyed torturing her." I looked around the room. "Is that what Keepers do around here? Because it's not what Keepers do where I come from. Back home they're good people, who care about things like right and wrong and good and evil and all that. Like my mom."

I looked at the crowd behind me. "Seems like you guys are pretty messed up."

The three spoke again, in unison. "That is not our concern. *Victori spolia sunt*. To the victor go the spoils. The debt has been paid."

"About that—" If this was my way back to Gatlin, I wanted to know.

Angelus raised his hand, silencing me. "In return, you have gained entry to this Keep, the Warrior's Way. You are to be commended."

The crowd fell silent, which didn't exactly make me feel all

385

that commended. More than anything, it felt like I was about to be sentenced. Or maybe that was how I was used to things going down in here.

I looked around. "It doesn't really sound like you mean it."

The crowd began to whisper again. The three Council Keepers stared at me. At least I think they did. It was impossible to see their eyes behind the strangely cut prism glasses, with the twisting strands of gold, silver, and copper holding them in place.

I tried again. "In terms of spoils, I was thinking more about going home to Gatlin. Wasn't that the deal? One of us goes to Eternal Darkness, and one of us gets to leave?"

The crowd burst into chaos.

Angelus stepped forward. "Enough!" The room fell silent again. This time he spoke alone. The other Keepers looked at me but said nothing. "The bargain was for the Cataclyst alone. We have made no such pact with a Mortal. Never would we return a Mortal to existence."

I remembered Amma's past, revealed through the black stone I still had in my pocket. Sulla had warned her that Angelus hated Mortals. He was never going to let me walk away. "What if the Mortal was never meant to be here?"

Angelus' eyes widened.

"I want my page back."

This time the crowd gasped.

"What is written in the *Chronicles* is law. The pages cannot be removed," Angelus hissed.

386

"But you can rewrite them however you want?" I couldn't hide the rage in my voice. He had taken everything from me. How many other lives had he destroyed?

And why? Because he couldn't be a Caster?

"You were the One Who Is Two. Your fate was to be punished. You should not have brought the Lilum into matters that were not hers to resolve."

"Wait. What does Lilian English—I mean, the Lilum—have to do with any of this?" My English teacher, whose body had been inhabited by the most powerful creature in the Demon world, had been the one who showed me what I had to do to fix the Order of Things.

Was that why he was punishing me? Did I get in the way of whatever he was planning with Abraham? Destroying the Mortal race? Using Casters as lab rats?

I always believed that when Lena and Amma brought me back from the dead with *The Book of Moons*, they had set something in motion that couldn't be undone. It started the unraveling that ripped the hole in the universe, which was the reason I had to right it at the water tower.

What if I had it backward?

What if the thing that was supposed to happen *was* the unraveling?

What if fixing it was the crime?

It was all so clear now. Like everything had been lost in darkness, and then the sun came out. Some moments are like that. But now I knew the truth.

I was supposed to fail.

The world as we knew it was supposed to end.

The Mortals weren't the point. They were the problem.

The Lilum wasn't supposed to help me, and I wasn't supposed to jump.

She was supposed to condemn me, and I was supposed to give up. Angelus had bet on the wrong team.

A sound echoed through the hall as the great doors on the far side pushed open, revealing a small figure standing between them. Talk about betting on the wrong team—I wouldn't have made this bet, not in a thousand lifetimes.

It was more unexpected than Angelus or any of the Keepers.

He smiled broadly; at least I think it was a smile. It was hard to tell with Xavier.

"He-hello." Xavier glanced around the intimidating room, clearing his throat. He tried again. "Hello, friend."

It was so quiet, you could've heard one of his precious buttons drop.

The only thing that wasn't quiet was Angelus. "How dare you show your defiled face here again, Xavier. If there is anything of Xavier left, beast."

Xavier's leathery wings shrugged.

Angelus only looked angrier. "Why have you involved yourself in this? Your fate is not intertwined with the Wayward. You are serving your sentence. You don't need to take a dead Mortal's battles on as your own."

"It is too late for that, Angelus," he said.

"Why?"

"Because he paid his way, and I accepted the price. Because"—Xavier slowed his words, as if he was letting them fall into place in his mind—"he is my friend, and I have no other."

"He's not your friend," Angelus hissed. "You're too brainless to have a friend. Brainless and heartless. All you care about are your worthless trinkets, your lost baubles." Angelus sounded frustrated. I wondered why he cared what Xavier thought or did.

What is Xavier to him?

There had to be a story there. But I didn't want to know about anything that involved Angelus and his minions, or the crimes they must have committed. The Far Keep was the closest thing I'd ever found to Hell in real life—at least in my real afterlife.

"What you know of me," said Xavier slowly, "is nothing." His twisted face was even more expressionless than usual. "Less than I know of myself."

"You are a fool," Angelus answered. "That I know."

"I am a friend. I have in my possession two thousand assorted buttons, eight hundred keys, and only one friend. Perhaps it is not something you can understand. I have not often been one before." He looked proud of himself. "I will be one now."

I was proud of him, too.

Angelus scoffed. "You will sacrifice your soul for a friend?"

"Is a friend different from a soul, Angelus?" The Council Keeper said nothing. Xavier cocked his head again. "Would you know if it were?"

Angelus didn't respond, but he didn't need to. We all knew the answer.

"What are you doing here, then? *Mortali Comes.*" Angelus took a step toward Xavier, and Xavier took a step back. "Friend of the Mortal," Angelus snarled.

I resisted the urge to insert myself between them, hoping that Xavier, for both our sakes, didn't try to run away.

"You seek to destroy the Mortal, do you not?" Xavier swallowed.

"I do," Angelus answered.

"You seek to end the Mortal race." It wasn't a question.

"Of course. Like any infestation, the ultimate goal is annihilation."

Even though I was expecting it, Angelus' answer caught me off guard. "You—what?"

Xavier looked at me like he was trying to shut me down. "It is no secret. The Mortals are an irritant to the supernatural races. This is not a new concept."

"I wish it was." I knew Abraham wanted to wipe out the Mortal race. If Angelus was working with him, their goals were aligned.

"You seek entertainment?" Xavier watched Angelus.

Angelus looked at Xavier's leathery wings, disgusted. "I seek solutions."

"To the Mortal condition?"

Angelus smiled, dark and joyless. "As I said. The Mortal infestation."

I felt sick, but Xavier only sighed. "As you wish to call it. I propose a challenge."

"A what?" I didn't like the sound of it.

"A challenge."

Angelus looked suspicious. "The Mortal defeated the Dark Queen and won. That was the only challenge he will face today."

I was annoyed. "I told you. I didn't kill Sarafine. She defeated herself."

"Semantics," Angelus said.

Xavier silenced us both. "So you are unwilling to face the Mortal in a challenge?"

There was an uproar in the crowd, and Angelus looked like he wanted to tear Xavier's wings off. "Silence!"

The chatter stopped immediately.

"I do not fear any Mortal!"

"Then this is my proposition." Xavier tried to keep his voice steady, but he was obviously terrified. "The Mortal will face you in the Great Keep and attempt to regain his page. You will attempt to stop him. If he succeeds, you will allow him to do with it as he likes. If you stop him from reaching his page, he will allow you to do with it as you like."

"What?" Xavier was suggesting that I face off against Angelus. My odds were not good in this scenario.

Angelus was aware that all eyes were on him as the crowd

and the other Council Keepers waited for his response. "Interesting."

I wanted to bolt out of the room. "Not interesting. I don't even know what you're talking about."

Angelus leaned toward me, his eyes sparking. "Let me explain it to you. A lifetime of servitude or the simple destruction of your soul. It doesn't really matter to me. I'll decide on a whim, as I like. When I like."

"I'm not sure about this." It sounded like a lose-lose proposition to me.

Xavier let one hand fall on my shoulder. "You don't have a choice. It's the only chance you have to get home to the girl with the curls." He turned to Angelus, holding out his hand. "Is it a deal?"

Angelus stared at Xavier's hand as if it was infected. "I accept."

⊰ CHAPTER 34 ⊱

The Caster Chronicles

Angelus swept out of the room, the other Keepers right behind him.

I let out the breath I was holding. "Where are they going?"

"They have to give you a chance, or they will be perceived as unjust."

"Perceived as unjust?" Was he serious? "Are you saying no one's caught on to that before?"

"The Council is feared. No one questions them," Xavier said. "But they are also proud. Especially Angelus. He wishes his followers to believe he is giving you a chance."

"But he's not?"

"That depends on you now." Xavier turned to me with

something resembling a sad expression on what was left of his human face. "I can't help you. Not beyond this, my friend."

"What are you talking about?"

"I'm not going back there. I can't," he said. "Not to the Chamber of the Chronicles."

Of course. The room that housed the book. It had to be close.

I looked at the row of doors beyond us, bordering one side of the room. I wondered which one led to the end of my journey—or to the death of my soul.

"You can't go back there? And I can? Don't chicken out on me now." I lowered my voice. "You just took on Angelus. You made a deal with the Devil. You're my hero."

"I am no hero. As I said, I am your friend."

Xavier couldn't do it. Who could blame the guy? The Chamber of the Chronicles must have been some kind of house of horrors for him. And he had put himself in enough danger already.

"Thanks, Xavier. You're a great friend. One of the best." I smiled at him. The look he gave me in return was sobering.

"This is your journey, dead man. Yours alone. I can go no farther." He put his arm on my shoulder, pressing heavily.

"Why do I have to do everything alone?" As soon as I said it, I knew it wasn't true.

The Greats had sent me on my way.

Aunt Prue made sure I got a second chance.

Obidias told me everything I needed to know.

My mom gave me the strength to do it.

Amma watched for me, and believed it when she found me.

Lena sent me *The Book of Moons*, against all odds and all the way from the other side of the universe. Aunt Marian and Macon, Link and John and Liv—they were there for Lena when I couldn't be.

Even the River Master and Xavier had helped me move forward, when all along it would have been so much easier to give up and go back.

I had never been alone. Not for a minute.

I may have been a Wayward, but my way was full of people who loved me. They were the only way I knew.

I could do this.

I had to.

"I understand," I said. "Thanks, Xavier. For everything."

He nodded. "I will meet you again, Ethan. I will see you when next you cross the river."

"I hope it's not for a long time."

"I hope this as well, my friend. For you more than me." His eyes seemed to twinkle for a second. "But I will keep busy collecting and counting until you return."

I didn't say anything as he slipped through the shadows and back into the world where nothing ever happened and the days became the same as nights.

I hoped he would remember me.

I was pretty sure he wouldn't.

One by one, I touched the row of doors in front of me with my hand. Some felt as cold as ice. Some felt like nothing, like plain wood. There was only one that pulsed beneath my fingertips.

Only one burned at my touch.

I knew it was the right door, before I saw the telltale Caster circles carved into the rowan wood, just like the *Temporis Porta*.

This was the doorway to the heart of the Great Keep. The one place any son of Lila Jane Evers Wate would instinctively find his way, whether or not he was a Wayward.

The library.

Pushing my way through the massive doors directly across from the *Temporis Porta*, I knew it was time to face the most dangerous part of my journey.

Angelus would be waiting.

The doors were just the beginning. The moment I stepped into the inner chamber, I found myself standing in an almost entirely reflective room. If it was supposed to be a library, it was the strangest one I'd ever seen.

The crumbling stones beneath my feet, the stubbled cave walls, the ceiling and floor that grew into stalactites and stalagmites as the room circled back upon itself—they all seemed to be made of some kind of transparent gemstone, cut into a thousand impossible facets that reflected the light in every direction. It looked like I was standing in one of the eleven jewelry boxes in Xavier's collection.

Except less claustrophobic. A small opening in the ceiling let in enough natural light to catch the whole room in a dizzying glow. The effect reminded me of the tidal cave where we'd first met Abraham Ravenwood, on the night of Lena's Seventeenth Moon. In the center of this room, there was a pond of water the size of a swimming pool. The body of milky white water churned as if there was a fire beneath it. It was the color of Sarafine's sightless opaque eyes, before she died....

I shuddered. I couldn't think about her, not now. I had to focus on surviving Angelus. Defeating him. I took a deep breath and tried to get my bearings. What was I dealing with?

My eyes fixed on the bubbling white liquid. In the center of the pool, a small stretch of earth rose above the water, like a tiny island.

In the center of the island was a pedestal.

On the pedestal was a book, surrounded by candles that flickered with strange green and gold flames.

The book.

I didn't need someone to tell me which book it was, or what it was doing here. The reason there was an entire library devoted to only one book, and with a moat around it.

I knew exactly why it was here, and why I was.

It was the only part of this whole journey I understood. The only thing that was perfectly clear from the moment Obidias Trueblood told me the truth about what had happened to me. It was *The Caster Chronicles*, and I was here to destroy my page. The one that killed me. And I had to do it before Angelus could stop me.

After all I'd learned about being a Wayward and finding my way—this was where it led. There was no way left to go, no more path to find.

I was at the end.

And all I wanted was to go back.

But first I had to get to that island—to the pedestal and *The Caster Chronicles*. I had to do what I'd come here to do.

A shout from across the room startled me. "Mortal Boy. If you leave now, I will leave you your soul. How's that for a challenge?" Angelus appeared on the other side of the pool. I wondered how he got over there, and I wished there were as many ways to leave this room as there were to enter it.

Or at least, as many ways home.

"My soul? No, you won't." I stood at the edge of the pool and chucked a rock into the bubbling water, watching it disappear. I wasn't stupid. He would never let me go. I would end up like Xavier or Sarafine. Black wings or white eyes—it didn't make a difference. In the end, we were all bound in his chains, whether you could see them or not.

Angelus smiled. "No? I suppose that's true." He gestured with his hand, and at least a dozen rocks rose into the air around him. They fired themselves at me, one after another, hitting with uncanny accuracy. I flung my arms across my face as a rock sailed past.

"Very mature. What are you going to do now? Tie me up and stick me in your old boneyard? Blind and chained like an animal?"

"Don't flatter yourself. I don't want a Mortal pet." He twisted his finger, and the water began to spin into a kind of whirlpool. "I'll just destroy you. It's easier for all of us. Though not much of a challenge."

"Why did you torture Sarafine? She wasn't a Mortal. Why bother?" I shouted.

I had to know. It felt like our fates were tied together somehow—mine, Sarafine's, Xavier's, and those of all the other Mortals and Casters Angelus had destroyed.

What were we to him?

"Sarafine? Was that her name? I had almost forgotten." Angelus laughed. "Do you expect me to concern myself with every Dark Caster who ends up here?"

The water churned violently now. I knelt and touched it with one hand. It was freezing cold and sort of slimy. I didn't want to swim through it, but I couldn't tell if there was another way across.

I looked up at Angelus. I didn't know how this whole challenge thing was going to take shape, but I thought it was better to keep him talking until I figured it out. "Do you blind every Dark Caster and make them fight to the death?"

I looked back at the water. It rippled where I had touched it, turning clear and calm.

Angelus folded his arms, smiling.

I kept my hand in the water as the transparent current spread across the pool, though my hand was going numb. Now I could see what was really beneath the milky surface.

Corpses. Just like the ones in the river.

Floating upward, their green hair and blue lips looked like masks on their bloated dead bodies.

Like me, I thought. *That's what I look like, right now. Somewhere—where I still had a body.*

I heard Angelus laughing. But I could barely hear, barely think. I wanted to vomit.

I backed away from the water. I knew he was trying to frighten me, and I resolved not to look at it again.

Keep your mind on Lena. Get to the page, and you can go home.

Angelus watched me, laughing harder. He called to me as if I was a child. "Don't be afraid. Your final death doesn't have to happen like this. Sarafine failed to achieve the tasks entrusted to her."

"So you do know her name." I cracked a smile.

He glared. "I know she failed me."

"You and Abraham?"

Angelus stiffened. "Congratulations. I see you've been digging around in matters that are none of your concern. Which means you're no smarter than the first Ethan Wate who visited the Great Keep. And no more likely to see the Duchannes Caster you love than he was."

My whole body went numb.

400

Of course. Ethan Carter Wate had been here. Genevieve told me.

I didn't want to ask, but I had to. "What did you do to him?"

"What do you think?" A sadistic smile spread across Angelus' face. "He tried to take something that did not belong to him."

"His page?"

With every question, the Keeper looked more satisfied. I could tell he was enjoying this. "No. Genevieve's—the Duchannes girl he loved. He wanted to lift the curse she brought upon herself and the Duchannes children who would come after her. Instead, he lost his foolish soul."

Angelus looked down into the churning water. He nodded, and a single corpse rose to the surface. Empty eyes that looked too much like my own stared back at me.

"Look familiar, Mortal?"

I knew that face. I would've known it anywhere.

It was mine. Or actually, his.

Ethan Carter Wate was still wearing the Confederate uniform he died in.

My heart dropped. Genevieve would never see him again, not in this world or any other. He had died twice, like me. But he would never get back home. Never hold Genevieve in his arms, even in the Otherworld. He had tried to save the girl he loved, and Sarafine and Ridley and Lena and all the other Casters who would come after her in the Duchannes family.

He'd failed.

It didn't make a guy feel better. Not about standing where I stood. And not about leaving a Caster girl behind, the way we both had.

"You will fail as well." The words echoed across the cavern.

Which meant Angelus was reading my mind. At this point, it was the least surprising thing happening in the room.

I knew what I had to do.

I emptied my mind the best I could, picturing the old baseball diamond where Link and I used to play T-ball. I watched Link throw a bum pitch in the ninth inning as I stood on home plate punching my glove. I tried to picture the batter. Who was it? Earl Petty, chewing gum, since the coach had outlawed chaw?

I struggled to keep my mind on the game while my eyes did something else.

Come on, Earl. Knock it out of the park.

I glanced at the pedestal, then at the corpses floating at my feet. More bodies continued to rise, bumping into one another like sardines packed in a can. It wouldn't be long until they were so close that I wouldn't even be able to see the water.

If I waited, maybe I could use them as stepping stones....

Stop! Think about the game!

But it was too late.

"I wouldn't try it." Angelus watched me from the other side of the pool. "No Mortal can survive that water. You need the bridge to cross, and as you can see, it's been removed. A security precaution."

He held his hand in front of him, twisting the air into a current I could feel all the way across the water.

I had to brace myself to stay on my feet.

"You will not retrieve your page. You will die the same dishonorable death as your namesake. The death all Mortals deserve."

"Why me, and why him? Why any of us? What did we ever do to you, Angelus?" I shouted at him over the wind.

"You are inferior, born without the gifts of Supernaturals. Forcing us to stay in hiding while your cities and schools fill with children who will grow to do nothing more than occupy space. You've turned our world into our prison." The air picked up, and he twisted his hand further. "It's absurd. Like building a city for rodents."

I waited, picturing that stupid baseball game—Earl swinging, the crack of the bat—until the words formed, and I spoke them. "But you were born a Mortal. What does that make you?"

His eyes widened, his face a mask of pure rage. "What did you say?"

"You heard me." I turned my mind to the vision I'd seen, forcing myself to remember the faces, the words. Xavier, when he was just a Caster. Angelus, when he was just a man.

The wind increased, and I stumbled, the edge of my sneaker splashing at the edge of the pool of bodies. I braced myself, willing my feet not to slip.

Angelus' face had turned even paler than before. "You know nothing! Look what you sacrificed—to save what? A town full of pathetic Mortals?"

I closed my eyes, letting the words find him.

I know you were born a Mortal. All those experiments can't change that. I know your secret.

His eyes widened, hate raging across his face. "I am not a Mortal! I never was, and I never will be!"

I know your secret.

The wind picked up, and rocks flew again through the air—harder this time. I tried to shield my face as they pelted my ribs, smashing against the wall behind me. A trail of blood ran down my cheek.

"I will tear you to shreds, Wayward!"

I screamed over the din. "You may have powers, Angelus, but deep down, you're still a Mortal, just like me."

You can't harness Dark forces like Sarafine and Abraham, or Travel like an Incubus. You can't cross that water any more than I can.

"I am not Mortal!" he screamed.

Nobody can.

"Liar!"

Prove it.

There was a second, one terrible second, when Angelus and I stared across the water at each other.

Then, without a word, Angelus flung himself into the air, lunging across the corpses in the pool—as if he couldn't contain himself a moment longer. That's how desperate he was to prove he was better than me.

Better than a Mortal.

Better than anyone else who ever tried to walk on water.

I had been right.

The rotting corpses were packed so tight that he ran right over their bodies until they started to move. Arms reached for him, the hundreds of bloated hands rising up out of the water. This was not like the river I had crossed to get here.

This river was alive.

An arm slithered over his neck, weighing him down.

"No!"

I shuddered as his voice echoed against the walls.

The corpses tore at his robe desperately, pulling him down into the abyss of loss and misery. The same souls he had tortured were drowning him.

His eyes locked on mine. "Help me!"

Why should I?

But there was nothing I could do, even if I'd wanted to. I knew those corpses would drown me. I was Mortal, just as Angelus was—at least part of him.

Nobody walks on water, not where I come from. Nobody except the guy in the picture frame in Sunday school class.

Too bad Angelus wasn't from Gatlin; he would've known that.

His hands clawed at the surface of the water until there was nothing left but a sea of bodies again. The stench of death was everywhere. It was suffocating, and I tried to cover my mouth, but the distinct odor of rot and decay was too strong.

I knew what I'd done. I wasn't innocent. Not in Sarafine's death, and not in this one either. He was reading my mind and

I had pushed him to this, even if his hate and pride had propelled him into the pool.

It was too late.

A rotted arm slid around his neck, and within seconds he disappeared under the sea of bodies. It was a death I wouldn't have wished on anyone.

Not even Angelus.

Maybe just him.

Within moments, the pool turned milky white again, though I knew what was lurking underneath.

I shrugged. "Wasn't much of a challenge after all."

I had to find the bridge, or something I could use to cross.

The splintering plank wasn't well hidden. I found it in an alcove only a few yards from where Angelus stood moments ago. The wood was dry and cracked, which wasn't reassuring, considering what I had just witnessed.

But the book was so close.

As I slid the plank over the surface of the water, I could practically feel Lena in my arms and hear Amma hollering at me. I couldn't think straight. All I knew was I had to get across that water and get back to them.

Please. Let me cross. All I want is to go home.

With that thought, I took a breath.

Then a step.

Then another.

I was five feet from the edge of the water now, maybe six.

Halfway across. There was no turning back now.

The bridge was surprisingly light, though it creaked and wobbled with my every step. Still, it had held up so far.

I took a deep breath.

Five more feet.

Four—

I heard a crash like a wave behind me. The water began to thrash. I felt a shooting pain in my leg as it gave way beneath me. The old board snapped like a broken toothpick.

Before I could scream, I lost my balance, falling into the deadly water. Only then there wasn't any water—or if there was, I wasn't in it.

I was in the arms of the rising dead.

Worse.

I was face to face with the other Ethan Wate. He was as much a skeleton as he was a man, but I recognized him now. I tried to pull away, but he grabbed me around the neck with a bony hand. Water poured out of his mouth, where his teeth should have been. I'd had nightmares less terrifying.

I turned my head to keep corpse drool from my face.

"Could a Mortal Cast an *Ambulans Mortus*?" Angelus pushed past the dead who crowded around me, pulling my arms and legs in every direction with such force I thought my limbs would rip right out of their sockets. "From under the water? To wake the dead?" He stood triumphantly on the land, in front of the book. Looking crazier than I'd thought even a crazy-looking Keeper could. "The challenge is over. Your soul is mine."

I didn't answer. I couldn't speak. Instead, I found myself staring into Ethan Wate's empty eyes.

"Now. Bring him to me."

At Angelus' command, the corpses rose from the stinking water, pulling me with them up onto the shore. The other Ethan tossed me onto the dirt like I was weightless.

As he did, a small black stone rolled out of my pocket.

Angelus didn't notice. He was too busy staring at the book. But I saw it clear enough.

The river's eye.

I had forgotten to pay the River Master.

Of course. You couldn't just expect to cross the water anytime you wanted. Not around here. Not without paying a price.

I picked up the rock.

Ethan Wate, the dead one, whipped his head toward me. The look he gave me—if that's what you'd call it, considering the guy barely had eyes—sent a shiver down my spine. I felt sorry for him. But I sure didn't want to be him.

Between the two of us, we owed each other that much.

"So long, Ethan," I said.

With my last remaining bit of strength, I hurled the rock into the water. I heard it hit, making only the tiniest sound.

You wouldn't have noticed it unless you were me.

Or one of the dead.

Because they disappeared a few seconds after the rock hit the water. About as quickly as it took a rock to sink all the way down to the bottom of a pool of bodies.

I fell back on the tiny stretch of dry land, exhausted. For a second, I was too scared to move.

Then I saw Angelus standing there, glued to the book, reading in the light of the flickering green and gold flames.

I knew what I had to do. And I didn't have long to do it.

I pulled myself to my feet.

There it was. It was open on the pedestal, right in front of me.

In front of Angelus, too.

THE CASTER CHRONICLES

I reached for the book, and it burned my fingers.

"Don't," Angelus growled, grabbing my wrist. His eyes were shining, as if the book had some strange hold on him. He didn't even look up from the page. I'm not sure he could.

Because it was his page.

I could almost read it from where I stood, a thousand rewritten words, one crossed out over the next. I could see the quill, ink-stained at the tip, almost twitching in his fingers next to the book.

So this was how he'd done it. How he'd forced the supernatural world to bend to his will. He controlled the story. Not just his, but all of ours.

Angelus had changed everything.

One person could do that.

And one person could change it back.

"Angelus?"

He didn't answer. Staring into the book, he looked more like a zombie than the corpses did.

So I didn't look. Instead, I closed my eyes and pulled on the page, as hard and as fast as I could.

"What are you doing?" Angelus sounded frantic, but I didn't open my eyes. "What have you done?"

My hands were burning. The page wanted to rip free from me, but I wouldn't let go. I only held on tighter. Nothing was going to stop me now.

It came off in my hands.

The ripping sound reminded me of an Incubus, and I half expected to see John Breed or Link appear next to me. I opened my eyes.

No such luck. Angelus reached for the page, shoving me in one direction while pulling my arm in another.

I grabbed a dripping candle from the pedestal stand and lit the bottom of the page on fire. It began to smoke and flame, and Angelus howled with rage.

"Leave it! You don't know what you're doing! You could destroy everything—" He threw himself at me, punching and kicking, almost ripping my shirt off. His nails raked my skin, again and again, but I didn't let go.

I didn't let go when I felt the flames sear their way down to my fingers.

I didn't let go when the ink-smeared page crumbled into ash.

I didn't let go until Angelus himself crumbled into nothing, as if he was made of parchment.

Finally, when the wind had blown every last trace of the Keeper and his page into oblivion, I found myself staring at my burnt, blackened hands.

"My turn."

Ducking my head, I flipped through the delicate pages of parchment. I could see dates and names at the top, penned by different hands. I wondered which ones Xavier had written. If Obidias had changed anyone else's page. I hoped he wasn't the one who changed Ethan Carter Wate's.

I thought of my namesake and shuddered, fighting to keep the bile down.

That could have been me.

Halfway through the book, I found our pages.

Ethan Carter's was right before mine, the two pages clearly written by different hands.

I skimmed Ethan Carter's page until I reached the part of the story I already knew. It read like a script of the vision I had witnessed with Lena, the story of the night he died and Genevieve used *The Book of Moons* to bring him back. The night that started it all.

I stared at the edge where the page met the binding. I almost tore it out, but I knew it wouldn't have made a difference. It was too late for the other Ethan.

I was the only one who still had a chance to change his fate.

Finally, I turned the page to find I was staring at Obidias' script.

Ethan Lawson Wate

I didn't read my page. I couldn't risk it. I could already feel the pull of the book on my eyes, powerful enough to Bind me to my page, forever.

I looked away. I already knew what happened in the end of this revision.

Now I was changing it.

I tore the page, the edges pulling away from the binding in a flash of electricity stronger and brighter than lightning. I heard what sounded like thunder in the sky above me, but I kept tearing.

This time, I kept the candles as far from the parchment as I could.

I pulled until the words came loose, disappearing like they had been written in invisible ink.

I looked down at the page again and it was blank.

I let it drop into the water around me, watching as it fell through the milky depths, vanishing into the endless shadow of the chasm.

My page was gone.

And in that second, I knew I was, too.

I stared at my Chucks beneath me

until they were gone

and I was gone
and it didn't matter anymore....

because

there

was

nothing

beneath

me

now

and

then

no

me

◄ CHAPTER 35 ►

A Crack in the Universe

The toes of my Chucks hung over the white metal edge, a town sleeping hundreds of feet below me. The tiny houses and tiny cars looked like toys, and it was easy to imagine them dusted with glitter under the tree with the rest of my mother's Christmas town.

But they weren't toys.

I knew this view.

You don't forget the last thing you see before you die. Trust me.

I was standing on top of the Summerville water tower, veins of cracked white paint spreading out from under my sneakers. The curve of a black heart drawn in Sharpie caught my eye.

Was it possible? Could I really be home?

I didn't know until I saw her.

The fronts of her black orthopedic shoes were lined up perfectly with my Chucks.

Amma was wearing her black Sunday dress with the tiny violets scattered all over it, and a wide-brimmed black hat. Her white gloves gripped the handles of her patent-leather pocketbook.

Our eyes met for a split second, and she smiled—relief spreading across her features in a way that was impossible to describe. It was almost peaceful, a word that I would never use to describe Amma.

That's when I realized something was wrong. The kind of wrong you can't stop or change or fix.

I reached for her at the exact same moment she stepped off the edge, into the blue-black sky.

"Amma!" I reached for her, the way I used to reach for Lena in my dreams when she was the one falling. But I couldn't catch Amma.

And she didn't fall.

The sky split open like the universe was tearing, or like someone had finally picked that hole in it. Amma turned her face toward it, tears running down her cheeks even as she smiled at me.

The sky held her up, as though Amma was worthy of standing on it, until a hand reached out from the center of the tear and the blinking stars. It was a hand I recognized—the one that had offered me his crow so I could cross from one world to another.

Now Uncle Abner was offering that hand to Amma.

His face blurred in the darkness next to Sulla, Ivy, and Delilah. Amma's other family. Twyla's face smiled down at me, charms tied into her long braids. Amma's Caster family was waiting for her.

But I didn't care.

I couldn't lose her.

"Amma! Don't leave me!" I shouted.

Her lips didn't move, but I heard her voice, as sure as if she was standing next to me. *"I could never leave you, Ethan Wate. I'll always be watchin'. Make me proud."*

My heart felt like it was collapsing in on itself, shattering into pieces so small I might never find them. I dropped to my knees and looked up into the heavens, screaming louder than I ever thought possible. "Why?"

It was Amma who answered. She was farther away now, stepping into the sliver of sky that opened just for her. *"A woman's only as good as her word."* Another one of Amma's riddles.

The last one.

She touched her fingers to her lips and reached them out to me as the universe swallowed her up. Her words echoed across the sky, as if she had spoken them aloud.

"And everyone said I couldn't change the cards...."

The cards.

She was talking about the spread that predicted my death so many months ago. The spread she had bargained with the bokor to change. The one she swore she'd do anything to change.

She'd done it.

Defied the universe and fate and everything she believed in. For me.

Amma was trading her life for mine, protecting the Order by offering one life for another. That was the deal she had made with the bokor. I understood now.

I watched the sky knit itself back together one stitch at a time.

But it didn't look the same. I could still see the invisible seams where the world had torn itself in half to take her. And I would always know they were there, even if no one else could see them.

Like torn edges of my heart.

417

⊰ CHAPTER 36 ⊱

Translation

As I sat on the cold metal in the darkness, part of me wondered if I imagined the whole thing. I knew I didn't. I could still see those stitches in the sky, no matter how dark it was.

Still, I didn't move.

If I left, it would be real.

If I left, she would be gone.

I don't know how long I sat there trying to make sense of everything, but the sun came up, and I was still sitting in the same spot. No matter how many times I tried to work it out, I kept getting stuck.

I had this old Bible story in my head, playing over and over, like a bad song from the radio. I'm probably getting it wrong, but I remember it like this: There was this city of people who were so righteous, they got picked right up off the earth and taken to Heaven. Just like that.

They didn't even die.

They got to skip dying, the way you pass Go and head directly to Jail if you pull the wrong card in Monopoly.

Translated—that's the name for what happened to them. I remember because Link was in my Sunday school class, and he said *teleported*, then *transported*, and finally *transportated*.

We were supposed to act real jealous about it, like those people were so lucky to get plucked up and taken into the Lap o' the Lord.

Like it was a place or something.

I remember coming home and asking my mom about it, because that's how creeped out I was. I don't remember what she said, but I decided right then and there that the goal wasn't to be good. It was to be *just good enough*.

I didn't want to risk getting translated, or even teleported.

I wasn't looking to go live in the Lap o' the Lord. I was more excited about Little League.

But it seemed like that's what happened to Amma. She was lapped right up, transported, transportated—all of it.

Did the universe, or the Lord and his lap, or the Greats expect me to feel happy about it? I had just been through hell to get back to the regular world of Gatlin—back to Amma, and Lena, and Link, and Marian.

How long did we have together?

Was I supposed to be okay with that?

One minute she was there, and then it was over. Now the sky was the sky again, flat and blue and calm, as if it really was just painted plaster, like my bedroom ceiling. Even if someone I loved was trapped somewhere behind it.

That's how I felt now. Trapped on the wrong side of the sky.

Alone on the top of the Summerville water tower, looking out over the world I had known my entire life, a world of dirt roads and paved routes, of gas stations and grocery stores and strip malls. And everything was the same, and nothing was the same.

I wasn't the same.

I guess that's the thing about a hero's journey. You might not start out a hero, and you might not even come back that way. But you change, which is the same as everything changing. The journey changes you, whether or not you know it, and whether or not you want it to. I had changed.

I had come back from the dead, and Amma was gone, even if she was one of the Greats now.

You couldn't get more changed than that.

I heard a clanging on the ladder beneath me, and I knew who it was before I felt her curling around my heart. The warmth exploded across me, across the water tower, across Summerville. The sky was striped with gold and red, as if the sunrise was reversing itself, lighting up the sky all over again.

There was only one person who could do that to a sky or my heart.

Ethan, is that you?

I smiled even as my eyes turned wet and blurry.

It's me, L. I'm right here. Everything's going to be okay now.

I reached my hand down and wrapped it around hers, pulling her up onto the platform at the top of the water tower.

She slid into my arms, falling into sobs that beat against my chest. I don't know which one of us was crying harder. I'm not even sure we remembered to kiss. What we had went so much deeper than a kiss.

When we were together, she turned me completely inside out.

It didn't matter if we were dead or alive. We could never be kept apart. There were some things more powerful than worlds or universes. She was my world, as much as I was hers. What we had, we knew.

The poems are all wrong. It's a bang, a really big bang. Not a whimper.

And sometimes gold can stay.

Anybody who's ever been in love can tell you that.

CHAPTER 37

What the Words Never Say

Amma Treadeau has been declared legally dead, following her disappearance from Wate's Landing, the home of Mitchell and Ethan Wate, on Cotton Bend, in Central Gatlin'—" I stopped reading out loud.

I was sitting at her kitchen table, where her One-Eyed Menace waited sadly in the mason jar on her counter, and it didn't seem possible that I was reading Amma's obituary. Not when I could still smell the Red Hots and the pencil lead.

"Keep readin'." Aunt Grace was leaning over my shoulder, trying to read the print that her bifocals were ten strengths too weak to read.

Aunt Mercy was sitting in her wheelchair, on the other side

of the table, next to my dad. "They best say somethin' about Amma's pie. Or the Good Lord as my witness, I'll go down there ta *The Stars 'n' Bars* and give them a piece a my mind." Aunt Mercy still thought our town newspaper was named after the Confederate flag.

"It's *The Stars and Stripes*," my father corrected gently. "And I'm sure they worked hard to assure Amma is remembered for all her talents."

"Hmm." Aunt Grace sniffed. "Folks 'round here don't know a lick about talent. Prudence Jane's singin' was looked over by the choir for years."

Aunt Mercy crossed her arms. "She had the voice of an angel if I ever heard one."

I was surprised Aunt Mercy could hear anything without her hearing aid. She was still carrying on when Lena began to Kelt with me.

Ethan? Are you okay?

I'm okay, L.

You don't sound okay.

I'm dealing.

Hold on. I'm coming.

Amma's face stared out at me from the newspaper, printed in black and white. Wearing her best Sunday dress, the one with the white collar. I wondered if someone had taken that photo at my mom's funeral or Aunt Prue's. It could've been Macon's.

There had been so many.

I laid the paper down on the scarred wood. I hated that obituary. Someone from the paper must have written it, not someone who knew Amma. They'd gotten everything wrong. I guess I had a new reason to hate *The Stars and Stripes* as much as Aunt Grace did.

I closed my eyes, listening to the Sisters fuss about everything from Amma's obituary to the fact that Thelma couldn't make grits the right way. I knew it was their way of paying their respects to the woman who had raised my dad and me. The woman who had made them pitcher after pitcher of sweet tea and made sure they didn't leave the house with their skirts hitched up in their pantyhose when they left for church.

After a while, I couldn't hear them at all. Just the quiet sound of Wate's Landing mourning, too. The floorboards creaked, but this time I knew it wasn't Amma in the next room. None of her pots were banging. No cleavers were attacking the cutting board. No warm food would be coming my way.

Not unless my dad and I taught ourselves how to cook.

There were no casseroles piled up on our porch either. Not this time. There wasn't a soul in Gatlin who would have dared bring their sorry excuse for a pot roast to mark Miss Amma Treadeau's passing. And if they did, we wouldn't have eaten it.

Not that anyone around here really believed she was gone. At least that's what they said. "She'll come back, Ethan. 'Member the way she just showed up without sayin' a word, the day you were born?" It was true. Amma had raised my father and moved out to Wader's Creek with her family. But as the story goes, the day my parents brought me home from the hospital, she showed up with her quilting bag and moved back in.

Now Amma was gone, and she wasn't coming back. More than anyone, I knew how that worked. I looked at the worn spot on the floorboards over by the stove, in front of the oven door.

I miss her, L.

I miss her, too.

I miss both of them.

I know.

I heard Thelma walk into the room, a hunk of tobacco tucked under her lip. "All right, girls. I think y'all have had enough excitement for one mornin'. Let's go on in the other room and see what we can win on *The Price Is Right*."

Thelma winked at me and wheeled Aunt Mercy out of the room. Aunt Grace was right behind them, with Harlon James at her feet. "I hope they're givin' away one a those iceboxes that makes water all on its own."

My dad reached for the newspaper and started reading where I left off. " 'Memorial services will be held at the Chapel at Wader's Creek.' " My mind flashed on Amma and Macon, standing face to face in the middle of the foggy swamp on the wrong side of midnight.

"Aw, hell, I tried to tell anyone who would listen. Amma doesn't want a service." He sighed.

425

"Nope."

"She's fussing around somewhere right now, saying, 'I don't see why you're wastin' good time mournin' me. Sure as my Sweet Redeemer, I'm not wastin' my time mournin' you.'"

I smiled. He cocked his head to the left, just like Amma did when she was on the rampage. "T. O. M. F. O. O. L. E. R. Y. Ten down. As in, this whole thing's nothin' but hodgepodge and nonsense, Mitchell Wate."

This time I laughed, because my dad was right. I could hear her saying it. She hated being the center of attention, especially when it involved the infamous Gatlin Funerary Pity Parade.

My dad read the next paragraph. "'Miss Amma Treadeau was born in Unincorporated Gatlin County, South Carolina, the sixth of seven children born to the late Treadeau family.'" The sixth of seven children? Had Amma ever mentioned her sisters and brothers? I only remembered her talking about the Greats.

He skimmed the length of the obituary. "'By some count, her career as a baker of local renown spanned at least five decades and as many county fairs.'" He shook his head again. "But no mention of her Carolina Gold? Good Lord, I hope Amma's not reading this from some cloud up on high. She'll be sending lightning bolts down, left and right."

She's not, I thought. *Amma doesn't care what they say about her now. Not the folks in Gatlin. She's sitting on a porch somewhere with the Greats.*

He kept going. "'Miss Amma leaves behind her extended family, a host of cousins, and a circle of close family friends.'"

He folded up the paper and tossed it back onto the table. "Where's the part where Miss Amma leaves behind two of the sorriest, hungriest, saddest boys ever to inhabit Wate's Landing?" He tapped his fingers restlessly on the wood tabletop between us.

I didn't know what to say at first. "Dad?"

"Yeah?"

"We're going to be okay, you know?"

It was true. That's what she'd been doing all this time, if you thought about it. Getting us ready for a time when she wouldn't be there to get us ready for all the times after that.

For now.

My dad must have understood, because he let his hand fall heavily on my shoulder. "Yes, sir. Don't I know it."

I didn't say anything else.

We sat there together, staring out the kitchen window. "Anything else would be downright disrespectful." His voice sounded wobbly, and I knew he was crying. "She raised us pretty well, Ethan."

"She sure did." I fought back the tears myself. Out of respect, I guess, like my dad said. This was how it had to be now.

This was real.

It hurt—it almost killed me—but it was real, the same way losing my mom was real. I had to accept it. Maybe this was the way the universe was meant to unravel, at least this part of it.

The right thing and the easy thing are never the same.

Amma had taught me that, better than anyone.

"Maybe she and Lila Jane are taking care of each other now. Maybe they're sitting together, talking over fried tomatoes and sweet tea." My dad laughed, even though he was crying.

He had no idea how close to the truth he was, and I didn't tell him.

"Cherries." That was all I said.

"What?" My dad looked at me funny.

"Mom likes cherries. Straight out of the colander, remember?" I turned my head his way. "But I'm not sure Aunt Prue is letting either one of them get a word in edgewise."

He nodded and stretched out his hand until it brushed against my arm. "Your mom doesn't care. She just wants to be left in peace with her books for a while, don't you think? At least until we get there?"

"At least," I said, though I couldn't look at him now. My heart was pulled so many different ways at once, I didn't know what I was feeling. Part of me wished I could tell him that I'd seen my mom. That she was okay.

We sat like that, not moving or talking, until I felt my heart start to pound.

L? Is that you?

Come out, Ethan. I'm waiting.

I heard the music before I saw the Beater roll into view through the windowpanes. I stood up and nodded at my dad. "I'm going up to Lena's for a while."

"You take all the time you need."

"Thanks, Dad."

As I turned to leave the kitchen, I caught one last sight of my dad, sitting alone at the table with the newspaper. I couldn't do it. I couldn't leave him like that.

I reached back for the paper.

I don't know why I took it. Maybe I just wanted to keep her with me a little while longer. Maybe I didn't want my dad to sit alone with all those feelings, wrapped in a stupid paper with a bad crossword puzzle and a worse obituary.

Then it came to me.

I pulled open Amma's drawer and grabbed a #2 pencil. I held it up to show my dad.

He grinned. "Started out sharp, and then she sharpened it."

"It's what she would have wanted. One last time."

He leaned back in his chair until he could reach the drawer and tossed me a box of Red Hots. "One last time."

I gave him a hug. "I love you, Dad."

Then I swept my hand across the length of the kitchen windows, sending salt spraying all over the kitchen floor.

"It's time to let the ghosts in."

I only made it halfway down the porch steps before Lena found me. She jumped up into my arms, circling her skinny legs around mine. She clung to me and I held on to her, like neither one of us was ever letting go.

There was electricity, plenty of electricity. But as her lips found mine, there was nothing but sweetness and peace. Kind of like coming home, when a home's still a shelter and not the storm itself.

Everything was different between us. There was nothing keeping us apart anymore. I didn't know if it was because of the New Order, or because I'd journeyed to the end of the Otherworld and back. Either way, I could hold Lena's hand without burning a hole in my palm.

Her touch was warm. Her fingers were soft. Her kiss was just a kiss now. A kiss that was every bit as big and every bit as small as a kiss can be.

It wasn't an electrical storm or a fire. Nothing exploded or burned or even short-circuited. Lena belonged to me, the same way I belonged to her. And now we could be together.

The Beater honked, and we broke off kissing.

"Any day now." Link stuck his head out the window. "I'm gettin' gray hairs sittin' here watchin' you kids."

I grinned at him, but I couldn't pull myself away from her. "I love you, Lena Duchannes. I always have, and I always will." The words were as true today as the first time I'd said them, on her Sixteenth Moon.

"And I love you, Ethan Wate. I've loved you since the first day we met. Or before." Lena looked straight in my eyes, smiling.

"Way before." I smiled back, deep into hers.

"But I have something to tell you." She leaned closer.

"Something you should probably know about the girl you love."

My stomach flipped a little. "What is it?"

"My name."

"You're not serious?" I knew Casters learned their real names after they were Claimed, but Lena was never willing to tell me hers, no matter how many times I asked. I figured it was hers to tell when she felt like the time was right. Which, I guess, was now.

"Do you still want to know?" She grinned because she already knew the answer.

I nodded.

"It's Josephine Duchannes. Josephine, daughter of Sarafine." The last word was a whisper, but I heard it, as if she had shouted it from the rooftops.

I squeezed her hand.

Her name. The last missing piece of her family puzzle, and the one thing you couldn't find on any family tree.

I hadn't told Lena about her mother yet. Part of me wanted to believe that Sarafine had given up her soul so I could be with Lena again—that her sacrifice was about more than just revenge. Someday I would tell Lena what her mother did for me. Lena deserved to know Sarafine wasn't all bad.

The Beater honked again.

"Come on, lovebirds. We gotta get to the Dar-ee Keen. Everyone's waitin'."

I grabbed Lena's other hand and pulled her down the front

lawn to the Beater. "We have to make a quick stop on the way."

"Is this gonna involve any Dark Casters? Do I need the shears?"

"We're just going to the library."

Link leaned his forehead against the steering wheel. "I haven't renewed my library card since I was ten. I think I'd have better odds with Dark Casters."

I stood in front of the car door and looked at Lena. The back door opened by itself, and we both climbed in.

"Aw, man. Now I'm your cabdriver? You Casters and Mortals have a really screwed-up way a showin' your appreciation to a guy." Link turned up the music, as if he didn't want to hear whatever I had to say.

"I appreciate you." I smacked his head from behind, good and hard. He didn't even seem to feel it. I was talking to Link, but I was looking at Lena. I couldn't stop looking at her. She was more beautiful than I remembered, more beautiful and more real.

I curled a strand of her hair through my fingers, and she leaned her cheek against my hand. We were together. It was hard to think or see or even talk about anything else. Then I felt bad for feeling so good when I was still carrying *The Stars and Stripes* in my back pocket.

"Wait. Check it out." Link paused. "That's exactly what I needed to finish my new lyrics. 'Candy girl. Hurts so sweet she'll make you want to hurl—' "

Lena put her head on my shoulder. "Did I mention that my cousin's back in town?"

"Of course she is." I smiled.

Link winked at me in the rearview mirror. I smacked him in the head again as the car pulled down the street.

"I think you're gonna be a rock star," I said.

"I gotta get back to workin' on my demo track, you know? 'Cause as soon as we graduate, I'm headin' straight to New York, the big time...."

Link was so full of crap, he could pass for a toilet. Just like the old days. Just like it was supposed to be.

It was all the proof I needed.

I was really home.

CHAPTER 38

Eleven Across

You kids go on in," Link said, turning up the latest Holy Rollers demo. "I'm gonna wait here. I get enough a books at school."

Lena and I climbed out of the Beater and stood in front of the Gatlin County Library. The repairs were further along than I remembered. All the major construction was finished on the outside, and the fine ladies of the DAR had already started planting saplings near the door.

The inside of the building was less finished. Plastic sheets hung across one side, and I could see tools and sawhorses on the other. But Aunt Marian had already set up this particular area, which didn't surprise me at all. She would rather have half a library than no library, any day.

"Aunt Marian?" My voice echoed more than usual, and within seconds she appeared at the end of the aisle in her stocking feet. I could see the tears in her eyes as she rushed in for a hug.

"I still can't believe it." She hugged me tighter.

"Trust me, I know."

I heard the sound of dress shoes against the uncarpeted concrete.

"Mr. Wate, it is a pleasure to see you, son." Macon had a huge smile plastered across his face. It was the same one he seemed to have every time he saw me now, and it was starting to creep me out a little.

He gave Lena a squeeze and made his way over to me. I held out my hand to shake his, but he swung his arm around my neck instead.

"It's good to see you, too, sir. We kinda wanted to talk to you and Aunt Marian."

She raised an eyebrow. "Oh?"

Lena was twisting her charm necklace, waiting for me to explain. I guess she didn't want to break the news to her uncle that we could make out all we wanted now without putting my life in danger. So I did the honors. And as intrigued as Macon seemed, I was pretty sure he liked it better when kissing Lena posed the threat of electric shock.

Marian turned to Macon, at a loss. "Remarkable. What do you think it means?"

He was pacing in front of the stacks. "I'm not entirely sure."

"Whatever it is, do you think it will affect other Casters and Mortals?" Lena was hoping this was some kind of change in the Order of Things. Maybe a cosmic bonus, after everything I'd been through.

"That's doubtful, but we will certainly look into it." He glanced at Marian.

She nodded. "Of course."

Lena tried to hide her disappointment, but her uncle knew her too well. "Even if this isn't affecting other Casters and Mortals, it is affecting the two of you. Change has to start somewhere, even in the supernatural world."

I heard a creak, and the front door slammed. "Dr. Ashcroft?"

I looked at Lena. I would've known that voice anywhere. Apparently, Macon recognized it, too, because he ducked behind the stacks with Lena and me.

"Hello, Martha." Marian gave Mrs. Lincoln her friendliest librarian voice.

"Was that Wesley's car I saw out front? Is he in here?"

"I'm sorry. He's not."

Link was probably scrunched down on the floor of the Beater, hiding from his mother.

"Is there anything else I can do for you today?" Marian asked politely.

"What you can do," Mrs. Lincoln fussed, "is try to read this book a witchcraft and explain to me how we can allow our children to check this out a the public library."

I didn't have to look to know what series she was referring

to, but I just couldn't help myself. I poked my head around the corner to see Link's mom waving a copy of *Harry Potter and the Half-Blood Prince* in the air.

I couldn't stop myself from smiling. It was good to know some things in Gatlin would never change.

I didn't take *The Stars and Stripes* out during lunch. They say that when someone you love dies, you can't eat. But today I had a cheeseburger with extra pickles, a double order of fries, a raspberry Oreo shake, and a banana split with hot fudge, caramel, and extra whip.

I felt like I hadn't eaten in weeks. I guess I hadn't actually eaten anything in the Otherworld, and my body seemed to know it.

As Lena and I ate, Link and Ridley were joking around together, which sounded more like fighting to anyone who didn't know better.

Ridley shook her head. "Seriously? The Beater? Didn't we go over this on the way here?"

"I wasn't listenin'. I only pay attention to about ten percent a what you say." He glanced at her over his shoulder. "I'm ninety percent too busy lookin' at you sayin' it."

"Yeah, well, maybe I'm a hundred percent too busy looking the other way." She acted annoyed, but I knew Ridley better than that.

Link only grinned. "And they say you don't use math in real life."

Ridley unwrapped a red lollipop and made a show of it, like always. "If you think I'm going to New York with you in that rust bucket, you're crazier than I thought, Hot Rod."

Link nuzzled her neck, and Rid swatted him. "Come on, Babe. It was awesome last time. And this time we won't have to sleep in the Beater."

Lena raised an eyebrow at her cousin. "You slept in a car?"

Rid tossed her blond and pink hair. "I couldn't leave Shrinky Dink alone. It's not like he was a hybrid back then."

Link wiped his greasy hands on his Iron Maiden T-shirt. "You know you love me, Rid. Admit it."

Ridley pretended to scoot away from him, but she barely moved an inch. "I'm a Siren, in case you've forgotten. I don't *love* anything."

Link kissed her on the cheek. "Except me."

"You got room for two more?" John was balancing a tray of freezes and french fries in one hand, his other hand locked around Liv's.

Lena smiled at Liv and moved over. "Always."

There was a time when I couldn't get the two of them to stand in the same room. But that felt like a lifetime ago. Technically, for me, I guess it was.

Liv tucked herself under John's arm. She was wearing her periodic table shirt and her trademark blond braids. "I hope you don't think we're sharing those." She slid the paper boat full of chili fries in front of her.

"I would never get between you and your fries, Olivia." John leaned over and gave her a quick kiss.

"Smart boy." Liv looked happy—not make-the-best-of-it happy but the real kind of happy. And I was happy for both of them.

Charlotte Chase called out from behind the counter; looked like her summer job had turned into a year-round after-school job. "Anybody wanna slice a pecan pie? Fresh outta the oven?" She held up the sad-looking boxed pie. It wasn't fresh out of anybody's oven, not even Sara Lee's.

"No, thanks," Lena said.

Link was still staring at the pie. "Bet it's not good enough to be Amma's worst pecan pie." He missed Amma, too. I could tell. She had always been on him about one thing or another, but she loved Link. And he knew it. Amma let him get away with things I never could, which reminded me of something.

"Link, what did you do in my basement when you were nine years old?" To this day, Link had never told me what Amma had on him. I had always wanted to know, but it was the one secret I'd never been able to get out of him.

Link squirmed in his seat. "Come on, man. Some things are private."

Ridley looked at him suspiciously. "Is that when you got into the schnapps and puked everywhere?"

He shook his head. "Naw. That was someone else's basement." He shrugged. "Hey, there's a whole lotta basements around here."

We were all staring at him.

"Fine." He ran his hand over his spiky hair nervously. "She caught me…" He hesitated. "She caught me dressed up—"

"Dressed up?" I didn't even want to think about what that meant.

Link rubbed his face, embarrassed. "It was awful, dude. And if my mom ever found out, she'd kill you for sayin' it and me for doin' it."

"What were you wearing?" Lena asked. "A dress? High heels?"

He shook his head. His face was turning red with shame. "Worse."

Ridley whacked him on the arm, looking pretty nervous herself. "Spill. What the hell did you have on?"

Link hung his head. "A Union soldier's uniform. I stole it from Jimmy Weeks' garage."

I burst out laughing, and within seconds so did Link. No one else at the table understood the sin in a Southern boy—with a father who led the Confederate Cavalry in the Reenactment of the Battle of Honey Hill, and a mother who was a proud member of the Sisters of the Confederacy—trying on a Civil War uniform for the opposing side. You had to be from Gatlin.

It was one of those unspoken truths, like you don't make a

pie for the Wates because it won't be better than Amma's; you don't sit in front of Sissy Honeycutt in church because she talks the whole time right along with the preacher; and you don't choose the paint color for your house without consulting Mrs. Lincoln, not unless your name happens to be Lila Evers Wate.

Gatlin was like that.

It was family, all of it and all of them—the good parts and the bad.

Mrs. Asher even told Mrs. Snow to tell Mrs. Lincoln to tell Link to tell me that she was glad to have me home from Aunt Caroline's in one piece. I told Link to thank her, and I meant it. Maybe Mrs. Lincoln would even make me some of her famous brownies again one day.

If she did, I bet I would clean the plate.

When Link dropped us off, Lena and I headed straight for Greenbrier. It was our place, and no matter how many terrible things happened here, it would always be the place where we found the locket. Where I saw Lena move the clouds for the first time, even if I didn't realize it. Where we'd practically taught ourselves Latin, trying to translate from *The Book of Moons*.

The secret garden at Greenbrier held our secrets from the beginning. And in a way, we were beginning again.

Lena gave me a funny look when I finally unrolled the paper I had been carrying around all afternoon.

"What's that?" She closed her spiral notebook, the one she spent all her time writing in, like she couldn't get everything on the page fast enough.

"The crossword puzzle." We lay on our stomachs in the grass, curled up against each other in our old spot by the tree near the lemon groves, near the hearthstone. True to its name, Greenbrier was the greenest I'd ever seen it. Not a lubber or a bunch of dead brown grass in sight. Gatlin really was back to the best version of its old self.

We did this, L. We didn't know how powerful we were.

She leaned her head on my shoulder.

We do now.

I didn't know how long it would last, but I swore to myself that I wouldn't take it for granted ever again. Not one minute of what we had.

"I thought we could do it. You know, for Amma."

"The crossword?"

I nodded, and she laughed. "You know, I never even looked at those crossword puzzles? Not once. Not until you were gone and started using them to talk to me."

"Pretty clever, right?" I nudged her.

"Better than you trying to write songs. Though your puzzles weren't that great either." She smiled, biting her lower lip. I couldn't resist kissing it over and over and over, until she finally pulled away, laughing.

"Okay. They were much better." She touched her forehead to mine.

I smiled. "Admit it, L. You loved my crosswords."

"Are you kidding? Of course I did. You came back to me every time I looked at those stupid puzzles."

"I was desperate."

We unrolled the paper between us, and I got out the #2 pencil. I should have known what we'd see.

Amma had left me a message, like the ones I left for Lena.

Two across. As in, to be or not to.

B. E.

Four down. As in, the opposite of evil.

G. O. O. D.

Five down. As in, the victim of a sledding injury, from an Edith Wharton novel.

E. T. H. A. N.

Ten across. As in, an expression of joy.

H. A. L. L. E. L. U. J. A. H.

I crumpled up the paper and pulled Lena toward me.

Amma was home.

Amma was with me.

And Amma was gone.

I pretty much wept until the sun fell out of the sky and the meadow around me was as dark and as light as I felt.

❧ CHAPTER 39 ❧

A Hymn for Amma

order is not orderly
no more than things are things
hallelujah
no sense to be made of water towers
or christmas towns
when you can't tell up from down
hallelujah
graves are always grave
from inside or out
and love breaks what can't be broken
hallelujah
one I loved I loved, one I loved I lost

now she is strong though she is gone
found and paid her way
she flew away
hallelujah
light the dark — sing the greats
a new day
hallelujah

⊰ EPILOGUE ⊱

After

That night, I lay in my ancient mahogany bed in my room, like generations of Wates before me. Books beneath me. Broken cell phone next to me. Old iPod hanging around my neck. Even my road map was back on the wall again. Lena had taped it up herself. It didn't matter how comfortable everything was. I couldn't sleep—that's how much thinking I had to do.

At least, remembering.

When I was little, my grandfather died. I loved my grandfather, for a thousand reasons I couldn't tell you, and a thousand stories I could barely remember.

After it happened, I hid out back, up in the tree that grew

halfway out of our fence, where the neighbors used to throw green peaches at my friends and me, and where we used to throw them at the neighbors.

I couldn't stop crying, no matter how hard I jammed my fists into my eyes. I guess I never realized people could die before.

First my dad came outside and tried to talk me down out of that stupid tree. Then my mom tried. Nothing they said could make me feel any better. I asked if my grandpa was in Heaven, like they said in Sunday school. My mom said she wasn't sure. It was the historian in her. She said no one really knew what happened when we died.

Maybe we became butterflies. Maybe we became people all over again. Maybe we just died and nothing happened.

I only cried harder. A historian isn't really what you're looking for in that kind of situation. That's when I told her I didn't want Poppi to die, but more than that, I didn't want her to die, and even more than that, I didn't want to die either. Then she broke down.

It was her dad.

I came down from the tree on my own afterward, and we cried together. She pulled me into her arms, right there on the back steps of Wate's Landing, and said I wouldn't die.

I wouldn't.

She promised.

I wasn't going to die, and neither would she.

After that, the only thing I remember was going inside and

eating three pieces of raspberry-cherry pie, the kind with the crisscross sugar crust. Someone had to die before Amma would make that pie.

Eventually, I grew up and grew older and stopped looking for my mom's lap every time I felt like crying. I even stopped going in that old tree. But it was years before I realized my mom had lied to me. It wasn't until she left me that I even remembered what she'd said.

I don't know what I'm trying to say. I don't know what any of this is really about.

Why we bother.

Why we're here.

Why we love.

I had a family, and they were everything to me, and I didn't even know it when I had them. I had a girl, and she was everything to me, and I knew it every second I had her.

I lost them all. Everything a guy could ever want.

I found my way home again, but don't be fooled. Nothing's the same as before. I'm not sure I'd want it to be.

Either way, I'm still one of the luckiest guys around.

I'm not a church kind of a person, not when it comes to praying. To be honest, for me it never gets much past hoping. But I know this, and I want to say it. And I really hope someone will listen.

There is a point. I don't know what it is, but everything I've had, and everything I've lost, and everything I felt—it meant something.

Maybe there isn't a meaning to life. Maybe there's only a meaning to living.

That's what I've learned. That's what I'm going to be doing from now on.

Living.

And loving, sappy as it sounds.

Lena Duchannes. Her name rhymes with rain.

I'm not falling anymore. That's what L says, and she's right.

I guess you could say I'm flying.

We both are.

And I'm pretty sure somewhere up there in the real blue sky and carpenter bee greatness, Amma's flying, too.

We all are, depending on how you look at it. Flying or falling, it's up to us.

Because the sky isn't really made of blue paint, and there aren't just two kinds of people in this world, the stupid and the stuck. We only think there are. Don't waste your time with either—with anything. It's not worth it.

You can ask my mom, if it's the right kind of starry night. The kind with two Caster moons and a Northern and a Southern Star.

At least I know I can.

❧

I get up in the night and make my way across the creaking floorboards. They feel astonishingly real, and there isn't a moment I think I'm dreaming. In the kitchen, I take an armful of spotless glasses out of the cupboard that hangs over the counter.

One by one, I set them on the table in a row.

Empty except for moonlight.

The refrigerator light is so bright, it surprises me. On the bottom shelf, tucked behind a rotting head of unchopped cabbage, I find it.

Chocolate milk.

Just as I suspected.

I might not have wanted it anymore, and I might not have been here to drink it, but I knew there was no way Amma had stopped buying it.

I rip open the cardboard and fold out the spout—something I could do in my sleep, which is practically the state I'm in. I couldn't make Uncle Abner a pie if my life depended on it, and I don't even know where Amma keeps the recipe for Tunnel of Fudge.

But this I know.

One by one, I fill the glasses.

One for Aunt Prue, who saw everything without blinking.

One for Twyla, who gave up everything without hesitating.

One for my mom, who let me go not once but twice.

One for Amma, who took her place with the Greats so I could take mine in Gatlin again.

A glass of chocolate milk doesn't seem like enough, but it isn't really the milk, and we all know that—all of us here, anyway.

Because the moonlight shimmers in the empty wooden chairs around me, and I know, as always, that I am not alone.

I'm never alone.

I push the last glass through the patch of moonlight across the scarred kitchen table. The light flutters like the twinkling of a Sheer's eye.

"Drink up," I say, but it's not what I mean.

Especially not to Amma and my mom.

I love you, and I always will.

I need you, and I keep you with me.

The good and the bad, the sugar and the salt, the kicks and the kisses—what's come before and what will come after, you and me—

We are all mixed up in this together, under one warm piecrust.

Everything about me remembers everything about you.

Then I take a fifth glass down from the shelf, the last of our clean glasses. I fill it to the brim with milk, so close that I have to slurp the top to keep it from overflowing.

Lena laughs at the way I always fill my cup as full as it can go. I feel her smiling in her sleep.

I raise my glass to the moon and drink it myself.

Life has never tasted sweeter.

HERE ENDETH

THE
CASTER
CHRONICLES

Fabula Peracta Est.
Scripta Aeterna Manent.

A Seer's moons, a Siren's tears,
Nineteen Mortal, Wayward fears,
Incubus graves and Caster rivers,
The Final Page the End delivers.

Acknowledgments

We've loved every minute of this.
Every character, every chapter, every page.
More than anything, all we need to acknowledge now is
the one person who made it all happen—
YOU.
Our favorite Caster Reader(s).
Thank you. For everything. For all of it.
It's been a wild ride—
we hope you'll keep reading
and keep believing
in true love,
things hidden in plain sight,
the world between the cracks,
and, more than anything, yourself.
We know we will.

Love always—and we do mean that—

KAMI & MARGIE

Special thanks to:

OUR EDITOR—JULIE SCHEINA

OUR LATIN TRANSLATOR—DR. SARA LINDHEIM

OUR CREATIVE DIRECTOR—DAVE CAPLAN

OUR COPY EDITOR—BARBARA BAKOWSKI

OUR PUBLICITY MANAGER—JESSICA BROMBERG

OUR MARKETING MANAGER—LISA ICKOWICZ

AND THE ENTIRE BEAUTIFUL CREATURES NOVELS TEAM
AT LITTLE, BROWN BOOKS FOR YOUNG READERS!

About the Authors

Like Amma, KAMI GARCIA is very superstitious, and like any self-respecting girl with Southern roots, she makes her biscuits by hand and her pies from scratch. She has relatives in the Daughters of the American Revolution, but has yet to participate in a reenactment herself. Kami attended George Washington University and has an MA in education. She is a teacher and reading specialist, and leads book groups for children and teenagers.

Like Lena, writing has gotten MARGARET STOHL in and out of trouble since she was fifteen. She has written and designed many popular video games, which is why her two bad beagles are named Zelda and Kirby. Margaret fell in love with American literature at Amherst and Yale, earned an MA in English from Stanford, and studied creative writing under poet George MacBeth at the University of East Anglia, Norwich.

KAMI AND MARGARET both live in Los Angeles, California, with their families.